"I loved you, Theo, and it broke my heart when you left."

Her voice had grown soft and low as if the confession was a secret she didn't want to share.

He closed the distance between them, swimming toward her. Searching her face for more answers than she could give, he asked, "Why couldn't you wait for me, Ree?"

He leaned closer, his mouth hovering above hers. Her barely covered breasts brushed against his chest, and a moan escaped from her throat before she could stop it. Touching him seemed unwise, but her hands went to his shoulders to keep herself above the pool water. Drowning would be the coward's way out. He took her touch as an excuse to wrap her in his arms and kiss her. They went under water, and still he kissed her. Wet, and slick, and hungry. She kissed him back not sure at all of the game they were playing, not caring if there were costs to pay later.

Praise for Molly Cannon's Novels

Crazy Little Thing Called Love

"Marvelous. Cannon incorporates an entertaining heroine, a charming hero, and a quirky supporting cast that adds color and depth…Readers will love this book and eagerly anticipate the next installment."

—*RT Book Reviews*

"Sweet, funny…It is incredibly easy to fall in love with all the characters…I highly recommend this charming romance!" —HarlequinJunkie.com

"If you want a book that's delightful, fun, and full of romance, then this might be the book for you."

—LongandShortReviews.com

"A great storyline as well as great writing. I can't wait to read more of Molly Cannon's books."

—FreshFiction.com

Ain't Misbehaving

"An endearing heroine, an honorable hero, sizzling sexual chemistry, and writing full of sassy charm add up to a romance readers will treasure." —*Chicago Tribune*

"A story full of warmth, wit, and charm."

—Jill Shalvis, *New York Times*
bestselling author

Flirting with Forever

MOLLY CANNON

FOREVER

NEW YORK   BOSTON

Forever
Hachette Book Group
237 Park Avenue
New York, NY 10017

www.HachetteBookGroup.com

Printed in the United States of America

First Edition: April 2014
10 9 8 7 6 5 4 3 2 1

OPM

Forever is an imprint of Grand Central Publishing.
The Forever name and logo are trademarks of Hachette Book Group, Inc.

The Hachette Speakers Bureau provides a wide range of authors for speaking events. To find out more, go to www.hachettespeakersbureau.com or call (866) 376-6591.

The publisher is not responsible for websites (or their content) that are not owned by the publisher.

ATTENTION CORPORATIONS AND ORGANIZATIONS:
MOST HACHETTE BOOK GROUP books are available
at quantity discounts with bulk purchase for educational,
business, or sales promotional use. For information,
please call or write:

Special Markets Department, Hachette Book Group
237 Park Avenue, New York, NY 10017
Telephone: 1-800-222-6747 Fax: 1-800-477-5925

To Bill: Let others share the moon. We will always have the Treasure City sign.

Acknowledgments

Life got in the way while writing this book, so I have many people to thank for helping me through it.

First my husband Bill, the most unselfish, loving man I know. Smooches. My kids and grandkids for lighting up my life and giving me balance.

My sisters, Sherrionne and Patricia. Thank goodness for you both. You are my anchors in many a storm, this year more than ever. And Maddie—you are a rock star! Moo and Dick—I love you both.

My daughter Emily—thanks for everything—the reading, the girls' days that kept me sane, and especially that thing you do where you stay all reasonable and calm while I'm pulling out my hair!

Support comes from other quarters, too. NTRWA, the Lit Girls, the Texas Tarts, the Harmy Board. I couldn't do without any of you.

Special thanks to Debra Dennis and her patience answering my questions. Thanks, CatMom!

Chris Keniston and Mabsie Bonnick—we are about six months behind on the celebrating, girls!

My super agent, Kim Lionetti. Your willingness to let me bend your ear is invaluable.

All the fine folks at Grand Central Publishing, including Megha Parekh, Jessica Bromberg, Diane Luger, Kallie Shimek, and Kathleen Scheiner.

And finally my wonderful editor, Michele Bidelspach. I appreciate your keen eye and attention to the story as always, but this time I want to thank you for your patience. You went above and beyond on this one!

Flirting with Forever

Chapter One

⁓

She hadn't bothered with a bathing suit.

Irene floated in her swimming pool, letting the hot Texas sun lull her into a lethargic daydream state. She closed her eyes and listened idly to the chirping birds and the chattering squirrels. Peace and quiet.

Exactly what she needed.

No one could see her way up here at her hillside home. The front of the house looked down on the small town of Everson. She could stand on her front porch and watch the traffic move through the streets, but the back of her house was completely private, backing up to an undeveloped area of small hills and trees. No, she was quite safely out of view, drifting languidly in her own private world.

The rumbling sound of a small plane overhead disturbed her tranquillity. As she shaded her eyes it flew closer and then buzzed directly overhead. She made no attempt to cover herself. In fact, she was tempted to sit up and wave. She had never been known for her modesty, and if some bozo pilot was out for a joyride, he might as well enjoy a cheap thrill. But she didn't react at all, instead deciding she wasn't going to let the uninvited visitor ruin her day. She watched as the plane tilted its wings, in a way of a greeting, it seemed, and then circled around heading in the direction of the small airfield on the outskirts of town.

In a flash she realized exactly who was flying that noisy, intrusive airplane. Theo Jacobson. She knew he was coming back to town. According to his brother Jake, he was due back in town for the wedding sometime this week. It was just like him to make a splashy return, arriving like some winged warrior mocking her from on high.

Good, she thought defiantly. Let him have a good look. He should get an undisguised eyeful of the woman he hadn't wanted all those years ago. The woman he hadn't bothered to acknowledge since. He'd broken her heart and never looked back. A big fluffy cloud wafted by, momentarily covering the sun. She trailed a hand through the relaxing water, but it suddenly felt too cold. She slipped off the float and pulled herself from the pool. A terry cloth robe lay draped across a lounge chair, and she picked it up, wrapping it around her chilly body. With one more look at the now empty blue sky, she opened the back door and went inside her house.

• • •

"Welcome to the Rise-N-Shine. My name is Nell, and I'll be your server today."

Theo looked up at the waitress standing by the booth at the back of the local diner. She was willowy and tall with a ponytail of thick, red hair trailing down her back. Her expression was carefully polite.

"Well, hello, Nell." He added a smile to soften the impact of his wild and woolly appearance. He knew he must look like a grizzled mountain man who'd just stumbled back into town after a long, cold winter's hibernation. That wasn't too far from the truth. His full, dark beard and unruly mess of long, black hair were a testament to the untamed months he'd just spent running backcountry tours up in Alaska. As soon as he'd landed he had called his brother to let him know he'd arrived and then called Everson's only taxi to take him into town. He was starving, so he'd had Bo Birdwell drop him at the diner. Later this afternoon he'd meet up with Jake and Marla Jean.

The smile must have helped because the waitress smiled back. "Are you ready to order?"

"Sure, I'll have the meat loaf and mashed potatoes. And a side of mustard greens." He took a quick glance at the menu and then refocused his blue eyes on her again. "And I think I'll try some of that peach pie, too. What do you think?"

"Good choice. My mom makes the best meat loaf in the world, and her peach pie is my personal favorite."

"Okay, then. That's good enough for me. I'm hungry enough to eat a bear. So, Bertie's your mother?" He nodded toward the Rise-N-Shine's owner loudly holding court at the front counter.

"She sure is. And I was just telling her we should add bear to the menu." They both laughed in the way people do when they're flirting rather than because something is actually funny. Still smiling, she asked coyly, "Are you new in town?"

He soaked up her interest and winked. "Actually, I'm just passing through. I'll be here for a week or two, and then I'm taking off again to parts unknown." He gestured out the window indicating the far horizon.

She peered out the window and then looked back at him. Moving closer, she said, "Parts unknown. That sounds mighty adventurous."

He leaned closer, too, like he had secrets to share. "It certainly can be, Nell. I'm Theo Jacobson by the way."

Her eyes widened. "Jacobson? Wait a minute. As in Jake Jacobson?"

He grinned like she'd won the grand prize. "The very one. He's my big brother. I'm here for his wedding."

She held the order pad against her breast as she studied him more closely. "I knew you looked familiar. Underneath all that hair, that is."

"So you know Jake?" He wasn't surprised. Everson was a small town after all.

"Of course. And Marla Jean, too." She gave his shaggy head of hair another once-over. "Maybe you should stop off at her place for a haircut."

His future sister-in-law owned the local barbershop. "Are you suggesting I look uncivilized?" He leaned back in the booth with an unrepentant grin.

She raised her eyebrows, fully flirting now. "Uncivilized isn't necessarily a bad thing, Theo Jacobson. I was just thinking you might be worth asking out if I could see what you look like under all that shaggy growth."

"Are all the women around these parts as bold as you, Nell?"

She laughed. "Hold your horses, mister. Let's not get ahead of ourselves. I haven't asked you out yet, have I?

And I better go put in your order." She winked and turned to go.

He watched her walk back toward the front of the diner, taking his time, admiring the way her waitress uniform skimmed tightly over her perky, little butt. This visit to Everson might turn out to be a lot more fun than he'd expected.

Nell was pretty damn cute, and he wouldn't mind spending some time getting to know her better while he was in Everson. He wouldn't mind that one little bit. After all, he was here to have a good time. Enjoy the wedding. Help Jake with some jobs. Keep it all easy and uncomplicated.

But Jake had already complicated this visit when he'd said he wanted Theo to stay on after the wedding. He was offering him a full-time job and a place to settle down with family close at hand. Theo had to admit he'd been tempted, which surprised him. Since leaving the Navy, he'd never stayed in one place for long. He always had one foot out the door, but this time he hadn't turned his brother down flat out. He'd actually promised to give the idea some thought. But still, the odds were pretty good that he'd be moving on when the time came.

Which was why he'd been out of his mind to buzz Irene Cornwell's house on the way into town. Because he certainly didn't plan to spend the short time he was here reflecting on the time in his life that included her. Some things were better left in the past where they belonged. But the last time he was in town she'd ignored him completely, didn't even give him the passing courtesy she would extend to a stranger, and he could admit he'd let it get under his skin. It chafed, and festered, and bugged the hell out of him. He was determined not to let her get away with doing it again. Not that he expected her to run and jump into his arms. He didn't want that, either. A simple hello or nod of the head would do.

But the image of her floating buck naked in her swimming pool would be hard to forget. As soon as he'd spotted her, he reacted with something close to physical pain and an old, ancient longing that he thought had died out a long time ago. His body didn't seem to get the message that she was off-limits now.

•　•　•

"Well, well. If it isn't the best man."

As Theo made his way through the gate and into the backyard of the Hazelnut Inn, a soft, feminine voice hit him like a nasty punch to the gut. A voice that had haunted his dreams for years, a voice he'd recognize anywhere. Irene Cornwell. He must have been thinking about her so much that she'd materialized right in front of him like a magic trick gone wrong. Shit. Irene Cornwell. Fully clothed as well. Double shit. And she was actually speaking to him as well. Mission accomplished. He could check that off his list. Not just a hello or a nod of her head, but an entire sentence. For some reason it didn't feel like a victory. It felt like he'd jumped out of his airplane without a parachute. Free-falling, waiting for the painful impact that was sure to follow. But he wasn't about to let her see him sweat, so he slapped a cocky grin on his face and said, "Well, if it isn't Irene Cornwell! How the heck have you been, Ree?"

She sat at an outside patio table with a thick file folder open in front of her and a pair of big, black-framed sunglasses shoved on top of her head. Her long, dark hair was caught up in a messy bun that he guessed was her attempt at looking serious. He allowed himself a minute to stare. She was still the most beautiful woman he'd ever seen, but he would be careful to keep that opinion strictly to himself. Seeing her from a distance had been bad enough. But now, here she was close enough to touch. He was determined not to even consider that idea. Not even if someone offered him a ten-foot pole.

Her bright smile turned brittle. "No one calls me Ree anymore, Theodore. And I'm fine, thanks."

He laughed, thinking how easy it was to get a rise from her. "Well, no one but you ever called me Theodore, and that was only when you were mad at me. I hope you're still not mad at me after all this time?"

"Don't be silly." She waved her hand as if she thought he was being ridiculous. "Of course not."

He dropped into the chair across from her. "I'm glad to hear that. And this is great. We're actually sitting here having a conversation. Last time I was in Everson you pretended I didn't exist." He kept smiling like he was tickled pink by their unexpected reunion.

Her chin lifted regally. "I don't know what you're talking about." He didn't push it when she changed the subject. "Jake will be glad you made it home for the wedding."

He looked at his watch. "Yeah, I'm supposed to meet him and Marla Jean here at four."

She nodded at the back door of the Inn. "They're inside talking to Etta about the food for the wedding reception, but they should be out any minute. We need to finish going over the details of the ceremony."

"We?" He couldn't think of any reason she'd be involved in the wedding.

She closed the folder on the table and held out her hands in a "look at me" gesture. "Haven't you heard? I'm their wedding planner."

An involuntary bark of laughter escaped his throat. But she looked completely serious, so he asked, "You? A wedding planner? Since when?" Even to his own ears it sounded like he was accusing her of some sinister crime.

She crossed her long legs to one side. "Actually, it's a fairly recent development. It came to me in a flash. When the Inn opened and I found out Etta planned to hold weddings here, I thought it sounded like something I'd be good at doing."

"You don't say? You don't need the money, do you? So what? You just happened to have some extra time on your hands?" He didn't try to hide his skepticism.

"Something like that." She stuck out her chin, looking like she was ready to engage in a battle over the subject. "Why do you find that so peculiar?"

"No reason. Don't go getting all defensive, Ree. Forget I said anything." He shrugged as if it didn't really concern him.

He could tell she wasn't ready to forget it, though. "I'm not defensive, but you obviously have a strong opinion on the subject. So, please share. I'm simply dying to hear what you have to say."

Theo knew he'd be smart to keep his mouth shut, but he plunged ahead anyway. "Okay, and don't take this the wrong way, but it seems to me that a certain respect for the institution of marriage should be necessary in order to do a good job as a wedding planner."

The look she gave him clearly let him know his sarcasm had been noted. "Okay, and don't take *this* the wrong way, but I'll have you know my respect for the institution of marriage has increased by leaps and bounds since you knew me, Theo. Besides, you remember how I love a good party. A wedding and the reception aren't that much different."

He was about to stick his foot further into his mouth by saying that her feelings about marriage must have improved once he was out of the picture, but he was saved when he spotted Jake and Marla Jean coming out the back door and he stood up from the table. They were talking about the advantages of a sit-down dinner versus the simplicity of a buffet.

Marla Jean was saying, "I don't want people to think we're being cheap, Jake."

"No one will think we're cheap. But a buffet is less stressful. Less waitstaff to hire. People can help themselves," Jake said. "Don't you agree, Irene?"

Before the words were completely out of his mouth, Marla Jean spotted Theo. She ran toward him in a full sprint and jumped into his arms. "Theo, you're actually here. Oh, Jake, look, it's Theo."

Theo laughed as he caught her in midjump and spun her around. "That's the way I like to be greeted. You sure you're marrying the right brother, Marla Jean?"

Jake reached the two of them just as Theo set Marla Jean's feet on the ground. "Take your hands off my future wife, little brother."

Theo turned and grabbed Jake in a bear hug. "I'm glad she's going to make an honest man out of you, Jake. It's about time." His big brother meant the world to him. While Theo was growing up, Jake had been the one person he could count on for love and to support him with no questions asked. Seeing him happily married to Marla Jean was a cause for real celebration.

"Now that you're here everything is going to be absolutely perfect," Marla Jean said.

"Once Jake asked me to be his best man, you know nothing could have kept me away," Theo assured her.

"With all the stops you had along the way, we weren't sure exactly when you'd get here, though. I was so happy when Jake told me you landed this morning. I couldn't believe it when he said you were flying your own plane all the way from Alaska."

"Oh, really? You flew in this morning?" Irene asked from her patio chair. "I think I saw your plane."

Theo smiled widely. So she realized it was him flying over her house. "It's a nice view from up there."

He watched her chin jut out as she declared, "Nice? I've heard it's nothing short of spectacular."

Marla Jean turned to Irene. "Have you met Theo, Irene?"

"As a matter of fact, Theo and I are old friends." Irene stood up and walked over to the group.

Jake looked at Theo in surprise. "Is that so? How come I didn't know that?"

"Old friends." Such a catchall phrase, such a generic, inadequate term for what they'd been. But now was not the time or place to squabble over how to define their past. "Yeah, Ree and I go way back. You remember when I got that job working at the Piggly Wiggly after school? Ree was a checker while I was a lowly grocery sacker."

Jake looked from one to the other. "That grocery store was over in Derbyville. You lived in Derbyville, Irene? I never realized that, either."

She nodded. "I grew up there. But I couldn't wait to

escape to the big city. I moved to Dallas right after high school."

Jake narrowed his eyes like he was sensing a deeper undercurrent. "And so did Theo."

Theo nodded. "Yep. That was a long time ago, though. A lot of water under the bridge."

"In all your visits you never mentioned you knew Irene," Jake said suspiciously.

Theo wished they would all just drop the subject. He glanced at Ree, who seemed completely unmoved by the conversation. On the other hand, he felt as if he was tee-tering on the edge of a cliff, scrabbling to get his feet back on solid ground. "It just never came up, and, well, our paths haven't crossed much since those days."

Marla Jean swatted Jake's arm. "Quit being so nosy, Jake."

Theo smiled at Marla Jean gratefully. "Yeah, Jake, we all have a few secrets in our deep, dark past." He was talk-ing to Jake, but he looked directly at Irene while he spoke.

Irene met his eyes and lifted her chin as if she was ready to challenge any version of things he might offer. Abruptly, she turned and marched back to the patio table. She grabbed the wedding folder and announced, "I hate to interrupt this walk down memory lane, folks, but we should head over to the pavilion and walk through the cer-emony. We have a lot of ground to cover before it starts getting dark." She started off down the backyard path without waiting to see if they would follow.

"We're coming." Marla Jean grabbed Jake's hand, and they bounded after her like puppies let off their leashes. Theo found their enthusiasm for the upcoming wedding to be downright heartwarming. He planned to concentrate on their happiness while he was here and, as much as possible, ignore the woman who had broken his heart without a backward glance all those years ago. That might have been easier to do if the recent picture of her wet, naked body hadn't been seared permanently into his brain.

Chapter Two

❧

And Jake didn't want a bachelor party at all, but my big brother is insisting," Marla Jean explained. "Linc said even though Theo was the best man, as Jake's lifelong best friend he was taking charge of the party. And he wouldn't listen to any arguments against it. So there will be a bachelor party, but I told him if Jake was a minute late for the ceremony he'd have to answer to me."

Irene nodded and smiled patiently while Marla Jean carried on about this newest wrinkle of possible trouble. The wedding was only five days away now, and all of their careful planning was practically finished. At this point Marla Jean just needed someone to listen while she tried to anticipate anything that could possibly throw a monkey wrench into things. Like her big brother Linc, for instance. He was happily married and a soon-to-be new father, but that didn't mean he wouldn't miss a chance to show Jake a good time on the eve of the wedding.

"Theo will be there. He'll watch out for him, right?" Irene threw that out as reassurance, and it seemed to do the trick.

"You're right, and Linc has to answer to Dinah, too. She does a good job of keeping him in line. Especially now that she's pregnant."

Irene laughed and looked over the checklist for Marla Jean's wedding. It promised to be simple and tasteful— a chock-full-of-love affair. Not that most weddings didn't start out chock-full of love, she supposed, but sometimes in the middle of haggling and hammering out all the details, harmony seemed to fly out the window. And in Irene's opinion a lot of those marriages would be plagued by the same problems after the ceremony was said and done.

Her very first adventure into the wonderful world of wedding planning had been the ceremony and reception she'd arranged for Beulah Cross and Noah Nelson. Theirs was a late-in-life marriage, but the utter sweetness of the couple and the obvious love they shared had brought tears to her eyes. It had spoiled her. The affair had gone off without a hitch. No fussing or fighting. No last-minute snafus. A real heartwarming success.

So she'd been supremely confident when she'd tackled the Mullins-Pickering nuptials next. What a mistake. It had been nothing but squabbling and backbiting and carrying on about every little detail. Talk about a nightmare. Bridesmaids rebelling at the last minute, refusing to wear their pink and purple dresses, the groom's father showing up drunk, and the band they'd booked veering from the agreed-upon playlist to show off their original math rock compositions. But in the end, she thought with some pride, she'd managed it. She'd learned she could be tough with people if she had to be. And when all was said and done, it had been a beautiful wedding. Most importantly Brenda and Eddie had never turned on each other throughout the turmoil, so she gave their probability of longtime happiness a better-than-average chance of success as well.

But Marla Jean and Jake's engagement had been the thing that originally inspired this new venture of hers in the first place. They'd been the first to agree to use her services, and their seal of approval had pointed more business her way. It was a fledgling venture, but it surprised her just how much she enjoyed it.

Marla Jean and Jake's ceremony and reception were going to be a piece of cake. The happy couple had decided on only one attendant each. Marla Jean's hugely pregnant sister-in-law Dinah was her matron of honor. Jake's brother Theo was his best man.

Theo. She had to brace herself just thinking his name.

She tried unsuccessfully to concentrate on what Marla Jean was saying. When she'd first corralled Marla Jean at the Inn's Valentine's Dinner and convinced her she would be the perfect person to plan her wedding, she hadn't been thinking about Theo or how since he was Jake's brother he would most likely and in all probability be a part of the wedding party. Or maybe subconsciously she'd been fulfilling a long-buried wish. A chance to not just see Theo again, but a reason to interact with him.

Marla Jean regained Irene's attention when she clapped her hands declaring, "I'm delighted to report that my mother has finally stopped giving me a hard time about wearing my cowboy boots under my wedding dress."

Irene shouldn't have been letting her mind wander while Marla Jean had been babbling happily along, jumping from subject to subject without rhyme or reason. She refocused on what her client was saying. "Oh, really? What made her change her mind?"

Marla Jean's mom Bitsy had been a big help with every-thing during the planning process. The cowboy boots had been the one sticking point for her. She'd been absolutely appalled at the idea, and she hadn't minded telling her daughter loudly and often that she thought Marla Jean should wear something more delicate and feminine under her beautiful white dress. These kinds of skirmishes popped up with every wedding Irene had planned so far. It amazed her how seemingly simple things could get blown way out of proportion. Helping negotiate these battles was part of the job, and she was good at it. But Marla Jean didn't need her help.

"I told her Jake really wanted me to wear them, and when I started to tell her the fantasy he had about taking them off, that stopped her in her tracks. She squealed and started shushing me. Then she threw her hands up and said, 'Okay, Marla Jean, wear the silly boots, for Pete's sake.'"

Irene laughed. "Your poor mother. She'll have that image in her head forever."

"Serves her right." Marla Jean laughed, too, enjoying her small victory.

They were sitting in Irene's newly opened office of I Do, I Do. Her wedding planning business now had an offi-cial address, a storefront located right on the town square on Main Street in Everson, Texas. She was nestled in between the Three Sisters Bookstore on her right and the *Everson Daily* newspaper office on her left. Her space had been a dress shop in another life and now needed some shelves and display cases where she could feature some wedding-type froufrou decorations that would lend the impression that she knew what the heck she was doing.

Because she didn't. Not really. She'd been flying by the seat of her pants up until now. Brazenly faking her way through two weddings with the help of the Internet and every bridal book she could get her hands on. Marla Jean and Jake's would be her third. Today they were finalizing the table placement around the dance floor. But for a few minor details it was all decided. White tablecloths with burlap runners. Centerpieces made from logs sliced into rough rounds would hold burlap-wrapped candles and pale green mason jars filled with white flowers. Instead of renting dishes, they purchased from thrift stores mismatched plates that would be stacked at the front of the buffet. The reception would be fun and down-to-earth.

From the start Marla Jean had been ever conscious about this being her second go-round at marriage. So now she bent over backward to approach this wedding in a mature, responsible way. Irene understood and appreciated her need to keep things low-key, but she'd finally told her that it was Jake's first wedding, and if the fates were smiling, it would be Marla Jean's last. She told her she should forget about what anyone else thought. If her choices made her happy, then everyone else could go screw themselves. Recently Marla Jean had confided that that was the minute she knew she'd made the right choice in wedding planners.

The two women had been acquaintances but never particular friends before. But this experience had forged a strong bond that would last long after the ceremony was over and done with. Irene cherished the idea. After all these years she still didn't have many women friends in town. For the most part everyone treated her with polite civility, but a few made no bones about what they thought of her.

Those few still treated her like an outsider and considered her a greedy, gold-digging opportunist because of marrying a wealthy man three times her age. But they were wrong about her. Her marriage to Sven might not have been typical, but it was full of love, and she missed him every single day.

Sometimes she wondered if that hadn't played a part in her decision to take up wedding planning. She certainly didn't need the money. But weddings in a small town like Everson were a big deal, and it was an innocuous way to insert herself into the middle of these social occasions that made up the heart and soul of small-town life.

"I'm supposed to meet Jake and Theo for lunch. You should join us," Marla Jean said as she gathered her purse and stood.

Irene kept her expression neutral, though her pulse kicked up again at the mention of Theo's name. "Thanks, but I have another appointment in just a bit. Margo Douglas says she's sure Jim Murray is about to pop the question, and she wants to get a head start, even though I'm pretty sure she's had her wedding planned to the last detail forever now."

"Good grief. Those two have been going together for over ten years, haven't they?"

"At least that long. And now she's saying when he asks, she doesn't plan to say yes right away, just to make him wonder. She wants him to grovel a bit."

"But she's going ahead with the wedding plans, anyway?"

"Oh, sure. Don't ask me to explain the games of people in love."

"Okay, I won't. I wish you could come to lunch. I still

want to hear some old stories about you and Theo sometime. I didn't even know Jake had a brother before last year, and it turns out you've known him forever."

"We haven't kept up with each other, so I couldn't add much. Besides he's always been pretty private." Even though Irene couldn't stop thinking about Theo, that didn't mean she was ready to talk about him. Especially not to Jake and Marla Jean.

"Okay. I'll mind my own business, then. But the rumor mill will go into full gear if anyone finds out you two knew each other way back when."

"Well, ever since I moved to this town married to a man three times my age, my whole life exists solely to keep the rumor mill churning. I think I can manage the few days Theo is in town for the wedding."

"Oh, but he'll be here longer than that," Marla Jean said slyly.

Irene didn't try to hide her surprise. She didn't know if she was experiencing pure panic or some out-of-bounds feeling of joy. "What do you mean? You two will be gone on your honeymoon. Why would he hang around?"

Marla Jean dug her keys from her purse. "That's the reason he's hanging around. Jake talked him into working on the unfinished jobs he already has lined up while we're gone. He didn't want all those projects to come to a screeching halt. And thank goodness Theo was willing to step in and help. I think that's the only reason Jake agreed to a two-week honeymoon."

"Oh, I guess that makes sense," Irene mumbled. Theo was staying in town for a while. Okay. She could handle it. She'd have to double reinforce the walls of her emotional armor, but she would manage.

"It makes perfect sense, and we both plan to convince him to stay for good if we can."

That idea stunned Irene into silence, and she always had plenty to say. Theo Jacobson back in town for good. *No, no, no.* That was a completely different story. For years she'd wished for an opportunity to sort things out with him. And she hadn't backed away from the idea that he would be part of Jake's wedding. It seemed like the perfect opening to heal an old rift. But Theo's life had always been about moving on. To the next place. To the next adventure. To the next woman, she assumed. Theo moving on had always been an essential element for her peace of mind.

Finally Irene asked, "Do you think he'll actually consider it? Staying here, I mean?"

Marla Jean sighed. "Who knows? I just know it would make Jake happy. And whatever makes Jake happy? Well, these days that makes me happy, too."

"Ah. It must be the curse of true love."

Marla Jean smiled and didn't deny it. "Must be, and I better get going. I wouldn't want to be late."

"Okay. I think we have everything under control on my end, but I'll check in with you again tomorrow." Irene stood up and walked her to the door.

"Sounds good, Irene. See you then."

• • •

Theo sat on a sofa in Mr. Smythe's tailor shop. He and Jake were having a final fitting on the monkey suits they'd wear on the big day. He'd already gone through the process of being poked and prodded, and now Jake stood on a short stool while Mr. Smythe measured and pinned and fussed over the fit of his tuxedo.

"So, I have plenty of work lined up to keep you busy while we're gone, Theo."

"That's great, but you better watch out. If your customers get too used to seeing what quality work looks like, they might hold a full-scale rebellion when you get home."

Jake's laugh filled the small space. "Fat chance. I just hope I don't have too many do-overs when I get back."

Mr. Smythe glared at him for moving around so much. "Please, Mr. Jacobson, you must resist the urge to wriggle."

Jake smirked at Theo and straightened up like a soldier. "Sorry, Mr. Smythe. I'm so eager to get married it's made me downright giddy."

Theo laughed from his spot on the couch. "He's in love, Mr. Smythe. You'll have to forgive him." It meant the world to Theo to see his big brother so happy. While in college Jake had discovered that his father had been living a double life for years and had another family in the neighboring town of Derbyville. That family had been Theo and his mother. Two families were destroyed by the revelation, but when their father died, Jake stepped up, making sure Theo got the emotional support he needed. Theo knew he'd never be able to completely repay Jake for all he'd done.

"Humph. My experience with Mr. Jacobson tells me that he always has some excuse for making my job more difficult. But I'll admit he has a good reason this time." Mr. Smythe draped the measuring tape around his neck and got to his feet. Smoothing the fabric across Jake's shoulders a final time, he said, "There now. We're all done, young man. And I'd like to earnestly express my good wishes regarding your upcoming nuptials."

"Why, thank you, Mr. Smythe. But you're coming to the wedding aren't you?"

Mr. Smythe adjusted his half-glasses further up his beaklike nose, looking curiously touched. "I was honored to be invited. Of course I'll be there." He scurried behind the counter and handed Jake a claim ticket. "The alterations on the tuxedos will be complete by tomorrow afternoon."

Jake handed the ticket to Theo. "Your first job as best man, Theo."

Theo put the ticket in his jeans pocket and put his hand over his heart. "I'll make it my number one duty to make sure you are properly attired when Marla Jean walks down the aisle."

"Sounds good. I'll be lucky if I can tie my shoes that day." Jake ducked into a dressing room and came out dressed again in his own clothes. "Thanks, Mr. Smythe. We'll get out of your hair now. Come on, Theo. Let's go meet Marla Jean for lunch."

• • •

Marla Jean was already sitting in a booth when Theo and Jake walked into the Rise-N-Shine Diner for lunch. She waved, and Theo slipped into the seat across from her while Jake slid in next to his fiancée and greeted her with a kiss that was a little too steamy for a middle-of-the-day, right-out-in-public kiss. Theo's eyes widened, and he cleared his throat, but he was ignored while everyone in the diner watched the display and cheered.

Jake ended the kiss and looked like a man satisfied with his lot in life. He made a gesture indicating that all the smiling, happy diners should return to eating their lunch now that the show was over. "If I don't lay a big kiss on her the minute I see her, they'll just goad me until I give in. My new strategy is to start beating them to the punch."

"That must be a real chore." Theo was happy that they seemed so happy.

Marla Jean nestled close to Jake's side beaming like a woman in love. "It's awful what we go through to keep folks in this town content."

Theo smiled at their antics. "When I left town you two were barely friends anymore. I thought I was going to have to come back and lock you both in a room until you came to your senses."

"Oh, I think I'd like that." Marla Jean elbowed Jake. "Your brother is full of good ideas."

"Don't encourage him, please." Jake pulled out a list from his pocket. "Theo, I thought I'd run down the jobs I've got lined up for you to finish while I'm gone."

Theo took the list and scanned it quickly. "These don't look like anything I can't handle. Once I see you two safely off on your honeymoon, I'll start contacting your customers and get to work."

"I've already warned most of them, so they shouldn't be surprised," Jake said.

"Hello, folks. Can I get your drink orders?"

Theo looked up from the list and was happily surprised to see Nell standing by their booth.

Marla Jean spoke up first. "Hey, Nell. I'll have an unsweetened iced tea."

"Me too," Jake said with a smile.

Nell turned to Theo. "And what about you, Mr. Mysterious Man of Adventure?"

Jake laughed. "So, you've met my brother, I see."

Nell grinned. "I've had the pleasure. I have to say, you clean up real nice, Theo."

Theo lounged against the booth, pleased with her attention. "Why, thank you, Nell. Make that three iced teas."

She grinned and said, "Will do. I'll be back in a sec to get your order."

Theo watched her go. "She's cute."

Jake unwrapped his silverware from the paper napkin. "Are you planning on breaking a few hearts while you're in town?"

"No, but there's no law against having a good time while I'm in Everson, is there?"

"Just remember Marla Jean and I have to live here with these good people after you are long gone, little brother."

Marla Jean put her hand on top of Jake's. "Don't be such a stick-in-the-mud, Jake. I'm sure there is more than one woman in this town that would love to show Theo a good time. And Nell's a big girl. I'm sure she can handle herself."

"Thank you, Marla Jean. I'm glad someone has faith in my sterling character."

She laughed. "Let's not get carried away. But I don't think you should let Jake guilt you into making your time here all work and no play."

Jake shook his head. "I couldn't if I tried."

Theo went back to reading the list of jobs. "Number one: painting Lily Porter's new garage, number two: new bookshelves for Lee Wheeler. Okay, wait a minute. What's this?"

He handed the paper back to Jake and pointed to the notation three places down.

Jake took a minute to read it and then looked up. "Oh yeah. 'ID, ID office and float.' That's some work I'm doing for Irene Cornwell's business, I Do, I Do. We made a bargain in trade for part of her wedding planning fee. Her new office needs a few built-in shelves and some storage areas. Simple stuff. Since you two already know each other this will work out nicely."

Theo didn't say anything. He sat staring at the list like it was suddenly radioactive.

Marla Jean chimed in, "Oh, goodness. I forgot all about the float. For the Fourth of July parade. Building that should be lots of fun. I bet Irene will go crazy with wedding decorations."

Theo didn't know anything about building a float, and he didn't want to build one for Irene. "Will you have a float for the barbershop?"

Marla Jean nodded her head. "Hoot and Dooley will help my dad throw something together. Since we'll barely be back from the honeymoon, Jake will just decorate one of his old cars for the remodeling business. He can wave to the crowd from there. It will still be lots of fun. You can ride with him, Theo. The parade is always a highlight of the Fourth around here."

Theo turned his head to stare out the window. Across the square he could see the sign. I Do, I Do. White letters bordered in black on a bright pink background. To be honest he'd stopped processing anything anyone said after he realized he was going to have to work with Ree. That hadn't been part of the bargain. She must not realize that Jake planned to foist this work off onto his brother, because Theo had trouble believing she'd ever agree to this arrangement. But then again maybe she hadn't wanted to cause a fuss right before Jake left for his honeymoon. No doubt she'd wait until they were gone to tell him his services wouldn't be necessary.

Nell came back to the table. "Are y'all ready to order?"

Marla Jean clapped her hands. "I'm so ready. I'm starving. I want a double cheeseburger with no onions and sweet potato fries."

Jake smiled like her appetite was one of her many charms. "I'll have the chicken fried steak, Nell."

Theo didn't feel all that hungry anymore. Thinking about Irene had dulled his appetite, so he just ordered the same thing as Jake. "I'll have the chicken fried steak, too." He could always get a doggie bag and send it home to Sadie if he couldn't eat it. Irritated that he was letting Irene ruin his day, he took a deep breath, and before Nell could walk away, he asked on a whim, "So, Nell, how would you like to go out tonight? I haven't made it to Lu Lu's yet since I've been back in Everson, and I could use a night out. How about it?"

Nell stuck her pencil behind her ear and put her hand on her hip. With a saucy smile she said, "Well, now, you must be reading my mind, Theo. I was all ready to ask if you wanted to help me paint the town tonight, but you went and beat me to it."

Theo allowed himself to be flattered by her enthusiasm. A little fun with a woman like Nell was the very thing to keep his mind occupied. With someone—anyone—other than Irene Cornwell. "Great. Just tell me where and when to pick you up."

She scribbled her address on an order pad, tore off the sheet of paper, and slipped it to him before skipping back to the front of the diner.

Theo watched her go and then turned back to face Jake and Marla Jean. "Hey, bro, I need to borrow one of your cars. If that's okay with you."

"Sure. You can use Jasper. The keys are at my office," Jake said. "We'll stop by and get them after lunch."

"Jasper?"

Marla Jean patted Jake's hand and explained, "Jasper is the Jeep, Theo."

Theo laughed. "Great, because it looks like Jasper and I have a hot date tonight."

Chapter Three

~∽~

Irene checked herself one last time in the mirror before heading out the door. She was wearing a tight black dress designed to give all but the hardiest of men heart failure on sight. Her lipstick was blood red, and her long black hair was straightened into a sharp blade hanging halfway down her back. With her armor firmly in place, she grabbed her purse, climbed into her Shelby, and backed out of the garage. Her headlights sliced past the tall trees that lined the road, piercing through the dark night and guiding her car downhill toward town.

All in all, it had been a productive day. In addition to her meeting with Marla Jean, she'd taken copious notes on Margo Douglas's dream wedding. The woman wasn't fooling around. It promised to be a gigantic affair. Now as soon as good old Jim proposed they'd be all ready to get to work on their big day.

After that she'd had a long conference call with her banker regarding several of her charity foundations. She had several ideas on the children's hunger initiative she wanted to implement, but that meant a trip to Dallas to discuss the details with the board. She scheduled several other meetings for next week. One was to discuss her proposal to provide prom dresses for girls who couldn't afford them, but that was going to take some convincing. The old men she had to deal with didn't appreciate how a decent dress could make all the difference when a girl was poor and trying to fit in with her peers. As always there was a lot to do, but today her concentration had been scattered, her thoughts tumbling in a million different directions.

All day long she'd been plagued by a feeling of light-headedness. A bumble-headed, unfocused vagueness that wouldn't go away. If that wasn't bad enough, the surface of her skin prickled with awareness that something had changed. Something in the air was different. Any other time she would have thought she was coming down with the flu. But she knew she wasn't getting sick. No, she knew it was because somewhere within the ten-mile radius that made up the town of Everson, Texas, Theo Jacobson was out there. Looking up at the same sky, walking the same streets, breathing the same air she did.

It made her want to jump right out of her skin. And it was probably just fanciful thinking on her part, but the world around her suddenly seemed to sparkle and shine with life. Brighter colors. Deeper shadows. Everything seemed less dull simply because Theo was nearby. In the flesh. Not just in her head where he'd lived for the longest time. It was as if her body knew he was somewhere close, and that old longing to touch and be touched had come roaring back to life.

While getting ready tonight she'd spied an old beat-up

box in the top of her closet. Her heart beat out a crooked rhythm while she pulled it down and opened the top with trembling hands. It had been a long time since she'd bothered to look inside. She'd almost thrown it away several times, but could never bring herself to do it. She couldn't part with this final piece of her past—a past that now fit so easily inside the small cardboard container.

So instead of drying her hair, she found herself sifting through old notes, a few pictures, and a small stuffed teddy bear. She picked up the fuzzy purple bear, straightened the aqua bow tied around his neck, and hugged him to her chest. Clarence. Sweet, silly Clarence. While they lived together in Dallas, Theo had won the bear for her at a small carnival by knocking over milk bottles. He'd been so proud, and she'd been thrilled. They'd been happy back then. A picture of her standing with Theo drew her attention. It had always been one of her favorite pictures of the two of them. Instead of smiling at the camera, Theo had his arm around her shoulder, and they were caught up completely in each other, smiling into each other's eyes, shutting out the rest of the world as only young lovers could. She closed her eyes remembering that sweeter time.

Seeing him again had hit her a hell of a lot harder than she'd expected it to. When he'd walked into the backyard at the Inn, the sight of him was like a shot of whiskey rushing to her head. Intoxicating and dangerous. Dammit, he looked so good her teeth hurt. That dark head of hair curling at the back of his neck just like she remembered. His long, lean body calling to her in all the old familiar ways. Easygoing and carefree, that's how Theo faced the world. But when his blue eyes raked down her body, pinning her in place like a butterfly on a mounting board, his words made it clear that any love he'd felt for her was long gone.

In any case he would be in town for only a few days. And she could manage anything for a few days. But what if he stayed longer? What if he stayed forever? According to Marla Jean that's what Jake wanted, wasn't it? There was no point worrying about it before it happened. After all, she knew from hard experience that Theo didn't do forever. No, he'd stay a few weeks at most, and then he'd be gone. And *that* she could survive. She'd done it before, and she could do it again.

So tonight she needed the comfort and ease she always found at Lu Lu's. The local bar had become a sanctuary over the years where she could kick back and block out all of her troubles for a few hours. She didn't drink much. Maybe an occasional beer, but the rhythms of the place soothed her like a colicky baby. The constant hum of low conversations, the smell of stale beer and being surrounded by all of the regular bar patrons. Nothing ever changed at Lu Lu's, and she appreciated that. But the thing she loved most of all was the dancing. Moving, spinning, and waltzing mindlessly around the floor to the music.

Up until a few months ago she could always count on Donny Joe Ledbetter to provide her with a dance partner. Despite what folks around town had believed, they were just friends. It was true neither of them had done anything to disabuse the good people of Everson of the notion they might be more. Having someone to hang out with gave both of them an escape from the pressure of the singles scene with no questions asked. Neither of them had wanted a relationship, so their friendship served their purposes. But now Donny Joe had fallen head over heels for the owner of the town's new bed-and-breakfast, and he spent all of his time wooing Etta Green. So she'd head into town and find someone harmless to fill out her dance card, because tonight she longed for the mindless part more than ever.

• • •

Lu Lu's was loud for a Tuesday night. Theo guided Nell around the dance floor, and for the first time since he'd hit town, he felt a sense of relief. He was in his element. A pretty woman in his arms, some lively music to set the mood, and a happy crowd of mellow people letting off steam after a day's hard work.

Nell was friendly and flirty, just the way he liked a woman to be. She wanted to have a good time, and he was more than willing to show her one.

"So, Theo, tell me about Alaska. Are you going back after the wedding?"

"Nah. I loved it up there. But I'm thinking I might head for someplace warmer."

"Everyone is buzzing about you flying your own plane into town. That must be terribly exciting." Her eyes gleamed like she thought that made him pretty exciting, too.

It wasn't the first time a woman had been turned on when they found out he was a pilot, and he never minded using it to his advantage. "Flying is my one true love. Nothing like soaring through the clouds to make all your troubles fall away."

She let her arm slip from his shoulder to his waist. "I think I'd be too scared. A small plane like that."

He snuggled her closer. "You might be surprised. Would you like to go up sometime?"

"Oh, gosh. If you were doing the flying maybe." She giggled like she couldn't control her delight at the idea.

The sound of another laugh—an all too familiar laugh—drew his attention, and his good mood took a nosedive. Irene was holding court in one corner of the bar. He tried to ignore the way his breath caught when he spotted her, tall and regal, surrounded by men.

During his visit to Everson the summer before he'd suddenly caught sight of her on the street one day. Back then he had no idea she even lived in Everson. He assumed she was still living in Dallas with her rich husband. And even if she was going to move back to this area of the state, he would've thought she would move home to Derbyville.

But there she'd been big as life, walking alone down the street with her head held high like a queen, nodding occasionally to her loyal subjects. He'd stopped in his tracks feeling breathless as she approached, overcome with a mixture of excitement and terror, not having a clue what he would say. But it hadn't mattered. She looked straight through him and walked by like he was invisible.

True, he was older, but he didn't believe for one second that she didn't recognize him. It was a deliberate snub, and he'd been surprised at first and then a little angry. But from that moment on he'd said the hell with her, taking his cue from her and simply acting like they were strangers when they crossed paths. But every time she ignored him, every time she pretended he didn't exist, she tore another strip of flesh from his soul.

No doubt those slights from last summer had spurred him to buzz her house on his way into town. This time he'd been determined that she would acknowledge him one way or the other. But in the end that proved to be unnecessary. She must have known he'd be part of Jake and Marla Jean's wedding, so ignoring him wouldn't be an option she could exercise. For him the challenge was to find a way to appear cool and calm whenever she was around. And tonight was a good time to start.

He planned to have a great time dancing with Nell, even though he would be acutely aware of Ree and who she was dancing with at every moment. Nell deserved his undivided attention, but it felt like a sort of self-defense to keep an eye on the woman across the room, too.

The song ended and he escorted Nell to their table. "How about another beer?"

"Thanks. I would love one, Theo."

"You got it." Theo smiled and left her at the table. He made his way to the bar and ordered a pitcher. As he waited he watched Irene take the dance floor with some old geezer. The old guy was grinning like he'd struck gold, and she was having a high old time, too. He remembered very clearly how much she loved to dance. It was like the music buried itself inside her and had to come out as she moved around the floor. Most people danced. Irene became the dance.

She must have felt him watching because she turned her head and their eyes collided. She raised an eyebrow, questioning his attention. He waved and tipped his hat just for fun. He wasn't about to let her ignore him again. She returned his greeting with a tiny nod, and then he smiled and turned away.

The bartender put a pitcher of beer on the bar. "Here you go, Theo."

"Thanks, Mike." He grabbed the pitcher and mugs and made his way back to Nell.

He'd barely gotten settled in his chair when Nell said, "I saw you waving at Irene Cornwell."

"Pardon me?" He poured some beer into their frosted mugs.

"Irene Cornwell. She's a beautiful woman, so I can understand why she would get your attention, but I probably should warn you about her."

His hackles went up, and his first instinct was to defend Irene. And he didn't even know what he was defending her against yet. "That's okay, Nell. I'm sure I don't need any kind of warning. She's planning Jake's wedding. That's all."

Undeterred, she leaned closer and said conspiratorially, "You know everyone calls her the black widow."

Theo leaned away and looked at Nell like he'd heard her wrong. "Like the spider? I thought that was saved for women who marry a string of men for their money, and they all end up dying."

She nodded. "Exactly. Old Mr. Cornwell grew up around here, but then he goes off to Dallas and makes his fortune. He marries and has a kid. The first wife dies, and before the dust settles, he comes back married to her." She nodded toward Irene in case he'd lost track of who they were talking about. "He built that big house on the hill for her, and next thing you know he was dead, too. He didn't even live a year after they moved back to Everson. It was quite a scandal."

Theo knew most of this story, and the word "scandal" hadn't come up until now. During his last visit, he'd asked a few discreet questions about Irene and learned the basics. He hadn't been able to help himself. But the exquisite pleasure Nell was having at sharing the story with a total stranger rubbed him the wrong way. "Humph. Didn't you just say he was old?"

Nell smiled with delight at this chance to air someone else's dirty laundry. "Old enough to be her grandfather."

"Wow. So maybe his dying had more to do with his age than it did with his young wife." He could feel his blood start to boil at the unfair rumors swirling around about Ree. Not that he hadn't had more than a few uncharitable thoughts about her himself. But that was personal and somehow altogether different than this.

Nell took a drink of her beer and said coyly, "Hey, I'm not actually accusing her of anything."

"Aren't you? It sort of sounded like you were." The words came out harsher than he'd intended, and she recoiled.

Crossing her arms across her chest, she said, "Just forget I said anything. I just thought you'd want to know."

"Oh, I do, darlin'. How many other dead husbands do you think she's hiding?" Theo smiled like they were on the same side, and he could see her begin to relax again.

Nell grinned, getting back into the spirit of things. "Who knows? That's just it. No one knew anything about her before she moved here, and so people have good reason to be leery of a woman like that. She obviously married Sven Cornwell to get her hands on his money."

Theo nodded toward the man she was dancing with and the others who seemed lined up ready to take his place. "The men in this place don't seem all that leery. In fact, they seem anxious to ask her to dance."

Nell pursed her lips in disgust. "A bunch of old fools.

That's Arnie Douglas dancing with her now. He gets all dopey when she barely smiles at him. The men around here are completely blinded by her beauty."

"I can see how there might be a lot of truth in what you're saying, Nell. Men can be plumb crazy when it comes to a good-looking woman. And beauty can hide any number of character flaws. So thank you." He reached over and tucked a loose curl behind her ear.

"You're welcome, Theo." She beamed like she was happy to be the provider of such a service.

His barb went right over her head. "I have something else you can add to that story when you're spreading it around the old rumor mill."

She showed no shame at his implication, but eagerly prodded, "Oh, really? What's that? I'm all ears."

He leaned closer. "Well, Nell, after hearing your tale, I guess I'm one lucky guy."

She smiled in anticipation. "You are?"

He nodded and added gravely, "Yep. By all accounts, I narrowly escaped a horrible fate."

Her eyes got wider. "You did? Oh my gosh. What do you mean?"

He leaned in and confessed, "Because I almost married that woman."

"What?" Nell pulled back, looking appalled.

He stood up. "That's right. Irene and I used to be engaged. Now if you'll excuse me, I think I'll go ask my ex-fiancée to dance."

Chapter Four

❧

"May I cut in?" Theo's deep voice cut through the noisy din inside Lu Lu's, interrupting Arnie, who was offering to make his brand-new serenading service available for her wedding planning business at a reasonable fee, of course. He'd just started his spiel, and she hadn't quite gotten the gist of what he was talking about when Theo barged up and planted himself beside them like he belonged there.

Irene didn't do a very good job of hiding her utter dismay at Theo's audacity. She shook her head at him and narrowed her eyes. "No thank you. I'm dancing with Arnie right now." Irene recovered enough to smile at her dance partner. Then she took control of the situation and whirled herself and Arnie away from the spot where Theo stood rooted to the floor. What in the world was he doing? If he wanted to ask her to dance, that was one thing. He could just wait his turn. Not that she planned on saying yes if he asked.

But from the looks of it, he didn't seem put off in the

least by her refusal. He sidestepped and danced his way around Agnes May French and Norbert Anderson, and then with a few "excuse me's" he made it past Benny and Lois Miller and continued stalking them around the floor. He tapped Arnie on the shoulder again.

Arnie shot him an apologetic glance since it went against ballroom etiquette not to surrender your partner when asked, but with Irene's encouragement he kept her in his grasp and danced away again. *Stubborn as ever,* she thought, as Theo tracked them down once more. When he caught up with them, he said, "Okay, I won't try to cut in anymore, but Ree I'm claiming the next dance. It's important we talk, and this time I won't take no for an answer."

"Is it about the wedding?"

"No, but—"

Irene cut him off, declaring, "Then I'm afraid you'll have to, Theo. After this I'm dancing with Mick Ponder, and after that I promised Dan Ford. In fact, I seem to be booked all the way until closing time." She smiled at Arnie, and they waltzed away before he could say anything else. What could he possibly have to say that was so important? She didn't buy that tactic for a minute.

Important, my ass.

It wasn't as if she hadn't known he was here at Lu Lu's even before he'd waved hello. She'd seen him come in with Nell Harcourt, and that tingling she'd been suffering from all day had multiplied by a thousandfold. Her first instinct had been panic. Maybe she could go hide in the bathroom and then sneak out when he wasn't looking.

Sure, she'd put on a brave face when she'd seen him at the Hazelnut Inn. But that was a relatively private meeting, and since he was part of the wedding party it couldn't be avoided. She'd been prepared for that. But if it didn't involve the wedding she didn't plan to give him the time of day. So after a swift mental lecture, she pulled herself together and reminded herself that hiding wasn't her style. Lu Lu's was her stomping ground. Dammit. Not his. If anyone was going to leave, it would be Theo and Nell. She'd come to dance, and by golly, that's what she intended to do.

But of course she'd watched the way he held Nell on the dance floor, watched the way he'd thrown back his head and laughed at something clever Nell said. And it was clear to see that Nell thought she'd hit the jackpot being held in Theo's arms.

So Irene laughed harder than anyone in the room, and danced with whoever asked her, and decided she was absolutely without a doubt having the best time of anyone in the whole damn place.

In fact, she'd been having such a good time she hadn't noticed Theo approaching her on the dance floor until it was too late to avoid him. And now that she'd brushed him off, instead of going back to sit at the table where he'd been earlier with Nell, he was sitting at the bar. Waiting and watching her. She couldn't prevent him from doing that. It was a free country, but his gaze scraped across her skin like a razor, sharp and stinging.

The man still had the power to unsettle her, and she couldn't deny it.

The song ended and Arnie guided her to the edge of the dance floor. "Thanks for the dance, Irene. We can talk about Arnie's Serenades later, okay?"

"Sure, Arnie. I didn't know you sang."

"I don't, but I play the guitar and make the guy proposing do the singing. How do you think Donny Joe Ledbetter won Etta Green's heart?"

"I heard something about that. Okay. We can talk about it. Come by my office this week if you'd like. And thanks for not letting that rude man cut in. I appreciate it."

Arnie looked over where Theo sat at the bar staring at them. "Isn't that Jake's brother? I remember when he was visiting last summer."

"Yes, that's Jake's brother, Theo, and he's just irritated because I told him throwing firecrackers instead of rice at the wedding was a dumb idea." She was shoveling BS now, but when it came to Theo, she wasn't willing to delve into anything resembling the truth.

Arnie nodded slowly like he didn't really buy her explanation. "You don't say. I guess it makes sense he'd be back home for the wedding. If he bothers you again, just let me know."

She smiled at Arnie Douglas who weighed a hundred pounds soaking wet. He'd never manage to lay a hand on Theo if there was any kind of confrontation, but she appreciated the offer just the same.

"Thanks, Arnie, but I can handle Theo. I just didn't like him being so pushy. Besides, I wanted to dance with you."

Happy to accept her flattery, he smiled and floated away as Mick Ponder came up to claim his turn. Closing her eyes, she heaved a weary sigh. She was going to hate herself. She really, truly was, but she patted her new dance partner on the arm and against her better judgment asked, "Mick, do you mind if I sit this one out? I have some business I need to handle first."

Mick stuck his thumbs in his belt loops and leaned

back on his bootheels. "Sure thing, Irene. You go ahead. I'll catch you later."

With a pat on his arm, she said, "Thank you. I appreciate it."

Mick left to find another dance partner while she fumed. It would serve Theo right if she left him sitting on that barstool all night until his bony ass went numb. She sighed while admitting he'd piqued her curiosity. What in the world had gotten him so riled up that he was willing to make a spectacle of himself by stalking her around the dance floor? The sooner she talked to him, the sooner they could settle this supposed "important" issue, and she could go back to having fun.

She turned and found he hadn't moved. He was still watching her. How those cool blue eyes could transmit so much heat had always baffled her. It was disturbing to discover she wasn't immune to the thrill of being the center of his focus. The arousal that swept through her was just as devastating as it had been all those years ago. She made her way to the bar and stopped in front of him.

"Where's your date, Theodore? Did you manage to run her off already?"

He stood up as she approached. "Who, Nell? She got a ride home with someone else."

Irene took the barstool next to his. "Still charming as ever, I see."

He sat back down beside her. "You know, I'd sort of hoped Nell and I could have some fun while I was here in Everson, but it doesn't look like that's going to work out."

"So, it's true then. Your mother told me you had a woman in every port. She also said you'd broken hearts all over the world."

He looked at her sharply. "I'm afraid my mother likes to embellish. And when exactly did you talk to my mother?"

Irene had meant to keep that information to herself. He didn't need to know she'd kept tabs on him over the years. "I haven't spoken to her since she moved to Colorado with husband number three."

Theo raised an eyebrow. "Colorado is husband number four, but who's counting?"

She decided she might as well come clean. "Your mother used to give me updates on where you were and what you were doing."

He harrumphed. "As if you cared."

Of course she cared. That had always been the problem. "We used to be friends, Theo."

"Ree, you have the strangest way of treating your friends. Last time I was in town you acted like I didn't exist."

"Don't call me Ree," she insisted.

He ignored her and kept talking. "And we used to be engaged."

She turned her stool to face him. "We were engaged for about five minutes."

He laughed. "We were engaged for the better part of a year, and you know it."

She sighed. "Well, it was a mistake, and we both know that. And by the way, I think ignoring you worked out pretty good last time. If it weren't for your brother's wedding, I'd be ignoring you this time, too."

"Whatever you say." He leaned in closer and said in a confidential tone, "But here's the thing. That so-called mistake is what I wanted to warn you about."

She sat up straighter, easing away from the heat radiating from his big body. "Warn me about what? You've completely lost me, Theo."

He grinned sheepishly like a kid about to confess he'd thrown a rock through a plate glass window. "Don't get mad, Ree, but I'm afraid I let the truth about our old relationship slip."

She turned to face him more fully. "You did what? Who did you tell? And what exactly did you tell them?"

He raised his eyebrows. "Hmm. You didn't call me Theodore, but still, you seem mad."

She grabbed his arm as the truth hit her. "Oh my gosh. You told Nell, didn't you?"

He grimaced and held his hands out as he confessed, "I'm afraid so."

"Nell, of all people. Why didn't you just take out a billboard on the highway?"

"Come on. Is she that bad?" He seemed to underestimate the fallout that could result from his big blabbermouth.

Irene wanted to throttle him. "Oh, come on, yourself. Her mother is Bertie Harcourt. The Rise-N-Shine Diner runs on gossip. It's part of Nell's DNA. Everyone and their next of kin will know by morning. What exactly did you tell her?"

He shrugged. "The truth. I told her we were engaged for a while before you up and married Sven Cornwell."

She stared at him blankly, so he kept talking. She was having trouble processing his words.

"In a way I was defending you," he said with a wink as if it let him off the hook. Now he was going to try to spin this so he came out looking noble. She groaned and laid her head on her crossed arms on the bar. He kept jabbering on. "She actually accused you of murdering all your old husbands, if you can believe that."

She raised her head. "The black widow thing? I've heard it before. A million times. Good grief." A frustrated growl escaped from her throat. "It's old news, and around here people will believe what they want. But I'm not in jail, am I? Obviously, I don't need to be defended, Theo."

"All of those old protective instincts kicked in, I guess. Jeez, you can't be mad because I stood up for you." He had the nerve to act like she should thank him.

"Sure I can. Exactly how did this conversation go, anyway? Were you bragging? Or did you tell her for shock value? Give me a break. Why would you tell her of all people? Your brother doesn't even know."

His face screwed up in a pained expression. "That's why I wanted to warn you. I don't really care if the whole town knows, but after I let it slip, I realized I'm going to have to tell Jake. I should have just told him the whole story the other day, but I didn't. And now..."

"And now?"

"And now I wanted you to know I'm sorry." He didn't sound sorry. "And I'll tell Jake tomorrow."

"Wait. We'll just deny it. I'll tell everyone you were drunk and Nell misunderstood." For a second that seemed like a real good option, but he started shaking his head as the words were still leaving her mouth.

"That sounds like more trouble than it's worth, Ree. And why would we bother? It's not like we did anything illegal or anything."

"No, but the fact that we kept it secret makes it seem

like there's something to hide." She jumped off the barstool and paced back and forth. "Crap, Theo. You fly into town and instantly complicate my life. Why couldn't you just do your best man duties and be on your way?"

Theo twirled his stool around to face her. "Settle down, Ree. It doesn't have to be complicated. I'm just an ex-boyfriend. End of story."

She had her doubts that it would be so simple. She stopped and glared daggers at him. "I want to be there when you tell Jake."

He grinned. "Why? Don't you trust me?"

She put her hands on her hips. "I just want to make sure my side of the story is reported accurately. He may be your brother, but he's also my client. We happen to be up to our ears in wedding plans at the moment, and I want to assure him this won't be a problem."

He pulled his phone from his pocket. "Let me give him a call. It's not that late, and we can go give them the news now."

She listened to the short conversation Theo carried on with his brother. When he ended the call, she opened her eyes and asked, "Well?"

"He said to come on over."

"Okay," she declared. "You can ride with me." She walked to a corner table and grabbed her purse.

Theo followed her while protesting, "I've got a car, you know."

She headed for Lu Lu's front door. "I'll bring you back to your car when we're done. I don't want you out of my sight until this mess is settled. You might stop at the town square and announce it to the world from the gazebo."

"You are being overly dramatic as usual, but fine. Do

you still drive like a maniac?" he asked as they walked out to the parking lot.

She ignored his question, which wasn't worth dignifying, and stopped at the Shelby. She unlocked the doors and started to climb behind the wheel.

He gave the car an admiring once-over. "Wow. Nice car. I don't suppose you'd let me drive her?"

She patted the car fondly as she got behind the steering wheel. "Not a chance in hell, buddy. Get in and fasten your seat belt."

She started the car and pulled out of the parking lot, spraying gravel beneath her tires. Her emotions were jumping around like cold water on a hot griddle. It was disconcerting having him sit so close. The heat from his body invaded her personal space. Theo was an impressive-looking man, the kind that turned heads and inspired fantasies. By tomorrow everyone and their grandpappy was going to know they'd once been involved and tongues would start wagging.

Theo had obviously never told a soul. Until tonight when he decided to share the information with a total stranger. Nell. Irene figured if she was really lucky the hubbub would die down about the same time Theo decided to pull up stakes and move on. She could hope, anyway. She glanced at his face illuminated by the dashboard lights and asked the question that had always bugged her.

"Why haven't you ever told Jake about us? I thought you and Jake shared everything." She'd wondered for years now, worrying over it like a knot she couldn't unravel, never coming up with a satisfactory answer. The only conclusion she could reach was that the time they'd spent together didn't matter much to him and wasn't important enough to share. Even knowing how they'd parted, that idea made her sad. She would never be able to file their past away as unimportant.

He didn't answer her question, but clutched the armrest as she sped around a curve and countered with a question of his own. "Why haven't you told him? You've lived in the same town with Jake for years. After you moved here, you must have figured out pretty quickly that he was my brother."

"Oh, sure. The great and wondrous Jake Jacobson. I remember how you worshipped him. The first time I saw him walking down the street I nearly fainted. From a distance he looks so much like you." She remembered how her heart started beating like a frantic, trapped bird when she thought Theo was standing down the street. And she remembered how it slowed to a wounded, dull ache when she realized it wasn't him.

"But you didn't say anything?" He grabbed his seat belt as she braked suddenly.

She turned to stare at him. "It wasn't my place, was it?" And at the time, standing in the middle of the sidewalk, she could barely breathe, much less talk.

He shrugged. "I don't know. You could have introduced yourself."

"And said what? I'm your brother's ex-fiancée? The one he never bothered to mention?" The car behind them honked.

"The light's green, Ree."

She gritted her teeth and then pressed on the accelerator making a jackrabbit start. "I didn't think it was my place if you didn't want him to know."

He grabbed the armrest again. "Why is our past relationship so hush-hush, anyway?"

She laughed. "That's a good one. We are rushing through the night to tell your big brother our secret before he hears it from someone else, and you're asking me that? I was merely following your lead."

"Don't blame me. First I was Jake's secret brother, and now I'm your secret ex-fiancé. Maybe I'm tired of being the person no one wants to acknowledge."

She turned into Jake and Marla Jean's driveway and made her way down the winding lane. "Believe me, by tomorrow that will no longer be something you have to worry about."

He sighed. "Ree, listen. If we can pretend to get along for the next week or so, I'll bet you a million bucks this will blow over like nothing ever happened. I don't want any old animosity between us to ruin Jake and Marla Jean's wedding."

"Neither do I." She stopped in front of the big white house and twisted in the driver's seat to face him. "They are paying handsomely for me to provide a fairy-tale wedding with peace and love abounding."

"Exactly. I'm just here to do my best man duties. That's it."

"And I'm the wedding planner. That's it."

He held out his hand. "So, can we call a truce, for Jake and Marla Jean's sake?"

She held out her hand and cursed the shivers that raced up her arm as he shook her hand. "For Jake and Marla Jean's sake."

He opened his door and got out. She opened the driver's door and climbed out, too. Once he'd come around the car to join her, she started up the front steps. "Let's get this over with, honey."

"I'm right behind you, sweetie."

His words rang in her ears as she knocked on the front door and waited for an answer.

Chapter Five

⁓

The front door opened and Sadie bounded out onto the screened porch before Jake could stop her. The dog made a beeline for Theo and started howling like she'd found her long lost friend. Theo knelt down wrestling with her like a little kid. Since he'd been back in town, she'd acted the same way every time he'd been to the house. They'd bonded when she'd been an abandoned puppy rescued by Jake and Marla Jean. He had no idea she would remember him, but he was glad she did. At least someone was glad to see him again.

"Come on in," Marla Jean said. She was wearing bunny rabbit slippers and a robe thrown over shorts and an old hockey jersey.

"Did we wake you up?" Irene asked. "I told Theo this could wait until morning."

Jake got everyone inside and shut the front door. "We were awake. What's this about? Does it have something to do with the wedding?"

Marla Jean directed them to a couch in the living room.

They sat down and waited while Jake and Marla Jean settled into side chairs. Sadie stuck her head in Theo's lap, wagging her tail while he scratched her head.

Theo smiled tentatively. "It's not about the wedding. At least not your wedding, anyway."

"Whose then?" Jake asked.

Theo jumped off the couch and paced around. He wanted some distance from Irene when he revealed the truth. "Ours."

Marla Jean looked like he'd spoken a foreign language. "What do you mean, yours?"

Irene stood up, too. "He doesn't mean ours, not exactly. But he's talking about the two of us, as in me and him."

Jake joined the standing ranks and asked, "You and Theo?"

She nodded. "Well—"

Marla Jean jumped up and interrupted her before she finished explaining. "You mean you eloped tonight? I could tell there was something between you two. Oh my goodness, that's so romantic. Isn't it, Jake? Crazy but romantic." She was beaming at them like she'd just been given an early Christmas present.

Horrified, Theo stopped in his tracks and turned to face her. "Good God, no. It's nothing like that."

"Oh." Marla Jean seemed majorly disappointed and sat back down.

Jake crossed his arms over his chest. "So, let's try this from the start. What's so important that both of you felt the need to drive all the way out here in the middle of the night if it doesn't involve our wedding."

"It's only nine, Jake, and like you said, we were awake," Marla Jean scolded him and then turned to Theo. "We're listening, Theo. What is it you need to tell us?"

Theo stopped pacing and sat back down on the couch. "Okay. You already suspected that besides working together at the grocery store, Irene and I knew each other when we lived in Dallas, too."

"That seemed like a good guess," Jake said.

"We were both going to community college. I had a partial scholarship, and Ree was waitressing at the golf club. But you know how it is. We were young and broke, both barely scraping by. So, we decided to share an apartment to save on expenses, and one thing led to another. After a while I asked her to marry me, and she said yes." He'd compressed a lot of their history, saying the last part in a rush like it wouldn't count if he blurted it out fast enough.

Irene decided to add something to the account. "We were both so young, and it turned out to be a mistake."

Theo glanced at her, trying to hide his reaction. It wasn't like he disagreed, and it was certainly no surprise she felt that way. He supposed in hindsight the idea to get married had been an ill-thought-out, impulsive, youthful mistake. But at the time he'd been deeply in love with her. And he'd thought she loved him, too. It hurt to finally hear Irene bluntly say otherwise.

Jake finally sat back down, too. "And you never bothered to tell me? I know we didn't see each other as much when you lived in Dallas, but you still had a phone. Something that important? Why wouldn't you tell me?"

"I would have, but Ree got cold feet and called it off. I joined the Navy. She married someone else. All in all, in the scheme of things it turned out not to be important. Besides, I had no way of knowing you two would end up living in the same town."

Irene crossed her arms across her chest and gave Theo a hard look. "That's not exactly how it happened, but for now I won't bore you with details. You get the gist of it."

Marla Jean got up and moved to the couch to sit by Irene. "So, does that mean you knew Jake was Theo's brother the whole time?"

"It wasn't hard to figure out. Theo talked about him all the time back then. And look at them. Two peas in a pod. But I figured Theo should be the one to share our secret, and he never did so I kept quiet, too."

"Now it seems sort of silly," Theo admitted.

"So, why the urgent need to tell us now?"

Irene crossed her legs and started swinging her foot. "Theo was trying to impress Nell Harcourt tonight, and he told her we used to be engaged."

Theo put his hands on his hips. "I wasn't trying to impress her."

"Whatever. The point is everyone in town will have heard the news by morning."

Theo sighed. "Jake, I thought you should hear it from me. I'm sorry I never told you before. But it was a long time ago."

Irene nodded. "Ancient history."

Jake blew out a deep breath. "Well, I appreciate the heads-up. We'll be prepared to deal with any remarks we hear. If we all react casually, I don't know why this shouldn't all blow over in no time. It's still hard for me to believe. You and Irene. But so what? The two of you had a thing a million years ago. What's the big deal? Right?"

"Right." Theo smiled at his big brother. Jake always kept things in perspective. And this was the time to celebrate the future. Marla Jean and Jake's future. Not dwell on his unhappy past.

Irene sat on the couch, chewing on her thumbnail and looking worried. She didn't seem to share Jake's optimism. She grabbed her purse and stood up. "Well, now that everything is out in the open, we should leave. Come on, Theo, I'll take you back to your car."

Marla Jean and Jake walked them out to the front porch. Marla Jean said, "Instead of coffee, we should all have breakfast together at the diner tomorrow morning just to get an idea of what everyone is saying."

"That's a good idea," Jake said. Then he added as if it just occurred to him, "Will it be a problem for the two of you to work together while we're gone?"

"Of course not," Theo said quickly. He didn't want them to worry about a thing back home while they were off on their honeymoon.

"Not at all," Irene said, too, but Theo thought she sounded like she'd rather enter the lion's den with a raw steak hung around her neck.

After they got in the car, she turned to him and said glumly, "Are you happy now?"

He tried to stretch out his long legs in the small car. "Are you asking in general? My life's pretty good, so sure, I'd say I'm happy. How about you, Ree? How's life treating you these days?"

"Until you showed up my life was just peachy." She started the car and started down the driveway. "Now I'm not so sure."

"Maybe we should talk about that." They'd never hashed anything out, never discussed how it all fell apart.

"There's nothing to talk about, Theo. Let's just get

through this, okay? I promised to be civil for the sake of Jake's wedding, and that's all I promised."

It seemed to him there was a lot to talk about, but he could feel her pulling down a curtain, shutting him out. "Fine. If that's the way you want it. I'll try to stay out of your way as much as possible."

The rest of the ride was tense and the silence thick with unasked questions and unresolved emotions. She pulled into Lu Lu's parking lot, and he got out, climbing into the Jeep without saying good night. Watching her taillights disappear as she pulled out onto the road, he kicked himself up one side and down the other. He didn't know why he'd felt the need to take up for her tonight with Nell. He'd only opened a can of worms, and Irene certainly wasn't thanking him for it. In fact, it looked like her only plan was to tolerate him—just barely.

• • •

Irene tossed and turned, trying to sleep. It was no use. Listening to Theo spout his version of their past to Jake had made her furious. She'd gotten cold feet? He had some nerve blaming her for everything that had gone wrong.

Growing up poor with no parents to support her, Irene's guiding goal early in her life was finding and holding on to security. Like the gold ring on the merry-go-round, she wanted to grab it with both hands and never let go. She hadn't apologized for putting it at the top of her list back in those days. As a young girl, she'd bounced around between different relatives. No one really wanted her, much less could afford to take her in, but eventually she ended up with her aunt Jo and uncle Ed. It hadn't been terrible. Aunt Jo did her best to make Irene feel welcome, but she had been painfully aware of the burden she placed on their family. They already had two girls to raise, and her cousins resented having to share a bedroom because of her too. She vowed when she got older she would never have to worry about having the simple basics that any kid should be able to expect. Enough to eat, a place to sleep that was all her own, and decent clothes to wear. Not ever again.

Love hadn't been anywhere on her radar. At least not the romantic kind. Back then she was pragmatic, focused, and told herself she didn't have room in her life for that kind of complication. But then she met Theo, and everything changed. Their slow, steady, dependable friendship exploded into a love so passionate, so deep, that she thought she might die from wanting him. When he asked her to marry him, all of her old resolve faded away. She said yes, realizing with a bone-aching need that the other thing she'd never had in her life was someone to really care about her. Theo cared. In fact, he loved her wholeheartedly, and it was a balm to her battered soul.

Even when they'd worked together at Piggly Wiggly, she'd liked him more than she wanted to admit. For hours he would listen to her talk about her dreams, and on top of that, he seemed to be as anxious as she was to get out of Derbyville and make something of himself. Tackling the future with Theo by her side made her feel brave and strong. She'd had to be strong all of her life, but suddenly with Theo she didn't have to do it alone. And she did love him. It was scary, but loving Theo, trusting him, almost felt like the same thing as security. It was such a relief to lower the tall walls she'd built around her heart and let him inside. When she'd accepted his proposal, he hadn't seemed to realize how much courage that had taken. And she should have known better. Without a second thought he left and joined the Navy, and she was alone all over again. So when it came to an honest recounting of the story of their past, it seemed to her he was the one who'd gotten cold feet.

• • •

Theo was glad Lincoln had insisted on this bachelor party. Even if it was only pool and pitchers of beer in Lu Lu's back room. It wasn't a wild orgy, like some he'd attended, and that was fine by him. Jake wasn't the wild orgy kind of guy even before he became an engaged man. But he was kicking back, blowing off a little steam, and relaxing before the big day. And he was grinning like a fool. Nonstop. The man didn't have a single doubt that he was doing the right thing by marrying Marla Jean, and it made Theo grin, too, seeing his big brother so content with his lot in life.

Jake was listening to Linc tell a story about some prank they'd pulled back in high school, something about stealing another school's mascot and hiding it before the big game. A goat named Annabelle, Linc said. Jake corrected him, saying no, the goat was named Butthead. The cheerleader that dumped Linc was named Annabelle. They corrected each other every other sentence and cracked up the way two friends do when they know where the story is going but love reliving it anyway.

Theo's attention was drawn to an older, frail-looking woman who wandered inside looking like she was lost. "Excuse me," she called out. "I'm looking for the groom-to-be. My name's Ethel, and I'm the entertainment for the night."

Jake looked alarmed while all the guys whooped it up. Lincoln stood up and guided her into the room. "Right over here, ma'am." He was grinning from ear to ear, and Theo was pretty certain he was up to no good.

Donny Joe Ledbetter pulled up a chair and sat down beside him just as the old lady pulled an iPod out from her baggy shirt. Donny Joe cackled. "She must be one of those strippers disguised as an old lady. This should be good."

Theo shot Donny Joe a sharp look. "I thought there weren't supposed to be any strippers."

She hit the play button and music poured out into the room. The woman started gyrating to the drumbeat of the song. Her hands were in the air, and her hips bounced around like basketballs being dribbled double-time. Theo didn't know whether to laugh or cover his eyes.

Donny Joe shrugged and tipped his hat back, enjoying the show. "Don't look at me. This is all on Linc."

Theo wanted to see how Jake was reacting. His brother looked horrified and amused and like he might kill his best friend. Just when it couldn't get any weirder, Ethel stunned them all by pulling off her short gray wig to reveal long strands of salt-and-pepper hair underneath. Without her disguise the woman was still at least sixty-five if she was a day.

First her blouse came off, and she flung it toward Jake. He put up his hands in an attempt to ward off her flying blouse just as her skirt landed on his head. Now dressed only in a blue polka-dot one-piece skirted bathing suit, she winked while going into a shimmy, moving directly in front of Jake, her honored victim. The guys hooted and hollered while Jake remained still as a statue. As the song came to an end, she spread her arms wide and attempted to do the splits, which never made it all the way to the floor. With her legs spread in an awkward wobbly V, she yelled, "And many more!"

Lincoln was doubled over laughing. "And many more?" Theo was afraid he was going to bust a gut. "And many more?"

Ethel staggered to her feet, panting and out of breath. "I usually do birthdays." She stopped in front of Jake and kissed him on the cheek. "Congratulations, young man."

Jake managed a courtly response. "Thank you, Ethel. You've made the night one I won't forget."

She gathered her clothes and started handing out business cards. "Tell all your friends, and have fun, boys." Theo, along with everyone else, stood and clapped. With a final wave she scampered out of the room.

As soon as she was gone, Jake grabbed Lincoln. "I'm going to kill you."

Linc didn't seem worried. "Aw, come on, *young man*. What's a bachelor party without a stripper?"

Jake shook his head. "That stripper might have broken a hip doing those splits. I hope you paid her enough money to cover medical bills."

Linc caught him in a bear hug. "Nothing's too good for you, buddy."

Theo was listening to their good-natured ribbing when Donny Joe said, "So, I hear you used to be engaged to Irene Cornwell." Donny Joe was smiling as they settled back into their chairs, but there was an edge to his words, a warning that he hadn't decided if he approved of the situation.

Theo didn't think it was any of Donny Joe's business,

but Donny Joe had known Irene for a long time, so he decided to give him the benefit of the doubt. Besides, he didn't want to start trouble at Jake's party, so instead of telling Donny Joe to shove it, he nodded and said, "Many moons ago."

"She's a wonderful woman." Donny Joe announced this solemnly as if he was preaching to a hell-bent sinner.

Theo took a sip of his beer. No one needed to sing Ree's praises to him. "You are telling me this because?"

Donny Joe's aw-shucks demeanor disappeared, and he pinned him with a glacial stare. "Because I expect you to be on your best behavior while you're in Everson."

Theo straightened. He was ready to change his mind about causing trouble if Donny Joe kept pushing it. "Are you threatening me, Donny Joe?"

Donny Joe shrugged. "Not at all. I'm just saying Irene could be vulnerable where an old flame's concerned. If you fly into town and stir up old feelings and then disappear again, I'll find you and beat you within an inch of your life. That's all."

Theo laughed. It was nice to know Irene had a champion, but Donny Joe was crossing the line. "Okay. For a minute I thought you were threatening me."

If possible, Donny Joe's expression grew sterner. "Just watch yourself."

Theo had had enough. "Look, Donny Joe, if I'm not mistaken you have a history of your own involving Irene. And now you're engaged to Etta Green. Maybe I should be beating you within an inch of your life."

Donny Joe tipped his hat back on his head. "Okay. Point taken, but you can't believe everything you hear through the grapevine."

Theo didn't try to hide his disdain. "That grapevine seems to be the main source of information for you folks in this town."

Donny Joe threw up his hands. "Guilty as charged." He punched Theo on the shoulder while slipping his good ol' boy grin back in place. "But I mean it. If you hurt her, you'll answer to me."

Theo rubbed his shoulder. "You've made your feelings clear. I'll take it all under consideration. Now if you'll excuse me." Theo was growing weary of Donny Joe's lecture and started to get up, but Donny Joe stopped him with a hand in the air.

"Hang on a minute. Now that we've got that straight, there's something else I want to ask about."

Theo sat back down. "What about?"

"Well, I've heard there's a chance you're considering settling down here for good. I know you'd be working with Jake, but I wonder if you'd consider another offer."

"You heard wrong. Jake mentioned the idea, but I'm not planning on sticking around." Jake needed to stop spreading that idea around town. "After the wedding I'll be heading to Australia."

Donny Joe nodded. "That's too bad. We could use a pilot to make a few runs to Dallas for the Hazelnut Inn. I thought you might be interested."

Out of curiosity Theo asked, "For guests or supplies?"

"Both. We have quite a few guests who would pay to fly from Dallas, and if we could offer that as a regular service, it would be a boon. But supplies would be something we'd consider, too, if it was cost-effective."

"You should talk to Bart at the airfield. He could probably help you out with that." Theo pondered the idea briefly before dismissing it. If he planned to stay he might be interested, but he wasn't so there was no point in discussing it further.

"Okay, but if you change your mind, let me know."

"Sure, Donny Joe. But as of now I plan to sell my plane and head to Australia." Theo stood up. "Now I need to make a toast celebrating my brother's big day tomorrow."

Donny Joe nodded and stood up, too. "I'll drink to that. To Jake and Marla Jean. Now there are two people who actually belong together." Theo watched him walk away before clearing his throat and raising his glass.

• • •

She should have been worrying about some unattended detail. There was bound to be something important to take care of. But she'd been over her checklist a dozen times and the wedding was well under way. Everything looked beautiful.

At this very moment Marla Jean stood at the outdoor altar with Jake beaming by her side. Their love for each other was obvious, almost painful for Irene to see. She'd given up long ago on ever having that kind of love again in her life.

Once again, in the same way it had been doing all day, her gaze strayed to Theo. He stood tall and proud by Jake's side. She found it hard not to stare at him. Impossible really. And right now she could probably get away with it without anyone noticing. All the good folks of Everson were rightfully focused on Marla Jean and Jake, so Irene could safely steal a moment to study Theo without being caught.

The first thing that struck her was a certain sense about

him, an air he carried, that he'd lived life to the fullest. He was a bit older obviously. No longer the young man she'd fallen in love with all those years ago. And she'd seen more than one woman sitting in the audience check out the way his body filled out his tuxedo. The afternoon was warm, but Irene wasn't sure if the women were fanning themselves because of the heat or from the sheer impact of seeing the two Jacobson brothers standing side by side in front of them. They made quite a picture.

Irene thought it was almost unfair for two men to be so good-looking. Jake was a little taller, his frame a little broader, but Irene preferred Theo's slim elegance. The leanness of youth had turned to muscle, and he carried himself with a confident grace that said he'd seen the world and was sure of his place in it.

And then there was his face. A strong jaw, a slender nose, and a mouth that could tempt any woman with a pulse. That dark hair she remembered so well falling down onto his forehead and brushing his collar. The way it curled when she used to run her fingers through it. His eyes hadn't changed. They were still as blue as the sky on a bright, sunny day. After all these years she still dreamed about getting lost in those laughing eyes. Now a few lines fanned out from the corners when he grinned. And he seemed to grin all the time. Those lines hadn't been there back in the days when they shared an apartment. They gave him a dashing, happy-go-lucky air that dared the world to join him on his next adventure. With Theo there was always a next adventure.

At that moment he looked up and caught her staring. He winked. Damn him. She could already tell he was not going to make the next few weeks easy for her.

Breakfast at the Rise-N-Shine hadn't been the nightmare she'd expected. Everyone stopped by to say howdy and stare at them like they'd escaped from the circus. She was already a bit of a curiosity to folks in town, so finding out about Theo was just another piece added to her shadowy past. Marla Jean and Jake helped, though. They took it all in stride, and soon the gossipmongers went away disappointed at not finding anything scandalous to report. For his part, Theo smiled and chatted with his arm draped across the back of the booth, just grazing her shoulder, and Irene shivered from the barely there touch. Since then he'd been friendly, maybe a little too friendly for her peace of mind.

Irene snapped out of her daydream when the preacher announced grandly, "I now pronounce you man and wife. You may kiss your bride."

Jake smiled and leaned down, placing a gentle kiss on Marla Jean's lips. She was having none of that. She threw her arms around his neck kissing him passionately, and the crowd went hog wild, and then they made their trek down the grassy aisle as newly united Mr. and Mrs. Jacobson.

Irene got ready to corral the newlyweds and the members of the wedding party so the photographer could finish getting pictures of the big day. And the minister was directing the guests to the pavilion where dinner would be served by Etta and her staff.

Irene beamed. The ceremony had gone off without a hitch. Everyone was so happy for Marla Jean and Jake. It was contagious. Now everyone was ready to kick up their heels and enjoy the reception inside the pavillion. A big party where the guests would eat, drink, and dance the night away. But she couldn't stand around patting herself on the back. She still had work to do.

• • •

"As best man, it's not only my duty, but my honor to toast the bride and groom." The wedding guests turned their attention to the front table where Theo stood with a glass of champagne in his hand. "I'm not the best public speaker in the world, but I want everyone to know the kind of man Jake is."

He turned to face his brother, and the two men exchanged a significant look. Theo's voice was full of love and pride as he continued, "He's my big brother, but you might not know that we didn't meet until after our father died. Jake, even though he was still in college, took it upon himself to be there for me, no matter what. He came to all my baseball games, he helped me out with my first car, let me crash on his couch when I got drunk after my first girlfriend dumped me." He paused and added with a grin, "I know it's hard to believe any woman would ever dump me."

While everyone laughed he spotted Irene at the back of the room. She glanced up and their eyes collided, locking in a heated stare. She raised her glass of punch in acknowledgment. The flower arrangement on the table suddenly seemed to require all of her attention, and she looked away.

He continued, "Some of you have actually known Jake longer than I have, and everyone agrees he's a great guy. I wasn't sure he was ever going to smarten up and ask Marla Jean to marry him, but I'm glad he finally did. I don't know of any two people who belong together as much as you two do." He clapped Jake on the back and raised his glass. "Here's to Jake and Marla Jean. I love you both."

Everyone raised a glass to the newlyweds. Marla Jean hugged his neck and Jake did, too. He looked like he had a tear in his eye. "Thanks, little brother. I am the happiest man in the world today."

Theo looked him straight in the eye and said sincerely, "You deserve it. Thanks for everything, Jake."

After that there were more toasts, more well-wishers telling stories about the couple. Marla Jean and Jake danced their first dance as a newly married couple. Soon everyone else joined them on the dance floor.

As the maid of honor, Dinah, despite her hugely pregnant condition, decided to lead the group in a line dance. Lincoln joined his wife, and Theo laughed, watching Hoot and Dooley with their wives doing the Cupid Shuffle. Even Milton and Bitsy joined in.

Theo looked around for Irene, but she seemed to have disappeared.

He hadn't realized how much this wedding would make him think about what could have been. Considering the life he could have had if they'd gone through with their plans to marry. He'd given up that dream years ago, and these days he was all about keeping things light and casual. But if he was honest, no woman had ever lived up to his memories of Ree and the days they'd spent together.

There was always a chance since he'd be working for her now that he'd discover he was painting the past with a rosy glow that wouldn't live up to the harsh light of the present day. They were both older now and different people than the two kids who'd thought they'd been in love. Reality would probably give him a nice kick in the head and show him that she wasn't the same woman he'd dreamed about. And if he was lucky, he hoped he could finally say he was over her once and for all. Spending time with her would be good. Build up some immunity so she didn't have the power to lay waste to his emotions with every smile or glance. At least it sounded like a good excuse to do what he really wanted to do. He spotted her across the room and headed in that direction.

Chapter Six

~~~~~~

"Can I have this dance?" Theo approached Irene while she was checking on the punch bowl. As soon as the ceremony was over, he'd watched her bustling around, making sure everything was running smoothly. He had to give her credit. She'd done a nice job with the wedding. Maybe her new career wasn't such a crazy idea after all.

"Go away, Theo. I'm the hired help. I can't take time from my duties to dance with you." She laughed like he'd just suggested the silliest thing.

"Sure you can." He took an empty glass from her hand and returned it to the table. He tossed his head in the direction of the couple that owned the Inn. "Donny Joe and Etta are dancing. I think that means you can, too." He held out his hand.

"People are starting to stare, Theo. Now just go away."

"They are only staring because they can't believe how beautiful you look today. Green was always a good color on you." She was wearing a short dress the color of apples, and it looked like it would be silky to the touch.

She laughed, but he thought she blushed, too. "Wow. You're dragging out the charm for me? Why don't you go dance with someone else? I'm sure they'll be more susceptible."

"You don't need to remind me how completely immune you are to my charms. Ree, I have deep scars to prove that." He put his hand over his heart as if she'd wounded him.

Her eyebrows shot up. "Deep scars? Don't make me laugh. And when did you become so dramatic?"

His grin was unapologetic. "Okay, the truth is I'm only asking for Jake and Marla Jean's sake. If everyone sees us getting along, they won't have anything to gossip about. That way the focus can stay entirely on the happy bride and groom. Where it belongs."

"So noble of you, Theo." She turned to watch the happy couple, who swayed in the middle of the crowd. "They do look happy, don't they?"

Theo turned, too, and leaned over to whisper in her ear, "They look as if they're the only people on the planet." He heard her sigh and pressed his advantage. "That's true love. It took them awhile to find each other, but I'd say that's a case of happily ever after if there ever was one."

Before she could protest again, he drew her out onto the dance floor. The song was a country two-step, and he wrapped her up in his arms. She fit perfectly. Randy Travis was singing about loving someone forever. Amen. He held her hand in his remembering the delicate shape, her slender fingers, the soft skin of her palm nestled against his. His other hand rested on her waist, and he could feel the warmth of her body through the material of her pale green dress. He'd been right. It was silky. And smooth, just like the skin it was lucky enough to skim over.

"Remember when we used to go dancing at the Blue Lagoon?" He didn't know if he should be bringing up old times or not, but when they'd been young and broke and crazy happy, they'd spent a lot of time spinning around the dance floor of the club close to their apartment in Dallas.

"I remember." Her voice was soft.

"We had some good times back then, didn't we, Ree?" He pulled her closer, and she reacted by pushing away.

"Don't do this, Theo. Don't try to soften me up with a half-assed corny walk down memory lane."

He did a quick spin and grinned. "Are you saying we didn't used to burn up the dance floor back in the good old days?"

"If they were so good, why haven't we talked to each other in all these years?"

He stopped dancing and moved to the edge of the dance floor. "I believe that was your choice, Ree."

"I was only following your lead." She smiled breezily at the folks dancing past them, but they still gawked at the two of them like they'd shed their clothes and were dancing around naked.

Theo narrowed his eyes and dropped her hand. "You can revise our history all you want, but I'm the one who got a letter saying it was all over. Just like that."

"Theo, lower your voice, please. It wasn't just like that, and you know it. Now is not the time to rehash all of this. I'm working and your plan backfired. People are staring at us. Not in a good way, either."

Theo glanced around and saw that it was true. He pasted on a big smile for show. "You're right. I apologize. Next time I ask you to dance we'll just talk about the weather."

"What in the world makes you think there will be a next time?"

"Darlin', as long as we're in the same town, there will always be a next time." As long as they were on the same damned planet, he thought, next time was all but inevitable.

She reached up and patted him on the cheek. "Don't hold your breath, darlin'. Now if you'll excuse me, it's time for the bride and groom to cut the cake."

• • •

Irene walked into the empty pavilion and looked at the ravages left behind by the wedding revelers. She couldn't remember ever being so tired.

She dropped into a chair, allowing herself a minute to sit down and look over her checklist. She decided right then and there that planning and executing a wedding was a snap compared to cleaning up the aftermath. Not that she didn't have plenty of people helping, of course, but there was so much to be done and a short amount of time to do it. Part of her contract with the Hazelnut Inn was a promise to return the pavilion back to normal as quickly as possible. It wouldn't help to have weddings at the Inn if they were too disruptive to the other guests staying there.

Thank goodness Etta and her kitchen staff from the Inn had taken care of gathering up all the dirty dishes, and they'd also packaged up any leftover food, including the cake. Irene had hired some college kids, one who happened to have a pickup truck, to help with the chairs rented for the ceremony. The pavilion had tables and chairs for the reception, but it didn't make sense to keep two hundred or more chairs around for outdoor ceremonies, too. Besides brides liked to choose the type of chairs they wanted. Renting them was the most sensible thing to do. Marla Jean had opted for simple chairs with cloth covers. So all of the covers had to be carefully removed first, and then the chairs had to be folded and stacked and loaded into the truck. The boys had finished their task awhile ago and immediately left to take the chairs back to the rental place. She looked at her list. Check. That was taken care of.

The reception space had looked spectacular, an exploding summer garden with flower arrangements gracing every table and surface. Now they were all gone. Oliver Barton was a local handyman she used for odd jobs around her house. Since starting her new business she paid him to help with setting up before the ceremony and taking everything down afterward. She had already helped him fill the bed of his truck with the flowers, and he was on his way with them now to the hospital to spread cheer and happiness to lonely patients. There was no reason for them to go to waste. That was another large job checked off her list.

But she was far from finished. The remaining decorations still needed to be boxed up and stored. She'd have to strip the tablecloths and napkins from all the tables. She'd be facing a mountain of laundry tomorrow. The list was long and seemingly never ending, but she couldn't help feeling a grand sense of satisfaction. The wedding had been wonderful. Everything had gone smoothly with only minor hiccups. But she'd handled them before they turned into major problems, and no one was the wiser. From what she could tell, everyone had a fine time, and most importantly, Marla Jean and Jake's special day had gone off beautifully.

"Excuse me, ma'am, but sitting down on the job is not allowed."

Irene looked up to see Theo grinning down at her. He'd taken his tuxedo jacket off and had his shirtsleeves rolled up, showing his bare forearms. He looked more handsome than ever if that was possible. She sighed. She didn't have the energy to spar with him.

"Hey, Theo, I thought you left as soon as Marla Jean and Jake rode off into the sunset."

"Nah, I was on tux and wedding gown duty. Have you ever wrestled a wedding dress into a dress bag?"

"How in the world did you get that job?"

"Actually, I was just helping Mrs. Jones. I happened to be passing by when I saw Marla Jean's mother struggling with it, so I helped. It took both of us. I have to take Jake's tux to their house, anyway. It just made sense to take her dress, too. I am happy to report they are now both safely tucked away in my car."

"See what I mean? No one truly appreciates all the tiny details that have to be handled behind the scenes."

"Hey, what did you think of the getaway car? It was pretty cool, huh? I was in charge of tying the tin cans and balloons to the back. Linc made the Just Married sign and handled the shaving cream."

She couldn't keep from smiling. He was like a proud little boy. "The car was a work of pure art, and if it was up to me, you'd both win an award. I have to tell you the 'Just Married' decorations have been pretty feeble at some of the other weddings I've done."

"It's an underappreciated part of the ceremony, but Marla Jean and Jake deserved to make a grand exit."

"Well, they did that, thanks to you and Lincoln. So, what are you still doing here now?"

He glanced around at the reception area. "It looked

like there was a lot of work to do. I consider it part of my best man duties to pitch in and help."

She hopped up from the chair, putting some distance between them. "That's really not necessary, Theo. It's all part of the service provided."

"I promised Jake, so I'm afraid you're stuck with me until everything is squared away. What can I do?"

She grabbed a box and handed it to him. "Well, I'd be silly to turn down an extra pair of hands. If you'll grab all the votive candles on the tables and put them in this box. I'll come behind you and begin gathering up the table-cloths and napkins."

"Aye, aye, captain. We'll have this done in no time."

He moved quickly clearing the tables almost before the request was out of her mouth. She expected him to hang around and try to flirt. She didn't know why he would want to flirt with her of all people, but since he'd been back in town, his attitude toward her seemed to fluctu-ate. One minute he'd be working the charm, teasing her, trying to get under her skin. The next he was skirting the edge of hurling insults, not even trying to hide the resent-ment he still harbored about their shared past. Thank-fully, right now he only seemed to be concentrating on the task of clearing the tables and didn't seem to care about anything else.

"Here you go. I'd say we make a good team, but I don't want to stir up trouble." He carried the box of candles over and stowed it on the floor out of the way. "What next?"

She finished stuffing the last tablecloth into the laun-dry bag and set it on the floor by the box of candles. "Can you take these out to my van? It should be unlocked." She'd pulled it up outside the pavilion once the wedding was over and had been loading it full of all the stuff that would go back with her to the I Do, I Do office.

"I'm on it." Without another word he picked up the box in one hand and the laundry bag in the other and hauled them outside.

She looked around deciding what to tackle next. Etta and Donny Joe had some twinkle lights they left up all year-round outside the pavillion, and that was fine for the entrance and the paths leading up to the structure, but Irene was discovering that brides had specific ideas about what they wanted in the way of lighting, so supplementing what was already provided was almost a given. Marla Jean liked the kind of string lights with the bigger bulbs. She said they made her think of Italy, though she'd never been. Irene didn't mind making the investment as part of her wedding inventory. She knew she would use them in future weddings.

She'd paid Oliver to hang them before the ceremony, but he'd already left to take the flower arrangements to the hospital, and she couldn't spare the time waiting for him to get back. The lights weren't going to jump down from the ceiling by themselves. Before she could talk herself out of it, she dragged the ladder over to the corner of the pavilion and climbed up the first two rungs. She needed to start with the string of lights that crisscrossed the ceiling. Heights weren't her favorite thing in the world, but it wasn't all that high, and she knew the ladder was sturdy. Telling herself not to be a wimp, she took a deep breath and climbed up high enough to reach the first strand of lights. She relaxed when they came off the hooks without a problem. This was going to be a cinch.

She climbed up and down the ladder, moving it around

the room, feeling more comfortable with each strand she pulled down. She'd moved to the last wall and reached for the last hook, even though it was a little out of reach. She leaned out further, hating the idea of getting down and moving the ladder for one last bulb. The ladder started to tip and she felt herself slipping.

"Ree!" Theo's panicked voice suddenly filled the space. "Dammit, woman, what do you think you're doing? Are you trying to kill yourself?"

Irene suppressed a scream and felt the ladder falling away. She felt herself falling, too. Before she could follow it down to the ground, strong arms grabbed her around the waist and plucked her out of midair. With a loud clatter the ladder hit the floor. But she didn't. Theo cradled her in his arms as if she weighed nothing at all. As if she was light as a feather. Which she wasn't.

"Oh my Lord," she whispered, holding on for dear life.

"Are you okay?" Theo's voice was shaking. "You scared the life out of me."

"I was doing fine until I decided to reach for that last bulb. Look. I almost had them all down." She motioned to the light strands that rested on the floor.

"Next time you want to climb a ladder, make sure you have a spotter. Or better yet just don't do it. You could have broken your neck." He didn't loosen his hold on her but sat down in a chair holding her on his lap.

Irene thought he looked a little pale. "Are you saying a woman can't climb a ladder without help? For your information, Theo Jacobson, I'm as capable as any man, and if I want to climb a ladder, I'll do just that."

"Don't start with me, Ree. I'm saying you shouldn't be climbing ladders at a time like this. And in that dress.

Jeez. From what I can tell you've been working nonstop since yesterday morning at least. Did you get any sleep last night? You have to be exhausted. Where's Oliver, anyway? I thought you were paying him to do this type of stuff."

The concern in his eyes was hypnotic. She shifted on his lap, but didn't get up. It felt good having him hold her, even if it was for all the wrong reasons. "He's taking care of other things, and I didn't want to wait for him to get back. I thought I could finish everything up, and we could all go home."

"Why didn't you ask me for help?" She could hear frustration in his voice.

He was right, at least this time, but she didn't like admitting it. "You were already helping, but you're right, I was being stubborn. I'm just so tired, and I got impatient. If I'd moved the ladder over one more time, this wouldn't have happened."

"Did you just say I was right?" His eyes twinkled with amusement and something more. Something dangerous and compelling.

"I might have," she whispered.

His mouth moved toward hers, and she found herself moving closer as well. It couldn't hurt to find out if his lips were as soft and as talented as she remembered, could it? He'd always kissed with a passion that knocked her off her feet. A passion that could also easily lay waste to her good sense all over again. She stopped herself in the nick of time. With a quick indrawn breath, she pushed herself off his lap, getting to her feet with effort, while her traitorous body woke up from a long wintry slumber. Reminding her that she was a woman. And that he was most definitely a man.

He let her go.

Disappointment warred with relief. Smoothing down the skirt of her dress, she declared with fake nonchalance, "Well, I suppose it's a good thing you came in when you did."

"Glad to be of service." He sat on that chair watching her with stormy blue eyes.

She moved away from him, trying to ignore the flames of desire he'd stirred so easily. In an attempt to get things back on track, she asked, "Since you're here now, would you mind climbing up there and getting that last string of lights down for me?"

"Why not?" He stood up and walked over to where the ladder lay fallen on its side. He hoisted it back to an upright position and climbed up easily. Theo unhooked the stubborn strand without any problem, and before she knew it he was back on the ground. Together they wrapped the lights into coils and stashed them in a storage bin.

She looked around and didn't see anything else that needed to be taken care of. He'd unsettled her and she tried to sound unaffected. "Thanks for all your help, Theo. I think I'm ready to call it a day."

"That's a good idea." He picked up the bin. "Let me carry this to your van."

"I will be happy to let you do that without a single objection." As much as she hated to admit it, his help had been a godsend. She made a note to hire more help for cleanup after the next wedding. "See, I'm not stubborn about everything all the time."

"I'm stunned. Falling off that ladder must have scrambled your brains. You're usually stubborn about being stubborn." He playfully jabbed her with his elbow.

She grinned. "You used to say I'd argue if someone told me the world was round."

"And you told me your fourth-grade science teacher told you it was more of a pear shape." He smiled and pushed the bin into the van's back storage space. "I don't think I ever won a single argument with you."

"Well, you won today. And thanks for catching me, in case I didn't say it earlier." They stood by the open van, staring at each other.

"Anytime. I'm just glad I was there to break your fall."

"Me too." She supposed she owed him now. At least a bit of gratitude. "Well then, I guess that's it."

"Yep. Guess so." A slight breeze ruffled his hair while the glow from the nearby Inn windows cast light and shadows across his face.

His too-handsome face, she thought with mock irritation. Why couldn't he have grown short and wrinkled and sloppy in the years they'd spent apart? "So, I'll see you around then, I guess."

He nodded. "You'll see me Monday morning. I'm starting the work at I Do, I Do. I'll be there at nine o'clock, bright and early."

She had been so busy with the wedding, she'd managed to put that out of her mind. "Oh, I forgot. We haven't even talked about this yet. Are you sure you want to do work for me? It won't be awkward?"

"Not unless we let it, and I don't see why it should be. I promise to stay out of your way as much as possible. Besides, I'm not letting Jake down. I don't want him to come home from his honeymoon and find any unfinished jobs. He told me your plans. Shelves, display cases, storage closets, that sort of thing. It doesn't sound too complicated. I'll have the work done before you have a chance to get tired of having me underfoot."

She figured she might as well resign herself to dealing with him a little longer. "Okay, then. If you're sure. I guess I'll see you bright and early Monday morning."

He started to walk away but stopped and turned back to face her. "Hey, Ree. I know I gave you a hard time when I heard you'd become a wedding planner."

She lifted her eyebrows. "I'd say that's a bit of an understatement. You intimated that I'd spread tears and marital blight far and wide."

"Well. I don't think I went that far, but I want to apologize and say right now that I was obviously too quick to judge. You did an outstanding job today. Everyone is saying it was a wonderful wedding. And they are all right. On behalf of my big brother, I want to thank you."

She smiled as she closed the back of the van and walked around to the driver's door. "Oh my goodness. I'm not sure I can handle the compliments. But thank you, Theo. That means a lot coming from you."

She got behind the steering wheel and started the van, easing across the uneven yard until she reached the pathway that led out to the street. It was insane, but she couldn't stop smiling. What Theo said did mean a lot. Even though she shouldn't care two flippin' cents what he thought about her and her new career. But evidently she did. Otherwise her face wouldn't be lit up like a dad gum Christmas tree. He still had the power to charm and unnerve her without even trying.

Alarmed by her ridiculous reaction to the man, her sunny smile dissolved into a worried frown. Why exactly was he being so nice to her, anyway? Hell, it was probably just because they'd be working closely together for the next week or two. He was making nice to smooth the way. That was all. Glancing up at her rearview mirror, she could see him standing tall, arms crossed over his chest, watching her as she drove away. She'd be smart to remember to keep Theo firmly in her rearview mirror.

Because that was exactly where he belonged.

Chapter Seven

Theo hardly got a wink of decent sleep during the rest of the weekend after Jake's wedding. It was late by the time he'd taken the tux and the bridal gown and dropped them off at Marla Jean and Jake's house. Then he'd loaded up Sadie, along with her bed, her food, and her toys, and driven over to the house on Overbrook Street. He'd spent a lazy day on Sunday getting settled into the house and playing with Sadie.

The renovations on the house were nearly complete, and except for an old bed in the bedroom and a sagging couch in the living room, it was empty of furniture. The kitchen had a refrigerator, a stove, and a card table with a couple of folding chairs for eating, but that was about it. Marla Jean had loaded him up with dishes and utensils, not to mention a bunch of casseroles and a big basket of fruit. Theo didn't mind the Spartan conditions. He needed to finish some painting and trim work in a couple of rooms, but this house was ready to go on the market as soon as Jake got home. No, an empty house and Sadie's company suited him just fine. It was just a place to crash until it was time to move on to the next place he'd call home.

Sunday night after he got Sadie settled in her dog bed, he climbed onto the lumpy mattress set up in the bedroom and tried to go to sleep. It had been a relaxing day, but shutting his brain down proved to be almost impossible. He turned onto his stomach and punched his pillow. He flipped over onto his back and kicked at his covers. Normally, he slept like a happy baby. Theo was an easygoing guy, laid-back, and he embraced whatever life brought his way. He wasn't one to analyze every decision he made. He didn't pick his life apart or second-guess his choices. But it seemed that coming back to Everson had changed all that. Tonight he was finding out that it was hard work fighting off the lost dreams of his youth, and at the same time suppressing a wild glimmer of hope for a different future.

And it was all Irene Cornwell's fault.

Just before she climbed into her van and drove away today, Ree had gone and smiled at him. A real, honest-to-goodness smile. Not one of those fake, insincere things she'd been pasting on her face for the last few days. He knew it was her attempt to keep him at arm's length and, at the same time, keep the curious folks in Everson at bay.

It had worked.

But then she'd gone and blown the game wide open. With that simple act. That smile. The honest light shining from her bright eyes had sent him reeling back in time. Back to the very first time he'd seen Irene Cunningham. Cunningham was her name back in those days, not Cornwell. He'd just been hired to sack groceries at the Piggly Wiggly after high school and had been dreading the whole thing up until the moment he laid eyes on the girl behind the cash register. It was a girl from high school. He'd never had the nerve to talk to her before, but it was impossible not to notice her when he passed her in the halls. And now, here she was, wearing an ugly pale blue uniform. But it didn't matter. She could have been wearing a burlap sack, and she still would have been the most beautiful girl he'd ever seen.

He tried to act cool. He tried not to act like the biggest nerd around, but he barely managed to introduce himself. She had a way of making him forget everything, including his own name.

She had these big brown smiling eyes, and the impact of those eyes on a high school kid was like a punch in the stomach. He stared at her, barely able to answer her questions. But she pretended he wasn't the biggest goofball to ever walk the planet, and instead she was nice and kind and helped him learn the ropes. Bread and eggs go on top. Don't overload the bags, especially for older customers. And that more than anything helped him feel comfortable around this dazzling creature. Getting to the store to spend time with Irene became the high point of his day. Soon they were hanging out after work, sitting on the tailgate of her old pickup truck, talking for hours about their hopes and dreams.

She told him a little about her family. How her uncle couldn't ever keep a job, while her aunt worked her butt off to keep food on the table. About how having enough money to get through the month was always an issue hanging over their heads, like an axe ready to fall without warning. She did what she could to help, but it wasn't enough.

Theo and Ree both planned to attend community college in Dallas after high school. They couldn't wait to escape from Derbyville and small-town life. But Theo had resigned himself early to his place in Ree's life. There was never a question that they'd be anything but friends. At least not as far as she was concerned. But still, he jumped on the idea of sharing an apartment in the big city when it came up. It made perfect sense. They would face the next phase of life together. Anything to make their dreams come true sooner. She planned to get her business degree and make enough money to take care of her aunt and uncle. He didn't know exactly what he was going to do with his life, but he had time to weigh his options.

Theo shook his head, chasing away the daydreams from the past. He finally gave up on the idea of sleeping and got out of bed. Getting up early was a good idea, anyway. He'd have plenty of time to feed Sadie and take her for a walk. So far, she seemed to be adapting to her new surroundings without too much trouble. She would wander to the front window and whine occasionally, no doubt wondering why Marla Jean and Jake had abandoned her, but Theo made a point of spending plenty of time with her, enough so she still felt loved.

After they came in from their walk, Sadie pranced around and barked until Theo got down on the living room floor and wrestled around with her like a goofy kid. Sadie ran off and came back with her favorite toy, an old chewed-up red tennis ball. She dropped it at his feet, and Theo threw it down the hallway, laughing as Sadie chased after it.

It had come as a big surprise, but he actually enjoyed having someone to take care of. Even if that someone was a dog. He'd never been big on the idea of getting tied down with responsibilities. "Travel light and stay unencumbered" had been his motto. But Sadie was such a great dog. The best dog ever. With her brown eyes and smiling face. Who wouldn't want to have a dog like that? And it was nice to have someone who was happy to see him when he walked in the door. If he ever did think about settling down in one place, he was going to get a dog. A sweet companion just like Sadie. Maybe that was a sign he was growing up.

He glanced at his watch. It was time to take a shower and have breakfast before he got ready to head over to I Do, I Do. He didn't want to be late the first day on the job. Irene still didn't seem too happy about the idea of having him underfoot, but he vowed to get in and get the job done and be out of her hair in no time. The only problem was every time he had been around her the last few days, all he wanted to do was get in her hair and stay there. He could admit he was having too much fun pushing all of her buttons.

And his motives weren't completely pure. He couldn't ignore the feelings she stirred inside him just by being anywhere in the near vicinity. But there was also a touch of resentment, a dash of vengeance, and a big scoop of desire. Not a healthy mixture. He was probably going to be crazy as a loon by the time Jake got home from his honeymoon. But his plan was to deal with Irene in a strictly professional manner. Unless she decided to give him another one of those genuine, honest-to-goodness smiles. Then all bets were off. After all, he was only human.

• • •

Irene had been at the store since eight o'clock. She didn't have any appointments scheduled, but it gave her some quiet time to finish up the paperwork on Marla Jean and Jake's wedding. They'd managed to stay within their budget and still have the wedding they wanted. She considered that a success by any measure.

Of course the real reason she'd gotten here early was to brace for the stress and strain of having Theo around working on the renovations. It was silly really. He'd be building shelves, and once he got started there would be no reason at all to talk to him. She hated to admit it, but since the wedding she'd thought of almost nothing but him. The way it felt to be back in his arms out on the dance floor. The way it felt to be held by him when he caught her fall from the ladder. She'd almost kissed him. Or he'd almost kissed her. She wasn't quite sure.

But the most disturbing thing of all was the way her heart raced when he told her she'd done a good job. Those kind words from him had her sailing through the rest of the weekend on a cloud. It really was just so silly. How could this man who'd walked out on her all those years ago waltz back into her life and make her long for things that had been over a long time ago?

She looked up when he knocked on the glass door. And there he was, big as life, making her heart speed up. Simply having him appear outside her store made her feel more alive. She took a fortifying breath and thought, *Get it together, Irene*. Waving him inside, she got up from her desk and walked to the door. "Good morning, Theo. You're right on time."

He was wearing a tool belt, which should have been illegal. It hung low on his hips over tight-fitting jeans. She dragged her gaze back to his face when she realized he was talking to her and she hadn't heard a word he'd said.

He had his hands on his hips, looking around the space. "So where do you want the shelves? You have lots of room in here."

"I have the preliminary plans I showed Jake, but he said you should feel free to offer other ideas, too." She walked to her desk and pulled out the plans.

He sat down across from her and studied the drawings. "This looks good. I'll need to make a run to the lumber-yard, but then I'll get back and get started. I hope it's okay if I'm in and out. I don't want to disrupt your business too much." His tone was overly polite.

"Of course, Theo. That's fine. I don't have any appointments scheduled today, and I'll put a sign up saying I'm closed for renovations."

He stood up and refolded the plans. "Okay, then. I'll be back in a bit."

"Would you like some coffee? I'm making a run to the Rise-N-Shine."

"Sure. That would be great." His tone was solemn. He didn't sound like he thought coffee was a great idea.

She watched him walk out the door without a smile or a backward glance. She should be happy. He was behaving himself. Treating this professionally. Which was exactly what she wanted. Wasn't it? Maybe instead she entertained a fantasy that he'd fall to his knees and confess that he should have never left her. That the years without her had been hell, and now seeing her again, he realized what a fool he'd been. Then he'd sweep her into his arms, kiss her, and beg for another chance.

She shook the fanciful notion from her head with a little laugh and walked out into the square. Standing still, she breathed in the summer morning. It wasn't scorching hot yet. That was something of a miracle. A mild June morning in Texas was something to enjoy. Maybe she should take Theo his coffee and then go drink her coffee at the gazebo and stay out of his way completely. She pushed open the door to the diner and was greeted right away by the owner Bertie Harcourt.

"Good morning, Irene. That was a real nice wedding you threw for Marla Jean and Jake."

"Thank you, Bertie. I need two coffees to go. Both black."

"Two? Is one for Theo Jacobson? I've heard he was going to be working over at your place today."

What a surprise. Irene should be used to the speed news traveled at in this town, but it never failed to catch her off guard. "He's building some shelves for me since Jake is on his honeymoon."

"Oh, darlin'. Is that difficult for you?" Sympathy oozed from her words accompanied by naked curiosity.

Irene braced herself. "Difficult? What do you mean?"

Bertie leaned over the counter and spoke conspiratorially. "Well, I'm not sure I could deal with spending so much time with someone I nearly married."

Irene shook her head, dismissing Bertie's concerns. "Now, Bertie. That was years ago. It's old news. Water under the bridge. We were both young, and we've both moved on since then."

"All I know is I saw a few sparks flying around when

you two were dancing at the wedding. And I say it's about time, too. Relax and enjoy it. A young woman like you should be out having a good time. Putting some romance in your life." Bertie put lids on the coffee cups and sat them on the counter.

"We are just old friends, Bertie. Nothing more." Irene knew she wasn't telling the whole truth, but she couldn't say exactly what she was being dishonest about. "I know how people in this town love to speculate, but Theo will be moving on once Jake gets back. So, I'm afraid everyone will be very disappointed if they expect anything to happen. Because it won't." Irene felt like she was rambling and decided to shut up, wondering if she was protesting too much.

Bertie smiled and with a knowing nod said, "If you say so, sweetie. The coffee is on the house this morning."

Irene could tell she hadn't changed Bertie's mind about anything. "Thanks for the coffee. I'll be back for lunch."

"Bring Theo with you. Smothered steak is the special, and Theo loves my smothered steak."

Irene didn't answer but headed for the door. Maybe she should start making a brown-bag lunch and eating it in her office from now on. But avoiding the diner would only lead to more gossip. In this town she was damned no matter what she did. When she got back to I Do, I Do, Lizzie Harris was waiting outside the door.

"Hi, Mrs. Cornwell. I know I don't have an appointment, but could I talk to you about my wedding?"

"Congratulations, Lizzie. I didn't realize you were engaged." She set the coffee cups down on the windowsill and unlocked the door. "Come on in. I'm about to have some construction going on in here, but we can talk until the builder gets back."

"Thank you. Matthew asked me to marry him right after graduation. I know we're young and our parents want us to wait until our careers are established, but we don't want to wait. If we are going to struggle, we want to struggle together."

Irene knew that Lizzie Harris and Matthew Long had both graduated from college in May, and their parents had been understandably proud. Irene wasn't in the business of giving advice on the wisdom of whether someone should get married. It wasn't her place to say, but she could see storms on the horizon if she took Lizzie on as a client.

"I can understand how you feel. Do you and Matthew want a big wedding?" Feeling her out seemed like the best course to take.

"We don't have a bunch of money to spend, but we thought you might help us come up with a plan so we can do a lot of the work ourselves."

"I've never helped with a do-it-yourself wedding, Lizzie."

"We'd pay you for your advice. I don't expect your help for free."

"I don't think that's necessary. I can point you in the right direction with a few books and online sites." They sat down at Irene's desk. "What kind of ideas do you have?"

"Something simple, not very formal, but we'd want to invite all our friends and family."

"For that you'll need a venue. Know anybody with a big backyard? And what about a reception?"

"Besides the cake we were thinking finger foods and beer and soft drinks."

"Okay. That all sounds like things you can do without my help."

"Well, we need someone to perform the ceremony."

"You can ask any minister in town, Lizzie. I'm sure they would be happy to preside."

Lizzie and Irene both turned to look out the window as Theo drove up in his truck up and parked in front of the office. "We don't want a minister."

"Okay, there are laypeople who can do that as well."

"We were hoping for something particular." She continued to stare as Theo climbed out of his truck.

"So, tell me. I can't begin to guess." Irene joined Lizzie in watching Theo unload the lumber from the back of his truck.

"We want an Elvis impersonator. Could you find one? I thought that might be on your list of services."

"An Elvis impersonator?"

"Like they have at those chapels in Las Vegas."

"Goodness." Irene had never anticipated such a request.

"Yes, young Elvis. Matthew loves him."

"I could try, but off the top of my head, I have no idea where I might find one."

Theo opened the door, balancing the long boards as he carted them through the door. "Excuse me, ladies. I didn't realize you had a meeting, Irene." He stacked the wood against the back wall.

Lizzie stood up. "What about him?"

Irene's eyes widened and she stood up, too. She turned to study Theo like he was a specimen in a test tube.

He pulled off his work gloves and stuck them in his back jeans pocket. Looking bewildered, he asked, "What *about* me?"

Irene smiled and walked over, clasping him on the shoulder. "Hey, Theo. How's your Elvis impression?"

Chapter Eight

I actually do an outstanding Elvis impression, but I only bring it out on special occasions. Why do you want to know?" Theo wasn't about to let Irene know her question had thrown him for a loop.

Irene was laughing, obviously enjoying herself. "Not me. Lizzie wants to know. Oh, sorry. I don't suppose you two have met."

The young woman walked over and held out her hand. "Hi, I'm Lizzie Harris. I'm trying to find an Elvis to perform my wedding ceremony."

He took her hand and introduced himself. "Theo Jacobson."

Wide-eyed, she said, "Nice to meet you, Theo. I think you'd be perfect."

Theo looked from one woman to the other. "I'm not qualified to marry anyone."

Irene raised her eyebrows. "Actually these days you can be ordained online."

"Whoa. Let's back up a minute. You don't know me

from Adam. Why in the world would you want me at your wedding?"

"Well, I guess Irene can try to find someone else. But you're tall and good-looking, and you have dark hair falling onto your forehead. Don't you think he's perfect, Mrs. Cornwell?"

"I'll admit he has potential." Irene wasn't even trying to hide her glee at this turn of events.

Self-consciously, Theo pushed his hair back from his forehead. "Lizzie, I'm flattered, but I'm sure Irene can find someone who does that sort of thing for a living. That's her job now. To plan the perfect wedding. Do your job, Irene." There was a note of panic in his voice as the young girl continued to appraise him for his Elvis factor.

Irene took Lizzie by the arm and led her toward the door. "Let me see what I can find out, okay? We should let Theo get to work now."

"So, you'll call?" Lizzie asked.

Irene grabbed a business card from her desk. "I will, I promise. And here's my card if you want to discuss any other questions you and Matthew might have."

Lizzie thanked her and with one more longing look in Theo's direction left the office. Irene turned around to find Theo watching the young woman go.

"She's getting married? How old is she? She looks about sixteen."

Irene bustled back to her desk and started clearing off the paperwork. "Lizzie just graduated from college, so she's at least twenty."

Theo grunted. "That still seems awfully young to me."

"They are both older than we were when you asked me

to marry you, Theo." She ducked her head, seeming to regret bringing up their past.

He shrugged and said thoughtfully, "We were old for our age. Life forced us to grow up fast and learn to take care of ourselves sooner than most kids."

"That is true. And we didn't go through with the marriage, so I guess we were smart enough to realize it didn't have a snowball's chance in hell of working."

"Is that why I got a Dear Theo letter? You smartened up before we could make a big mistake?" He watched her face flush and wanted to apologize. He'd promised himself not to go down these personal roads with her, but every time he turned around, something reminded him of the way things used be between them. And he still had so many unanswered questions.

Irene picked up her briefcase. "Listen, Theo, I know there's going to be a lot of sawing and hammering going on today. So since I'm not a big fan of sawdust, I'll clear out and let you get to work. It's a nice day, so I'll be working at the gazebo this morning if you need anything."

Theo nodded. "Okay. I'll try not to take too long. I'll get the construction finished today and the staining and varnishing finished tomorrow."

"That will be just fine. By the way, Bertie said to tell you smothered steak was the lunch special today."

"Oh, Bertie knows smothered steak is my favorite." In an attempt to apologize for letting things get personal, he decided to stick his neck out. "In that case, can I offer to buy you lunch?"

Irene studied him for a long moment before saying, "We'll go Dutch. How about twelve thirty?"

She gave in without a fight, and it took him off guard. He started to say, "It's a date." Instead, he wisely said, "Okay, Ree. I'll see you then."

She left the office, and he got to work. The first job was to construct built-in shelves all along a sidewall. Jake had done the measuring ahead of time, but Theo had learned to double-check any kind of measurements before he started cutting any boards.

He set up sawhorses out in the alley behind the store and got to work. He made all his cuts and was ready to start on the installation. He moved back inside and started construction. The morning went quickly. A couple of Irene's potential customers stuck their heads inside the door, and he directed them to the gazebo in the middle of the town square, saying they could find her there.

The next time the door opened, it wasn't a potential wedding customer, but Hoot and Dooley. The two old guys normally spent their day playing Parcheesi in the front of the barbershop.

"Hey, Theo."

"Hey, Hoot. Nice to see you, Dooley. Taking a break from Parcheesi?" He stood up and walked over to shake their hands. "I'm afraid Irene's not here right now."

"We didn't come to see Irene."

"Oh?" Warning bells went off in his head. These two were usually up to something.

Hoot explained, "The barbershop is closed on Monday, so it's our day off."

"So, what are you boys doing here?" He figured he might as well come out and ask.

"Well, now, we thought we'd come by and see how things are going over here."

"You mean the remodeling?" They were definitely up to something.

"Yes, sir, we're both pretty good amateur carpenters, so we thought we'd drop in and maybe pick up a few tips on the art of construction. But don't mind us. We'll stay out of your hair." They each pulled up a chair and sat down like they'd come to watch a show.

The two old men were fixtures in the town. Besides their daily Parcheesi game in the front of the barbershop, they published a town newsletter with coupons, an events calendar, and an advice column. Jake didn't really want an audience, but what was he going to do? Hoot and Dooley did pretty much whatever they wanted around Everson.

Theo picked up a drill. "Jake's the real carpenter in the family. But he's taught me everything he knows, so I do an adequate job."

"Don't sell yourself short, son," Hoot said. "Jake wouldn't have left you in charge of his business if you couldn't do the work."

"Thanks, Hoot."

"Do you think those shelves are going to be deep enough, Theo?" Dooley asked.

Theo stopped what he was doing to ponder Dooley's question. He stood back, appraising the work he'd done so far. "Jake drew up the plans based on Irene's suggestions before he left town. I'm sure they took the depth requirements into consideration."

"You're probably right. I don't know what kind of matrimonial geegaws Irene plans to put on there. And Jake usually seems to know what he's doing."

"He knew what he was doing marrying Marla Jean. That's for darn sure," Hoot volunteered. Marla Jean owned the barbershop where they whiled away the hours every day. She could do no wrong in their eyes. "Have you heard from the newlyweds?"

"Jake sent a text to say they'd arrived. I don't expect I'll hear anything else until they are on their way home. They have better things to do than talk to me."

"Well, if you do happen to speak to them, tell Marla Jean that Milton is doing a fine job holding down the fort at the barbershop. It's just like the old days." Milton was Marla Jean's dad. He owned the barbershop before he retired and passed the place on to his daughter.

"I'm sure she's not worried." Theo drilled some holes and lined up the shelf for installation.

The men crouched down to get a better look. "Good job, Theo."

"Thank you." He moved on to the next shelf.

Dooley squatted down beside him. "So, Theo, is it true you and Irene used to be engaged?"

Theo put down his tools and stood up. Maybe now they were getting down to the real reason for the visit. "I know it's hard to believe, but yes, it's true, Dooley. We were engaged for a short time many years ago." Everyone knew Hoot and Dooley weren't above spreading gossip. Especially if it was juicy enough.

"That's what we heard, but we wanted to hear it from the horse's mouth." So they didn't spread rumors unless they verified them personally.

"Out of respect for Irene's wishes, I'm not going to discuss it. It would be nice if everyone else would stop discussing it, too."

"Now come on, Theo. Irene has lived in Everson long enough to know that when a new scandalous rumor comes along, the more a person tries to squash it, the more it fans the flames."

"There is no scandal here. Lots of people get engaged and don't go through with the wedding. That's the end of the story."

"Except here you are, building shelves in her new business." Dooley raised his eyebrows as if that proved some important point.

Hoot nodded. "Are you sure there's not still some tiny spark burning that's never been extinguished? Irene's an amazing woman."

He wondered if they were in cahoots with Donny Joe. "I agree. She's amazing."

"Do tell," Dooley said while fingering the whiskers on his chin.

Theo watched their faces light up like they'd just uncovered a deep dark secret. But what was he supposed to say? That some part of him would always love her in some way? Not likely. He was just going to nip this in the bud. "We are just friends. So anyone who says anything else is just trying to stir up trouble. I would appreciate it if I thought you fellas had my back on this."

Hoot took his time considering it and then said, "You know, we were pretty well acquainted with Sven Cornwell while he was alive."

"Is that so?" Theo wasn't sure he wanted to hear about Ree's husband. On the other hand he'd be lying if he said he wasn't curious.

"We were." Hoot smiled and patted him on the shoulder. "And so the question that comes to mind is 'What would Sven say?'"

"About what?"

Dooley chimed in. "About you and Irene. She sits up there all alone in that big house on the hill year after year. It doesn't seem right somehow."

Theo stopped and looked at them pointedly. "She seems fine to me."

"Well, if you say so, Theo. But in our opinion, we feel certain Sven would approve of her moving on with her life." Hoot made the announcement like it had come from on high.

Theo was happy to hear it. "She has moved on. Besides everything else, she's planning weddings now. So she is plenty busy."

Dooley slapped his knee. "Good golly, we aren't talking about her businesses. We're talking about a new man. A new man like you, Theo."

Hoot was nodding his head as if Dooley was spouting gospel. "You'll find some in town who will disagree, but don't let those Debbie Downers get in the way of true love."

Theo felt a headache coming on. Who knew that besides gossip, these two good old boys dabbled in matchmaking, too. "I hate to disappoint Sven or anyone else, but I'm here to build shelves. That's it." He glanced at his watch. "Well, would you look at the time? I'm supposed to meet Irene for lunch in about five minutes."

"You're having lunch with Irene?" Their gray, wiry eyebrows shot up in unison.

"That's right. A business lunch over at the Rise-N-Shine." He herded them toward the door. "Will I see you over there?"

Dooley shook his head. "No, no, I gotta get home and eat with the wife. Linda's making bacon sandwiches. And tomato soup."

Hoot nodded. "Yeah, Maude wants me to drive her to Derbyville this afternoon. Gomer's Dry Goods is having a sale on shower curtains. I swear that woman is always redecorating the bathroom."

Theo shrugged. "Tell me about it. My mom was the worst when I was growing up. Always buying those little decorative soaps and candles. What are you going to do?" he asked sympathetically. He'd rather talk about decorating than his love life any day of the week.

Hoot patted him on the back. "Amen. So, we'll get out of your way. It was nice catching up, Theo. And take some time to think about what we said."

Theo walked out onto the sidewalk with them as they left and used the key Irene had given him to lock up the place. Then he headed across the town square, somehow feeling that despite the words that had come out of his mouth, as far as Hoot and Dooley were concerned, he'd just declared his undying love for Irene in no uncertain terms.

• • •

Irene settled into a booth at Rise-N-Shine and waited for Theo to join her. She'd caught up on some paperwork sitting at the gazebo, and two new brides-to-be had stopped by wanting to set up appointments. They'd both reported that Theo was hard at work in her store. She smiled, pleased with the day so far. The best part had been Lizzie thinking Theo would make the ideal Elvis to perform her wedding ceremony. The truth was he would be perfect, but the horrified look on his face had been priceless. She didn't think he'd be volunteering for the role.

"So, I suppose you plan to break his heart again?"

Irene looked up to find Nell Harcourt glaring at her like she'd murdered someone's pet goldfish.

"Excuse me?"

"He might have everyone else around here fooled, but I know for a fact that Theo still has feelings for you."

"Is that a fact? He told you all that in the five seconds you've known him? I find that hard to believe." Irene wasn't in the mood to deal with Nell. "By the way, does your mother know you talk to customers this way?"

Nell glanced nervously toward the counter at the front of the diner. Bertie was holding court with several regulars. "Leave my mother out of this."

"Ah, so she wouldn't approve, would she?"

"I'm just worried about Theo, that's all." Nell's voice was sullen as she trotted out what she surely considered a noble defense for her behavior.

At that moment Theo pushed through the front door of the diner. Irene smiled and waved at him. "I've known Theo a lot longer than you have, Nell. And I can assure you he's always been able to take care of himself."

"Irene Cornwell, you don't deserve a nice man like that." Nell certainly had no problem speaking her mind.

Irene laughed. "Thanks for sharing your thoughts, but what I deserve is a nice lunch without being harassed. Why don't you ask Jill if she wouldn't mind waiting on us today instead of you."

Nell scurried away as Theo sat down across from Irene. "I think we have a problem," he said.

"I know," Irene agreed.

"You do? Did you talk to Hoot and Dooley, too?"

"Hoot and Dooley? No, but Nell was giving me an earful before you got here, though."

He groaned. "I would have thought she'd have learned her lesson by now. What did she say now?"

"Not much. She warned me not to break your heart again. What's going on with Hoot and Dooley?"

He arranged his silverware and opened his menu. "They stopped by the store while I was working. Just in case I needed any carpentry pointers."

Irene smiled, knowing how opinionated the two of them could be. "How thoughtful of them."

"Yes, indeed. While they were at it, they made several pointed inquiries about our engagement. They seemed to believe I still carry a torch where you are concerned, and I might have a chance to win you back if I put my mind to it. They also ventured the opinion that Sven would approve."

Irene was dismayed by their pushiness. "Oh, good gosh. I'm sorry, Theo."

"Don't be sorry. It's not unreasonable to think I'd have trouble getting over someone like you." His blue eyes narrowed as he gave her a long, lingering look.

Irene rolled her eyes. "I bet you'll be happy when Jake gets home so you can get out of here."

"You know Jake wants me to stay, don't you?"

"Marla Jean said something about that before the wedding." She could see he was measuring her response.

He looked at her seriously. "So, what do you think about that?"

She shifted in her seat. The idea of Theo being around all the time made her restless. "It doesn't matter what I think, but I assumed you'd be ready to move on. I heard something about Australia."

"That's right. My friend Mitch Baker runs tours taking groups into the outback."

"Really? That sounds like quite an adventure. Right up your alley, Theo. Staying in a dinky place like Everson can't hold much appeal compared to that."

"I don't know. I've had my share of adventures. Sometimes I think I'm ready to settle down. So, I'm asking again. How would you feel about that?"

Jill came to the table and took their drink order.

After she left, Irene asked a question of her own. "Tell me, how long are you in one place before you start getting the itch to move on?"

"I don't get itchy. I get another offer. A better offer that I don't see the need to refuse."

"Are you ready to order?" It was Bertie. It seemed the owner of the diner had decided to wait on them herself.

"Hi, Bertie," Irene said. "I'll take a Cobb salad."

Theo smiled and said, "I'm having the special. Smothered steak with mashed potatoes and Texas toast."

Bertie nodded approvingly. "You got it, darlin'. You get one more side with that."

Irene butted into the conversation. "You might try having a vegetable."

He wrinkled his nose. "You mean something green, don't you?"

"It's good for you." Irene smiled at his reluctance. He'd always been a meat-and-potatoes man.

"Okay. By chance, do you have any more of those mustard greens?"

"I do, for a fact. Been simmering on the stove with a hunk of ham since this morning."

"Well then, Bertie, give me a mess of greens." He smiled at Bertie like she'd made his whole day complete. He was such a flirt, Irene thought.

"Coming right up." Bertie left, and Theo got right back to the subject at hand. Pushing Irene for an answer, he asked, "No more evasions. How would you feel if I stayed around?"

Irene stared at Theo while a million possible answers swirled around in her head. Instead she asked, "So, how do you feel about impersonating Elvis?"

Chapter Nine

He laughed. "I think that qualifies as an evasion. Are you saying if I stay here I'll have to perform weddings as Elvis?"

"It's an option. It's good to have options." She didn't want to answer his real question. It would open all the old wounds. Old wounds she'd managed to keep bandaged up and out of sight so far. It would open her up to more heartbreak, and she wasn't sure she could handle that a second time in one lifetime.

She wanted to pour all her time and energy into the new wedding business. It was the one thing in this town that was all hers. The one thing that didn't have Sven's name and money attached to it. She was happy to keep using his money to help good causes. But it wasn't her money and it never would be. Maybe planning weddings wasn't an earthshaking career choice, but it was all hers. And when she did her job properly, she spread happiness and got to share in the love of couples starting out in their life together. That seemed like a worthy endeavor in her mind.

Theo was a distraction. Plain and simple. She'd been playing with fire since he'd been home. Even mentally giving in to that old attraction was a glorious temptation, and at the same time, the worst idea she could possibly consider.

Not that he'd done anything out of line. Except for some harmless flirting at Jake's wedding he'd been a complete gentleman. She could admit she was guilty of giving mixed signals. Flirting with him one minute and pushing him away the next. That needed to stop now.

"Look, Theo, we're old friends. There used to be something between us, but we haven't seen each other in ten years and both of us have lived our lives without the other. So, if you want to stay here and work with Jake, you should."

He studied her closely. "Okay. That's plain enough. I admit I'm giving it some thought, at least considering my options for Jake's sake, but most likely I'll be moving on once they get back to town."

Whether he talked of staying or leaving, her heart lurched all the same. Changing the subject seemed like the safest idea. "I figured as much, Theo. And now we need to talk about the parade float. That's the reason I agreed to lunch."

Theo grinned. "So, it actually is a business lunch? Forget Dutch, then. In that case you can pay for the whole thing."

She appreciated that he was going to let the other conversation go. She returned his grin. "That's no problem. Now, what experience do you have with building floats?"

He seemed to ponder the question and then declared, "None. I can't say I have any. But I rode in a parade once with my high school baseball team if that helps."

She pulled out some business cards from her purse and handed them to Theo. "Here. You can talk to these people. They have floats every year."

He sifted through the stack. "Okay, let's see here. Binnion's Lumber, Romeo's Pizza, the Posey Pot. Lord, this looks like every business in town."

"Just about, but when you talk to these people be diplomatic. This is a very competitive, cutthroat event, so they won't be giving away any of their trade secrets."

"Cutthroat? Trade secrets? Great. What am I getting myself into?"

She leaned forward enthusiastically. "First prize gets bragging rights for the entire year."

His eyes widened like it was all clear now. "Well, who wouldn't cut a few throats for that?"

She sat up primly. "Make fun if you like, but the Fourth of July parade Penelope Bottoms Grand Prize trophy is a big deal around here, and I plan to win it this year."

He leaned back in the booth and slung one arm across the back. "Listen to you. Who exactly is Penelope Bottoms?"

Irene could tell he wasn't properly impressed, but she didn't care. "She was the first official queen of the parade back in the 1950s. Penelope personally presented the trophy to the winning float until her death in 2002. But her legend lives on in the quest for the trophy each year."

Bertie showed up at the table to deliver their food. "I didn't mean to eavesdrop, but I heard you say you think you can win the Penelope trophy this year."

"I'm going to give it a try," Irene said.

Bertie sat Irene's salad down in front of her. "Well, now, I don't mean to rain on your parade, so to speak, but we've won it for the last three years." She stopped and pointed to the four-foot trophy that sat behind the diner's lunch counter. "Ain't it pretty?"

"Impressive," Theo agreed as she slid his smothered steak onto the table.

"Anyway, our float will be more elaborate than ever. Nell's already working on the costumes and some top secret special effects. But good luck, Irene. You go ahead and give it your best shot, darlin'. It'll be real nice to have some new blood in the arena." Confident as the reigning owner of the award, she grinned and waltzed away.

Irene slapped the table. "Oh, they are going down. Three years is too long for the same place to win. It's time for a new grand prizewinner. It'll boost the morale of the town folks if a new float is declared champion. And it might as well be mine."

Theo grinned. "I like this side of you, Ree. Full of spit and vinegar. I hate to break into your dreams of future glory, but if we can get back to the real world for a minute. I have another full day working on your shelves before I start on the storage closet tomorrow. Then I promise I'll get to work researching parade floats."

She leaned across the table, pinning him with the determined gleam in her eyes. "Not just parade floats, Theo, but floats that can win the Fourth of July Penelope Bottoms Grand Prize trophy. Now eat your lunch."

"Yes, ma'am." Not needing any more encouragement, he dug into his smothered steak.

• • •

Irene stood on the front porch of her childhood home and knocked on the front door. She called out, "Aunt Jo? Are you home?" Jo Anne Cunningham was the closest thing to a parent she'd ever known.

Irene's real mother had given birth to her when she was seventeen. Her father wasn't interested in having a baby, so when he left town her mother left with him. Irene was left with her grandmother. Grandma Grace had been sweet, but she was also old and in bad health. She died when Irene was seven. That's when she went to live with her aunt and uncle. They had two kids of their own, and her uncle made it clear that taking Irene on to raise was a complication the family didn't need. But her aunt tried to make her feel welcome, make her feel like part of the family. She loved her for that.

The small house she'd grown up in over in Derbyville boasted a fresh coat of paint and a nicely manicured front lawn these days. Irene had tried to convince her aunt to allow her to buy her a nicer house in a better neighborhood, but she always refused. Since the death of Irene's uncle a few years back, Jo thought it was silly to live in anything bigger. The little three-bedroom cottage suited her just fine. Anything larger would just be more to take care of. Irene had offered to have a housecleaning service come in once a week, but Jo Anne seemed to resent the suggestion. Irene only wanted to help, but her aunt thought Irene was ashamed of where she came from.

That might have been true when she was growing up in this house. Even back then it was old and falling apart. And she never knew if she'd come home from school to find the electricity had been cut off or the phone disconnected because her uncle had used the money meant for utilities on one of his get-rich-quick schemes. Irene's aunt worked hard to keep a roof over their heads, but her uncle believed in keeping his head in the clouds, dream-

ing of hitting the ever-elusive jackpot. Eddie Cunningham
always thought his big break was around the next bend in
the road. The idea of holding down a nine-to-five job that
would help put food on the table paled next to that.

Irene was about to knock again when the door opened.
"Hi, Aunt Jo. I had a meeting down at city hall and thought
I'd see if you wanted to keep me company at lunch before
I head home." She knew she had to state it as if her aunt
would be doing her a favor before she'd say yes.

Jo Anne Cunningham was a tall woman like Irene. It
ran in the family. When she'd been a young woman, she'd
been quite a beauty, too. Now her dark hair was cut into a
short bob, showing a bit of gray, and a few wrinkles lined
her face, but she still attracted the attention of the older
men in town. "I wish you would have called, Irene. I look
a mess." She smoothed down her crisp pink button-down
blouse over her neatly pressed gray slacks.

"You look fine. In fact, you always look fine. And when
I call ahead of time you always make up some excuse not
to go with me."

Her aunt opened the screen door and invited her inside.
"What makes you think I'm making them up? You aren't
the only one around here with a schedule, girly."

"I know. You are busier than most people I know." And
she was. With all of her volunteer work she put in more
hours now than she did before she retired from the law
office she'd managed for forty-something years. "But you
can't blame me for wanting to spend time with you, can
you? So, I thought I'd take my chances."

Her aunt's attitude seemed to soften. "Well, there is a
new place over in Derbyville Square I've wanted to try.
The Snooty Fox. They have English pub food, and Lila

Gifford has been carrying on about the fish-and-chips to everyone who'll listen. Seems her husband took her to England for their thirtieth anniversary so now she considers herself an expert on everything English."

"Why don't we plan a trip together somewhere sometime, Aunt Jo? Just me and you. It would be fun. Or maybe Bonnie and Carrie would want to go, too, if we timed it right. What do you think?" Bonnie and Carrie were her cousins, and Aunt Jo doted on them still.

"I think you need to slow down. Every time I make a simple remark about this or that, you try to turn it into a whoop-de-do major event. For one thing I don't need to start gallivanting around the world at my age. Goodness gracious. And I'm sure you have better things to spend all that money of yours on."

"I can't think of anything better to spend it on. What's the use of having it if I can't make life easier?"

"My life is easy. It's just fine, Irene. I've got a roof over my head, food in my pantry, and both my girls are healthy and happy. On top of that, you're about to take me out to eat. Who could ask for more?"

Irene knew she wasn't counted as one of her girls, and she also knew when to stop pushing. Now that the idea of a trip had occurred to her it seemed like a wonderful plan. At this point her aunt would resist any attempts at persuasion, but Carrie or Bonnie might be able to convince her. She made a note to call her cousins later.

The restaurant was charming and made a nice change from the hamburger joints and pizza parlors that filled Derbyville. They both ordered fish-and-chips, dousing them with malt vinegar, and even though they were stuffed, they shared bread pudding for dessert.

"How's your wedding planning business going?"

Her aunt shared little interest in the various charity boards Irene served on, but since she'd mentioned her newest venture, she seemed unusually curious about the day-to-day details.

"Business is starting to pick up. This last weekend was Jake Jacobson and Marla Jean Bandy's wedding, and I have several more scheduled this summer."

"I think that's wonderful, Irene. You're using your talent to help people."

Irene could read between the lines. What she meant was she wasn't using Sven's money. Aunt Jo had never come to terms with her marriage to Sven. Since his death, she still felt uncomfortable with all the money Irene had inherited. "I help people all the time, Aunt Jo."

"Of course you do, but this is more personal. I'd be happy to help if you ever need another pair of hands."

Irene was surprised and pleased. "You would? That would be a big help. I'm still putting together a staff that can be available to help regularly."

"I think I'd enjoy it. So, keep me in mind. And you wouldn't have to pay me, so that would be a savings right there."

"The couples do pay me for my services, you know. It's not a charity, so if you work for me, you will be paid for the work you do. No arguments."

"Okay. We can settle that later. But it sounds like fun."

"I'm having some work done at the office right now. Jake's brother Theo is building some shelves for me. Maybe you'd like to come over next week and help me set up the displays."

Irene's aunt smiled. "I do have a good eye for design.

Just tell me when you want me to come by, and I'll be there."

Irene was ridiculously pleased at her aunt's interest. "Okay. It's a deal."

"You mentioned Jakes' brother, Theo? That's not a name you hear every day. Wasn't that the name of the boy you ran off with to Dallas after high school? The one you were engaged to? Good grief, the one you mooned over for months after you broke things off?"

Irene sighed. Her aunt had a memory like a steel trap, especially about things concerning her past transgressions. "Nothing gets by you, does it? Okay, it's the same Theo. He was Jake's best man so he had to come to Everson for the ceremony."

Her aunt sat up straight in her chair. "Irene, are you telling me the first man you were ever engaged to is back in town and working for you? After all this time, he's back in your life. Goodness, how do you feel about that?"

Irene shook her head. "He's not back in my life. He's passing through at most. He'll be in Everson for a couple of weeks, and then he'll move on to some new adventure."

"So, it's no big deal." Her aunt raised her eyebrows and studied her curiously.

Irene shrugged and ducked her head. She could never hide much from her. In fact, she was one of the few people she'd confided in when she broke things off with Theo. "Seeing Theo again has brought up some memories, but it was a long time ago. We have both had interesting lives since those days, and neither of us have been walking around heartbroken. Theo's behavior has been very civilized."

"Civilized? Is that what you want?" Her aunt's smile was uncharacteristically wicked.

"Aunt Jo, really." Irene blushed because she couldn't deny the feelings he still inspired.

"I'm not convinced you ever stopped loving that boy."

Irene raised her chin stubbornly. "I married Sven, and he was a wonderful husband."

"But you didn't love him. Not like a woman should love a man." Aunt Jo Anne didn't mince words.

Irene closed her eyes. This was a discussion they'd had before, and Irene wasn't going to explain why she'd married Sven. If her aunt knew the truth, she would be even more upset. "Don't start on Sven, please."

"Sven was a nice man, but he was old enough to be my father, much less your husband."

"Yes, you've never hidden the way you felt about him, but he's gone now, and he left me with a great responsibility."

"He left you with lots of money. The one thing you always believed would make you happy."

"You make me sound so coldhearted. His money continues to do a lot of good in this county. I won't apologize for being proud of that."

"I'm not criticizing, but if that man hadn't had money, you wouldn't have agreed to become his child bride."

Her aunt had no idea. "Okay, we are rehashing old territory now. We are never going to agree on this point. Are you ready to go?"

Jo reached across the table and took Irene's hand in hers. The show of affection was unusual and took Irene off guard. "Listen, I won't say another word about Sven Cornwell. But you promise me that you'll make sure that Theo doesn't disappear again until you find out if there is anything still there."

"Oh, you are impossible. When did you turn into such a romantic? What I'm going to do is concentrate on my new business, and if you are serious about helping, I'll be glad to put you to work."

"I have lots of good ideas for decorations." Aunt Jo smiled. "Weddings are just the loveliest occasions. Just give me a theme, and I'll bet I can come up with some fabulous designs."

Irene nodded. "I'll bet you can, but first I have to come up with a theme for my parade float. Why don't you help me think about that?"

"A float for the Fourth? You've never done one before, have you?"

"No, this will be for I Do, I Do."

"You know, that sounds like a great project. Okay, I'm going to put on my thinking cap."

"You can ride on it too if you'd like. After all, you'll officially be part of my staff."

"Me? On the float? Lila Gifford would be green with envy. But oh, I don't think so. Really?" Her aunt was clearly flustered.

Irene grinned at her aunt's mixture of enthusiasm and caution. "We can decide on the details later. Let me take you home now. I have another meeting this afternoon."

Chapter Ten

Theo sailed through the clear blue summer sky. He needed to clear his head, and flying was the best way he knew how to do that. Working so close with Irene the past few days had stirred up a thousand buried memories. Memories he'd refused to relive over the years, but now they came to him unbidden at unsuspecting moments. When he was awake, when he was asleep, and any state in between. Old memories haunted him.

He remembered the day they'd finally found an apartment in Dallas they thought they could afford. Irene had been excited, jumping around like a little kid. It was a shabby two-bedroom place with one bath and a tiny kitchen that was so small they had to take turns opening the refrigerator and oven door to inspect them. None of that mattered to him, either, because he would be sharing it with Ree.

He's done a good job of keeping his feelings for her hidden. Especially since he knew without a doubt that he was nowhere on her radar when it came to anything romantic.

She considered him a buddy, a friend, a nice guy to split the rent with. And he was happy to be that guy.

In fact, he was more than happy. He was out of Derbyville, and Irene, like no one else, understood what that meant for him. She had aspirations of her own, too. They would both attend the junior college and work part-time. When she got the job waitressing at the country club, she made a joke about finding a rich husband, but he never took her seriously. He knew she was serious about getting through college with a business degree and making enough money to help her family. Working hard to secure a stable economic future was the thing that drove her.

And he understood that.

Theo approached the Everson airport and made an effortless landing. He taxied over to the hangar and saw Nell Harcourt standing outside. He'd done his best to steer clear of her since their date at Lu Lu's, but Everson was too small to avoid her completely.

He climbed out of the plane and greeted her neutrally as he passed. "Nell."

She smiled like they were old friends. "Hi, Theo. I've wanted a chance to talk to you."

"Oh? I thought we'd said all there was to say." He kept walking, but she trotted along at his side.

"I should start by apologizing. I have a tendency to run my mouth too much."

He raised his eyebrows, not disagreeing.

She tried making a joke. "Not that it's an excuse, but with Bertie for a mom, I come by it naturally."

He kept walking.

She seemed determined to keep talking. "So, like I said, I want to apologize for the things I said about Mrs. Cornwell."

Theo sighed. "Maybe you'd like to say that to her instead of me."

Nell nodded in agreement. "You're right. I'll do that next time she comes into the diner."

He was almost to the airfield office. "Really? She said you warned her about breaking my heart or some garbage like that just the other day."

She tugged on his arm until he stopped. "I don't know what comes over me. I get all protective when you're around. That's why I told you all those stories about her in the first place."

"You're protecting me. From Irene." He stopped and laughed in her face. "That's the most convoluted excuse for spreading rumors I ever heard."

She made a pleading face. "So, can we start over?"

He started walking again. He didn't have time for this. "We never started, Nell."

She dogged his heels. "And that's my fault."

He stopped and faced her. "Look. I'm only here for a couple of weeks, so I'll make a deal with you."

She lit up like a streetlamp. "What's that?"

"You stop spreading lies about Irene, and I won't cross to the other side of the street when I see you."

"Wow, you're really upset with me, aren't you?" She seemed confounded by his attitude.

He was on a roll now, so he kept preaching. "You need to remember you are talking about real human beings when you open your mouth, Nell."

"You are so right, Theo. I'm going to reform my ways."

He looked at her skeptically. "What are you doing out here at the airfield, anyway?"

"Don't worry. I'm not stalking you. The empty hangar over there is where we build our parade floats."

"Is that so? Can I take a look? And who is 'we'?"

She took off, waving at him to follow. "Sure, come and have a look. Everyone's in the basic foundation stage, so no one will think you're a spy."

He stopped. "You're kidding, right? Why would anyone think I'm a spy?"

She turned to face him. "It's no secret you are helping Mrs. Cornwell with her float this year. Folks around here take the competition for the Penelope Bottoms trophy very seriously, so I would never kid about a thing like that."

He started walking again toward the hangar, and before he reached the door he could hear the sound of hammering, sawing, and good-natured banter filling the air. He walked inside and saw ten floats in various stages of construction lining the walls. He waved at Larry Binnion from the lumberyard. Hoot and Dooley supervised the work on a float toward the back of the hangar. He didn't recognize anyone else.

Nell stopped by his side and proudly pointed out the Rise-N-Shine float in the front. "We are going to have a kick-ass float this year."

Right now it didn't look like much. Theo noted the basic structure for future use. "Your mom was showing off the trophy last time I was in the diner. She seemed determined to win it again."

"Of course she is, but I admit, it's getting harder to top myself every year. I'm expected to come up with bigger and better ideas every year. I'm still ironing out the details, but we'll get there. Do you know what Irene's planning?"

"You just told me this was highly competitive. Why in the world would I let the current trophy holder in on our plans?"

Nell rolled her eyes. "As the current trophy holder I'm hardly going to be threatened by a first-time entry."

"That sounds like a challenge," Theo said distractedly as he looked at the different floats taking shape and made mental notes in his head.

"Not at all. I actually thought I could offer some pointers. All in the spirit of being neighborly." Nell was persistent. He'd give her that.

"I see. Well, we'll manage on our own. How does a person go about getting work space?"

"All the spots in the hangar are filled, I'm afraid. Mrs. Cornwell will have to find a space to rent. Does she have her permit yet?"

"Permit?"

"Participation permit. Every float has to have one to be included in the parade."

Theo wondered what else he needed to know. "I have no idea, but just in case, where do you get one?"

"City hall. Irene probably already took care of that, but you might want to double-check. And good luck. A new entry will be fun. We tend to be stuck in our ways sometimes in Everson."

Nell, despite her odd apology, rubbed him all the wrong ways. He'd love nothing better than to yank that dumb trophy out of her grasping hands and watch as it was presented to Irene.

But it would be an uphill battle. Theo was starting to wonder what he'd gotten himself into with this parade business. He recognized that new entries faced a big disadvantage from the start. No work space for building being the number one problem. He needed to discuss their options with Irene right away. She had that big old house and a big old garage. Maybe they could build the fricking float up on that hilltop of hers. He jumped in his truck and turned it in the direction of town.

• • •

"It's not trivial, Mr. Roach. If you'd ever been a young girl faced with going to a prom, you'd understand."

He frowned and tapped his fingers on the side table. "I just think our resources could be better used somewhere else."

Irene stiffened at his words. They were words she'd heard many times before. "They are my resources, and I'm putting my foot down where this project is concerned."

Joe Higginbotham cleared his throat before speaking. "What would Sven have to say about this?"

"Sven would say that providing prom dresses for underprivileged girls is a worthy project. I'm not taking away money from the food pantry or the veterans' foundation, so he would say that spreading happiness is an easy thing to do. He'd tell you to smile and give me what I want. And in case you've forgotten, Sven doesn't get a vote anymore." Sven had taught her not to let the guys in suits intimidate her. He'd told her when he was dying that she would hold the power, and he trusted her to use it as she saw fit. Bless him, he'd trusted her completely.

"Of course, Mrs. Cornwell, my apologies. But you pay us to give you financial advice." Mr. Roach remained stubborn for the moment. It was a familiar dance.

She leaned toward him. "Am I running out of money?"

He shook his head. "No, but every time we turn around you are spending it on a new project and too many of them aren't self-sustaining."

"I see. So when do you think I'll run out?"

Mr. Roach pressed his lips together and didn't answer.

"The answer is not for a long time." Irene set him straight. "The investments you've made on my behalf are performing according to projections. I'm not about to run out any time soon. Isn't that correct?"

"Yes, ma'am," Joe agreed.

"My name is Irene, Joe. How many years have I asked you to call me by my first name?"

He smiled. "Irene, I'll look into the pilot program they have in Dallas and get back to you."

"That would be great. I want it up and running by the time school starts in the fall."

Mr. Roach jumped into the conversation. "What about the boys? Every boy can't afford to rent a tux."

"That's the spirit, Mr. Roach. Let's get started on that, too. I don't want money to keep these kids at home from the dance if they want to go just because they are ashamed of what they have to wear."

A knock on her front door interrupted the meeting.

"Gentlemen, excuse me, please."

Irene smiled as the men started reminiscing about their high school proms and left them in the den. She answered the door, surprised to find Theo standing on her front porch.

"Theo? Did we have an appointment?"

Theo was looking around at the massive front porch and two-story house that towered over the surroundings. "Good God, this place is huge. Don't you ever get lost?"

"Leaving a trail of bread crumbs helps. Why are you here?" Irene was proud of the house Sven had built for her, but it felt odd for Theo to be standing at the front door, taking it all in. If he was going to be judgmental, she didn't want to hear it.

"I need to talk to you about the parade float."

"Right this minute? I'm in a meeting at the moment."

"I guess I should have called, but I ran into Nell, and she put a bee in my bonnet."

"About the float? Oh, dear. Well, come on in. I'm almost finished if you don't mind waiting a few minutes."

He walked into the foyer, still looking around this way and that. "I don't mind. Where do you want to park me in the meantime? Someplace out of the way?"

"In here is fine. You don't need to hide." She led him to a formal living room and waved him inside. "Can I get you something to drink while you're waiting?"

"I'm good. I'll be here when you're ready."

She walked back to the study, surprised to feel so disconcerted about having Theo in the house. It was her refuge from old memories and anything that had to do with her past. And now Theo, the most painful reminder of those days, sat in her living room big as life.

Walking back into the study, she said, "I'm sorry for the interruption, gentlemen. Do you have any more questions?"

Gordon Roach stood up as she entered. "No, we will look into some of these other foundations that do this sort of thing and see what works and what doesn't."

Joe Higginbotham added, "Then we'll get back to you."

They both gathered their folders and stuffed them back in their briefcases. Irene walked them to the door and thanked them for coming. When they'd gone she turned around, and with a stiffening of her spine, she went to find Theo.

He'd taken advantage of the time while she was gone. His head was thrown back on the cushions of the couch, and his hat covered his face. His long legs were stretched out in front of him, boots crossed at the ankles. His hands were clasped across his flat stomach, and he seemed to be enjoying a nice nap. Heat curled in her belly as she took the time to study him. He was a beautiful man, long and lean. Nothing about the way she reacted to him physically had changed in all these years.

She used to come home from work and find him asleep on their couch in the apartment they'd shared in Dallas. She would try to sneak in so she wouldn't wake him, but he always seemed to sense her presence. He'd sit up and yawn and ask her about her day. She loved that. The time they spent talking almost every night. It was during those talks that her feelings for him started to change. She realized he'd had a crush on her since he started working with her at Piggly Wiggly. She hadn't encouraged it. She didn't have time for an emotional attachment. Getting out of Derbyville was her only aim at the time. But she couldn't lie. She'd been flattered by his devotion. It was nice to have someone think you hung the moon.

But he'd always been so respectful of her dreams and never pushed himself on her in any way. She could relax with Theo, so when the idea came up of sharing an apartment, she jumped at the opportunity. She should have known it would end badly.

She didn't try to be sneaky now.

"Wake up, cowboy. You said we had things to discuss."

He jumped and pushed his hat back on his head. "Sorry about that. I didn't get much sleep last night."

She sat down beside him on the couch. "So, what's this about our float?"

He straightened up. "Not our float, lady. I'm just the hired help."

"Okay. My float, then."

"You need to find work space."

She smiled. "That's not a problem. Everyone uses that empty hangar at the airfield."

He corrected her. "That is the problem. Everyone's already claimed all the space. As a new entry you'll have to find someplace else to construct this thing. I thought you might have room up here. A garage or we could put up a large tarp."

"Way up here?" She'd liked the idea of being surrounded by other float builders. She'd thought it would be fun and full of camaraderie.

"You won't have to worry about spies that way."

"Should I be worried about spies?" She looked at him like he'd been drinking.

He grinned as though the whole process was a big joke. "According to Nell, no one will consider you a threat, but apparently spying is rampant when it comes to the Penelope Bottoms trophy."

"I never realized." She tapped a finger against her lip while considering the situation.

Theo continued to paint a dire picture. "I wouldn't be a bit surprised if sabotage wasn't a concern as well."

She stood up, pooh-poohing that idea with a wave of her hand. "If I'm no threat, I don't expect anyone would bother to go that far."

"You're probably right, but once we have a working plan in place, we should take precautions."

"So, now we're back to 'we'?"

Theo shook his head. "What about it? Do you have a spot to use or not?"

"Of course. My garages are full, but there is a covered carport around back. Sven thought it would be handy for boats and or visitors to use, but it's empty."

Theo frowned at Sven's name but said, "That looks like a six-car garage. Is it full of cars?"

"I have a variety of vehicles. Why do you ask?"

"Just curious. Hey, since I'm here why don't you give me a tour of the house?"

"You want to see the house?"

"Sure. I'm curious to see what I was dumped for."

Irene wanted to slug him. Instead she herded him to the front door. "Go home, Theo. I'll be in touch about the float."

He held up his hands. "Okay. I'm going. You don't have to push."

"That was a low thing to say, Theo." She stood facing him with her arms crossed over her chest.

He sighed. "You're right. Sometimes old resentments spill out before I can stop them."

She didn't care to hear his lame excuses. "I'm not going to apologize for anything I have. Not to you. Not to anyone."

He settled his hat on his head. "Understood. Good night, Ree." He started walking toward his truck, his long legs carrying him into the falling darkness.

"Theo?" She walked out onto the porch, calling his name. When he turned around, she said, "I want to win that trophy. I know it's silly and doesn't mean much, but I want it. I don't have to worry about sabotage from you, do I?"

He walked a few steps back in her direction. "You can always count on me, Ree." His face was solemn, his tone sincere.

She studied him for a minute, and then she nodded. There had been a time when she'd believed that without question. She'd believed Theo would always be there, always and forever. And she'd been absolutely wrong. But she was tired of singing that same old song. This was a new day and maybe the start of a new verse. "I'm glad to hear it. Good night, Theo."

Chapter Eleven

Theo hauled the lowboy trailer up the hill using one of Jake's old work trucks. The road was steep and winding. At least he didn't have to worry about traffic. He'd been an asshole the last time he'd seen Ree. He couldn't look at that big, fancy house and not think how much more it had meant to her than their relationship. He'd been off at basic training, missing her like crazy, and she'd been getting cozy with that old goat Sven and all his money. It shouldn't matter anymore. But the moment he stepped inside that place, it was like little explosions going off inside his head. He sat in that living room surrounded by expensive vases, original paintings, and silk throw pillows, and it was a painful reminder of all the "stuff" he hadn't been able to give her.

In all the time they talked, she'd never really acted like she longed for luxury. He knew money was always a concern for them both. The security she'd longed to have while she was growing up was a deep-seated need for her. He hadn't even asked about her family since he'd been back, but he couldn't imagine anything had changed. Her uncle had been spineless and her aunt had been over-worked, and they argued a lot. Her cousins would have been caught in the middle of all that the same way Ree had been growing up. But these days, he supposed, if nothing else, she didn't have to worry about being able to provide for them anymore.

The hill flattened out as he approached her house, and he pulled around back to the carport. It was a wide struc-ture open on four sides, and the plan was to drape it in plastic sheeting to protect their work from the elements.

Irene hadn't shown him her design yet. He didn't have any idea how to decorate a wedding planner's float to make it stand out in the crowd. Maybe a giant revolving cake or bride and groom statues. He would wait and see what she had planned for an award-winning float.

He lined up the pickup with the front side of the car-port and drove straight through, stopping when the eight-foot trailer was under the roof. He got out and unhitched the truck. Then he pulled it around to the side where it would be out of the way. The back door opened, and Irene walked out past the swimming pool gate and came out to the carport.

"Oh, good. You already have it in place. That's great, Theo."

"I aim to please, ma'am."

She rolled her eyes. "I'll show you the design, but first let's have lunch. You haven't eaten yet, have you?"

He'd been working all morning on the house on Over-brook Street, and he was hungry enough to eat a moose. "I'm starving. What are we having?"

"I made cucumber sandwiches and tea cakes." She

looked extremely pleased with herself as she headed back into the house.

"I can't wait," he grumbled. He called after her, "I hope you made a lot." He'd have to stop off at the diner as soon as he left.

She laughed as she held the back door open for him. "I remember how much you can eat. I thought we'd eat on the sunporch."

He walked through the kitchen out onto a glass-enclosed room filled with flowering plants and lounge chairs. A glass table sat in the middle surrounded by spindly cushion-covered chairs. Place settings were arranged artfully for two.

"Sit down and I'll serve. Be right back."

He frowned, pulling out a chair, and sat down gingerly. The chair was sturdier than it looked so he relaxed. Irene came out from the kitchen carrying a covered casserole dish. "I was just kidding about the cucumber sandwiches. I made your favorite."

He waited as she removed the lid. "Cheese enchiladas? Oh, man, I haven't had any that hold a candle to yours since—well, since we were back in Dallas."

She scooped a large serving onto his plate and then put a couple on hers. From a sideboard she grabbed a basket of chips and hot sauce and put them in front of him. Then she put some refried beans on his plate and a scoop of guacamole.

"I would have given you a beer, but I thought that was unwise if we plan to get any work done this afternoon."

He toasted her with his glass of iced tea. "Who needs beer? I can't believe you did this, Ree."

She blushed a bit, looking embarrassed. "It was nice to

have a reason to cook. If we are going to be working up here on the float, it doesn't make sense to stop and go all the way into town for a lunch break. Don't expect enchiladas every day, though."

"I can always brown-bag it."

She waved a hand to dismiss that idea. "Don't be silly. Consider it a perk of the job."

"Yes, ma'am." He took a big bite of enchilada, savoring the taste. "Man, I've missed your cooking." He ducked his head, knowing that admission was just the tip of the iceberg. He'd missed everything about her.

She didn't seem to read anything into the remark, though. She simply smiled and started eating, too.

It was harder for him *not* to read anything into the big plate of enchiladas parked in front of him. She'd taken the time to cook for him, and she knew they were his favorite. She'd remembered that after all this time.

Okay. Big deal.

He remembered that she loved spaghetti and meatballs. It didn't mean he was still madly in love with her or anything. That was nonsense. Mad-dog-baying-at-the-moon nonsense. Irene was merely making an effort to be civil, to make sure that the time they spent working together up here all alone on her hill wouldn't be bumpy. Hell, if they could get along and not jump down each other's throats every five minutes that would make this project easier for them both.

But dang it, she'd prepared one of his favorite dishes. She could have thrown some sandwiches together with a bag of chips, and he would have been happy as a clam. The extra effort threw him more than a little. She was wearing jeans and a pale yellow tank top. Her version of work clothes, even though that skimpy top alone probably cost more than his work boots. The tank top showed off her strong, shapely arms and just enough cleavage to distract him. He wasn't a teenage boy who lost the ability to function in the face of a little boobage, but this wasn't just anyone. This was Ree. And that little display of her creamy, inviting skin was enough to drive him crazy if he let it. He jerked his eyes up to her face when she spoke. Maybe she hadn't noticed his ogling.

"Theo, you keep eating, and I'll go grab the plans I've been working on. I'm excited to get started." She left the sun porch, taking her dishes with her.

Exercising restraint, he decided to stop eating before he made a pig of himself. He gathered his plate and glass and followed her into the kitchen. "That was great, Ree. The best meal I've had since I've been back in Everson."

"Are you sure you got enough?" She took his dishes and stacked them in the sink.

"I'm sure. If I eat anymore, I'll need a nap, and you'll have to put me to bed. We won't get any work done at all."

Her eyebrows went up like she thought he was suggesting something naughty with his nap remark. Let her think what she liked. He wasn't going to tiptoe around, watching every word that came out of his mouth.

"So, let's see those plans."

"Give me a second." She left the kitchen and was back in a flash with a file folder. She opened it and spread out the drawings on the kitchen table. "I thought you could build a wedding arbor on one end and a giant wedding cake on the back."

"I wondered if there would be a giant cake."

"Oh, so is that too obvious?"

"Isn't that the point? You don't want folks having to guess what the float represents."

"True, but I need to come up with something that will make it stand out above the rest. But you're right, it has to say *wedding* in a big way."

"I bet you'll figure it out."

He'd done some research on building a parade float. It recommended using a trailer no longer than eight feet and then building a platform sturdy enough to hold all the people and all the decorations. "That should be easy enough. I can get the decking and siding on today. It'll be up to you to help when it comes to applying all of the froufrou stuff."

She grinned. "That will be the fun stuff. I'll need to go shopping for the decorations. I might have to make a trip to Dallas. They have some wholesale shops that sell fake flowers and we are going to need lots and lots of flowers."

"I could fly you to Dallas if it would save some time. We could be up and back in no time."

She looked unsure. "Fly in your plane? With you doing the flying?"

"That's the way it works normally."

"Um. Let me think about it."

"Okay. But the offer is always open." He had to admit it had been an old daydream to get Irene up in the air someday. But in his vision they landed in a meadow covered in blue-and-yellow flowers and made love on a ratty old blanket until they were both sunburned from head to toe. But he had work to do now, so he'd bury his steamy fantasy back into his impossible dream file. Sawing some boards and pounding some nails might relieve some of the pent-up sexual frustration he suffered from when Ree was around.

"I'm going to get started," he declared.

"I want to help, so just tell me what to do."

"Can you swing a hammer?"

"It's been awhile, but I used to do a few home improve-ment projects around the house when I was growing up. I built a doghouse out of pallets I got from behind the grocery store." She was on his heels as he went out the back door.

"I remember that. Your dog's name was Macy."

"Yeah, my uncle wouldn't let her in the house, and our yard didn't have any shade. My cousin Bonnie used to sneak her food and a couple of times tried to sleep outside with her. She loved that dog."

"That's right. Well, let's get to work. If you can build a doghouse, this float will be a snap."

He had some supplies stashed in the back of the pickup truck and started unloading them, carting them over to the trailer. "We are using these wooden pallets to raise the floor so it will be level with the rails, and then we'll nail boards over the top of them."

Irene grabbed a pallet from the truck and dropped it on the ground beside the trailer. "How do you know what to do?"

"I looked on the Internet like everyone else does these days. I could tell I wasn't going to get any helpful hints from the experienced float builders around here. All very hush-hush, if you know what I mean."

"We don't need those buzzards, anyway. They'll be asking us for advice next year."

They started working together as a team. Irene handed wooden pallets to Theo, and he would hoist them up and arrange them until they were stacked two deep and cov-ered the entire trailer. "So far, so good," he declared.

"What's next?" she asked.

"I already cut those boards into sections to cover the whole thing. We will lay them out and nail them in place. That will be your floor. Then you can work your magic."

She picked up a hammer. "I like this part better. It's been too long since I've gotten to do anything physical that made me sweat. It's fun."

Theo made a show of adjusting the pallets in front of him and tried not to notice the beads of sweat dotting her face. He remembered doing all sorts of physical things to her that made her sweat. The idea of licking those beads of sweat from her long neck made him squirm. Following them with his tongue down across the rise of her breasts. He tried not to notice the way her tank top clung to her body, clearly showing the shape of those breasts. But he wasn't very good at ignoring what was right in front of him.

He lined up a board and began nailing it in place. She followed his lead, and they had the floor finished in less than an hour.

"Whew," she declared, smiling like she'd climbed the tallest tree in the forest. "It has to be a hundred degrees out here. Want to take a swim to cool off?"

His mind flashed back to the picture seared into his brain: Irene naked on a float. Before he could stop himself, he asked, "Are you going to wear a bathing suit this time?"

She gave him that haughty look she'd used when she thought he was acting childish. "And we were getting along so well, Theo. Maybe you should just go home and take a cold shower."

"Aw, come on, Ree. Can't you take a joke?"

"I'm going to change. If you want, there are several men's swimsuits in the bathhouse." She left without waiting for his answer.

If he was smart, he'd follow her suggestion. Get the hell out of here, go home, and take a cold shower. But he'd never been smart about Ree, and it was hot. Summer-in-Texas hot. And her swimming pool was just sitting there waiting to be of some use. He put his tools away and headed for the bathhouse. An odd assortment of suits hung from hooks on the wall, and he picked a pair that looked like long plaid walking shorts. They fit just fine, so he grabbed a towel and walked out to the pool.

Ree must have still been in the house, but he didn't wait for her. He dove into the deep end of the pool, letting the cool water shock his system. He stayed underwater, swimming with his eyes open until he reached the shallow end of the pool, and then he turned around without surfacing and swam the other direction. His lungs were burning from a lack of oxygen, so he was finally forced to come up for air. Good God. The sight before him nearly knocked the breath out of him all over again.

Wearing a purple bikini and nothing more, Ree walked out of the back door, gliding toward him like a model on one of his fantasy runways.

• • •

Irene walked out the door just as Theo was rising from the water like a sleek water god. Neptune's warrior. Or some mythical creature. His black hair was slicked back from his face. Water cascaded down his bulging arms, across his broad chest, and ran over his flat stomach. He'd gained more muscle since she'd first known him, and the result was extraordinary. Unfortunately for her peace of mind, he was gorgeous. Absolutely. Undeniably the epitome of male perfection. A beautiful boy grown into the manliest of men. Dammit all and a box of rocks.

She put her eyeballs back in their sockets and tried to act casual. If she didn't want to make a fool of herself, she'd have to keep things light—act unaffected. Working with him this afternoon had already put her into a state of unbridled ditziness. She kept sneaking peeks at the way the muscles in his arms bunched as he swung the hammer or the way he used his long legs, lifting the thick boards over his head before putting them in place. The hot Texas sun must have baked her brain because he suddenly seemed even more attractive than usual. She was supposed to be immune. But the way his dark hair artfully curled around the tops of his ears seemed designed to make her blood thicken with need. Those eyes. Cool blue and watching her, calculating her responses, but she'd lost track of what he wanted from her years ago, and the time she'd spent with him the last few days had done nothing to clarify anything at all. Especially what and how she felt about this man.

It had taken her way too long to decide what bathing suit to wear. Like it mattered. It wasn't like she was going on a date, for goodness' sake, but his remark about her not wearing a suit made her self-conscious, and resentful, and turned on all at the same time. She was letting the man screw with her head, and that was the one thing she'd promised she wouldn't do. First, she started to put on a black one-piece racing suit that covered as much skin as possible, but it felt like she was being manipulated into wearing it. Like she was ashamed that he'd seen her naked on his arrival into town. Then she grabbed a two-piece that had a little skirt. Modest, but showing a little more flesh. She held it up in the mirror and frowned at the polka-dot design. It looked like something a clown might wear. To hell with it. She picked up her favorite purple bikini, slipped it on, and marched outside with her head held high.

The impact of seeing him all wet and bare-chested was like taking a shot of tequila on an empty stomach. Hot quivers ran through her veins. Intoxicating. She'd been without a man for much too long if he could make her feel so out of control just by taking his shirt off. It took all of her mighty concentration not to stop and gawk. But she was proud of herself. She made it to the side of the pool but then stopped, having no idea what to do next. Conversation was way beyond her power. As a kid she'd always liked to make a splashy entrance, so she let out a yell and executed the perfect cannonball, rocking the pool, and hoping he might be gone when she surfaced for air.

Chapter Twelve

✦

He wasn't gone, but he'd retreated to the shallow end of the pool. Sitting on the steps, he watched her with a guarded expression. "So, did you invite me to swim just so you could drown me?"

"Don't be silly, Theo. I haven't wanted to kill you for nearly eight years now. Maybe only seven and a half."

"Aha. So, you admit you wanted to kill me. When you sent me the letter saying we were through?" He looked like he'd won an important contest.

"Who can remember, really? It's been so long since I've even thought about that time." That was a big fat lie. Even before he came home to Everson, there wasn't a week that went by that she didn't wonder about the man who'd gotten away. She was treading water in the deep end of the pool, keeping a safe distance from his ridiculous body with all its muscles and smooth, tan skin. "Obviously, it was the right thing to do, though. Look at what an exciting life you've had. You would have missed out on most of it if you'd been tied down in a marriage to me."

"So, you broke up with me because it was for my own good? So I'd have an exciting life?"

She didn't like where his questions were leading, so she asked a question of her own. "Hey, do you remember that old indoor pool we used to swim in at the Y? You'd swim laps, and I'd do water exercises and practice holding my breath underwater. You could always beat me at that."

"Are you changing the subject again?" He pushed himself off the steps and in a smooth gliding stroke made his way until he was directly in front of her. He bobbed there in one spot, piercing her with those blue eyes. She backed away from him until the side of the pool stopped her and she had no more room to retreat. He put an arm on either side of her, not touching her, but trapping her just the same. "Why won't you tell me what really happened, Irene? I thought we were happy, but somehow I had it all wrong. That kind of thing eats at a man."

"What good will it do to rehash everything? Why dredge up old wounds, Theo? It's pointless, and we can't change any of it now."

"You are the one that keeps pointing out that it all happened a long time ago. A little honesty between us right now might be a good thing."

"Okay. If honesty is what you want, let's go there." Her heart twisted inside her chest, and she tried to keep the hurt from her voice, but it was there, the pain, the ache. "You left me long before I wrote that letter. I was just cutting the cord so you could really be free."

He shook his head like he could erase the words. "I didn't want to be free."

"It sure felt that way to me. And I didn't want to be alone. When you asked me to marry you, I said yes because I thought we'd have a life together. Together. Not miles apart. Obviously you didn't want that."

"That's not true. I was trying to be responsible. Half the time we could barely make the rent, and that was exactly the kind of life we'd come to Dallas to escape. If I was going to marry you, I wanted to be able to support a family." He seemed incensed.

She felt all of the old frustration bubbling to the surface. "And that was a decision we should have made together. You were gone to basic training, and I didn't get a vote in the matter. And that was just the beginning of your five-year stint."

His voice was low and hard. "So, you married the first rich guy that came along."

She wasn't going to dignify that with an excuse, so she said the only thing that seemed true. "I made a mistake when I trusted my heart instead of my head. I decided not to make the same mistake again. Sven offered security."

"And you jumped at it." The words were an accusation.

She didn't deny it. "With both feet."

"So, you're saying everything between us was a mistake. That nothing you felt for me was real?"

"I loved you, Theo, and it broke my heart when you left. That's all I knew." Her voice had grown soft and low as if the confession was a secret she didn't want to share.

He closed the distance between them. Searching her face for more answers than she could give, he asked, "Why couldn't you wait for me, Ree?"

He leaned closer, his mouth hovering above hers. Her barely covered breasts brushed against his chest, and a moan escaped from her throat before she could stop it.

Touching him seemed unwise, but her hands went to his shoulders to keep herself above water. Drowning would be the coward's way out. He took that as an excuse to wrap her in his arms and kiss her. They went underwater, and still he kissed her. Wet, and slick, and hungry. She kissed him back, not sure at all of the game they were playing, not caring if there were costs to pay later.

Maybe this was the only honest thing left between them. The physical desire that swamped her couldn't be denied. When they broke the surface of the water, he rolled onto his back, keeping her above him. Both of his big wide hands tangled in her wet hair, holding her head in place so his mouth could ravage hers. She didn't fight it. In fact, she was a more than willing participant. Her hazy brain told her she deserved this. A chance to relive something that had been good about their relationship.

"Well, well. Isn't this cozy?"

Irene pushed away from Theo at the sound of a man's voice. Theo looked thunderous at the interruption. The man on the pool deck stared down at them from above, dismissing Theo with a withering glance. His attention was all on Irene when he said, "Hello, mother dearest. Is he your latest boy toy?"

Irene didn't say a word, but inside she was shaking. She calmly swam to the steps and walked out to face Charlie. In a cold voice she asked, "What are you doing here?"

He smirked. "I guess I should have called."

Theo got out of the pool behind her and handed her a towel. "What is this, Ree?"

Charlie looked at him like he'd crawled out of the sewer. "This is none of your concern, buddy boy."

Theo wedged his way in front of Irene even though she

tried to pull him back. He faced Charlie with a threatening glower. "Irene will always be my concern. I suggest you speak to her with a little more respect in your tone."

Irene could see things were unraveling quickly. "Theo, it's fine. Why don't you go on home? We've done enough work for the day."

"Is that what they're calling it now? Work?"

Before Irene could stop him, Theo picked Charlie up off his feet and threw him into the deep end of the pool. While Charlie was sputtering and cussing up a blue streak, Theo said, "I warned you to watch your tone."

"Theo, for God's sake. You're just making things worse." She had to admit she enjoyed seeing Charlie drag himself out of the pool with his designer suit drenched and his fancy loafers soaked. He might have even ruined a watch or phone to boot.

Charlie stood dripping on the decking, trying to look ferocious. It didn't work, but Irene knew he could cause her trouble if he wanted to. She threw him her towel and said evenly, "Go get out of those wet clothes, and we'll talk."

"He better be gone when I come back."

"You don't make demands around here. This is my house, remember."

He stalked to the back door and before he went inside said, "Just remember whose money built it."

When she turned around, Theo was headed to the bathhouse.

"Theo, wait. I'm sorry."

"Who is that jerk? Let me guess. He must be Sven's son. I didn't know he was part of the deal."

"He's not. I haven't seen him for three years."

"So why is he here now?"

"Once he dries off, maybe I'll find out."

Theo looked sheepish. "Sorry about that. I guess I over-reacted, but I didn't like the way he was talking to you."

She smiled reluctantly. "It was pretty funny seeing him splash around like a drowning duck. But it would be good if you left now."

"I don't like the idea of leaving while he's still here."

"I can handle Charlie. And I'll call you later so we can discuss the rest of the work on the float."

"You know we have more to discuss than the damned float." He opened the bathhouse door and went inside.

She found one of her long terry cloth robes and wrapped it around her bikini-clad body. She didn't want to deal with Charlie without having a lot more coverage.

Theo walked out dressed in his jeans and T-shirt. He walked over to where she was sitting at a poolside table. He didn't look happy. "Because you asked me nicely I'm going, but if I don't hear from you in the next couple of hours, I'll be back up this hill knocking on your door."

"That's not necessary, Theo."

"Consider it a favor to your old fiancé."

"I'll call. Now just go, please. It will be better if Charlie doesn't see you again."

"You got that right. It will be better for his health. Next time I won't be so gentle." And with that last warning, he leaned down and kissed her one more time.

She watched him roar off in his pickup truck, and her fingers covered her lips, savoring his taste. She was in big trouble where Theo was concerned, but for now she had to go inside and deal with Charlie.

• • •

When someone breaks up with you when you're away from home, there is a big disconnect. All your memories are happy ones, so it doesn't make sense. Theo couldn't remember anything bad about the time he'd been with Ree. They'd moved into that apartment, and for him it had been like playing house. Except in the beginning they hadn't shared a bedroom. She had been very clear that they were strictly roommates. But he was already madly in love with her, so he had agreed. They'd shopped for groceries together, counting their change and coupons to scrape up enough food for the week. They cleaned the apartment together every Sunday like clockwork. She would tie a bandanna around her head and attack the bathroom like a woman possessed. He would vacuum and whistle while she worked around him. They were happy days. At least he thought so. And the night she finally crawled into his bed blew every other day and night they'd shared together out of the water.

They'd argued over what show to watch on their little portable TV that evening. She wanted to watch a movie, and he wanted to watch baseball. It was all so silly, but he'd stormed off to his bedroom to do homework. He could hear the movie in the other room. It was a love story, which irritated him even more. She would moon around about some romantic movie for days, but she never even noticed how he suffered for her. But why would she? He was careful to keep his unrequited feelings to himself.

He'd barely dozed off when she'd knocked lightly on his door. He pretended to be asleep. By morning he'd be able to handle things with new resolve. Instead of going off to her own room, she'd opened the door and stuck her head inside.

"Theo, are you awake? I just wanted to say I'm sorry. I hate it when we fight." He didn't answer, but she came farther and farther into the room until she was standing right beside his bed. "Theo?"

She'd reached out, touching his shoulder, and then crawled onto the bed beside him. She was on top of the covers, but her head rested on his chest and his arms naturally went around her, pulling her close. Having her so close lying in his arms was a dream come true. But it didn't change the way she thought of him, so he reined in his rampaging hormones and tried to go back to sleep. Ree seemed to have other plans. She kissed him. Not a good buddy peck on the cheek, but the real thing, and the top of his head blew off.

Kicking off the blanket that separated them, he kissed her back, rolling onto his side so they faced each other. "Ree? What are you doing?" He pulled back to read her intentions and maybe protect his heart before she could break it, but she threw one of her legs over his and burrowed into him until all space between their bodies was erased. When she kissed him again, he stopped asking any questions. Hell, he was eighteen years old, and the girl he'd loved for years was in his bed.

After that they not only shared the apartment, but a bed as well. When they were together, they couldn't seem to keep their hands off each other. A simple glance while doing homework could turn into tearing off all their clothes without warning. Theo remembered it as a hot and heavy and intense time. Not to mention the happiest days of his life. But it wasn't all about the sex. They'd been good friends before, and they were better friends now. So when they talked about the future, they said "we" and "us." And they laughed about growing old together, though marriage wasn't mentioned. They were still so young, and they were still in school with things to accomplish. But life has a way of throwing curveballs when you least expect it. And this one changed everything. For both of them.

• • •

After getting dressed, Irene found Charlie sitting at the kitchen table wearing dry clothes and drinking a beer. He looked chastened, but she would expect an explanation before buying his act. And it better be a damned good one.

"I put my suitcase in one of the extra bedrooms. I hope you don't mind."

"So, you plan on staying? It's a little late to care if I mind, isn't it? What is going on, Charlie? I haven't heard from you in ages. And now you barge in here and embarrass me and my friend."

"He looked like more than a friend." His tone was sullen.

"What he is doesn't concern you, but for the record, I'm entitled to have someone that's more than a friend, too, if that's what I want. Your father has been gone for a long time now."

He held out a hand in her direction. "I know, and I'm sorry. I'll apologize to him too if that will help."

Irene didn't want his apologies. "Just tell me why you're here."

He looked embarrassed. "I got fired."

"Charlie? How many jobs is that now?" He'd always struck her as one of those men who thought he should start at the top without having to work his way up through the ranks. Maybe it was the curse of having a rich father who paved the way for him his entire life. Now that his father was dead, he was having trouble figuring things out on his own.

"I don't know. Lately, I've screwed things up and I know it."

Irene was amazed he was making this confession to her. He'd never been happy with his father's choice of a second wife, but while his father was alive, he kept his opinions to himself.

"So why come here?"

"I was hoping you'd give me a job." He smiled nervously like he'd wandered out onto a scrawny branch of a tree.

"A job?" She was surprised. She'd been expecting him to ask for a handout.

He nodded and launched into a spirited pitch. "I have some experience working with foundations. I'm a lawyer after all. I wouldn't expect to be a voting voice, but I know it was important to my father. Maybe it's time I respected his wishes and got involved."

Irene sat down at the table, not sure what to think. If he was really interested, she'd welcome him with open arms. Sven expressed more than once his disappointment that his son showed no interest in carrying out what he'd started. Sven would have been so pleased to have Charlie aboard. But if he was just using this as a port in the storm while he found something more worthy of his time and attention, then she didn't want any part of it.

"Let me think about it and talk to the board. I don't even know where you'd start. But in the meantime, you are welcome to stay here for a few days while we figure it out."

He smiled, looking genuinely grateful. "Thanks, Irene. After this afternoon, it's more than I deserve."

"Yeah, I haven't forgiven you for that stunt yet." She got up, leaving him sitting at the table. "I'm going out for a while. Make yourself at home."

For reasons that didn't make sense, she felt the need to discuss the situation with Theo. She wished she could discuss it with Sven.

She'd become acquainted with Sven while working at the country club. He was a regular on the golf course and many times would end his day by eating at the club. She'd waited on him a few times, and they'd chat a bit. He'd always been polite and respectful, not to mention a generous tipper.

And then she'd gotten a call saying her aunt Jo was sick. She needed an operation and didn't have insurance that would cover the necessary treatment. It made Irene furious that her aunt worked so hard, but couldn't afford to be sick. Her cousins were both still in high school, and both were scared. Aunt Jo was the rock of the family. And while some people show their character under duress, Uncle Eddie completely lost it. Instead of getting a second job or doing anything remotely helpful, he started drinking. Irene had missed so much school going home to try to help, she was afraid she would fail the semester.

Irene had finished her shift at the country club and was sitting at an empty table in the back corner of the dining room, trying to find the energy to go home to her empty apartment. Her cousin Bonnie had called that afternoon, upset because her mother insisted on going back to work even though she could barely sit up for more than an hour at a time. Irene felt overwhelmed and helpless. The tears she'd fought to hold back for so long finally fell. For her aunt, for her cousins, for herself, for Theo. He'd been gone several months at this point, and she'd written a letter, breaking things off with him. Giving him his freedom had seemed like the sensible thing to do. So now as usual, she faced her problems all alone.

Sven stopped at her table, and she'd tried to smile, wipe the tears away before she embarrassed herself, but he sat down and handed her his handkerchief. "Is there anything I can do to help?" His voice had been kind and sincere.

"Oh, I'm sorry, Mr. Cornwell. I could lose my job, and that's the last thing I need."

"I have a little pull around here. No one is going to fire you. Now what's wrong?"

Before she knew it, she'd told him about her aunt and school. She stopped short of telling him about Theo because that was all over now. The two of them talked for hours, and though nothing was solved, just getting it all off her chest made her feel better when she finally went home.

A couple of days later she got a call from her aunt saying that the law firm she worked for had come up with a bonus that would cover her medical bills. It was a miracle, but she couldn't believe it. Things were going to be okay.

Irene couldn't believe it, either. After all the pain and worry they'd suffered through, her aunt was going to get the surgery she needed. When she saw Mr. Cornwell at the club, he'd had a certain twinkle in his eye when he asked about her aunt that made her suspicious.

Suddenly the big miracle made sense. "What did you do, Mr. Cornwell?"

"I don't know what you mean." He sat down his iced tea and straightened the napkin on his lap.

She pushed him for answers. "I think you do. The question is why? You barely know me."

He said kindly, "I saw a problem I could fix, so I did."

"We can't accept your money," she insisted stubbornly. She didn't know how she was going to break the news to her aunt.

Mr. Cornwell looked at her with sad eyes. "Money is the one thing I have in abundance, Irene. Sharing it with others is one of the few pleasures I have left in this life."

"I can try to pay you back, then." Irene didn't like the idea of owing him.

"There are no strings, Irene. I don't want the money back. I want your aunt to get healthy, and I want to see a smile on that lovely face of yours again."

"There must be something I can do for you." She didn't have a clue what that might be, but she was willing to try.

"If I think of something, I'll let you know."

"Promise?"

"I promise."

A few months later he asked her to marry him.

Chapter Thirteen

Theo stood in front of the counter inside city hall, reading the name tag of the clerk. "Good afternoon, Carlotta. I need an application for a permit to build a parade float, please." He figured he'd take care of this little piece of business while he waited to hear from Ree. Otherwise, he'd find himself driving back up her long steep driveway to check on her whether she invited him or not.

Carlotta Todd, the middle-aged woman behind the counter patted her flaming red hair and peered at him curiously over her glasses. "Oh, well, let's see now. Will that be for a business, a community organization, or for some kind of personal expression?"

"The city has categories?"

"Certainly. Every year besides the high school bands and the commercial enterprises, we have a few entries from folks who like to show off their juggling or some such talent. A few years back Hogan Farley set his float on fire when his fire-eating endeavor went wrong. Now, for safety reasons, we have to keep a tighter rein on applications." She smiled, pleased at the city's efforts.

"Was anyone hurt?"

"Oh no, but the fire scared Grant Tucker's horse, and he reared up and knocked over the lemonade cart. Hogan escaped without a blister, but he had to pay for all the damages. It was a quite a boondoggle."

"Well, this application is for a nice, quiet business. No fire eating involved. Irene Cornwell's I Do, I Do. Her new wedding planning business?"

"Oh, of course. I attended my niece's wedding. Mrs. Cornwell did a lovely job."

"Great. So, anyway, I'm building her float, and I was told I needed a permit."

"Well, between you and me and the ten-foot lamppost, I honestly don't think you need to bother."

His first reaction was to defend Irene and her right to participate in the parade like anyone else in town. His indignation was clear as he spoke. "If it's because you don't think we can compete with the Rise-N-Shine Diner, think again. We plan to give them a run for their money this year."

Carlotta seemed startled by his vehemence. She reached out and patted his hand. In a voice one would use to soothe a snarling dog, she said, "Goodness, son, I hope you do."

Theo was caught short. "You do? Well, then what's the problem?"

"Oh, there's no problem. If you want to go through all the bother to fill out paperwork, knock yourself out. I just don't think it's necessary. That's all."

"I don't understand."

"Well, if you hadn't noticed, Irene Cornwell's late husband's name is on half the parks and buildings in town."

"I hadn't noticed, but what does that have to do with anything. If all of the other floats need permits, why wouldn't Mrs. Cornwell's?"

"I take it you're new around here?"

"In a manner of speaking."

"Otherwise, you'd know without asking that if it wasn't for Sven Cornwell, we wouldn't have a parade at all. Leastways, not on the grand scale that we do now."

"You wouldn't? Why not?"

"Because until he died, he provided the money for the whole shebang. The parade, the picnic, even the fireworks."

"You're kidding. I thought all towns funded their local celebrations through taxes or business contributions."

"No sirree. Not in our case. And since Sven died, his foundation has carried on in his footsteps like a trooper. Sven was born here, and the town owes him a lot. So, I figure if his wife wants a float in the parade, there's not a soul in Everson that would turn her down."

Theo was stunned. He knew her late husband had money, but he didn't know how much. The man had played benefactor to the whole town. He wasn't sure what to make of it. "I'll go ahead and do the paperwork just to be on the safe side. Is that okay, Carlotta?"

She opened a file and pulled out a form. "Sure, here you go. I guess sticking to the rules is a good idea. Just drop it back by when you're finished. And good luck."

He took the form and folded it in half. "Thanks, I appreciate your help."

Theo walked down the steps of city hall, and the

muggy summertime heat hit him in the face like a blast from a furnace. Taking a deep breath, he looked around the town square with new eyes. There was the Sven Cornwell Gazebo in the middle of everything. He wandered over and sat on a bench. It bore a plaque saying it had been donated by the Sven Cornwell Foundation. The building across the way was the Sven Cornwell Recreation Center. The community garden on the corner was named after none other than Irene's late husband. How had he never noticed that before? He was surprised the town hadn't been renamed in his honor while people were at it.

Theo hadn't given it a lot of thought, but he'd had the odd notion that Irene started the wedding planning business because she was starting to run low on funds. After all, Sven had been dead for over five years. Even a large inheritance didn't last forever. He'd been wrong apparently.

He got up from the bench and headed to his truck and drove to the house on Overbrook where he was camping out with Sadie. He could use a good run, and he knew Sadie would be raring to go after being inside all day. As he approached the house, he saw Irene's Shelby sitting out on the street. She was sitting on the front steps. She came toward him as he got out of the truck.

He slammed the door to the pickup. "Hey, Irene, is something wrong?"

"Nothing's wrong, but the world must be tilted on its axis." She frowned, looking unhappy.

He took her arm and guided her back toward the house. "Why's that?"

"Because I need some advice, and you are the only person I wanted to talk to. I must be crazy." She seemed embarrassed by the idea.

He was unaccountably pleased. He noticed Sadie jumping up and down in the front window. "Hold on a minute. Sadie is going to bust through the glass if I don't let her out."

She laughed. "Oh, sure. We've been having a nice conversation while we were waiting for you."

She waited while he opened the door. Sadie bounded out making a beeline for Theo. "How's my girl? How's my Sadie?" She bounced around sharing all of her doggy joy with Theo and Irene equally. "I was going to take her for a walk. She needs to work off some of this energy. Would you like to join us?"

She smiled like the idea was an answer to her prayers. "I'd like that very much, if you're sure you don't mind."

"Great. Let me get her leash." He hurried inside the house with Sadie at his heels. "Come here, girl. Are you ready for a walk?"

Sadie woofed her approval of the plan and stood still while Theo hooked her leash to her collar. They joined Irene outside and took off down the sidewalk at a brisk pace that Irene and Theo let the dog set.

"So, what kind of advice could you possibly need from me, Ree?"

She sounded cautious when she said, "It's about Charlie."

He gave her a sharp look. "Sven's son? I was afraid he was going to be a problem. Is he always such a jerk?"

She shook her head. "No. I'm not sure what's going on. He said he'd like to apologize."

Theo wasn't impressed with the offer. "I don't need an apology. But I'm not going to stand by while he insults you."

"That's very gallant, Theo, but unnecessary. I have to

admit I haven't spent much time with him. Before or after his father's death."

"Did he disapprove of the wedding, too?"

"Yes, but he didn't say much at the time. He and his father were estranged long before I came along. We were married in a private ceremony, but Charlie attended the reception. To be honest, I don't know him very well. Since the funeral I've only seen him once when the will was executed. That's it."

"And when Sven died, Charlie was fine with him leaving you all his money?"

"He didn't leave me all his money, and he was very generous with Charlie. I don't think he thought it was worth the trouble to fight the will. Back then Charlie seemed happy with his own life."

"So what does he want now?"

"He wants a job."

"A job doing what?"

"I don't know. He says he wants a job at the foundation."

"Is he qualified?"

"Oh, sure. He has all sorts of fancy degrees, including a law degree. He's worked at several big firms, but from what he said he must have burned some bridges. He seemed fairly humbled by his last experience."

"I'm not sure what you expect me to say, Ree." Sadie stopped to smell the base of a tree before lifting her leg.

"You are right. It was unfair of me to ask you, but of everyone in town, you are the only one who might have a clear perspective."

Theo laughed at that idea. "That's funny. Given our past, I'd say I have no perspective at all, but I'm happy to lend an ear."

They entered a small park, and Irene sank down onto the first bench they came to. Theo sat down beside her. "Thanks. The thing is, I know this would've made Sven so happy. He didn't feel like he'd been the best father when Charlie was growing up and said he'd spent too much time working. He had a lot of guilt about that. It was a wedge between them, and they were never as close as Sven would have liked, even when Sven got sick."

"Then that's your answer, isn't it?"

She nodded and sighed. "I feel like I should at least give him a chance."

Theo felt honored that she'd turned to him for advice, but it was clear she knew better than he did what to do. She just needed someone to tell her so. "Trust your gut, Ree. You can always tell him to get lost if it turns out he's pulling a fast one."

She smiled. "Thanks, Theo. I'll have to keep a close eye on him, though. But if it works out, it could take some pressure off me, too. I can concentrate on planning weddings."

"Explain to me again why you're spending time planning weddings? It's clearly not for the money."

She shrugged. "The money from the foundation is Sven's. I oversee the distribution, but it's not mine. Charlie has a better claim to it than I do, but Sven trusted me to keep things running smoothly. So that's what I do for the sake of the town. Planning weddings is what I do for myself."

"I think that's a healthy attitude. You should try doing more things just for yourself."

"It's not that simple. I have obligations."

"Then maybe Charlie will help with that. If he needs to be thrown in the pool again, I'll be happy to oblige."

She laughed. "Thanks, Theo. It helped to talk things out."

"Oh, before I forget." He stood up and pulled out his wallet. He ignored the folded, wrinkled letter that was always in his billfold and pulled out the permit instead, handing it to her.

"What's this?" she asked.

"A permit for building a parade float. Everyone is supposed to turn one in to city hall."

"Okay. I'll do that first thing tomorrow. I better go." She reached down and patted Sadie's head. "You're a good girl, Sadie." Then she got up and started to walk away.

Maybe it was seeing the Dear Theo letter that made him ask, but before she got too far, he called her name. "Ree?"

She turned back to face him.

"Did you love him? Did you love Sven?"

She stood stark still, her face a mask hiding all emotion from him. Finally she answered, "Yes. I did. I loved him very much." This time when she walked away she didn't give Theo another glance.

Chapter Fourteen

～

Irene couldn't go home yet. On her way through town, she stopped at the Hazelnut Inn to drop off menus for an upcoming wedding. While she was there, she decided on impulse to treat herself to a nice, relaxing dinner all by herself. Dining out alone always seemed civilized and sophisticated in the movies. She didn't feel sophisticated, but she forced herself up the steps of the old house and walked inside.

Etta's sister Belle greeted her. "Hey, Irene. Are you here on business?"

Irene had become familiar with the place because of all the weddings she planned using it as a venue. "Partly, but I'm here to have dinner, too. Do I need to have a reservation? It was a spur-of-the-moment decision."

"Of course not, Irene. Even if we were full, we'd let you eat in the kitchen."

"That's awfully nice, Belle."

"You're like family, and the weddings you've booked here kept us afloat the first few months after we opened."

Irene was touched by Belle's sentiments. "Well, thank you. And stick me anyplace you like. As long as Etta's cooking, I don't care where I sit."

Belle took her into the dining room. Most of the tables were filled with happy chatting diners, but she led her to a small open table by the back window.

"Let me go tell Etta you're here. She'll want to say hello."

"Oh, I'm sure she has her hands full."

"Don't be silly. She'll have my head if I don't, so relax. Can I bring you a cocktail or an iced tea?"

"Iced tea would be perfect. Thanks, Belle."

After Belle left, she took in the view out onto the grounds. Glorious flower beds and tall trees surrounded a swimming pool that had been recently installed in late spring. It was ready and waiting for the summer guests of the B and B to take advantage of during their stay.

A deep masculine voice interrupted her thoughts. "What do you think?"

Irene looked up to find Donny Joe standing by her table. She smiled. "The pool is a beautiful finishing touch. You should be proud of this place, Donny Joe."

"Thanks, Irene. Mind if I sit down? I don't think you've ever dropped in for dinner before." He sat down without waiting for her permission.

She smiled. "I've meant to, but you know how it goes. But boy, you look happy. Etta is good for you."

"I won't argue with that. I'm a lucky man. But I've wondered how you've been. We don't get the chance to keep up the way we used to, Irene."

Over the years since Sven's death, Donny Joe had provided a shield for her against the speculation of the people in Everson. And as a result he'd been the source of a different type of speculation. There were still plenty of townsfolk wrongly convinced they'd been lovers. Either way he'd been a good friend. She was happy that he'd found the love of his life, but she could be honest enough to admit she missed him.

"I'm fine. Planning weddings keeps me busy. And it's a nice change of pace. I stumbled onto something I really enjoy."

"You do a great job. Maybe you've found your true calling." He grinned. "So, what has you frowning?"

Donny Joe could always read her mood. "Charlie Cornwell showed up at my house this afternoon."

Donny Joe's eyes widened. "Sven's son? What did he want?"

"He wants a job at the foundation. And the crazy thing is I'm actually considering it."

Etta came out of the kitchen and approached the table. "Irene. What a nice surprise. You should come for dinner more often."

"Hi, Etta. I was dropping off the menus for the Stone-Rendell wedding and decided to stay for dinner. In fact, I was just about to order the special. Donny Joe distracted me with too much conversation." She dug in her purse and pulled out her notes.

Etta took them and said, "Thanks, and I'm so pleased you decided to eat."

"If you have time, you should join us." Irene knew that Etta had once been jealous of her relationship with Donny Joe. She wanted to take every opportunity to let her know she thought they made a perfect couple.

"You don't have to ask me twice. I'd love to sit down

for a minute." Etta waved at Belle. "Sis, would you bring Irene tonight's special? I'm going to take a little break."

Belle smiled and patted her sister's shoulder. "You've got it. And I'll bring you some tea, too."

"Thanks, Belle."

"I was just telling Donny Joe that Sven's son showed up today asking for a job."

Etta looked concerned. "Is that a problem?"

"If he's serious about taking a real interest in his father's foundation, it could be the answer to my prayers. If he's just here because he's run out of money, then it's going to be a real headache."

"It's always tricky dealing with family. Let us know if we can help."

Belle came back with Irene's food. The special was roast chicken with polenta and mushrooms. "Here you go. Can I get you anything else?"

"No, this smells wonderful. I didn't realize how hungry I was. Thanks."

"You're welcome." She left and returned momentarily, putting glasses of tea down in front of Donny Joe and Etta before returning to the kitchen.

Irene took a bite and moaned her pleasure. "Oh my goodness. This is incredible, Etta."

"Thanks. It's a simple dish, but it always seems to be a crowd-pleaser." Etta smiled, pleased at Irene's reaction to the food.

After another bite, Irene asked, "So, what about you two? When do you plan to tie the knot?"

"We've been discussing some dates," Etta said with a sappy smile.

Donny Joe reached over and grabbed her hand. "I'd

get married tomorrow, but Etta seems to think we need to have a big ceremony with fuss and family and lots of flowers involved."

Etta patted his arm. "Yes, I do, and that's why Irene will be our first call after we decide on a date. We'd love to have you plan our wedding, wouldn't we, Donny Joe?"

He nodded. "Absolutely. Nobody else will do."

Irene put her fork down. "Oh, what fun, and I'd be honored. Just say the word and we'll get started. I'll make it my top priority. My, my. Donny Joe getting married. I can't think of any wedding I'd like to plan more."

Etta laughed. "Me, either. But now I better get back to the kitchen. We'll talk soon, Irene."

Donny Joe stood up, too. "I'll let you finish eating, but if you need to talk about anything ever, you know my door is always open, Irene."

"Thanks, Donny Joe. That means the world to me. By the way, are you having a float in the parade?"

"Is grass green? Of course we are. Two of 'em in fact. One for the Backyard Oasis and one for the B and B."

"Are you building them out at the old airport hangar?"

"Yeah. I heard Theo was helping with yours."

"He is. We're building it up at my house."

"Why aren't you down at the hangar with the rest of us?"

"Nell told Theo there was no space left in the hangar. I was disappointed. Half the fun was going to be hanging out with everyone."

Donny Joe crossed his arms over his chest. "Well, Nell is wrong. What is wrong with that woman? There's plenty of room by our floats. Move it on down, and I'll make sure you get the space you need."

Irene should have known to question anything the girl said. She supposed she could chalk it up to sneaky sabotage. "Thanks, Donny Joe. You are a true friend." But Nell was the least of her problems. Right now she had to quit stalling. She had to go home and have a serious talk with Charlie.

Chapter Fifteen

⁓

The next morning Irene walked into the kitchen and found Charlie sitting at the table, drinking coffee and looking at his phone. "Oh, good. You're awake."

He put down his phone when he saw her. "I've been up for hours, so I hope you don't mind that I made coffee."

Irene got a mug from the cabinet and poured a cup before joining him at the table. "I don't mind at all. Are you ready to get to work?" They'd stayed up late talking and came to an agreement for a trial run. Today she planned to show him the ropes.

"Ready? I'm more than ready. I'm grateful for the opportunity."

She had to admit his eagerness seemed sincere. "I want you to know exactly what this job would entail before you accept."

"I told you I've had some experience working at foundations before."

"Well, this is a little more hands-on. I let the lawyers sit around in the office juggling the money. I prefer to stay involved on the local level."

"So, what does that mean?"

"Today we will visit the food pantry, deliver Meals on Wheels, and check in with the community garden manager."

"Okay. I guess it's important to supervise how they are spending their money."

"You don't understand. I'm not interested in just funding these programs, Charlie. If you are going to work for me, you have to be involved in the everyday work they do. Unless you weren't planning on living here?"

"Wait a minute. I thought I could live in Dallas. Isn't that where the other lawyers are?"

"I don't need another lawyer, Charlie. If you want to be part of your father's legacy, you need to learn it from the ground up."

He looked skeptical, but he said, "You're the boss."

She raised her eyebrows. "Let's see how today goes first. I want you to realize what you'd be getting into before you agree to anything."

He took a drink of coffee and then stood up, setting the mug in the sink. "Okay. I'm ready when you are. And Irene? I appreciate this. After yesterday you could have thrown me out on my ear."

Irene stood, too. "We've been over all that. Let's start fresh today. If you're serious, I know your father would be thrilled that you want to be part of what he started."

Charlie looked like a vulnerable kid. "Do you really think so?"

Irene wished once more that Sven was there to tell him himself. "Charlie, your father loved you. Of course he would."

"Thanks, Irene. That means a lot."

Irene smiled and said, "I'll be ready to go in fifteen minutes, okay?"

Charlie smiled, too. "I'll be ready."

• • •

Irene pulled her minivan around to the alley behind the Rise-N-Shine Diner. Opening her door, she turned to Charlie. "Come on. We have to pick up the bread for the meals program."

"The diner donates it?"

"Yes, they bake it fresh every day. I've managed to get different restaurants involved then we meet at the Methodist church to distribute the meals to the drivers."

"And you do this every morning?" He followed her to the back door.

She rang a bell on the service door. "No, we have different volunteers that handle the pickups and deliveries. But since I'm showing you the ropes, I called and changed the schedule. I usually try to drive three days a week if I can."

"Are you telling me my dad did this, too?"

Before she could answer, the door opened and Bertie Harcourt waved them inside the kitchen. It was crowded with staff preparing for the morning breakfast rush. "Come on in, Irene. I've got the yeast rolls wrapped up and ready to go. And I baked some chocolate sheet cakes last night. I was on a sweet kick and figured I'd share." She was staring at Charlie with wide-eyed curiosity.

"Thank you, Bertie. That will be a real treat."

"It's just as easy to bake a few extra. Who is he?"

"I'm sorry. Bertie, this is Charlie Cornwell. Charlie, this is Bertie Harcourt. Owner of this fine diner."

She looked surprised. "Cornwell, as in Sven Cornwell?"

"He was my father."

"Well, I declare. I knew your father when he was a boy. He was in high school with my older brother Ralph. They played baseball together."

Charlie perked up. "Really? I didn't even know he played sports. He never said much about growing up here."

"Well, come in for lunch someday, and I'll tell you a few stories. Are you just here for a visit?"

Charlie looked at Irene and shrugged. "I'm not sure yet. But I'll be sure to come by for lunch while I'm here."

Irene picked up the large tray holding the rolls and handed it to Charlie. "We need to get going." Bertie handed her several aluminum-covered pans containing the cakes. "Thanks, Bertie. Talk to you later."

• • •

Theo stood on a ladder painting Lily Porter's garage, thinking he really should have gotten an early morning start instead of baking his brains out in the noonday heat. But Lily was a talker. When he'd shown up that morning, she'd had him come in for a cup of coffee, and he'd gladly accepted.

Another thing he discovered about Lily Porter was that she loved her Siamese cat Mitzi. He'd never been around cats much, but Mitzi took to him right away. Wandering in and out of his feet, rubbing her fur against the legs of his blue jeans. And when Mrs. Porter had offered him a seat, Mitzi had jumped into his lap and curled herself into a ball, purring louder than his airplane engine on idle.

"I'm mighty impressed, Theo. Mitzi has given you her

stamp of approval, and I can tell you she doesn't give it lightly. She's likely to hide under the bed most times when anyone visits."

He scratched the cat between her ears. "She seems like a sweetheart."

Lily Porter seemed charmed, and as she talked Theo could see that she was lonely. So he didn't hurry with his coffee.

"Can I offer you a muffin? They're banana nut. That was my husband's favorite, rest his soul. Can't have coffee without a muffin."

"That would be great." He didn't say no to the stale muffin. And he didn't say a thing about needing to get to work before the day got any hotter.

When she dragged out a second picture album, Theo told her he hated to end their visit, but he needed to start painting if he wanted to finish in one day.

"I have a porch rail on the back porch that needs some repair work done, too. I was going to mention it to Jake, but what with the wedding and all, I never got around to it."

"I can come back later this week and take care of that for you. I'll look at it before I leave. How would that be?"

"Gracious, Theo. That would be fine. You're an answer to an old lady's prayers."

So now he had another job to add to the list, but the porch rail would be an easy fix. He made a note to come back with fresh muffins.

He turned from his perch on the ladder as a silver minivan pulled into the driveway. He was happy to see that Lily was having visitors. Irene and Charlie climbed out of the van. Charlie opened the back door and pulled out some cardboard containers.

Theo climbed down the ladder, set his paintbrush on the tray, and wiped his forehead on the sleeve of his shirt. Irene still hadn't noticed him. She was busy talking to Charlie, herding him toward the front door.

Charlie looked up and saw him. He stopped walking, and then Irene noticed him, too.

"Hey, Irene." He smiled at her and gave Charlie a hard look just in case he decided to cause any trouble.

Irene smiled as soon as she noticed him, too. "Theo. I didn't realize you'd be here."

He wiped his forehead on his sleeve. "Painting Miz Lily's garage was one of the jobs Jake asked me to take care of while he was gone."

"That's very kind of him. I mean of you. And it looks great."

She looked wonderful, dressed in a short black skirt with a crisp white blouse. Just seeing her made the whole day better. "Well, I guess I'd better get back to work."

"Of course. We won't keep you, then. But actually, wait a second. I need to talk to you about the float."

"Sure. What about it?"

"I spoke to Donny Joe, and he said there's plenty of room by them in the hangar."

"You're kidding. So Nell just lied to us?"

"Seems so. I'd like to be with all the other participants. I think that's half the fun, so I'm going to ask Oliver to drive it down for me this morning and get set up in a spot. I'll call you later with details."

Theo couldn't believe the nerve of that woman. "Okay. Just let me know."

She smiled. "I will. Come on, Charlie. Let's go."

Charlie nodded in his direction, but all the smart-assed attitude he'd presented the day before seemed to have disappeared. Theo still planned to keep his eye on the guy. They walked to the front door, and he heard Mrs. Porter greet them warmly. He heard a yowl. "Oh, that Mitzi. There she goes off to hide under the bed. Don't mind her. Oh my, what did you bring me today?"

Then the door shut, and he didn't hear anything else. He continued to work, trying to ignore the fact that Ree was inside the house. His body reacted just because she was near. About fifteen minutes later, Irene and Charlie emerged from the house and Theo could hear them saying good-bye. Mrs. Porter followed them out onto the front walkway.

"Thank you, Irene. I don't know what I'd do without you. And it was nice to meet you, Charlie. I hope you come again."

They waved good-bye and got in the van and drove off. Theo came down the ladder.

"I tell you, that Irene is an angel here on earth."

Theo watched the van disappear down the street. "You don't say."

"I do say. I wouldn't have anything to eat some days if she didn't bring me my meals."

"Your meals? She does that all the time?"

"I don't drive anymore and getting to the store is difficult. The meals program is a lifesaver."

"So, she's a volunteer driver?" Theo had never taken the time to learn what she did when she wasn't planning weddings.

Lily nodded. "Why, yes, but there's more to it than that."

"What do you mean?"

"She set up the whole program and made sure the elderly and shut-in folks of Everson got signed up and taken care of."

Theo was impressed. "Her husband didn't set it up?"

"Don't get me wrong. Sven Cornwell did a lot of good for this town, but I always got the feeling it was so he could slap his name on buildings and parks. Irene worries about ways to help people that need it. She's a treasure, that's for sure."

"She's full of surprises. I'll give you that." Theo started gathering his painting equipment and moved it out of the way. "So what do you think of your garage?"

Lily turned to survey her freshly painted garage door. It had started the day as a peeling, ugly eyesore. But now the old, dull brown paint had been scraped and covered with a nice shade of sage green. "Oh my, it looks wonderful, Theo. It makes me want to have company over now so I can show off my house. Thank you."

"You're welcome, and I'll be back on Thursday to fix your porch rail. Is that okay?"

"Of course. I can't tell you how much I appreciate it."

"And I'll bring the muffins, too." He loaded his equipment into his pickup. "See you then."

After he left Lily's house, he drove back to the house on Overbrook and took a shower. Then he loaded Sadie into the truck and headed to the airfield. He wanted to put out some feelers with Bart about selling his airplane. Sadie was happy to be out of the house, and she panted happily on the seat beside him. He couldn't stop thinking about Lily Porter. He wondered how many older folks could use some help around their houses. And Irene delivering food. It cast her in an additional light. According to Lily Porter, she was Everson's own saint living up in that big house on the hill above town. He'd never doubted her generosity, but it seemed she was personally involved in the program.

He pulled into the parking lot and parked in a spot close to the main hangar. As he was putting Sadie on her leash, he noticed a few people milling around outside the hangar designated for the floats and decided to have a peek inside.

He walked inside the hangar with Sadie trotting at his side. He spotted Donny Joe working on a float for his pool store in the far corner. Irene's bare-boned trailer was on the other side. "Hey, Donny Joe. Nice palm trees."

Donny Joe jumped down as he approached. "Thanks. It looks like we'll be neighbors."

"It looks that way. I'm glad to see Oliver already moved the float down from the hill."

"Yeah, I heard Nell sold you a bill of goods about that. Irene stopped by the Inn and mentioned it last night."

He knew Donny Joe had a real loyalty to Irene, so he decided to ask his opinion. "Did you know Charlie Cornwell is in town, and he's staying with Irene?"

Donny Joe put his hands on his hips now. "Yeah, she told me. She said he showed up out of the blue wanting a job."

Theo rubbed a hand across his face. "Do you trust him?"

Donny Joe narrowed his eyes. "I've met the man one time about five years ago. Do you know of a reason I shouldn't?"

"I have no idea. He just gives me a bad feeling. And

you seem to be full of protective instincts where she is concerned. I thought you might have some insight."

Irene's voice cut through the cavernous hangar. "Hey, guys. What's going on?"

Theo turned as she walked toward them, her long legs eating up the floor, her dark hair streaming out behind her. His main thought was that she looked magnificent.

"Oliver moved the float," he said. "I was checking out our new work space."

Sadie recognized Irene as her walking companion and yipped with excitement as she approached.

Irene stopped and knelt down, petting Sadie on the head. "Hey, girl. How's the good girl?" After a few more good rubs, she stood up and faced Theo.

"Charlie and I were making the rounds, and I thought I'd stop by and see if there was any problem moving the float."

Chapter Sixteen

⁓

Did I hear my name?" Charlie came strolling up with Nell by his side. "Nell was being nice and showing me around."

Irene watched with interest as Theo turned to confront Nell. "Hello, Nell. Look what we managed to squeeze inside this old hangar."

Nell looked flustered. "What are you talking about?"

"Irene's float. Inside the hangar you said was all out of rental space."

Nell turned to look at the float. Donny Joe and Theo both stood in front of it with their arms folded over their chests.

"I'm sure that's what Bart said." Nell smiled a sickly sweet smile.

Charlie clapped his hands together. "Well, no harm done, is there? The problem is solved now."

Theo fumed. "For someone who is so sure about winning that dumb trophy, you sure seemed to be worried about the competition."

Nell looked at everyone standing around. "You mean her? Irene?"

"Hey, I'm standing right here."

"She is no competition." Nell seemed obnoxiously sure of herself.

Charlie put his hand on Irene's arm, and in a tone that implied they were all being childish, he asked, "Are you all really fighting about a parade float?"

She shook his hand off her arm. "It's not just a float. It's for the Penelope Bottoms trophy."

"Oh, well, in that case." He smirked and shook his head.

"Your father loved the trophy and the parade. Are you going to be in town for the Fourth?" Nell asked.

Charlie winked at her. "If Irene decides to keep me on full-time."

"She's going to hire you? But it's your father's money."

"Nell, there you go sticking your nose into things that don't concern you." Irene was trying not to let the woman bother her, but every time she opened her mouth, it got more difficult.

Theo touched Irene on the shoulder. "Irene, could I have a word with you?"

She wrenched her attention away from Nell and said, "Sure. What is it, Theo?"

"Can you tell me anything about Lily Porter?" he asked. "You delivered food to her today."

"Yes, she's one of our meal recipients. Why?"

"No reason really. She just came up with another job for me to do, and I got the impression it was for the company as much as anything. She seems lonely."

"That's a real problem for the older folks in town that

live alone. We try to visit a bit when we drop off the food, but we have other meals to deliver so we can never stay as long as we'd like."

"That's what I figured. Thanks."

They walked back to the group. Nell was complimenting Donny Joe on his palm trees. "I plan to install a hot tub on this baby, too. It's going to blow the other floats out of the water."

"Don't bet on it, hotshot," Nell said. "The palm trees are a nice touch, but the Rise-N-Shine will be four-peating this year."

Charlie shook his head. "So, you've won before, I suppose."

"Yes, indeed." Nell was happy to brag.

"What about Irene?" Charlie asked. "Has she won before?"

"Oh, heavens no. This is her first time to enter the parade," Nell announced.

Irene answered, too. "Only because this is the first time I've had a business."

Charlie nodded. "Oh, I forgot. Your wedding planning business."

Nell snickered, and Irene pinned her with a withering glare. "Exactly. So Charlie, if you're ready, we have another stop to make before we go home." Irene headed out of the hangar without waiting to see if he was coming along.

Charlie stuck his hands in his pockets and with a grin said, "I'm right behind you, boss."

"Bye, Charlie," Nell said. "Come by the diner sometime, and the pie and coffee will be on the house."

Irene turned impatiently while Charlie finished with the social niceties. "Thanks, Nell, it was nice to meet you." Nodding toward Theo and Donny Joe, he added, "Gentlemen. I'm sure we'll meet again."

"I'd bet on it," Theo promised loudly. Irene didn't think he sounded too happy about it.

• • •

Charlie was showing a real interest in all the foundation's projects. Irene admitted she was surprised by his intense examination of every detail. When she'd taken him to the back room of I Do, I Do and showed him the prom dresses she'd collected so far, she expected him to finally bolt. But he didn't.

He sorted through the array of dresses hanging on a metal rod, making clucking noises and grimacing when he pulled out a purple puffy number. It was donated by a bridesmaid who cursed the bride who made her wear it. Irene hoped her aunt might refashion it into something more acceptable.

Charlie finished his inspection and asked, "Are you going to run it out of this building?"

"No, I want to keep it separate for tax reasons, but this makes a good collection center for now. There's a small storefront across the square that I can rent."

"I'm not sure my father would have approved."

She bristled at his remark. That had been her lawyer's opinion as well. "Why do you say that?"

"Because he always seemed to promote projects that exalted his good name."

"And providing prom dresses for girls that can't afford them doesn't qualify?"

"Oh, I think it exalts his name in exactly the right way. Helping people who really need it. It just doesn't have the panache of donating land for a park, does it?"

"Parks are wonderful additions to any town, and everyone in Everson benefits, but that can't be the only reason to consider the worthiness of a project."

He stopped and gave her a hard look. "Is this personal for you?"

"Do you mean, was I too poor to afford a dress for my senior prom? As a matter of fact I was, but I didn't have a date anyway, so it didn't matter."

"A beautiful girl like you didn't have a date? All the boys must have been panting after you."

"I had to work that night, but I don't want another girl to take an extra shift at her crummy after-school job if a dress is the only thing keeping her from going."

He gave her a thoughtful look. "I think I'm starting to see what my father saw in you."

"Your father took pity on a lonely girl who was struggling to get by. I miss him every day."

He looked uncomfortable. "That's really none of my business."

Irene had never figured out what Charlie expected from her. "You're right. I'm sorry. Are you ready to go home?"

"Lead the way. Oh, and I'll cook dinner tonight."

"Are you a good cook?" Irene didn't cook much for herself these days, but she enjoyed it.

"I am. Let's stop at the grocery store on the way home."

Charlie had struck her as spoiled and entitled in their few encounters. Maybe she'd been wrong about him, too.

• • •

The finishing touches were going on all of the parade floats. Everything was taking shape. There had been some small but irritating vandalism problems—supplies and tools being mysteriously moved around—but for the most part Theo was impressed at the cooperative spirit that seemed alive and well among the participants. For supposedly being such a cutthroat, competitive sport, almost everyone but Nell seemed to be willing to lend a hand or give a suggestion without batting an eye. Nell was the only one who shrouded her float in tarps, trying to keep her masterpiece out of sight. He was almost tempted to sneak a peek. He couldn't imagine what could be so amazing that she had to keep it hidden from view. Ree's float was coming right along. It boasted a giant four-layer wedding cake with wooden slots on one end and a vine-covered arch on the other where a bride and groom could stand and wave to the crowd. He hadn't asked for any details about who would be doing the waving.

Jake and Marla Jean were due back in town in a few days, and he wanted to finish up and spend a few quiet days with them before he took off. Irene had been a real sport while they worked together. He had to hand it to her. She'd done everything to make him feel comfortable. The lack of drama between them had been refreshing.

"Theo, I need a hand with these flowers," she called from somewhere out of sight.

Theo was in the middle of securing the poles people would hold onto while they rode along the route. "Hold on, I'll be right there. I just need to finish securing these handholds."

She walked around the corner carrying an overflowing armful of white paper flowers. She looked like a bride-to-be, and his heart jumped to his throat. She smiled and said, "Okay, I'll wait. I don't want my bride and groom falling off during a sudden turn."

"Safety first. Why don't we tape their hands to the handle just in case?"

"Don't be silly. They have to wave at the people on the sidewalk and throw candy."

"Candy? Is that to help win votes for best float?"

"Of course. That and the real wedding cake we'll be serving at each stop."

"Wow. I detect a sugar theme." He laughed and nodded toward Nell's shroud-covered float. "What do you think Nell will be throwing? Fried eggs and biscuits?"

"Who knows? I'm sure it is a highly guarded secret just like her float."

"If this thing is so competitive, why doesn't anyone else care about hiding their float?"

"I don't know. I guess Romeo's Pizza doesn't think anyone else is going to build a giant pizza to go on their float."

"You have a point. Cheese and pepperoni don't exactly say I do." Theo finished using the screwdriver to tighten the last bracket into the wood.

Irene laughed. "And Brick's Bait Shop doesn't have to worry about anyone stealing their decorating scheme, either."

Theo pretended to ponder that. "I don't know. Walking down the aisle through crossed fishing poles might be somebody's idea of a perfect wedding. But I think when it comes to the trophy, Lu Lu's might be the one to beat."

Irene looked concerned. "Why do you think that? What are they doing?"

"I haven't seen it, but if Mike's float has a bar and jukebox, that's going to be where I'm hanging out." Mike was the longtime bartender and part owner of Lu Lu's dance hall, and the parade would begin and end in his parking lot on the edge of town.

She pooh-poohed the very idea. "Don't be silly. I'm pretty sure Mike can't serve alcohol at nine o'clock in the morning along the parade route."

"Damn. I guess it's for the best, though. The folks here in Everson are a wild bunch, and things might get a little rowdy."

She acted indignant. "Are you making fun of my town?"

He climbed down and took some of the flowers from her arms. "So, it's your town now?"

She sighed. "It feels more like home than Derbyville ever did."

"I know what you mean. Since Mom is not there anymore, I don't have too many reasons to go back. Wally and Jeff from my old high school baseball team asked me to come out and sub on their softball team."

"Are you going to do it?"

"I don't know. Maybe. You could come sit in the stands and cheer me on. Since we've decided to be friends."

"I'll think about it. That might be fun. I still go back and see my aunt."

"You do? I wasn't sure you stayed in touch."

"Oh, sure. Aunt Jo always did her best for me, and since Uncle Eddie died, I try to make certain she has help with the house. Things like that."

"Where are her daughters?"

"They are both in Dallas. I'm closer and I can afford to pay someone to take care of her yard and paint the house every other year."

"That's very nice of you, Ree."

"She won't let me do any more, but she seems inter-ested in helping with the wedding planning business."

"And you like that idea?" He hadn't seen her look so happy about anything in a while.

"I do. She's family. You know?"

He did know. Jake was the main reason he'd consid-ered staying in Everson. Spending more time with his big brother had been an ongoing goal. Since he'd be leaving soon, spending time with Irene was easier, too. He didn't watch every word he said or even try to convince himself that he didn't want her with every fiber in his being. He just planned to take the time he had left and store it up. Maybe it would get him through the next ten years of liv-ing without her.

Irene interrupted his thoughts. "What about your mom? How's she doing?"

Theo shrugged. "She seems happy. But I've thought that before, and she always ends up turning in her current husband for a new one."

She looked concerned. "Because of your dad?"

"Probably. Finding out he had another family the whole time he was with us. I'd say she has trust issues."

Irene crossed her arms across her chest. "I can under-stand how she'd feel. She's protecting herself."

Theo wasn't so sure. "But in the long run she's being self-destructive. She won't allow herself a chance to be happy once and for all."

"Do you think most people ever have that chance?" She looked at him as if she might be lost. She looked at him as if his answer mattered.

He took the rest of the flowers away from her and laid them on the float. Then he did something completely selfish. He wrapped her in his arms and rocked her back and forth. "I don't have a clue. But you are young and beautiful, and someday you will meet someone to share your life with." And he wouldn't be around to see it.

She pulled back so she could look into his eyes. "Are you going to turn into my personal matchmaker now?"

"Not a chance. I'm sure I wouldn't find anyone I considered good enough for you."

She laid her head against his chest. "Did I give up on us too easily?"

"That's a loaded question, and I don't want to argue with you anymore. If we can scrape out some semblance of friendship by the time I leave, I'll consider that a victory."

She pulled out of his arms. "You and me. Friends. That's a concept that would take some getting used to."

"It might be nice since I know I'll be back occasionally to see Jake and Marla Jean."

"Especially if they start having kids. They'll need to know their uncle Theo."

That made him smile. "I can teach them some bad habits. They'll be crazy about me."

"I always thought you'd be good with kids."

He frowned and before he could think it through said, "Just not our kids?"

Chapter Seventeen

She looked like he'd slapped her.

He immediately felt remorse. "Ree, I'm sorry. I vowed I'd stay away from sensitive subjects."

"I'd say that's a pretty sensitive subject."

He walked over and sat down on the edge of the float. "I know, and I'm so sorry. When I found out you were pregnant, I was dancing on the moon. I felt ten feet tall. I was going to be a father. We were going to have a baby. You and me. It seemed like a miracle. But then you had the miscarriage, and I tried to be strong for you, but inside I was dying." He realized now he should have told her how he'd felt a long time ago.

She sat down beside him and took his hand. "You really wanted the baby, too?"

Her soft question ripped him apart, and he tightened his grip, holding on for all he was worth. He could see the pain in her eyes, and he hated that he'd had a part in putting it there. "Of course I did. How could you have ever doubted that?"

She let out a shuddering sigh. "Well, I knew the timing was all wrong. We were so young and still in school. But I was thrilled. And scared. And happy. And devastated when I miscarried." She leaned her head against his shoulder.

He turned, cupping her face in his hands. "Me too, Ree."

Her eyes were wet, but she seemed determined not to cry. "It seems there were lots of things we didn't talk about. I guess we were both caught up in our own pain."

"When we lost the baby, I started thinking I needed to be more responsible for you and any other children we might have. It played a big part in deciding to join the Navy. We were two young kids playing house, and when you got pregnant, I woke up and realized it wasn't a game. Why do you think I talked to that recruiter? I needed a plan for the future."

"I just thought you wanted out."

"After I got your letter saying it was over, I used to think about those kids we might have had. The family we might have been, and I couldn't understand why you didn't love me enough to give me that chance."

"Theo, we both ended up hurting each other, and that probably means we were too immature to deal with our feelings. When you left, I felt abandoned and completely alone. But now I can say I'm sorry for the way I handled it."

"I'm sorry, too." He pulled her into a hug, and they held each other, healing some of the old pain that had lain between them all these years.

Dooley walked by and yelled, "Hey, you two, no making out on the job. Get to work."

They pulled apart laughing, wondering what new rumor Dooley would spread about the two of them now.

Theo turned away and dashed the tears from his eyes. As a distraction he gathered up some of the flowers. "There's something I wanted to talk to you about. Wally said there's a big Derbyville High School reunion planned for the weekend before the Fourth. He said I should come."

Irene started poking the flowers into the chicken wire. "Are you going to go?"

"Maybe. Would you go with me?" Once the idea occurred to him he couldn't let it go.

She seemed surprised. "Me? I don't have a lot of good memories from high school. I had to work and didn't have many friends."

"Except for the guys on the baseball team, I didn't, either. But it might be fun. We could go back and you could say, 'Hey everybody, look at me now.' "

"Oh, that would be awfully petty of me, don't you think?"

"I think some of those snotty girls and boys have grown up and become nicer people. We won't know unless we go to the reunion. I'm game if you are."

Irene laughed and shook her head. "I don't know. Let me think about it."

Theo stood up and reached down and picked up more flowers. "Okay, now tell me what the heck we're doing with all these flowers."

• • •

Irene looked at her image in the mirror. Theo was picking her up for the reunion in about an hour. Getting ready to go out had been an exercise in mental gymnastics. She wanted to look elegant without being too dressy. Classic and tasteful without looking like an old lady. But then again she couldn't help but want to show a touch of sexiness without being trashy. There were so many lines she didn't want to cross. She'd gone online and looked at the reunion announcement. The dress code said semiformal.

She couldn't decide if that meant knee length or floor length. In a small town like Derbyville, it might mean not wearing flip-flops with your sundress.

She'd finally given up all pretense of not caring what she looked like and drove to Dallas the day before to shop for the perfect dress. She settled on a cobalt-blue above-the-knee dress with three-inch blue-and-coral heels. They made her legs look nine miles long. The dress was made from silky, swirly material that made her feel feminine and pretty. It wasn't the same type of armor she donned for a night on the town at Lu Lu's, but it was armor all the same. And if she was honest, she hoped to see a reaction from Theo when he came to pick her up for the date.

"A date with Theo." She said it out loud, letting the words hang in the air of her bedroom. She'd tried to downplay that idea, but Theo wouldn't let her. In fact, he'd crowed about it when she'd finally said yes.

He'd grabbed her around the waist and twirled her around. "I don't believe it. You'll go with me?"

She pounded on his chest until he put her down. "Stop it, Theo. I said I'll go."

"I need to tell someone." He looked across the hangar and yelled at Lincoln and Dinah. They were working on their float for the parade. It had a desk sitting in front of a giant calculator. "Hey, guys, Irene agreed to go out with me."

"Congratulations," Linc hollered back. Dinah turned with her hands on her giant pregnant belly. "Irene, you better watch that guy. I hear he can be trouble."

Irene waved in acknowledgment to them. "Hush, Theo. It's not a date."

"Of course it's a date. I'm going to wear a suit. You're going to wear a dress. If I'm wearing a suit and tie, then it better be a date."

She finally relented, and now she was looking forward to the night. Since they'd talked about the miscarriage, she'd felt more at ease with Theo. At the time she'd been so caught up in her own fog of sorrow and suffering that she hadn't been able to see that he'd been in pain as well.

Tonight should be fun. Except for the nagging feeling that she might throw up any minute. Seeing all those girls would bring back memories she wanted to forget. But it was too late to back out now. It would be cowardly and unfair to Theo.

She grabbed her purse and went downstairs to wait for Theo.

Charlie was on the couch in the living room reading and stood up as she came down the stairs. "My goodness. You look great."

"Thanks, Charlie." They needed to get some things settled about his working schedule. And while they were at it, they needed to address his living arrangements, too. It was a big house, but she wasn't comfortable sharing it with Charlie permanently.

"What's the occasion?"

"It's my high school reunion." She felt a little embarrassed.

"You went to high school here?"

"No, I went to school in Derbyville."

"I wouldn't mind tagging along if you'd like some company. I'm bored out of my mind sitting around this place."

"Sorry, but someone is picking me up."

"You have a date? Who's the lucky guy?"

"It's not a date. I'm going with Theo, if you must know."

"Theo. Your ex?"

"You don't have to say it like I'm committing a crime. He went to school in Derbyville, too. He heard about it from some of his old friends. He told me about it, and we both decided it might be fun. You know, see what kind of adults those kids turned out to be."

His voice was full of appreciation when he said, "Well, I know it's not your prom, but I think you'll turn a few heads."

"Thanks, Charlie. You might try hanging out at Lu Lu's if you're bored. That's where most folks go on a Saturday night in Everson."

He nodded. "I might just do that."

The doorbell rang, and she jumped, unable to hide her nerves. "My date," she said breathlessly.

He laughed. "Now it's a date. Do you want me to get it?" He stood up and started toward the door.

She hurried after him. "No, no, I'll do it." She gave him a pointed looked, and he took the hint.

"Okay, I can see I'm not needed. I'll make myself scarce. Have fun." He grinned and disappeared toward the kitchen.

Irene took a deep breath and walked to the front door. Pulling it open, she smiled at Theo.

His eyes were wide with appreciation. "Ree, you look amazing."

She did a little twirl, asking, "Do you like it?"

"You're going to knock a few socks off in that dress." His eyes raked her from head to toe, and she loved every minute of it.

Her heart sped up under his gaze. He wore a gray suit with a crisp white shirt and a blue tie. He was the one that looked amazing. She didn't try to hide the pleasure she would feel by just being on his arm tonight. "Thank you. But I'm afraid I wanted to look good for all the wrong reasons."

He laughed, and his eyes twinkled in a way that had her tummy doing backflips. "In that case, wrong never looked so right."

She grabbed her purse from the side table and joined him on the porch. "You're being nice, but I didn't want to walk into that room and give Christine Dempsey anything to be catty about."

"Christine Dempsey. I haven't thought about her in years. Didn't she have a mouthful of braces?" He took her arm as they walked down the steps.

"She did. But braces were all the rage back then." She smiled and pointed to a lightly crooked tooth. "We couldn't afford braces. That was only one of the many ways I didn't fit in."

He frowned. "I guess I never realized that. When I looked at you, I always saw the prettiest girl in school. Nobody else compared."

"Theo, you don't have to try to make me feel better."

"I'm not. You knew how I felt. Even way back then. Don't pretend it was a big surprise."

"Okay, but back to Christine. As soon as you mentioned the reunion, I remembered how she and her little clique of followers used to torment me every day of the school year."

"Why?" He opened the car door and helped her into the passenger seat.

Before he closed the door, she said, "Who knows? My clothes weren't fashionable enough. My hair wasn't cut the right way. Girls like that don't need a reason once they decide you aren't one of them."

He shut the door before trotting around the car and climbing into the driver's seat. Once he started the engine he said, "Well, they might as well wear paper bags tonight, because no one will give them a second look once you make your grand appearance."

"Well, that's the way I imagine it happening, anyway. But I'll settle for civil, polite behavior."

"That's awfully tame." He pulled out of the driveway, heading down the hill toward town.

"Well, I'm a mature woman these days. Even if I did have all sorts of trouble picking out the right dress, I'm not going let a few bad memories from years ago keep me from having a good time tonight. Do you think there will be dancing?"

He flashed a grin illuminated by the dashboard lights. "I'm counting on it."

To hide her smile, Irene turned to stare out at the dark night. Trees and the occasional streetlight passed in a blur as they drove out of Everson and headed toward their old hometown.

"Hey, do you remember the progressive double two-step we used to do when we lived in Dallas?" Theo asked.

"Oh, right. That dance instructor Barb gave free lessons at the Blue Lagoon every Friday night. How could I forget?"

Theo glanced away from the road. "And we'd get there early because they offered the free appetizer buffet."

She sighed. "I do believe that buffet kept us from starving the first year we were in Dallas."

"Between what we could eat at the buffet and the leftovers you brought home from the country club, we managed. But with the buffet we learned a new dance as a bonus."

Irene supposed a little reminiscing was in order while driving to a reunion. And those were fond memories. They'd had some good times in that club. "Okay, you convinced me. I'll save you at least one dance. Maybe two."

"Make one of them a slow dance." His smile teased her, sending wicked impulses chasing through her body.

The space inside the car suddenly seemed charged with intimacy. Irene sank into the soft leather seat. Theo smelled like clean soap and subtle cologne. She inhaled the scent of him, savoring the flutters that awoke in her stomach. It had been so long since she'd let herself feel like a woman. That yearning that Theo could create simply by sitting too close. "Don't start flirting with me now, Theo. I don't know what to do with it."

"I could make some suggestions, Ree." His words held danger and temptation.

She looked straight ahead, but she could feel his gaze brush across her skin. "Keep your eyes on the road, and keep your suggestions to yourself."

His voice grew serious. "I've told you I'm leaving once Jake's home, but in the meantime, I don't know how to pretend I don't still want you."

His words set off a physical ache that wrapped her in need. "That's what I'm talking about. You say these things, and what am I supposed to do? Say okay, Theo, take me, I'm yours until you leave town?"

He stepped on the brakes, guiding the car to the side of the road. As soon as the car stopped, he turned to face her. "I apologize. I'm sorry. I don't want to make you uncomfortable, but I know in a week or so I'll be gone, and I'll manage the same way I've managed all of these years."

"On to the next adventure. On to the next woman. And you'll forget about me all over again." Her voice was bright with the false impression that she approved and understood.

His eyes glittered in the dark as he sat still as a stone. But then he was moving, unfastening his seat belt and reaching for her. His mouth was a weapon, slashing and devouring hers like a conquering warrior. She kissed him back because she had wanted—no, needed—to kiss him again from the moment he'd flown back into town. She had no intention of resisting now. And her mouth opened under his, seeking the taste of him, wanting the contradiction of comfort and fire that only came from his touch.

He raised his head and moved back into his seat. In an almost angry voice he asked, "Do you honestly think I can forget that? Ever? Until the day I die, I'll never find a woman that makes me come undone the way you do. And believe me I've tried."

She was unreasonably flattered by his words and irritated by his tone at the same time. But she wasn't about to take the blame for everything. She wasn't going to let him get away with pretending he was the only one who'd been carrying baggage from their past all these years. "I'm sure it's been a chore for you, Theo, but you aren't the only one with regrets."

They stared at each other, eyes locked in defiance, neither backing down. He surrendered first.

"God." He put his head back against his seat and sighed. "Let's don't do this tonight. I'm weary of the battle. Aren't you?"

She sighed, too, as she reached over and took his hand from the steering wheel. Wrapping her fingers around his, she gave them a little squeeze. "More than you know."

He rolled his head to look at her. "So, can we just go and have a good time? I'll behave. I promise."

She nodded. "Okay. Let's go show Derbyville High how two of its finest turned out. Deal?"

He smiled and returned her hand softly to her lap. "You got it." Then he started the car and pulled back onto the road. They rode in silence as the lights of Derbyville twinkled in the distance.

Chapter Eighteen

The entrance to the gym of Derbyville High was decorated with an enormous green-and-white balloon arch. Irene also noted the crepe paper streamers hanging limply from the rafters and butcher paper posters lining the walls in an attempt to transform the old gymnasium into a festive party place for the reunion. She tried to ignore the mothlike fluttering of her chest as she and Theo approached the table set up to greet people on their arrival for the big event. She was surprised she recognized the woman at the table. Carol Boykin-Weems. Back in high school she'd been popular and nice to everyone. The perfect person to welcome the prodigal students back to the scene of their crimes.

Her smile was big and bright as she said, "Hello, y'all! Did you two preregister?" She waved a hand over the name tags spread across the table. "If you give me your names, I'll help you find your tags. They're alphabetical."

Theo said, "Hi, Carol. I registered us. Theo Jacobson and Irene Cunningham."

"Oh, here you are." Carol found Irene's name tag in the *C*'s and studied the yearbook picture before holding it out to her. "You are just as pretty as you were in high school, Irene! A lot of these people don't look the same at all."

"Thanks, Carol. How have you been?"

"I'm great. Married with two kids.

"Anyone I know?" Irene asked.

"No, I met Greg in college, and we moved back so I could take care of my mom. We need to talk more later on, once I'm through checking folks in."

Irene smiled. "I'd like that."

So far so good. Tonight might turn out to be better than she'd thought. She took Theo's arm and together they walked inside.

• • •

"Theo Jacobson, as I live and breathe!" Coach Barstow's voice boomed across the crowded room. Theo looked up to see his old baseball coach loping toward him with his arm held high in a friendly wave. He pounded him on the shoulder, saying, "I didn't know you'd be here. How've you been?"

"I'm great, coach. It's good to see you, too."

"And this must be your wife? This young man played baseball for me, and I tell you he was a real go-getter. I wish I'd had a bunch more like him."

Irene smiled. "I think one Theo is more than the world can handle, coach. And I'm not his wife. I'm just his date for the moment. I attended Derbyville High, too."

He blushed red. "I apologize for jumping to conclusions." He spotted her name tag and gave her a closer look.

"Irene Cunningham. I remember you now. It's heartening to see all the old students come back home."

"It should be fun," Theo agreed. He was happy Irene hadn't seemed bothered when the coach thought she was his wife. Despite his good intentions, a big part of him would have been happy to introduce her as his wife, show off to everyone his good fortune. But he reined his imagination back in and decided that they were sharing a temporary truce. Another one.

He was still reeling from that kiss. It rocked him to the core. He must have kissed dozens of women in his time and he'd enjoyed most of them, but Ree made the top of his head blow off. And he shouldn't have kissed her. He should have resisted the urge. She was addictive and that was the problem. He'd gone cold turkey a long time ago, but one taste and he was craving a whole lot more.

Coach Barstow shook his hand and moved on to some other former students. "Sorry about that, Ree." Theo made a wry face. "Thanks for not killing him for thinking you're my wife."

She patted his arm. "Don't worry about it. But it looks like I could use some help from you now."

He looked concerned. "What's up?"

She widened her eyes and nodded her head in the direction of the snack table. "Trouble at three o'clock and it's heading this way. Smile and look like I'm the most interesting person in the world, if you don't mind."

Theo glanced around and spotted Christine Dempsey and a gaggle of other women heading their way. They were whispering and smirking in a way that made Theo's blood boil. He turned back to Irene, placing his knuckle under her chin as he gazed into her eyes, looking at her as if she was the most magnificent creature on earth. He didn't have to work too hard to imagine that she was exactly that. "Don't let them see you sweat, Ree. We've got this."

She blessed him with a smile that melted his heart like a blown-out candle. "I'm going to owe you for this, aren't I?"

He tucked a loose strand of hair behind her ear. "This one's on the house, darlin'."

A feminine voice that floated on the air like spun sugar interrupted them. "Excuse me."

He turned to face the one and only Christine Dempsey. She was stunning at first glance. Blonde curly hair that gave her the appearance of an angel. A sexy, seductive body that most men would find impossible to ignore.

But all her efforts left Theo cold, and he realized he'd never give her a second glance even if Irene hadn't been in the room. Christine's blue eyes glinted as they calculated and schemed, constantly taking in her surroundings, trying to scope out and eliminate her competition.

Irene turned, too, exclaiming, "Why, Christine Dempsey! How are you?" She smiled and gushed like she'd just found an old, dear friend.

Theo could see the group of women hadn't been expecting her reaction to be so friendly, and they grew quiet waiting to gauge their leader's response so they could follow her example.

"Irene Cunningham. My goodness, it's been ages." Christine batted her eyes at Theo while she spoke. She eyed him like someone on a diet who suddenly spotted a chocolate cupcake. Theo raised an eyebrow. She'd certainly never noticed him back in high school. He'd been way below her on the social scale, and he almost laughed now at her interest. She read his name tag. "Theo Jacobson. Did we have classes together?"

Theo pulled Irene close and barely looked at the women around them. "I don't think so." In fact, they'd sat next to each other in Algebra, where she'd cheated off his papers, and were both in the same biology class. He was happy to let her think he hardly remembered her at all.

Irene snuggled into Theo's body and asked, "What have you been up to these days, Christine?"

"Oh, I have a little antique shop downtown. It's not much, but I like to dabble in business. You should stop in sometime if you ever visit your aunt. Where do you live these days?"

"I'm still in the area. I live in Everson. Theo was in town for a visit, so he convinced me to come to the reunion with him. It's been fun to see how we've all changed."

Christine nodded agreeably. "I didn't realize that. I see your aunt once in a while. We both belong to the Women's League. What do you do in Everson these days? I remember when you worked at Piggly Wiggly back in high school."

"No more grocery stores for me. I recently started a wedding planning business. It's a lot of fun." Irene smiled at the group. "Anyone planning to get married should give me a call."

Christine seemed less than impressed. "Well, that sounds precious. I'm sure you are very good at it, too."

Theo stepped in and decided to take the reins on this one. "She's being modest. The wedding planning business is just one of Irene's many accomplishments."

"Oh, really? What do you mean?" Christine feigned interest, but it was clear she doubted Irene could compete with her in any way, not even business.

Theo drew back to look at Irene as if she was the smartest woman in the room. "She also runs a successful charitable foundation that provides help not just to the folks in Everson, but provides assistance to people in the entire county. That includes Derbyville."

Beverly and Joan looked at each other before Joan asked, "Goodness, how did you get hired to do that?"

Theo grinned. "She's highly qualified for the job, but she wasn't just hired. It's her foundation, and she's quite the generous benefactor. Now, if you ladies will excuse us, Irene promised me this dance." Without waiting, he whisked Irene onto the dance floor, but he noticed Christine watching them with new interest. A fast song was playing, and he'd never been much of a dancer to rock and roll in high school, but he held one of her hands and bounced around to the beat. "That was fun. Did you see their faces?"

Irene bounced, too, looking much better at it than he did. "I did. You enjoyed that a little too much, Theo."

"Oh, come on. Don't tell me you didn't enjoy Christine looking like she had swallowed a bug. I wish I'd had a camera."

Irene giggled, and she never giggled that he could recall. "Okay. I'll admit it. I wasn't planning to flaunt my position in life, but since you did it instead..."

"No problem, darlin'. I'm available anytime."

She swung her hips seductively. "Thank you, Theo. I could have faced them alone, but it was more fun having you beside me."

"Arm candy?" He winked. "Is that all I am now?"

"Christine looked like she wanted to take a bite out of you."

"Remind me to keep my distance." He raised his arm and twirled her around. "I reckon I don't like mean women very much. I guess I proved that by the way I handled Nell. Or should I say screwed things up with Nell."

"I've almost forgiven you for that." Irene shook her shoulders and turned in a circle. "But I don't think Nell's really mean. She's just misguided."

He moved his elbows up and down and shuffled his feet in an awkward attempt to keep time to the music. He made a mental plea that the next song they played would be a two-step or something he could handle and maintain his dignity, but watching Irene dance with such wild abandon was a reward all its own. He did his best to imitate her movement, surrendering and enjoying the moment. "You are more generous than I am, then."

The music stopped and to his relief changed to a country song. Keith Urban was singing "Thank You" to someone. With pleasure he held out his arms in a wide invitation. "Shall we?"

• • •

She smiled and moved into his embrace without hesitation. After a moment they began to twirl and advance around the floor as if they'd been dancing together for years. Irene found it exhilarating, as if she was home at last. In Theo's arms, with music filling the air around them, filling her body and soul. She held on as he executed a man under and spun her around to the beat. Nothing else mattered. And she realized how silly she'd been to care what Christine and her minions thought of her. They weren't worth her time or energy, and she felt shallow for giving them that kind of power. Some things and some people should stay in the past.

She'd known since his return to Everson that she hadn't been able to say the same about Theo with any kind of certainty. She felt his strong arms anchoring her to the dance floor. The feel of his hand on her back was such a little thing, such a tiny touch, but it filled her with a raging happiness that made her feel as if she could've danced all night. Or instead when the reunion ended, she could climb back into his car and let him drive her back into the night. Hope he'd pull his car over and kiss her again the way he'd done earlier. She wouldn't stop him.

She knew he was leaving town soon and whatever happened tonight there wasn't a chance it would lead to anything that would last. But right now, she didn't care. Theo was a right now kind of man. And she wanted him.

Right now.

After this dance she would make the rounds. Make more of an effort to say hello to old classmates while he did the same. Chat with them all, make new contacts, and when it was time to leave, she would walk out with Theo by her side.

And whatever happened after that—well, she wasn't going to fight it anymore. The dance ended, and before they made it off the dance floor, Theo was surrounded by some of his old baseball buddies. Irene waved at him and left them to catch up with each other.

She was pulled back onto the dance floor by Carol Boykin-Weems and a group of women who decided it was time for a line dance. She laughed and slid and kicked and twirled, having a great time. After, Carol introduced her and she remembered a lot of the women. They were friendly and warm, and they outnumbered Christine and her snarky little bunch. She made a lunch date with Carol, and for the first time all night, she was glad Theo had convinced her to come.

All that dancing made her thirsty, so she wandered over to the table that held a punch bowl. It also held every kind of cookie, chips and dips, something that looked like meatballs, and a platter of wings. She poured herself a cup of punch, but passed on the food, and made a note to nix that kind of food for her wedding receptions unless they were served in silver serving dishes. It was all in presentation.

A male voice interrupted her musings about the snack table. "Irene Cunningham? Is that you?"

"Yes?" She looked up at the tall man by her side and smiled while reading his name tag. "Well, hello, Mark Connors. How are you?" He'd been in her chemistry class, and due to alphabetical seating, they'd been lab partners on several experiments.

"I'm great. It's really nice to see you here."

"It's nice to see you, too. How've you been?"

"I'm fine. Do you still live around here?"

"I'm in the area. I live in Everson. What about you, Mark?" She sat her punch on the table and turned toward him.

He beamed at her undivided attention. "I live in Dallas. I almost didn't come to the reunion, but now I'm glad I did."

She nodded. "I know what you mean. It's hard to know

what to expect at these things. A friend convinced me to come at the last minute."

"Anyone I know?"

"Maybe." She nodded over at the group of men, laughing and slapping each other on the back. "Do you remember Theo Jacobson?"

"Sure. He was one of the jocks. Theo's here? I heard he'd gone and joined the Navy."

"You heard right. He was home for his brother's wedding."

"So, are you and Theo..."

Irene answered truthfully, "We're just friends, and he'll be leaving soon."

Mark stuck his hands in his pockets, looking as if he was considering something important. "Would you like to dance?" He smiled and leaned toward her. "I'm not trying to be pushy, but I never had the nerve to ask in high school."

Before she could accept Theo reappeared at her side with a sharklike smile on his face. "Mark Connors. It's been a long time, buddy." He held out his hand.

Mark took it, and the two men shook hands. "Hello, Theo. Irene was just telling me you were in town for your brother's wedding."

"Was she?"

Irene jumped into the conversation. "Mark and I used to be lab partners in chemistry class. Old Mr. Floyd didn't like us very much. I think we played around too much."

"I didn't realize Mark was such a cutup." Theo looked at the man like he should be sent to the principal's office.

"Irene seemed to bring it out in me. Otherwise, I was a big nerd who never made a peep. Mr. Floyd was a good teacher, though. Those were some fun times."

Theo didn't look like he agreed, but he said, "The good old days, huh?"

"I was just asking Irene if she wanted to dance."

"Is that so?" Theo casually put his arm around Irene's shoulder. "Mark, are you trying to horn in on my date?"

Chapter Nineteen

Theo wasn't proud of the jealousy that surged through his body when he'd glanced over and seen Irene flirting with the man beside the punch bowl. Even as he walked over to where they stood, laughing and talking and carrying on, he knew he should mind his own business. He should be happy Irene had found an old friend to spend time with. He guessed they were old friends judging from their easy familiarity. Of course, he wasn't the only old friend she'd ever known, and their past didn't give him any kind of claim on her at all. He kept telling himself every bit of that with every step he took. He'd wanted her to have a good time when he asked her to come with him to the reunion. But now he realized he hadn't wanted her to have a good time with another man. He wanted her to have a good time with him and only him. He wanted to be the source of her joy and happiness and even something as mild as contentment.

He could tell he'd pissed her off when she shrugged out from under his arm. He tried to make up for it now.

"Mark, I don't know if you know this, but Irene loves to dance."

"That's why I'm hoping she'll accept my invitation. But if I was out of line for asking..."

Irene shook her head and didn't look too pleased with either man. "I'm standing right here. Stop talking about me like I'm invisible."

Mark looked embarrassed. "I'm sorry, Irene. And you could never be invisible."

"That's sweet, Mark." She graced him with a forgiving smile. "And I'd love to dance. Theo, if you'll excuse us."

"You bet." Mark allowed her to pull him onto the dance floor. "Nice to see you again, Theo."

Theo nodded in acknowledgment. The poor guy looked awkward but game as he moved around in front of Irene. Irene, of course, moved like she heard some inner beat, graceful and sexy at the same time. And in the end he was still the guy standing alone on the sidelines while they were having fun without him.

Theo checked around for his baseball buddies, but they'd dispersed, having been reclaimed by their wives or girlfriends. He wandered over to an empty table and sat down. He wasn't going to stand there like a dolt watching Irene dance with Mark. He was only going to take a break before he started circulating again. There were bound to be untold numbers of alumni he hadn't spoken to yet. They'd put up a bulletin board full of old pictures from back in their school days. That would kill a few minutes while he waited for Irene to decide it was time to leave. Because she was leaving with him. He had no doubt old Markie boy would be glad to see her home, but that wasn't going to happen if he had anything to say about it.

"Theo Jacobson."

"That's me." He turned to find a short woman with bright red hair standing in front of him. "I'm sorry. Did we know each other in school?"

She pointed to her name badge. "I'm sorry. I'm Susan Connors. My maiden name was Bolton. I don't know if you remember me, but we were in study hall together."

Theo looked closer and suddenly recognized the face on the name badge. "Susan, of course. How are you?"

"I'm fine. Well, not really. My ex-husband is out there on the dance floor making a fool of himself with Irene Cunningham. I'd hoped to spend some time with him, but I can't compete with her."

Theo felt sorry for the woman. She was cute in her own way. "So, you married Mark Connors?"

"Yes. We both went to college in Austin, and after we graduated we got married and moved to Dallas."

"I'm sorry things didn't work out for you and Mark."

"Me too. I guess I'm pretty pathetic, mooning over him like this, aren't I?"

Theo knew exactly how she felt. "I don't think you are pathetic at all. Would you like to dance with me? It's better than standing around like two bumps on a log."

"Really? Oh, I don't know." Susan looked like she was considering it.

"Come on. I think we should show Mark that you don't need him to have a good time."

She grabbed his outstretched hand and practically dragged him onto the dance floor. It was a slow song, and she was good at following his lead. "What do you do these days, Susan?"

"I teach at one of the community colleges in the Metroplex."

"What do you teach?" They danced around the floor while Theo deliberately moved them within sight of Irene and Mark. He focused his attention on the redheaded woman in his arms once his prey was in sight. No matter what happened, Mark needed to see that his wife was capable of attracting other men.

"Poetry and composition. In fact, I wrote a poem for Mark that I planned to give him tonight, but I guess I won't do that now. What about you, Theo? What do you do these days?"

"I'm trying to figure that out, Susan. I've been roaming around the world for the last few years. Lately I've been thinking it might be time to settle down."

"With Irene? I saw you come in together."

"We rode together from Everson. My big brother lives there now. Irene is an old friend. But let's not talk about her. Let's talk about you. Do you like your job?"

Susan seemed pleased to have someone want to know more about her job. "I really do. There's nothing more satisfying than helping a student learn to express their thoughts. And poetry can be very freeing. Young folks have so much raging emotion, and they don't always have a healthy way to release it."

"I never thought about poetry like that before. I go flying when I need an outlet for pent-up feelings. Way up in the sky, everything else seems to float away."

"You fly—as in your own plane? That must be incredible."

"I do. A buddy from the Navy was a pilot, and he taught me the ropes. I worked for him in Alaska until recently."

"I always wanted to learn to fly," Susan gushed, looking transported by the idea.

Theo smiled at her eagerness. This wasn't some pilot groupie. Susan really seemed interested in flying, and he could appreciate that. "I'd be happy to take you up sometime while I'm here. And you should take lessons. Life's too short to not go after our dreams."

The song ended, and Theo realized they were standing next to Mark and Irene. Mark's face looked like a thundercloud. "Since when have you wanted to fly, Susie?" His voice was loud and demanding.

"First you horn in on my date, and now you're horning in on my dance partner. Mark, old boy, we need to establish some boundaries."

"Susie is my wife. I don't need your permission to talk to her."

"Your wife?" Irene put some distance between herself and Mark. "You didn't say you were married."

Theo thought he'd make sure everyone knew everyone. "Irene, you remember Susan Bolton? We were in study hall together."

"We're divorced. Or at least we will be soon," Mark explained quickly. "Susie, I didn't know you'd be here tonight. You didn't say anything."

"That's what happens when people divorce. They don't have to get each other's approval before they make plans. Derbyville was my high school, too, you know."

"I know that. I wasn't trying to say you shouldn't be here."

"Theo was nice enough to ask me to dance."

"It was my pleasure, Susan." Theo still held onto her hand and gave it a little squeeze before dropping it.

Irene turned to Susan. "It's nice to see you again, Susan. So, Mark and I were just catching up on things."

Susan eyed her closely. "Theo and I were doing the same thing. That's what reunions are for, I suppose."

Mark looked at his ex-wife. "You look very nice tonight, Susie."

Susan blushed. "You never used to tell me that when we were married. Thank you, Mark."

"How have you been?" His voice dripped with concern and care.

Theo grabbed Irene's hand and tugged her away. Mark and Susan didn't notice. They were gazing at each other intimately as if everyone else in the room had disappeared. "I think we should give them some privacy," he insisted.

"I can't believe that." Irene allowed herself to be dragged off the floor, but she kept turning her head back to look at the couple who were now deep in an animated conversation.

Theo scoffed. "What? That a man might still be in love with his wife even after they separate?"

Irene turned abruptly to face him. "No, Theo, I believe that part, but while we were dancing, he mentioned we should meet for lunch sometime. I faded into the wallpaper as soon as he saw her dancing with you. Did you plan that?"

"And you aren't used to being part of the wallpaper, are you, Ree? Maybe he's been trying to move on. It's part of surviving." He didn't understand why he wanted to provoke her.

She gave him a sharp look. "I'm not as shallow as all that. I actually think it's sort of sweet."

"Only if things work out. She wrote him a poem, and she brought it with her tonight hoping to have a chance to read it to him." Theo watched as Mark and Susan disappeared out a side door. "It looks like she'll have that chance."

"A poem? Would something like that work for you?"

"I don't think it matters whether it's a poem or not. It's the effort she's putting into letting him know how she still feels."

"So, why did they let things get to the point of divorce?"

"Who knows? Things can spin out of control. Maybe that's what happened to them."

Irene walked over to an empty table and sat down. He followed and sat beside her. "Maybe," she said. "When you're in the middle of things, it's easy to lose perspective."

"Is that what happened to us?" Theo still wanted answers from her. Some easy explanation that would clear away the hurt and confusion surrounding their long ago breakup.

"Theo, we were young and dumb."

"And in love. Don't forget that part. You can't gloss over that like it didn't matter." Mentioning that, he felt exposed, like he was hanging on a slender branch that could snap under the weight of her next response.

Ree looked him directly in the eye without any attempt at evasion and reached for his hand. "Of course it mattered. Otherwise, we wouldn't have been able to hurt each other the way we did."

Theo felt like he'd won a victory. She might not have written a poem for him, but he felt like carving her admission in stone. She had loved him, too. Somewhere, sometime before she fell in love with Sven and married him. Maybe not enough, maybe not as much as he loved her, but it hadn't been all one-sided.

She ducked her head, looking at her watch. "I know it's still early, but do you want to get out of here?"

He grinned. "Yes, ma'am. I'm ready if you are."

He stood up, and she grabbed his arm. "I'm ready. Let's blow this pop stand."

He noticed Christine and her group of friends watching them, and he waved in their direction. Irene glanced at the women before turning back to Theo. "Thanks for inviting me, Theo. I had more fun than I expected." And then she kissed him.

It was short and sweet, and he wasn't sure if it was for his benefit or Christine's. He didn't really care. He tucked her into his side and waltzed out of the reunion like he was ten feet tall.

• • •

Irene sat in Theo's car watching the dark blur of trees slide by in the darkened night. The reunion had been a mixed bag. Some good. Some bad. Some highly satisfying. Dancing with Theo had been the highlight. Not much could beat gliding around the room in his arms. Even better than facing off with Christine. She'd found once she was face-to-face with the woman, it didn't really matter one whit what she thought anymore. It was funny how certain things from the past that seemed to matter so much went poof, disappearing into the mists when confronted head-on. Other things like her past with Theo only grew in importance the more time she spent with him. He'd be gone soon, but if he was leaving what was wrong with grabbing new memories to get her through the endless span of time that yawned out ahead of her. More lonely years, years that threatened to bury her alive in that house up on the hill.

"I'm sorry about Mark." Theo's voice washed over her, disrupting her thoughts.

She swiveled in her seat to face him. "It's okay. It was just a dance."

"And maybe lunch. You seemed happy talking to him." His fingers beat out a rhythm on the steering wheel.

She thought about it. "Not him particularly. Face it, I barely know him. I think it only woke me up to the fact that I need to get out more. And not just to Lu Lu's on Friday and Saturday nights. I've fallen into a pattern in Everson, and as a result, my social life sucks. It's time to change that."

"So, Irene Cornwell is officially going back on the market? Watch out world." His grin lit up the inside of the car.

"Oh, sure. I'm expecting parties in the street."

"Ree, you underestimate your effect on the male population."

"Is that so?" She would give twenty bucks if she could figure out her effect on Theo.

"That's the gospel truth."

"So, would you be interested in dating while you're still in town?"

He cut his eyes in her direction. "Me? In dating you?"

She shrugged. "I figure you would be a safe place to start. Nothing long term. That would be understood up front."

"If you think I'm safe, I'm doing something wrong." He sounded put out.

She laughed at his show of ego. "Down, boy. I'm not insulting your manhood. I'm just saying we already know each other so the initial awkwardness that can happen on a first date wouldn't be a problem. You could be my trial run."

"We just had a date and you tried to pick up another man. I'm not sure I'd survive another encounter like that one."

"Well, when you put it that way, you actually owe me. If you hadn't found Susan and danced her over right beside me and Mark, flirting with her like crazy so that Mark would be sure to notice, I wouldn't have to find other interested men, would I?"

"You are giving me more credit than I deserve. I was trying to make you jealous. The fact that Mark noticed was an added bonus."

She turned to face him. "You were trying to make me jealous?"

"Did it work?" Theo kept his eyes on the road, but she could sense tension radiating from his body.

Irene placed her hand on his arm and said, "Pull the car over, and I'll let you know."

Chapter Twenty

She probably should have kept her big mouth shut. Theo didn't even look her way. And he didn't swerve to a sudden stop the way he did on the way to Derbyville. Just when she thought he was going to ignore her, he slowed down and turned the car onto a small tree-lined lane.

Irene was acutely aware of her breath going in and out and of the seat belt holding her in place. She was aware of the cold air streaming from the car's air conditioner, chilling her overheated body that felt like it might burst like an over-ripe plum. And she would always remember the Motown song playing on the oldies station on the radio. Martha and the Vandellas singing about dancing in the streets.

He pulled to the shoulder, well off the road and out of the way of any traffic they might encounter. She watched Theo carefully as he put the car in gear. His jaw was clenched, and he took a deep breath before he unfastened his seat belt and turned to face her. "I'm ready. Are you?"

"Ready?" she asked tentatively. But she'd challenged him, and he'd called her on it.

"I believe you said if I pulled the car over, you'd let me know. What am I going to know, Ree?"

She decided to be brave and honest with him, no matter the cost. "Okay. If you want the truth, I hated watching you dance with her. I hated that she was a good dancer. That really, really bugged me. And I hated hearing you offer to take her up in your airplane. You're not supposed to take other women flying."

He leaned toward her. "Ree, you never said you wanted to go fly—"

She held up her hand. "Don't interrupt me. I'm on a roll, so hush and let me finish."

He sank back in his seat. "By all means, continue."

"So, yes. I was jealous. Are you happy now? You make me want things I shouldn't want anymore. I want to relive the past, our past, and I know that's not a smart thing to want since you'll be gone soon." She felt his shuttered gaze studying her while she talked, and her voice sounded husky to her own ears. "Or maybe that's the best reason. You'll be gone soon, so anything that happens is temporary and unbinding." She let out an exasperated growl. "All I know is I don't know anything for certain when I'm with you, Theo."

He stayed on his side of the car looking dangerous and unsettled. "That's quite a speech."

She shifted restlessly, not knowing if she'd made a fool of herself. "So now you're supposed to tell me what you're thinking. Don't leave me hanging, for Pete's sake."

He slung one arm up over the steering wheel with his wrist bent. After a few seconds, he said, "Okay, I'll tell you. You drive me freaking crazy, do you know that? One minute you're kissing me, the next you're dancing with

Mark. I could care less if Susan can dance. I only asked her to dance because I felt bad about the way she was mooning over Mark, and I'm thinking she doesn't have a chance now that he thinks he has a chance with you, because why in hell would anyone turn down a chance to be with you?" He finally wound down, coming to a halt.

They stared at each other, careful to keep their distance. She felt her blood thrumming through her veins, thick and slow, and she felt more alive than she had in years. Crazy bursts of piercing pain mixed with joy skittered around inside her chest. She'd been shut down, boarded up, nailed closed, refusing to acknowledge the part of herself that longed for love and affection, companionship, and yes, sex. Physical needs. She had them like anyone else. And sitting less than two feet away from her was the man who could make her blossom like a flower with his knowing touch. God, he had great hands. Because he did know her. He'd been her first lover, and even though they'd been young, they'd grown experienced together.

Theo broke the silence, his voice brushing across her skin like a velvet glove. "So, what are you suggesting? Dinner and a movie?" He was teasing her now, and she knew how to play that game.

She smiled, a slow smile that seeped out, spreading like honey. "That would be very nice."

He returned her smile. "How about tomorrow night?"

She sighed, the molten lava flow of passion sliding throughout her core. "I'll look forward to it."

"Great. I'll pick you up at seven." Theo's eyes were full of smoldering promises.

"I'll be ready." The need to reach for him was overwhelming, but she resisted. There was something to be said for practicing patience. Building anticipation. Some respect paid to the formalities before she fell into bed with him. Because she had no doubt that was where they were heading.

Flashing red-and-blue lights filled the car.

"Great," Theo said. "I don't believe this."

A policeman walked up to the window as Theo rolled it down. "Good evening, sir." He ducked down and looked briefly at Irene. "Ma'am."

"Good evening, Officer." Theo sounded friendly and congenial.

"You folks having car trouble?" He flashed a spotlight around inside the car, first into the backseat.

Theo sounded breezy as he said, "No, sir. We just stopped to have a conversation."

The policeman sounded disapproving. "Out here in the middle of nowhere? That's not a good idea."

"It was an important conversation, and I thought it was safer not to keep driving while we talked."

"Hmm. So you were arguing?"

"No, sir."

"Are you all right, young lady?"

"I'm fine," Irene assured him. "We were about to leave, so we'll be happy to be on our way."

The policeman wasn't going to let anyone else call the shots. "Hold your horses there. We've had some reports of suspicious characters around these parts. Can I see your driver's license and insurance card please?"

"Irene, the insurance card is in the glove box." Theo pointed to the dashboard as he reached into his back pocket for his wallet. She opened the glove compartment and found the form.

The policeman took the documents, taking his time to study them. "This insurance card is for Abel Jacobson. Your license indicates that you are Theo Jacobson. I take it this is not your vehicle."

"It belongs to my brother."

"Sit tight. I'll be right back."

"Holy shit," Theo muttered as the policeman walked back to his squad car. "We weren't doing anything. Thank God, we still had our clothes on."

Irene shot him a look and laughed. "What do you mean still? Did you have plans for our clothes to come off that I didn't know about?"

"A man can always hope." Theo checked the rearview mirror.

"I hate to tell you, Theo. But if you manage to get me without my clothes on, it won't be in the front seat of your brother's Jeep." Irene pretended indignation. She thought the whole thing was funny, but Theo didn't seem to agree.

"You have to admit, if we'd been naked this situation could have been a whole lot worse."

Irene tried not to think about Theo without his clothes. "I'm sure he comes across kids making out in cars all the time."

Theo glanced in the rearview mirror. "We aren't kids. He thinks we are suspicious characters."

Irene thought the whole thing was silly. "Why don't you let me talk to him when he comes back?"

"Let's just see what he has to say."

Before she could convince him, the officer was back. "Would you please step out of the car, sir?"

"What's the problem?" Theo asked cautiously.

"Just step out of the car. Slowly, and keep your hands where I can see them."

Irene jumped out and ran around the car as Theo opened his door and got out of the driver's seat. "What's wrong? Why does he have to get out of the car?"

"Please return to the car."

Theo started to get back in the car.

"Freeze. I said to get out of the car."

Theo stopped halfway in and halfway out. "So, do you want me in or out?"

"Sir, have you been drinking?"

"Drinking? No. Well, I had some of the punch at the reunion."

Irene piped up. "Oh, me too. Was it spiked?"

"No, it wasn't spiked," Theo insisted.

She finally got a good look at the policeman. "Owen? Is that you? It's me, Irene Cornwell." Owen was new to the Everson Police Department. Irene was friends with his mother. She owned the bookstore next to her in the town square. "How's your mama?"

Officer Owen Melber looked taken aback. She'd clearly flustered him. "My mama's fine, Ms. Cornwell, I mean ma'am. Could you get back inside the car?"

"Oh, surely this is some kind of mistake." Irene moved toward him, talking animatedly while waving her hands. "Why don't you let us go with a warning, and we'll promise not to park on dark roads anymore." She felt her high heels stick in the soft dirt on the road, and then she was off-balance lurching toward Officer Melber. She let out a yelp and made a grab for his arm to keep from falling.

Theo towered over them where they'd landed tangled in a heap on the ground.

Officer Melber scrambled to his feet, yelling, "You're both under arrest."

Theo stood stock-still with his hands raised. Irene raised her hands, too. She heard Theo mutter, "Something tells me we're in big trouble now."

Chapter Twenty-One

❧

I called Charlie. He'll get us out of here, but he said it might take awhile."

"Thanks. You know, I hate the idea of owing Charlie anything, but in this case I'll take any help I can get." Theo took a seat on the lumpy bunk in the holding cell.

Irene paced back and forth in an adjoining cell. "I know, but he was closer than any of my Dallas lawyers."

"You might as well make yourself comfortable, then." He glanced at the closed door that separated the jail cells from the lobby of the police station. Officer Owen Melber had locked them in and then disappeared, saying he'd be back to check on them shortly.

Irene sat down on the bunk and informed him, "Well, this is my first time in the pokey. It will make my memoir more interesting when I get around to writing it. How about you?"

Theo shook his head. "I know it's hard to believe, but this is a first for me, too. And don't try to find a silver lining in this, Ree. Jake is going to be pissed if his car is impounded."

"I'm sure we'll have everything straightened out before Jake and Marla Jean get home. You're taking this way too seriously." She sat down on the cot and arranged her skirt over her legs.

"Maybe so. I just don't want him to have any reason to be sorry he asked for my help."

"Don't worry. I'll tell him it was my fault. If I'd stayed in the car, we probably would have gotten a ticket, and that would have been the end of it."

He seemed to relax a bit. "Oh, you don't have to do that, but since you brought it up, why did you get out of the car, anyway?"

"It sounds dumb now, but when I recognized Owen, I just thought I could get out and straighten everything out. That backfired when my shoe got stuck in the dirt."

"Well, it did look like you just launched yourself at him for no good reason. I have to admit I was shocked."

She laughed. "Yeah, that didn't work out the way I planned. I think he was shocked, too." The silence stretched out between them. She wondered if he was rethinking his offer of dinner and a movie. She watched him lay down on the cot with his arms bent at the elbow, holding up his head.

Finally he asked, "So, other than landing in a jail cell, how did you enjoy the reunion?"

"As a matter of fact, I'm really glad I went, Theo. Almost everyone was nice and friendly. Carol was asking about some of the work the foundation does, so we plan to have lunch and discuss some ways she can get involved. She does work with seniors in Derbyville, and there might be a way to combine resources."

"That would be great. I know the more I've helped Lily

Porter, the more I see the needs of the other older folks in town. Just the other day I helped Clete Morrison with his fence, and that's just the tip of the iceberg. These senior citizens become isolated inside their homes."

"It sounds like you've thought a lot about this, Theo."

"I'm thinking I might talk to Jake about starting a low- or no-fee handyman service. Someplace they can call for basic house repairs. Things that will make it easier for them to stay in their homes longer."

"That's a great idea, Theo. I know the meals program tries to take note of problems we see when we visit, but we miss a lot."

"Most folks don't want charity, but I know Jake will have some good ideas on the subject."

"Tell him to talk to me, and we'll try to help, too."

"I will. Thanks, Ree."

They heard a commotion in the outer office, and voices drifted back to where they were locked up. "It sounds like Charlie made it in record time."

Officer Melber opened the door, followed by Charlie.

Charlie came striding in with a grin on his face. He seemed to enjoy seeing the two of them behind bars. Irene wanted to remind him who paid his salary, but she'd wait until she was free first.

"Charlie! I'm so happy to see you. Please, get us out of here. Quickly if possible." Nell Harcourt drifted in behind Charlie. "Nell? What are you doing here?"

Charlie looked over at the other woman and said, "We were on a date when you called. Nell was nice enough not to mind when I said I needed to stop by the local jail and bail you out."

Irene was sure Nell was gloating and salivating over

the new juicy gossip she could add to the rumor mill. "Wasn't that nice? Thanks, Nell." She tried to keep the sarcasm from dripping from her words.

"Don't mention it." Nell smiled at Irene, but then turned her attention to Theo. Waving, she said, "Hi, Theo." Her tone suggested they were bosom buddies.

Theo grunted in response.

Charlie looked at Theo. "I suppose you'd like me to get him out, too?" He jerked his head toward her jail mate.

Theo stood up from his bunk. "Very funny, Charlie. If you can spring us, I'll owe you big time."

"Yes, you will. Now then. Officer, I'm Ms. Cornwell's lawyer. What are the charges?"

"I'm still filling out the report. They have to go before the judge, and he won't be in until tomorrow morning."

"Officer Melber, are you sure we can't make some arrangement? You don't want to waste the judge's time, do you?"

"This is my first arrest." He sounded unsure.

"Hey, Owen." Nell walked over and touched his arm. "If you could let them go, I'd really appreciate it. I could see my way to make sure you get extra pie next week. I'll be baking in the morning. I know how you love lemon meringue."

His eyes lit up. "Extra pie?"

"Isn't that a bribe?" Irene asked Theo through the bars separating them.

"I'm not sure," he said. "Let's see if it works."

Nell continued her bargaining. "My mama always says our fine law officers deserve some consideration. It's the Rise-N-Shine's way of showing our appreciation."

"Where's the sheriff?" Charlie asked.

"He's on his way in. We don't usually have two arrests in one night."

"Well, then, let's wait and see what he has to say."

Irene liked the sound of that. She dealt with Sheriff Watson regularly as one of the sponsors for the annual Policeman's Ball.

The door opened and Sheriff Watson came barreling inside. "What's going on, Owen? I got here as soon as I could. We were in the middle of a dinner party, so Mrs. Watson isn't too happy with me right now. This better be good."

"Well, sir, I just finished my report if you'd like to look it over. Or I could just tell you what happened."

The sheriff's face was the color of cooked liver. "Just tell me, for Pete's sake."

"Well, sir. I caught these two making out on Bramble Bush Lane. And they tried to make a run for it."

"We weren't making out, and we were leaving anyway when you turned on your flashing lights. We weren't running from anything." Theo peered out from behind the bars while protesting Officer Melber's version of the events.

Charlie shushed him. "Just hold on, Theo. We'll have a chance to give our side in a minute."

Owen continued his recitation. "I asked Mr. Jacobson to get out of the car, and that's when Mrs. Cornwell rushed me."

"I didn't rush you. I couldn't hear what was going on inside the car. And I only got out so I could help straighten out what was obviously a terrible misunderstanding."

"Did I misunderstand when you grabbed my arm and knocked me to the ground?"

"Sheriff Watson, that's not what happened. Charlie, that's not how it happened at all. I slipped and grabbed his arm so I wouldn't fall."

"They were in a car registered to another person. And Mrs. Cornwell refused to stay in the vehicle."

Charlie spoke up at this point. "So, what are the charges?"

"Resisting arrest and assaulting an officer of the law."

Charlie laughed. "You're kidding, right? Sheriff, come on. This is a case of overreacting if I've ever seen one. I'd say the worst I've seen in all my years of practicing law."

"And the back taillight was burned out." Officer Melber added that as a final justification.

"So write a ticket, and let's all go home." Sheriff Watson reached into his pocket and pulled out a key ring. Unlocking the cell doors, he huffed, "Get the hell out of here. Both of you. Owen, I'll speak to you in the morning."

Officer Melber stood with his head hanging down. Nell stopped in front of him. "Don't forget about your pie, Owen. I fully support your effort to do your job. I'm sure we all do." The look Nell shot Irene could have scrambled an egg inside its shell.

Officer Melber seemed mollified by her words. "Thanks, Nell. I apologize, folks. I guess I was overeager."

Sheriff Watson paused while putting his keys back in his pocket. "Did I hear you mention pie, Nell? I hope that includes cherry pie."

Nell smiled like she'd negotiated world peace. "You bet, Sheriff. I've got a cherry pie with your name on it."

Charlie herded everyone toward the door. "I guess you need a ride back to your car, Theo."

"Thanks, Charlie. I barely had a chance to lock it

before he hauled us in like common criminals." Theo was still feeling put out over the incident.

Charlie decided it was time for a lecture. "Maybe you should think twice before parking in the boonies like a couple of teenagers. Aren't you two a little old for that kind of thing?"

Nell piped up. "What would Sven think?"

Irene could feel her hands curling into claws that would fit nicely around the woman's neck. "Sven would tell you to mind your own business. But you must hear that a lot, don't you, Nell?"

Theo held the door open for Irene while she climbed into the backseat of Charlie's car. "We weren't making out," he insisted once more with feeling.

"You don't have to keep saying that like you're bragging about it, Theo." Irene was a little sore from the spill she'd taken earlier, and her ego was taking a beating, too, with Theo's stubborn mantra of how he'd kept his hands to himself.

"I didn't mean it like that. I was only trying to keep your reputation untarnished."

Charlie scoffed and looked at them in the rearview mirror. "Too late for that, I'm afraid. Her reputation was tarnished as soon as she married my father."

Theo reacted sharply. "That's uncalled for. She loved your father. She told me she did, so as far as I'm concerned, I'd say her character is still intact."

Despite the darkness of the backseat, Irene could see Theo's tightened jaw.

The car got very quiet. Even Nell kept her mouth shut. Charlie headed out of town and made his way back to Bramble Bush Lane. Irene kept her hands clenched together in her lap. It was the only way she could keep from reaching over and hugging Theo. Why did he keep doing things that bordered on heroic? Right in front of Charlie and Nell he moved in front of her, protecting her from their snarky remarks. And at who knows what cost to himself, he invoked Sven's name and her love for him to do it. What was she going to do with this man?

Charlie stopped behind Jake's Jeep, and Theo and Irene got out.

"Theo, make sure you get our girl home safely. I'll see you at the house later, Irene." Charlie put his car in gear, did a U-turn and drove off with Nell waving good-bye at his side.

• • •

Theo had an unholy desire to punch Charlie in the face. But since he'd already driven away, he unlocked the car and they climbed inside. "Well, here we are again. This has been an unusual evening."

"It wasn't dull at any rate," Irene said as she put on her seat belt.

"I promise I'll do better tomorrow night."

She looked up, seeming surprised. "You still want to go out?"

Theo started the car. He wouldn't blame her if she'd changed her mind after tonight's fiasco. "Sure, if you do."

"I do, Theo. I think we need to forget about tonight and replace it with a better one."

He grinned. "I agree. But you did look pretty funny when you knocked Officer Melber over."

She laughed. "Poor Owen. I hope I can explain things to his mother. She really is a friend, and I hope he doesn't get into too much trouble with the sheriff."

"I hope he learns to show a little bit better judgment next time he stops someone."

Theo relaxed for the first time in hours as they drove toward Irene's house. As they got closer to her front door he could only think of one thing. He was going to kiss her good night. She'd made it clear that this whole thing between them was temporary, and if that was the case he didn't have a minute to waste on polite preliminaries. He put the car into park and jumped out of the car, running around to her side to help her down. He took her arm, tucking her close, and walked her up the long sidewalk that led to the front door. As they climbed the porch steps, the heat of her body seeped into his. Her long, dark hair cascaded like a curtain over his arm as he turned her to face him. They reached the top of her porch, and he couldn't help but notice the incredible vista spread out below them. The lights of Everson twinkled and glowed like tiny jewels.

He turned to face Ree, and her eyes twinkled just as brightly.

"Thank you for inviting me to the reunion, Theo. I learned some things about myself that I needed to face."

"It wasn't supposed to be any kind of lesson. I just wanted you to have fun."

"I had fun, too."

"Okay, then. I guess I should say good night."

"If Charlie wasn't here, I'd invite you in for a nightcap. Until tomorrow night, then?"

"You bet."

"Good night, Theo." She wasn't moving.

He leaned down until his mouth hovered over hers. "Good night, Ree." His kiss made it clear that this was the first of many more to come. Unlike the other kisses they'd shared since he'd been back in town, this one had no agenda other than to say "I want you." Plainly and simply. And it was all-consuming. With great effort he pulled away. "Damn that Charlie." But he smiled when he said it.

She laughed and moved to the front door. "I better go in before he blinks the porch light."

Theo raised his hand in a farewell gesture and loped down the steps to the Jeep. He sat watching until she was inside and the porch light went dark before he started the engine and drove down the hill.

Chapter Twenty-Two

He needed to buy a decent bed. That's all he could think about. And because that was his main focus, he should have felt shallow, but there it was nonetheless. Since the night before, he had no doubt where this thing with Irene was heading. It was going to end up in a bed with them rolling around, burning up the sheets, and rearranging some furniture. And he didn't have a bed that he could carry her to without being afraid she'd do permanent damage to her back. That lumpy twin bed he slept on now was totally unacceptable.

Her house was out of the question as long as good old Charlie was still in residence. She might have a gazillion bedrooms in that monstrosity on the hill, but he wouldn't be able to relax as long as Sven's son was parked somewhere nearby.

Ree obviously agreed since she wouldn't invite him in last night. So the solution was to buy a new bed and have it delivered to the house on Overbrook. The work on the house was complete. The outside was painted buttercup yellow, and the landscaping gave it a welcome-home feel. If he was staying in town, he might consider buying it for himself. It wasn't a huge house, but it was cozy and with the right furniture it would make a nice home.

He drove to Everson's only furniture store and got out of his truck. The store was on the square. In fact, it was almost directly across from Irene's I Do, I Do. But he hoped he could conduct his business without running into anyone he knew. He opened the front door and walked inside.

"Howdy-do, sir." A tall man with gray hair and red suspenders approached him as he came in the door. "Welcome to Carter's Fine Furnishings. How can I help you today?"

Theo looked at the man's name tag. "Hello, Gavin. I'd like to buy a new bed."

"Well, now. What did you have in mind? We have a nice variety to choose from. Are you just looking for a new mattress and box springs, or do you need the whole kit and caboodle?"

"What do you mean by kit and caboodle?"

Gavin walked over to where several bedrooms were set up complete with dressers, lamps, nightstands, and chests of drawers. "You know, everything to make your bedroom a relaxing haven at the end of the day."

The man was waxing poetic, but he did have a point. Theo was going to need more than a new mattress. He was going to need linens and decent pillows. He was going to need the whole kit and caboodle.

He must have looked overwhelmed because Gavin took mercy on him. "Let's take this one step at a time. What kind of mattress do you prefer? Soft, firm?"

Any mattress with Ree spread out on it.

He had to keep those kinds of thoughts tamped down if he was going to make it through this shopping expedition. "I have no idea."

"Tell you what. Try out a couple of these babies and we'll figure it out." He pointed to a section where bare mattresses were lined up like a dormitory. He pointed to the first one. "Lie down and see what you think."

Theo tried the first one and didn't have much of an opinion. This was going to be more difficult than he'd expected. Gavin must have read his reaction and moved him on to another. He finally ended up on a bed that made his whole body go "ah." He sat up and yelled, "This is it. I'll take this one."

Gavin smiled, knowing he was good at his job. "Yes, sir. What else can I help you with today?"

Theo hopped up and looked at the different bedroom setups. One featured a bedstead that had four thick solid columns on each corner. It was a solid, masculine bed without being too utilitarian. "I like this bed."

"What about a dresser or a nightstand. Need someplace to put a lamp or an alarm clock, don'tcha?"

Theo figured the bedroom would look more finished if the bed wasn't the only thing in it. He wouldn't look so obvious, maybe. What the hell? Might as well go whole hog. "And I guess I'll take the dresser and nightstands, too."

Gavin looked like he might pop all his buttons. "Yes, sir. Would you like to schedule delivery for sometime next week?"

Theo panicked at that question. "Oh, I really need to have it delivered this afternoon. I'm willing to pay for a rush job."

"I'll have to talk to my delivery manager and see what we can do." Gavin's face pinched together in thought, but Theo didn't see crowds of people milling around the store, so he didn't see why an immediate delivery should be much of a problem.

"I'll triple the delivery fee if your crew delivers everything this afternoon, sets up the new furniture, and hauls off my old bed."

Gavin smiled from ear to ear. I'll have my son, Gavin Jr., handle it personally. It's a pleasure doing business with you, Mr. . . . ."

"Jacobson, Theo Jacobson."

"Are you related to Jake?"

"Sure am. He's my big brother."

"Well, I declare. Give him my regards."

He left the furniture store and headed to a department store. He needed to buy sheets and blankets and one of those comforters. Now that he was committed to this deal he wanted it to look nice. He wanted Ree to be impressed. He wanted her to be comfortable. That was a bunch of bull. In reality he wanted her to be so besotted with lust that she wouldn't notice if they were making love in the middle of a rocky field. But just in case he wanted it to be nice.

The furniture was delivered and set up right on time. He made up the bed and asked Sadie what she thought. Sadie barked and curled up on her dog bed that sat in the corner of the room. She seemed to approve, but Theo still had his doubts. "Do you think she'll like it, Sadie, or is it way too pushy? Do I look like the biggest lecher in the world?"

He refused to question his motives anymore. He had to get some actual work done today. He'd promised Lily

Porter that he'd come look at her garbage disposal. He wasn't a plumber, but he'd fixed his mom's plenty of times while he was growing up. She promised to pay him with brownies, and he thought that was a fair deal. He had to finish in time to get home, walk Sadie, and jump in the shower. After all, he had a hot date tonight.

* * *

Irene was knee-deep in the middle of planning the Foster-McKinney wedding when the door to her shop opened. Lizzie Harris walked inside and plopped down in the chair next to Irene's desk.

"Sorry to barge in, Mrs. Cornwell, but I need your advice again."

"Call me Irene, please, and I'll help however I can."

"Okay, Irene. Matthew and I still want to get married right away, but our families aren't cooperating at all. We're thinking of eloping. In fact that's what Matthew is pushing for. At least that way he'll get his Elvis impersonator. But the idea that our relatives won't be there for the ceremony breaks my heart."

"I know you talked about doing something simple in someone's backyard."

"But no one can agree on a date or whose backyard to use. I just want to scream. They are throwing up roadblocks every time I turn around, and it's taking all the joy out of what should be the happiest day of our lives."

Irene tapped her fingernail on her cheek trying to think of a solution. Then she suddenly got a wild idea, one Lizzie might reject out of hand. But it would actually benefit them both. "Lizzie, I'm going to suggest something, and you are free to tell me no."

"Okay. What is it?"

Irene tried to keep the excitement in her voice from influencing the young woman. "Why don't you get married on my float during the parade?"

"On the Fourth? How would that even work?" Lizzie looked at her like she was crazy.

Irene smiled. "Before you decide I'm completely out of my noggin, let's talk it out."

"Okay. Anything that gets me married to Matthew—well, I'm all ears." Lizzie bounced up and down eagerly.

"Well, first of all most of your friends and relatives would be in town for the Fourth, anyway. They'd be scattered along the route, and we could perform a part of the ceremony at stops along the way. By the time you get to the end, you'd be man and wife."

Lizzie widened her eyes as she considered the idea. "Is that legal?"

Irene nodded. "Why not? And the picnic afterward could be a great reception. I'm having cake made to hand out on the route, and I'm sure we could have extra made for you and Matthew. I needed to find someone to stand in as bride and groom and wave to the crowd, anyway. A real bride and groom makes it even better. What do you say?"

Lizzie's eyes gleamed. "What about our Elvis?"

Irene grinned at the young woman. "I'll see what I can do."

Lizzie grinned back. "It still sounds nuts, but it might work. Let me talk to Matthew and see what he says." Lizzie left the shop practically skipping, and Irene could see that she was giving it some serious thought. It would give her float the wow factor she'd been missing. The more she thought about it, the more perfect the plan seemed to be.

The door opened again, and she expected to see Lizzie back with more questions. Instead her aunt Jo Anne walked inside, carrying a big stack of books and magazines.

"Aunt Jo! I'm so happy to see you, but what brings you all the way to Everson?"

"You do, of course. And I assume you meant it when you said you could use my help in this place." Jo Anne was dressed formally in a shirtwaist dress with heels and a pearl necklace around her neck. That was her idea of work attire, and Irene wasn't going to tell her any different.

Irene stood up and walked around her desk to give her aunt a welcoming hug. "Of course I meant it. I'm in the middle of making a wedding scheme right now, and I could use your opinion." She nodded to the stack of books her aunt carried. "What's all this?"

"Oh, just some ideas I found when I started doing some research. I wanted to come in with a little bit of knowledge about how things are done these days."

"That's great." She took the stack from her aunt and put them on an empty shelf. "I'd like to look through them, too."

"So, how can I help?"

"Here, have a seat by me, and I'll show you what I'm working on right now."

They sat down together, and she showed her aunt the plan she was drawing up for her current client. "The ceremony will be at the Methodist church, and the reception will be in the bride's parents' backyard. Since it is a small wedding they decided to splurge on the reception."

"In my day we got married at the church and retired to a banquet room for punch and cake. Nobody fooled with all this folderal and nonsense. It seems like a big waste of money to me."

"Well, I can say thank goodness for me the times have changed and folks want more of a celebration on their wedding day. Something to share with family and friends."

"I guess." Her aunt picked up a small circle of pearls. "What's this?"

"It's a napkin ring. The bride loves pearls, so I'm including them in the table settings wherever I can."

"So, we just find the theme and carry it out in the reception?"

"More or less. I have to learn to balance what the bride wants with what mama wants and what daddy's willing to pay."

"You were always a good negotiator."

"Thanks, Aunt Jo." She went over the rest of the wedding with her, noting that her aunt was full of good ideas and suggestions. It would be nice to have another brain to bounce things around with.

"So, how was the reunion?"

"It was fine." She had told her aunt she'd decided to attend.

"You don't sound too enthusiastic. Did you go with Theo?"

Irene sighed. "I did."

"And did you see some of your old friends?"

She sighed again. "I did."

"Anyone I would know?"

"Christine Dempsey. I understand she's active in the Women's League."

"I know Christine. She's a royal pain in the ass."

"Aunt Jo!"

"Well, she is. That girl acts like she's the queen of Derbyville and the rest of us are all her underlings allowed membership only to do her bidding. Just because she married that danged Cole fellow."

"I hate to tell you this, but she acted that way in high school, too. Seeing her again was a good thing. I've let her meanness live inside my head all of these years, and now she's lost all the power she had to intimidate me."

"Well, good for you, Irene. Maybe I'll tell her to take a flying leap next time she asks me to serve on one of her committees."

Irene laughed, happy to share something with her aunt. "I was about to take a coffee break when you showed up. How about some coffee and a piece of pie over at the diner?"

Jo Anne stood up and grabbed her purse. "I never say no to coffee. Pie sounds good, too."

Irene locked up the shop, and they made their way across the square to the Rise-N-Shine. As they slid into one of the red vinyl booths, Bertie came hurrying over. "Darlin', are you okay?"

Irene was alarmed by her tone of voice. "I'm fine. Why wouldn't I be? This is my aunt Jo Anne, by the way."

"How do you do? Bertie Harcourt," she said, introducing herself. The two women nodded cordially before Bertie was off to the races again. "Nell, told me all about how you were making out with Theo out on Bramble Bush Lane and how you got arrested for assaulting a police officer."

"What?" Aunt Jo Anne bolted to attention.

Irene shook her head at her aunt as if to say it wasn't what it sounded like. "She did, did she?"

Bertie acted all sympathetic. "Nell said it was just awful."

Irene wanted to say Nell's habit of telling tales was just awful, but she held her tongue. "Did she also tell you that it was all a big misunderstanding? And that no charges were brought?"

"No, but she did say she took you back to your car once that nice Charlie got you out of jail."

"Exactly. But he didn't have to get us out, because the sheriff showed up and let us go. End of story. Sorry, Aunt Jo." Her aunt's face had paled to the color of the coffee creamer. "I was going to tell you what happened, but we were having such a nice visit." She gave Bertie a pointed look, which had no effect on the woman at all.

Aunt Jo unrolled her napkin and arranged her silverware at her place setting. "It's not really any of my concern what you do, Irene."

Irene heard the note of disappointment in her aunt's voice. Nell and her big mouth. "Of course it is. Bertie would you bring us some coffee and two pieces of pie? What kind do you want, Aunt Jo?"

"I'll take peach, no ice cream." She sounded like she was ordering arsenic.

Irene smiled at Bertie. "And I'll have coconut cream."

Bertie seemed confounded at not getting any more juicy details, but she nodded and hurried off to fill their order.

"It sounds like you had quite an adventure. So, I guess this means things are heating up again with Theo. Making out in cars. My goodness."

She didn't want to talk to her aunt about Theo. Especially not the way he heated her up every time he was anywhere near her. Especially since whatever she planned to do with him would be a short-term affair at best.

"We weren't making out. We were merely talking. The police officer misunderstood. I do have a date with him tonight, though. Dinner and a movie. We are taking things slow, and we are hoping to reclaim our friendship. That means a lot to me."

Aunt Jo nodded her approval. "I think slow is a good idea. The last thing I want is for you to get your heart broken again."

Bertie came back with the pie and then grabbed the coffee urn filling their cups to the brim. "I'm sorry for being such a snoop, Irene. Anything going on between you and Theo Jacobson is nobody else's business. I'll remind Nell of that, too."

Irene couldn't believe her ears. "Thank you, Bertie. I appreciate that."

The front door to the diner opened and Gavin Carter came busting inside with a bouncy spring in his step. He grabbed a stool at the front counter. "Howdy-do, Bertie."

"You seem like you're in a good mood today, Gavin," Bertie said as she walked back behind the counter.

"Whooee, you're right about that. I just made a big sale, and I need to celebrate."

"Is that a fact?"

"Shore is. Nobody buys much furniture in this poky ole town, but Theo Jacobson just bought a complete bedroom set with a spanking new mattress and box springs. If that wasn't good enough, he then paid triple to have it delivered and set up by this afternoon."

Jo Anne stopped with a big bite of pie halfway to her mouth. Irene started choking on her coffee, until her aunt had to get up from her seat and come around to her side of the booth. She took Irene's arm and forced it up and down like she was priming an old water pump until Irene was afraid she'd pull it out of the socket. She'd done the same thing to her and both of her cousins when they were kids. "Are you okay?"

Irene managed to collect herself and took a sip from her water glass. "I'm fine, Aunt Jo. Can we just get out of here?" She noticed that the diner had gone deathly quiet. Everyone was watching her.

Jo Anne looked around and nodded. "That's a good idea." She helped Irene to her feet and then picked up both of their purses. They stopped at the front counter long enough to pay the bill. Bertie tried to say it was on the house, but Irene insisted on paying. As they were walking out the door, Irene heard someone say, "Well, at least they won't have to make out in his Jeep anymore." Laughter followed them out the door.

Chapter Twenty-Three

~~~

Theo had just finished at Lily Porter's and climbed into his truck when his phone rang. It was Ree saying, "I'm not sure I can go out with you now."

He was quiet for a second before asking, "Why not? You're not getting cold feet, are you?"

"It's because you bought a bed." She said it like she was accusing him of something sinister, but then she laughed and he relaxed.

He sighed. "News travels fast in these parts. I didn't realize that was a crime."

She seemed to be enjoying giving him a hard time. "In Everson, crime is loosely determined by how may tongues it sets to wagging."

"I'm assuming quite a few are wagging now?"

"You may have set a new record."

"That sounds like a reason to celebrate."

"Maybe if you hadn't paid triple to have it delivered. It makes you seem so . . . so . . . desperate."

He let out a bark of laughter. "To tell the truth,

Ree, I am feeling a little desperate. Besides, you're to blame, too."

"How do you figure that?"

"If you'd kick Charlie out of your house, we might have had other options."

"So now the big idea was we'd end up at my place? I thought dinner and a movie was our other option. I don't remember when we decided it would end up in bed."

"Are you saying you weren't hoping on some level for the same thing?"

"I'll admit it crossed my mind." His heart rate kicked up at her admission.

"I was mostly thinking of your comfort, you know."

"I see. You were just being gallant."

"Listen, lady, I can make love anywhere. On the bare floor, against a wall. On top of the bathroom sink—remember?"

"Stop it." She was laughing now.

He could tell from her voice that she did remember. "I can't forget how good we were together."

"But still, everyone in town will be monitoring our date tonight."

"Wait a minute. I just had a brilliant idea." He couldn't hide his excitement. He should have thought of it sooner.

"Oh, dear. Why does that worry me?"

He laughed while cajoling her. "Trust me. It doesn't include my brand-new, super-comfy bed in any way, shape, or fashion."

She turned stubborn on him. "Does it still include dinner and a movie?"

"I'll make good on dinner, I promise, but I'm afraid the movie will have to wait for another night. I'll pick you up at six if that's okay. We'll need to get an early start."

"I'll be ready." Her voice sounded soft and full of promise.

He needed to stop reading things into everything she said, so he simply said, "Thanks, Ree. I'm looking forward to it." He hung up the phone, but then looked at his phone contacts and made another call. He had some arrangements to make before tonight.

• • •

Irene watched as the airfield came into view. "Are we working on the float?"

"No way. I don't plan to share you with the rest of the town tonight." He pulled the Jeep around toward the main hangar and parked in an inconspicuous spot. He walked around and helped her out. "I guess I better ask. Making assumptions has gotten me into enough trouble."

She smiled, thinking she knew what he was up to. "So, Mr. Jacobson. What do you want to ask?"

"Do you want to go flying with me?" He grinned like he was offering the world.

"Really? Oh my. I've never flown in a small plane."

"I thought we could fly to Dallas and have dinner. No one from Everson anywhere in sight. What do you say?"

"It seems extravagant."

"You're worth it."

"You already spent so much on your new bed." She had to tease him about it.

"So I made a boneheaded move. My heart was in the right place."

"I'd love to fly off to dinner with you. You were right. This was a brilliant idea."

"I don't have much time to impress you before I leave. Wait right here." He walked over to the office and took a moment speaking with Bart. The two men exchanged a few words and then Theo trotted over to where she waited.

She stood and stared at the airplane. "This is a good start," she whispered.

He seemed so pleased with himself and it was contagious. He was smiling as he helped her into the plane. He got behind the controls and taxied out to the runway. As the landscape sped by, she looked out the window and then they were in the air. That moment when they defied the rules of gravity and took off filled her with awe. Theo seemed so in control. She looked down as they circled over Everson and headed toward the Dallas–Fort Worth Metroplex.

"We don't need reservations where we're going, so we have plenty of time to get there."

"Where are we going? Or is that a surprise, too?"

"It's nothing fancy. There's a hamburger joint I've heard good things about."

"I'm always in the mood for a good hamburger."

"I remembered that, but I wasn't sure if your tastes had become more refined these days."

She turned her head to watch him. "Not very much about me has changed since you knew me, Theo. I'm the same woman you lived with all those years ago."

He nodded. "So, hamburgers it is. I haven't changed that much, either."

Irene didn't know if he was trying to tell her something or not, but she decided to quit trying to read him like a puzzle. She was flying, and it was amazing. It was still light outside so she could see the trees and roads below as they soared through the sky. "This is incredible, Theo. Thank you for doing this."

"My pleasure, Ree. I've thought about getting you up in the air for a long time now. I figured you would like it."

They landed at a small suburban airfield, and Theo had arranged for a car to be waiting for them to make the short drive to the restaurant. It was a hole-in-the-wall in a strip shopping center, but the parking lot was packed, so it obviously had a dedicated clientele. They walked inside and stood in line to order their food from a blackboard behind the cash register. They had a variety of burgers to choose from and Irene finally decided on the chili cheeseburger with sweet potato fries. Theo got a ten-pepper burger with a side of regular fries.

"Are you sure you can handle ten peppers?" Irene remembered he overestimated his tolerance for hot food.

He tapped her on the nose. "Don't worry. I can handle it."

They found a table, and Irene dug in with the enthusiasm of someone who'd missed a few meals. She hadn't been hungry since the night before, but now her appetite was back with a vengeance.

"It's nice to eat somewhere outside of Everson for a change." Irene took a big bite, and chili dripped down her chin.

Theo grabbed his napkin. "Let me get that." He swiped it across her chin.

"I'm going to make a mess, and I don't even care. This is so good."

Theo took a bite and waved his hand in front of his

mouth. "Yowee, that's spicy." He took a swig of his iced tea and shoved some french fries in his mouth.

She smiled sweetly. "I warned you. Do you want to trade?"

"Like you could eat this. You'd be crying like a baby." He took another bite and chewed gamely. "I'm adjusting to the heat now. That first bite must have had extra peppers in it." His face was turning red, and beads of sweat popped out on his forehead.

"You could just order something different. You don't have to be brave for my sake." She enjoyed teasing him.

He waved his hand in front of his face again. "I'm not being brave. It's delicious. Do you want a bite?"

Now, he was challenging her. "Sure." She couldn't back down. She took a deep breath and took a small bite. It wasn't that hot at all. "Have some of mine." She pushed her basket in front of him and pulled his over in front of her.

He took a bite of her chili cheeseburger. "This is good. You don't think that's hot?"

She took a big bite this time and chewed with gusto. "I think it's just right. You've been away from Texas too long, buddy."

He grinned. "But I'm here now, and I plan to make the most of it."

"So, what's next on the agenda?" She didn't really care. Being in his company was enough.

He leaned back in his chair. "Well, I have a couple of ideas. How about a street carnival? They have a Ferris wheel."

"A Ferris wheel? I haven't been on one of those since we lived here." Old memories of being with Theo flooded back.

He seemed happy she remembered. Leaning toward her, he said, "I'll warn you right now, I plan to steal a kiss."

"Just one?" She smiled. Now was no time to act coy.

"I thought I'd start slow. I have a lot of ground to make up since the bedroom set incident."

She grinned. "Maybe we can negotiate a settlement." She'd overreacted a bit this afternoon, probably because Aunt Jo had been sitting across from her at the diner. But she soon saw the humor in the situation. It wasn't like she hadn't been thinking this date would end in someone's bed. Charlie absolutely needed to move out of her house. That was clear. He was cramping her style, and with what she was paying him, he could afford his own place.

She couldn't let Theo keep taking all the blame.

He stood up, gathering their trash. "The street fair is across town. Not too far."

"Let's go, then."

They drove to the fair and parked across the street from the rides. The Ferris wheel loomed overhead, twinkling with colored lights as it whirled round and round. They wandered down the midway and Theo found a ticket booth. He bought an arm's length worth of tickets, and they walked around deciding on which game booth to try out their skills.

She stopped at the ring toss. "Let's try this one. I remember you were pretty good at it."

He surveyed the setup and bragged, "No problem, little lady. You want that giant gorilla or the panda?"

She pointed to a purple fuzzy bear. "Remember Clarence?"

He nodded. "I sure do. He was on the small side."

She made a face. "No. He was perfect. In fact, I still have him."

"You do?" He looked surprised.

"I do, so I don't really need another one. Why don't we skip the games and head for the Ferris wheel?"

He grabbed her hand, holding it tightly in his, and they ran like little kids to get in line. She was floating, and Theo was anchoring her to the ground. Since she'd gone up in the airplane with him, she still hadn't come back down to earth.

And he'd made it clear he planned to kiss her. Maybe she should just lean over and kiss him now. Get it over with. Nip it in the bud. Or start a conflagration that wouldn't be proper in a public place in the middle of a street fair with parents and children all around.

The wheel stopped and the operator let the people off. They got on, and the attendant strapped them in and then their car moved up and around until the ride was full. When they stopped at the very top, Theo's arm went around her shoulders and it felt so natural, so right. Then they were spinning around and around moving higher and then back down toward the ground. She snuggled into his body, feeling the heat and muscle of the man she'd always loved wrap around her like a cocoon. This was like a dream out of time. If she closed her eyes she could pretend he'd never left her. She could pretend she hadn't married Sven. She could pretend they were two broke kids out on the town for a night of fun. She looked up to find him watching her.

He smiled and tilted her face up to his. The kiss was gentle, slow and simmering with passion. Unhurried, even while her body said, "Go faster. Don't waste time."

Time was her enemy now because in only days he'd be going away again, and she wanted to cram every bit of life and passion into the time that was left.

• • •

Theo wrapped her in his arms, knowing in this enclosed car he couldn't get too carried away. If all he could do was kiss her as they spun through the air, it would still be the best night he'd had in years. She was kissing him back, willingly, wholeheartedly, and with an enthusiasm that threatened his sanity.

He'd known she was never really mad at him about the bedroom fiasco. He could have talked her into keeping their date, but getting out of town had been the best idea he'd had in a long time. She shed Everson like an overcoat as they soared away in his airplane. The things that separated them—like Sven, like his son, like their past—didn't matter tonight.

So he kissed her like he had every right, and she folded into his body like she never wanted to leave. Her arms wound around his neck, her breasts brushed his chest, and her legs tangled with his as they sat side by side in the metal car. He tried to keep the kiss gentle, but his unruly nature had a mind of its own, and soon he was devouring her lips with his. His tongue dueled with hers, playing a game of chase. When the car came to a stop, she was practically in his lap. The ride had stopped with their car almost at the top. They were both breathing hard, and he struggled to find his composure. He smoothed his hands over her hair, whispering her name.

"Ree, I want you to spend the night with me. I don't care where. I'll get a room, and no one in Everson ever needs to know a thing about it. But I need you, and I think you feel the same way." He didn't try to keep the longing from his voice.

She buried her face in his neck before confessing, "I do, Theo. I tried to tell myself I didn't, but I don't seem to have much control where you are concerned. Take me to your house. Please."

He tilted her head up. "Are you sure?"

The ride moved again, and they were almost back on the ground. "I'm sure, Theo." Her smile was wicked when she said, "Besides, I have to get a look at this infamous bed."

"I'll be happy to show it to you." He winked, feeling dizzy with happiness and desire. The drive back to the airfield was quiet. Theo was afraid to ruin the mood. When they took off and headed back to Everson, the clear sky was filled with twinkling stars and a full moon the size of a giant grapefruit. It seemed magical, mysterious, and he felt like the luckiest man flying over the face of the earth.

They landed in Everson and taxied back to the main hangar avoiding the group of cars parked at the hangar holding all of the parade floats. Theo spoke briefly to Bart, and they were on their way.

"That was the most remarkable night of my life. Thank you for sharing that with me."

"You're welcome. Thanks for trading hamburgers. You may have saved me from burning a hole in my digestive tract."

"What a wimp." Irene's hand rested on his thigh while they drove through the streets of Everson. It was quiet for a Saturday night, so nobody was watching as they turned onto Overbrook Street and pulled into the driveway of the house painted buttercup yellow.

He put the car in park, turned off the engine, and turned in her direction. "Irene Cornwell, would you like to come inside for a nightcap?"

She unfastened her seat belt and put her hand on the door handle. "Theo Jacobson, if a nightcap is all you're offering, I'm going to be very disappointed."

Chapter Twenty-Four

~

Irene walked up the front sidewalk with Theo's arm around her. She expected to feel nervous, but it all felt so natural. She could imagine that this was their house and Sadie who was barking at the front window was their dog.

It was a life she'd imagined having with Theo once upon a time. They would get out of school, work at jobs they enjoyed, and buy a nice, little house just like this one. At the end of the day they'd come home, cook dinner together, and fall into bed and make love all night long. But life had thrown them a curveball, and none of that came true.

Until tonight. She planned to make love to Theo all night long. And maybe, just maybe she'd have some memories to get her through the next few lonely years without him. Maybe they could forge a friendship out of this visit, since she knew he'd come back occasionally to see Jake and Marla Jean. She would like to be able to count him as a friend when he returned.

Theo opened the door, and Sadie came bounding out to

greet him. Kneeling down to her level, he rubbed her fur with both hands. "Hey, girl. Did you miss me? I missed you. Yes, I did."

He was so cute with Sadie. She never considered a cat or dog for herself. She seemed to lack the gene that nurtured animals and small children. Besides Sven had been allergic. But Theo needed a dog of his own. That was plain to see. If he ever settled down anywhere permanently, she would recommend it. A sweet dog like Sadie. If they were still in touch. A really big if.

Theo got Sadie settled down and led Irene inside. It was sparsely furnished. A couple of folding chairs and a card table sat in the living room. A vase of mixed flowers sat in the middle and a bottle of red wine. Two wineglasses flanked the bottle.

"What's all this?" Irene asked.

"Sorry. I did all of this before you called off the date. I was trying to make a good impression." He seemed a little embarrassed by his attempts.

She leaned over and smelled the bouquet. "It's very nice, Theo. I'm impressed."

He smiled. "Would you like some wine?"

"I would like that very much."

He poured the wine and handed her a glass. "Let me make a toast."

"Okay." She held her glass out and waited.

"To you and me. And to whatever we may be to each other at this time in our lives."

"I'll drink to that." They both took a sip, their eyes locked on the other's.

Theo took her glass and set it on the table. "Friends?"

She nodded, and he kissed her on the cheek. His face

was all sharp angles and planes in the dimly lit room. His blue eyes narrowed with warning as he pulled back to measure her response.

Then his mouth moved from her cheek to her lips. "Lovers?"

She moaned. That was the only answer she could give him as they wrapped their arms around each other. It wasn't the first kiss of the night and it certainly wouldn't be the last, but Irene would remember the slight taste of wine on his lips, the sound of the ceiling fan lazily turning overhead, and the certain knowledge that she was exactly where she belonged. In this moment, nothing else mattered.

"I'm not trying to rush you," he whispered.

"Rush me," she said with a nip of his ear. Her smile was an open invitation.

He didn't need any more encouragement. With a whoop of laughter, he scooped her into his arms and headed toward the bedroom. At least that's where she assumed he was taking her. He paused at the doorway and set her on her feet. Then he opened the door with a sweeping flourish and led her inside.

"I'm not sure that it can live up to its reputation, but here's what all the fuss was about."

She walked inside, taking in the giant bed, the dresser, the nightstands, and lamps. "Wow, this works pretty good for a den of inequity. I guess you haven't even had a chance to try it out?"

"Only at the store. Gavin let me take it for a test-drive."

She wandered over and wrapped her hands around one of the massive corner posts. "This bed looks like it can handle just about anything."

He advanced on her with a wicked gleam in his eyes. "I'll take that as a challenge."

"Please do." Then he was kissing her again, and she didn't care about talking anymore. He backed her up until the backs of her thighs were pressed against the edge of the bed. And then it was so easy to fall backward. His arms cushioned her fall, and he followed her down. She unbuttoned his shirt, stopping to trace the small scar on his shoulder. She mapped and bookmarked all the old familiar places on his body that had once been as well-known to her as her own. The freckle on his rib cage. The flat muscles of his stomach. That hadn't changed. It all added up to Theo. The man she'd loved and lost.

He turned her around, moved her hair aside. Then he worked quickly, unzipping her dress and pulling it off her shoulders. He sprinkled kisses down her shoulder blade before pushing the dress down and off her arms. "You're beautiful, Ree."

"I feel beautiful when I'm with you, Theo." She turned in his arms, pulling him down for a long open-mouthed kiss. They fell into old patterns. He knew the places to touch her that made her dissolve with desire. He knew the rhythm that let her free fall, and then let her fly. She opened up under his sure touch, allowing herself to be vulnerable. His mouth worshipped her breasts, using his tongue and fingers, sucking until she thought she'd lose her mind. Insanity seemed like a tempting choice if the alternative meant he would stop touching her.

She was doing her best to drive him crazy, too. She feasted on his neck, kissing and licking, moving down his body until she reached the waistband of his blue jeans. She reached for the button, looking up into his face as she flipped it open, letting her hand travel down the length and breadth of his desire.

With a growl he jumped off the bed, pushing his jeans and his boxer shorts off of his long legs. She lolled on the bed, enjoying the sight of his naked body. He was tall and proud, a man whose gaze swept over her, adoring her without reservation. She sat up, moving to her knees as he returned to the bed, facing her on his knees as well. His hands went to her face, and he pulled her close until they were touching thigh to thigh, chest to chest.

"I've dreamed of this night for so many years now." His words were a balm to her homesick soul.

She couldn't hide the truth from him. "It was bound to happen. The moment you flew back into town, you've been seducing me."

"Have I?"

"You know you have. And I'm tired of resisting."

He kissed her cheek, and then her neck, and then her shoulder. With a grin he asked, "So, I've just worn you down?"

She sighed. "Not yet, but I expect you will before the night is over." She longed for his strength to take her over the edge that glimmered just out of reach. "Please, Theo. I want you now."

Theo pressed her into the mattress, covering her with his hard body. She spread her legs to welcome him, cradling him with her hips, smoothing her hands down his back stopping at the flare of his hips and moving back up to run her fingers through his hair. The curls sprang out, holding her subtly, without chains, binding her softly as he moved inside of her.

He moaned, sinking into her with sureness, with a

boldness that took her breath away. Irene closed her eyes, flying through a fog of passion, buffeted by updrafts, rolling in his arms as the earth tilted below, circling ever higher in a spiral that went on and on.

Then she came apart in his arms, a shattering moment that seemed to stop time. He followed, and his yell echoed through her head like a victory cry. She floated back to earth slowly, languidly, holding onto his body like stolen treasure.

"Theo." His name was like a prayer on her lips.

"Ree, oh, God, Ree. I've missed you so much." His voice was harsh, and his words pierced her to the core.

She didn't want to cry for what she'd lost. Or for what she'd been lucky enough to find again, so she kissed him. Stealing his breath for her own, snuggling into his heat, into his space as if she could crawl inside him and live there until it was time for him to go.

• • •

Ree was sleeping like a baby. Some things never changed. When they'd lived together all those years ago, she would fall asleep after they made love and an earthquake wouldn't disturb her. But in about an hour she would wake up, if things followed her normal schedule, and she'd be ravenous. Back in the day, bacon and eggs were her favorite, so he'd stocked up just in case. Again he wasn't sure if that made him creepy or thoughtful.

He stretched, easing himself from under her slumbering body. She whimpered and then curled up, hugging the pillow instead. Theo took a moment to watch her. She was the most beautiful woman he'd ever known, that had been his unwavering truth since the moment he'd first seen her.

Her lush, curvy body with her long legs and slender arms moved with a grace that made him wish he could write poetry. Her long, black hair against her pale skin, and now in sleep, those long, dark eyelashes lying against her cheeks. That cute nose and lips that were lush and pink and soft and aligned perfectly with his mouth. Magic. She stirred him in ways he didn't understand. He could sit and watch her all day long and never grow tired. But she was beautiful inside, too. Sweet, generous, funny, smart.

He tried to think of something wrong with her. It would make saying good-bye that much easier.

She'd loved another man after him. He'd never found anyone else that compared. It didn't seem to matter now. She was here in his bed, and he hoped that she would choose to stay there for at least a little longer.

Marla Jean and Jake were due home soon, and then it would be the Fourth of July. The time he had left in Everson would fly by now. Bart told him he'd found an interested buyer for his plane. He needed to e-mail Mitch down in Australia and keep him apprised of his plans. Every time he started to contact his old friend, he'd found a reason to delay.

He pulled a sheet over Ree, tucking it around her, brushing her hair from her face, and placed a gentle kiss on her cheek. She smiled without waking, and he shrugged into his jeans. He walked out into the hallway and took a deep breath. Making love to Ree had been better than he remembered. Maybe it was because before he'd thought she was his forever. He'd never pictured his future without her in it.

This time the fragile nature of their relationship had him holding onto his nights and days with her for dear life. He walked to the kitchen and pulled out a skillet from the cabinet. He got eggs and bacon and orange juice from the old refrigerator and then found whole wheat bread for toast in the pantry.

Sadie padded into the kitchen, watching him with a puzzled look on her face. She wasn't used to seeing him cook, especially not in the middle of the night. "It's okay, Sadie. I'm making an early breakfast."

Sadie seemed to take him at his word and curled up in the corner of the kitchen and went back to sleep while he cooked. He was going to miss Sadie when he left, too. Of course, even if he stayed, she would go home to Jake's house where she belonged. He'd miss Lily Porter and her stale muffins. He'd miss all the folks he'd met while working on the danged float. Everson would be a nice place to live. But that wasn't going to happen, so he needed to stop dwelling on it and figure out what his future looked like without this town. And without Ree.

The toast popped up, and he grabbed a plate to put the slices on. The bacon was crisp, and the eggs were done. He buttered the toast and arranged everything on the plate. He carried it into the living room and got a single flower from the arrangement sitting on the card table. A nice little touch to add to the meal. He turned toward the bedroom, and that was the moment Irene appeared in the doorway.

She was wearing his shirt and her hair was mussed. Theo thought she'd never looked more beautiful.

"Hi," she said with a soft smile. "I'm hungry, and I smell bacon."

He held out the plate, and she squealed like he'd offered her diamonds and pearls.

"Oh, you are the most amazing man."

"I know." He was going to bask in all the extra points he was getting for doing this part right.

She grabbed his arm and dragged him back to the bedroom. "Come with me. After I rebuild my energy, I have plans for you."

Chapter Twenty-Five

⁓

"Hey, Theo." Irene nudged him with her elbow.

"Hmmm?" He didn't open his eyes.

It was the second night she'd spent at his house. After work they'd met at Lu Lu's and danced while the whole town watched with undisguised curiosity. She didn't care. It was past time to worry about the gossip in this old town. After that they'd driven to Theo's house, fallen into bed, and made love. Twice. Theo had just dozed off when she got a brilliant idea.

"Theo?" She tried again.

He made a sleepy noise, but she wasn't ready to give up yet.

"Let's sneak out to the hangar, and see if we can catch anyone causing mischief." She whispered the suggestion into his sleeping ear. Irene was stretched out on Theo's super-comfy bed. He was wrapped around her. They were both naked.

"Huh? What time is it?" He tried to pull a pillow over his head.

She pulled it off and kissed the side of his neck. "It's three in the morning. The perfect time to steal out to the airfield."

He turned, wrapping both arms around her, pulling her snugly against his side. "Dunno. We'd have to get up," he mumbled. "And get dressed."

She rubbed his bare chest. "I know, and that part sucks, but it could be fun. We could wear all black and tiptoe around with flashlights." Someone was still stirring up trouble at the hangar around the floats. So far, it had mainly been moving things around, hiding tools, minor pranks. But still, things had to be sorted out every time anyone tried to get to work. It was a pain in the butt, and Irene suspected Nell. She'd love to catch her in the act.

Theo seemed to be more awake now. "Uh-uh. Bad idea. If we get caught, everyone will think we're the ones causing mischief. We already went to jail once this week."

"Come on." She was halfway off the bed before he could argue anymore. She stopped stark-naked by the side of the bed. In her most seductive voice, she said, "It will be an adventure, I promise."

He stared at her like he'd never seen a naked female before. "You make it awfully hard to resist."

"I hope so," she said as he got off the bed. He didn't have enough black clothes to go around, so they wore their blue jeans, and a couple of his dark-colored T-shirts. "We'll do," she declared as she inspected them in the mirror. Then she grabbed her car keys from the dresser and held them in the air. "And to make it worth your while, I'll let you drive the Shelby."

• • •

Theo parked at the front of the airfield across a parking lot with a good view of the entryway. He pulled the car next to a shed that would shield them from anyone watching. Irene grabbed some binoculars and peered across the lot, eager to catch anyone up to no good.

Theo rolled down the windows, and a warm wind brushed their faces and rustled through their hair. The moonless night shaded everything in a gray gloom, making it difficult to make out details. Everything was quiet except for a couple of dogs barking in the distance.

"I don't see anything," she said, sounding disappointed.

Theo rested his arm on the steering wheel. "And maybe you won't. They might have done their handiwork already and gone home. Or maybe this is their night off."

She hit his arm playfully. "You're such a pessimist, Theo."

He grinned. "No, I'm optimistic we won't see a thing. And if we do, what's your plan? Make a citizen's arrest?"

She put the binoculars down. "I don't know. I was just feeling all Nancy Drew. She'd catch them red-handed and turn them over to the authorities. Everyone has worked too hard for someone to be causing trouble."

"Speaking of hard work, have you come up with your wow factor yet?"

She gave him a sly grin. "I think so. Lizzie Harris came to see me the other day."

"The young woman I met in your shop?"

"That's the one."

Theo narrowed his eyes. "The one that wanted me to marry them dressed as Elvis."

She nodded eagerly. "That's right."

Theo didn't like where this was going. "What did she want?"

"Well, they haven't been able to get their wedding together yet, and I asked her if she'd consider getting married on the float."

"During the parade?"

Irene gushed with excitement over the plan. "Exactly. All of her family will be in town, and the town picnic will serve as a giant reception. She loved the idea."

"I have to admit it's different," he said cautiously.

She clapped him on the arm. "I know. It's going to be fantastic, but..."

"But what?" He knew he shouldn't ask.

"If you'd play Elvis that would put us over the top. I think we'd win the trophy without a doubt." She looked at him like he held her fate in his hands.

He held up a hand. "Oh no. I thought I made it clear I wasn't interested."

She sighed. "I understand. I'm looking at other options, but since they are willing to do this for me, I'd like to give them what they want. Without Elvis it won't be perfect."

Headlights sliced across the parking lot. Theo grabbed her arm and pulled her down in the car. They slumped down while still peeking out the windshield, trying to tell what was going on. But they were too far away. The car cruised around the hangar and then suddenly headed straight for the place they were parked.

Theo tried to start the Shelby and make a getaway, but red-and-blue flashing lights filled the night sky.

"Tell me this isn't happening again." Theo banged his head on the steering wheel.

Irene bit her lower lip. "I'm sure we can explain everything."

"Whatever you do, just stay in the car."

The cop car stopped in front of them, and they sat quietly as Officer Melber walked up to the side of the car. "Excuse me, sir, but can you tell me what you're doing out here in the middle of the night?"

"Good evening, Officer."

The policeman flashed his light inside the car, and his eyes widened when he recognized Theo. "Not you again. What's going on this time? I see you're in a different car. Does this one belong to you?"

"No, but—"

Irene spoke up. "It's mine, Officer Melber."

He leaned down and looked inside. "Is that you, Mrs. Cornwell?"

She waved. "It's me. Good evening, Owen."

He sighed. "And I suppose you have a perfectly good reason for being here?"

Theo spoke up. "Yes, sir. We were guarding our float from vandals."

Officer Melber leaned toward the window. "Vandals? Did you see anyone?"

Theo shook his head. "No, we just got here."

"Well, the department is making regular passes. We've heard about the problems."

Irene stuck her head over so she could see him. "You are? That makes me feel much better. As you can see, I could hardly sleep worrying about it. My float is in good hands if you are guarding the premises, though."

"It's just part of the job, ma'am."

"Thank you, Owen. You aren't planning on hauling us off to jail this time?"

"Any reason why I should?"

"Not a one," Theo assured him quickly. "If it's okay, we'll go home and leave this to you."

"Get out of here. But I don't want to find the two of you parked in any more dark places. Understand?"

"Yes, sir." Theo started the car and they drove off. He sounded kind of grumpy when he said, "Next time you want to wake me up in the middle of the night, don't. We're lucky we didn't end up in jail again."

"I know. I'm sorry." Irene was frustrated that her plan had been foiled before it ever got off the ground. But maybe the sabotage would stop now that the police were keeping an eye on the hangar, and that was the important thing. "What if the next time I want to wake you up in the middle of the night it involves staying in bed?"

He sighed and reached over and grabbed her hand. "I guess that would be okay."

Her hand slipped from his and found his thigh. With a squeeze she asked, "Just okay?"

His answer was to step on the accelerator and hurry back to the house on Overbrook.

•   •   •

Irene waited on the front porch in the white rocker. Sadie lounged at her feet. They were both watching for Theo's Jeep to turn the corner. It had become the best time of the day lately. Knowing he'd be coming home any time now. Knowing he'd be coming home to her. Seeing the big grin that spread across his face the second he spotted her. Admitting there was no place else on earth she'd rather be. Since the night they'd spent together, she would finish work and head to his place. His workday varied, and sometimes he'd be waiting for her instead. Either way, she was happy. She knew Theo would be leaving soon, and she tried not to let it dampen the mood. But she knew she'd miss him even more than the first time he'd gone away. She knew and tried to pretend it would all be fine. Otherwise she might howl with the sheer misery of it all.

She saw the Jeep and stood up and waved. He pulled into the driveway and got out. She drank in the sight of him. He was wearing a white T-shirt tucked into work jeans and had work boots on his feet. Taking the porch steps two at a time, he grabbed her and swung her around, while she squealed with delight. Sadie bounced around wanting to be part of the greeting. Theo set her back on her feet and then took a few minutes to greet Sadie properly. Squatting down and rubbing her head, he asked, "How's my girl? How's my Sadie?" Sadie barked and wagged her tail, telling him she was glad to see him, too.

Theo stood up, his eyes twinkling. "And how are you, beautiful?" he asked before kissing her hello.

"I'm good." Irene thought she might die from the simple joy of the moment. "I brought pizza and wine for dinner."

His arms went around her waist. "Pepperoni and mushrooms?"

She leaned back so she could see his face. "Is there any other kind?"

"I could use a shower first," he said with a smile.

"That's funny. So could I." She led him into the house, shutting out the rest of the world.

• • •

"Theo, I'm not going to spend the night here anymore." They were lying in bed, snuggling. Tomorrow was the Fourth. The big day.

He looked down so he could see her face. "Is it something I said?"

She shook her head. "No, but you'll be saying good-bye in a few days. And I might cry. I can't promise I won't."

He smiled at her honesty but felt a tug on his heart-strings. "I might cry, too."

She cupped his face with her palm. "We don't want that."

He turned so they were nose to nose. "No. Just happy memories, right?"

"Right. You'll be busy getting Jake up to speed, and I still have a million things to do for the parade."

He nuzzled her neck. "Only a million?"

In the end, he'd had no choice but to agree with her decision to go home. She wanted the Fourth, a day full of parades and picnics and fireworks, to be the day they formally said good-bye. Not that they'd avoid each other if they ran into each other before he left. They'd speak. Maybe even share a joke or two. It would all be very civilized, he thought savagely. He rolled her into his arms, determined to make the next few hours count.

Chapter Twenty-Six

~~~~~~

The Fourth of July finally arrived. It was a hot, clear day that boded well for the parade and all the planned activities for the day ahead. Theo stretched out all alone in his humongous bed, listening to the quiet house. He'd woken up early to walk Sadie as was his habit only to realize Sadie was back home with Jake and Marla Jean.

They had shown up yesterday afternoon, and she'd gone into doggy fits of heaven when she'd seen them. Barking and squirming, not being able to get enough of their touch and attention.

Jake finally sat on the ground, letting the poor dog climb into his lap. Marla Jean hugged the dog's neck as though she'd reclaimed a long lost child. Sadie did stop for a minute and woof at Theo, wondering why he wasn't joining in the joyful reunion.

Theo was happy to see them, too.

They looked tanned and relaxed and gloriously in love.

Jake wrestled Sadie to the ground while saying, "See, Marla Jean. I told you Theo would take good care of

Sadie." He winked at his brother, letting him in on the joke.

Marla Jean stood up watching the man and his dog. "I wasn't worried. You were the one who wanted to Skype with Sadie so often I finally had to put my foot down." She looked at Theo and said, "Don't ever go on a honeymoon with this man."

Jake abandoned Sadie to chase his wife around the yard. "Is that right?" He caught her and swung her around by her waist.

Theo felt like an intruder watching them laugh and kiss like teenagers.

Marla Jean protested, "Stop it, Jake. Your poor brother probably has better things to do than watch us slobber all over each other."

"I don't slobber, but you're right. We need to get home and unpack and figure out what we are going to do for the parade tomorrow. Did you finish Irene's float?"

Theo nodded. "I haven't seen the finished product, but she was working on last-minute details last I heard."

"Are you going to ride in the car with me? Jake's Remodeling? Or we can change the name to Jacobson Brothers and announce it with our sign. Just say the word."

"I appreciate the offer, Jake, but my plan to go to Australia hasn't changed. And I'm afraid I'll be riding on Irene's float tomorrow."

Marla Jean looked disappointed. "Well, you aren't leaving right away, are you? Give us a chance to change your mind."

"I'll be here for another week or so, but I can't promise anything more than that."

Jake walked over and held out his hand to his younger

brother. "Thank you for holding down the fort while we were gone. I can't tell you what it meant to me."

"You're welcome, Jake. I couldn't let everything fall apart while you were off lollygagging around."

Marla Jean put her arm around her husband's waist. "Hey, Theo, why don't you come over for dinner tonight, so you can tell us what we missed while we were gone."

He agreed, and they climbed back in their car, taking Sadie with them. As they drove away, Theo felt more alone than he had the entire time he'd been in Everson. He'd been e-mailing back and forth with his friend Mitch, and his friend from Australia was enthusiastically looking forward to his arrival. Theo kept waiting for the bubble of anticipation that he'd always experienced before embarking on a new adventure to build. So far, he felt nothing at all. Maybe he'd become jaded. The places might change, but the vacant place in his soul stayed empty and unfulfilled.

He looked at his watch and jumped up—this time for good—and took a long shower, got dressed, and then climbed in the Jeep, heading to Lu Lu's parking lot. All of the floats were supposed to be in place by 9:00 a.m. to be ready for the parade. It would start at ten and wind through town around the Main Street Square and end up back at Lu Lu's. He would meet up with Irene and make sure everything was ready to go. He'd finally agreed to play Elvis and had gone online to be ordained. Now he was wearing the outfit Ree had come up with and was getting a variety of looks from people he passed. Some did a double take. Some looked startled. Some smiled and waved like he was a parade all his own.

This whole wedding-on-board thing was top secret.

Only the bride and groom, Irene, and Theo were in on the plan. But now, before long the cat would be out of the bag. When he pulled into the parking lot, it was already more than half full. He spotted Jake and Marla Jean and parked in a place out of the way.

He got out and greeted them warmly. "Happy Fourth of July."

"Theo? Is that you? Why are you dressed like Elvis?" Marla Jean laughed, inspecting him like he'd just stepped off an alien ship.

Jake was arranging the sign on the side of one of his cars but stopped when he saw Theo. "What the hell is that getup? Is this for Irene's float?"

Theo looked down at his outfit. Thank goodness they'd decided on early Elvis so he didn't have to wear the skin-tight white outfit with the cape. Instead he was more "Jail-house Rock," with the black-and-white striped T-shirt and black jeans and jacket. Aviator sunglasses and a black bouf-fant wig completed the look. "Yep. What do you think?"

"I don't understand, but I love it," Marla Jean declared.

"Thank you very much," Theo mumbled with a curled lip.

"I can't believe Irene talked you into doing this." Jake crossed his arms over his chest and laughed.

Marla Jean was bouncing up and down. "Oh, I love this parade. Did you see what Hoot and Dooley managed to do for the barbershop?"

Theo looked around to where she was pointing. A cardboard pair of giant scissors painted silver opened up as an arch with a barber's chair sitting underneath. "I get to sit in the chair and wave. Mom and Dad are going to sit on either edge and hand out candy."

He laughed. "Very nice. Are you handing out candy, Jake?"

Jake reached into Lucille and hauled out a giant bag of mixed candy and lollipops. "It's the only way to get out of the parade in one piece."

"Well, I better go find Irene. I'll see you two after the parade." He waved and walked off looking at the different entries. The high school marching band was organizing to his left. Young kids practicing on their instruments in a cacophony of noise. Old Martin Quinn was there riding his antique tractor. A line of shiny convertibles waited to carry local officials. The first one sported a sign indicating it would hold the mayor. Another one would carry the county judge. Then there were more cars carrying a variety of junior princesses—dairy, strawberry, blackberry, and rose. Any number of agricultural royal representatives.

A veritable garden of blooms and flowers covered the Posey Pot float. Romeo's Pizza was easy to spot. A giant pizza served as the background. And then he saw Irene's float. The giant wedding cake rose above the other floats. He could see her climbing up on the side.

Theo trotted over to her float. "Hey, Ree. The float looks great."

His heart lightened as she turned and spotted him. Her face lit up like the morning sun breaking over the horizon. "Theo! Happy Fourth. Isn't this wonderful?" She stood up proudly holding her arms out to her side indicating her finished float.

"It looks terrific, Ree."

She climbed down and, smiling with real delight, touched his collar. "And so do you. Are you ready to do this, Elvis?"

"It's too late to back out now, so I'm ready. Have you seen your competition yet? I don't see Nell's masterpiece anywhere in the parking lot."

"It's over in the far corner shrouded from the public eye. I'm sure she wants to make a grand entrance."

"I've got to admit I'm curious. But I think you have a good shot at the trophy."

"Thanks, Theo. But at this point I'm just happy to be a part of everything. Too many years I've sat on the sidelines. Not anymore. Now I really feel like part of the community."

Theo saw the young couple dressed as a bride and groom milling around to one side. "There's the happy couple."

Ree laughed. "They haven't seen you yet. I wanted to surprise them." She pulled him out of sight around to the other side.

An older woman Theo didn't recognize stood there, holding a cupcake. "Irene, I have all the cupcakes loaded into the slots. We can hand them out whenever we stop."

Irene grinned. "Thanks, Aunt Jo. I don't think you two have met. Aunt Jo, this is Theo Jacobson. Theo, my aunt Jo Anne Cunningham."

Theo watched as the woman's eyes widened and her mouth formed a perfect O. He held out his hand. "I've heard a lot about you, Mrs. Cunningham. Irene has spoken highly of you over the years."

Jo Anne took his hand, studying him like a bug under a microscope. "So, you're Theo. Finally, I get a good look at you. She said you were a handsome devil, and she was right."

Grinning, he glanced at Ree who looked embarrassed. "Well, thank you, ma'am."

She looked over at the float. "I can't believe I let Irene talk me into riding on this thing. I'm probably going to fall off and break my neck." Aunt Jo laughed like a young girl.

Theo smiled and reassured her. "I made sure those handholds were good and secure, so you should be okay."

Ree's aunt leaned closer and spoke as though she was confiding precious secrets. "I can't tell you how much she appreciated all your help since you've been back in town. I think she's just blossomed since she started this new business. She's like a new woman."

Theo spoke honestly. "She's always been special to me."

That put a twinkle in her eye. "Well, now, we need to talk later. Maybe later at the picnic."

"Yes, ma'am," Theo agreed.

Jo Anne turned, patted Irene on the back, and disappeared around the other side of the float.

Irene made a face. "Sorry, Theo. She's always romanticized our relationship."

Theo was surprised. "Why? She didn't even know me."

"No, but she didn't approve of my marriage to Sven. She takes every chance she can to point out my mistakes. Now that she's gotten a good look at you, she'll be even worse."

"Because I'm such a handsome devil?" Theo winked and hooked his thumbs in his belt loops.

Irene shook her head. "No, because she used to be a huge Elvis fan. So, don't let it go to your head, mister."

"Too late." His grin was cocky, and he enjoyed seeing her squirm.

She gave him a small push. "Come on. It's time I introduced you to the bride and groom."

They walked around the float and Lizzie gasped. "Oh my gosh, it's Elvis. You found him. Mrs. Cornwell, I mean Irene, thank you!"

Irene smiled. "Actually, you found him. But he looks great, doesn't he?"

Matthew Long stepped up and held out his hand. "We appreciate this. The wedding was already perfect since I'm marrying Lizzie, but now this is awesome."

"I'm happy to help." Theo shook his hand, and for the first time since he'd put on the Elvis getup, he was glad he'd let Irene convince him to do it. "We should go over the plan. I know there will be eight stops along the way. We can do the whole ceremony at the first stop and then just pronounce you man and wife and kiss the bride at all the rest. Otherwise we can break it up and just do a bit at each stop."

"I vote for kissing the bride at each stop," Matthew said with a grin.

Lizzie wrapped her arms around his waist. "Me too."

Theo took out the paper that had his part written on it. "Okay, then let's review my part and yours."

• • •

Irene made sure her aunt had a good seat on the float and then climbed on board. Theo stood under the wedding arbor, facing Lizzie and Matthew. Everyone was in place, and she was excited. Up at the front of the parking lot, the line of cars started moving. First the car with the mayor left the parking lot. The county judge's car followed, and the ancient tractor pulled out behind that. Bo Birdwell, the town's only cabdriver, rode a unicycle and juggled at the same time. Irene was impressed. The marching band marched out of the parking lot next with only the percussion section setting a rhythm, and the high school twirling team came next. She knew from other years they'd make two stops on each block and play something patriotic to the folks gathered along the street. Irene knew they'd be far enough ahead that they could use those stops to perform the wedding ceremony.

Finally, it was time for the business floats to leave the parking lot. Oliver was driving the truck pulling their float. He waved at her and climbed into the cab. He honked his horn as they started moving, and everyone grabbed onto their handholds. Ahead of them she could see Linc and Dinah on their float followed by Marla Jean in a barber chair flanked by her parents under her giant scissors. Hoot and Dooley played Parcheesi on a table at the front. It was very cute. A group of men and women riding horses from the Landon Riding School followed at a safe distance; Romeo's Pizza, the Posey Pot, the Rise-N-Shine float, which was still shrouded in secrecy, and then Irene brought up the rear.

She was amazed by the number of people crowded along the street since it seemed like everyone she knew was already in the parade. She and her aunt tossed candy in the direction of kids holding big empty bags in hopes of filling them with their share of the sweet bounty being handed out along the way. Lizzie, Matthew, and Theo waved.

They made the turn onto Main Street, heading around the square, and stopped while the band played and the twirlers twirled their batons. They were still on the side street with only a few people lining the way.

"This is going to take awhile, isn't it?" Theo shouted back to her.

She took the opportunity to walk up to the front of the float. She squeezed Lizzie's arm. "Just keep smiling and waving. Theo, you can start the ceremony once we make our first stop on Main Street. That's where most of the people will be. Including Lizzie and Matthew's folks, right?"

Lizzie nodded. "I told them we had a surprise and told them where to sit."

Theo smiled. "Sounds good, then. Irene, you better sit down. It looks like we're moving again."

Irene hurried to sit back down. She could see Romeo's Pizza float around the first corner. Romeo was tossing dough in the air, thrilling the crowd as the pizza dough flew high before he caught it with one hand. The women from the Posey Pot were handing out flowers to the crowd. She was still hoping to get a glimpse of Nell's Rise-N-Shine masterpiece. Nell had certainly done a good job of building suspense. And then the shroud came down as they moved onto Main Street.

It turned the corner ahead of them and a big, shiny chrome diner came into sight. The sun came out from behind a cloud to bathe it in heavenly light. Irene had to admit it was breathtaking. It was an open-faced replica of the Rise-N-Shine. A broad counter stretched across the float while Bertie with her ever-present pencil stuck behind her ear, wearing her standard apron, served pie to customers sitting on the stools.

Irene couldn't deny that it was impressive. But she didn't know if being shiny was what it took to win the trophy. She still thought a real honest-to-goodness wedding gave them a fighting chance. As far as she was concerned, the Penelope Bottoms trophy was still up for grabs. A young couple saying vows evoked feelings of young love that would inspire the sentimental in the crowd. And the cupcakes were another secret weapon. Wedding cake white cupcakes decorated with white icing and the words "I Do" written on the top of each one. Those should get her a few votes, too.

But no matter what happened, she was thrilled to be helping Lizzie and Matthew get married, and with Theo's help it was going to be great. They moved along the route until they came to their first stop on Main Street. Theo gave her a signal, and she helped her aunt down so they could hand out cupcakes. Theo smiled and turned on his microphone.

"My friends, we are gathered here today to celebrate one of life's greatest moments, to give recognition to the worth and beauty of committed marital love, and to add our best wishes to the words, which shall unite Matthew and Lizzie in marriage."

An audible gasp escaped from the people lining the street. Then a smattering of applause started when they realized what was happening. Lizzie and Matthew smiled and waved at their parents who all looked shocked. Lizzie's mom started crying. "My baby girl."

Irene handed her a cupcake, hoping that would help.

Matthew's mother, not to be outdone, reached for two cupcakes. "Matthew looks so handsome." Then she started bawling, too.

"The commitment that the two of you are about to make is the most important commitment that two people can make. You are about to create something new, the marriage relationship, an entity that never ends. I would ask that you both remember to treat yourself and each other with dignity and respect; to remind yourself often of what brought you together today."

Irene's heart caught in her throat, thinking how

the time she'd spent the last few weeks with Theo had reminded her of all of those things. She looked up, and he caught her eye and smiled.

"Matthew Michael Long will you have this woman to be your wedded wife?"

The groom spoke clearly. "I will."

"Will you love and comfort her, honor and keep her, in sickness and in health, and forsaking all others, keep yourself only unto her as long as you both shall live?"

He looked at her, love shining from his face. "I will."

"Lizzie will you have this man to be your wedded husband?"

The bride answered happily. "I will."

"Will you love and comfort him, honor and keep him, in sickness and in health, and forsaking all others, keep yourself only unto him as long as you both shall live?"

"I will." Her smile lit up the already sunny day.

Since it is your intention to enter into marriage, join your right hands, and repeat after me:

"I, Matthew, take you, Lizzie, to be my wife, to have and to hold from this day forward, for better or for worse, for richer or for poorer, in sickness and in health, to love and to cherish, as long as we both shall live."

Matthew repeated the words and placed a ring on her finger.

Lizzie did the same.

"Matthew and Lizzie, I now pronounce you husband and wife. Congratulations, you may kiss your bride."

Matthew grabbed Lizzie and kissed her with a passion that had the crowd cheering.

Theo smiled and said, "May I present to you, Mr. and Mrs. Matthew Long."

The couple smiled like their faces might break and waved some more. Lizzie's mother ran up to the side. "Oh, sweetie, why didn't you let us know? I would have worn a dress and had my hair done."

"You look great, Mama. I love you."

Her father came up and took her by the arm. "Come on, Mama. We'll talk to her after the parade. We're happy for you, honey."

"I love you, both," Lizzie yelled as the float started moving again.

Aunt Jo said she wanted to keep handing out cupcakes, so Irene got back on the float. The bride and groom looked like they might float away with happiness, so Irene considered it a huge success. Theo looked happy, too. She used the rail to join them at the front. Theo was congratulating the couple. "And next stop will be shorter, since you are already married."

It seemed the word had spread because the applause along the route grew and grew. Folks shouted congratulations and good wishes as they passed. Irene took the time to speak to Theo.

"Good job, Elvis. You were wonderful." She did a little jig.

Theo smiled, clearly pleased with the situation. "So, what do you think? Are we going to bring home the Penelope Bottoms trophy?"

She beamed. "You know, we just might."

He laughed. "I can't believe I married them."

"Only seven more times to go. I better get back so I can hand out more cupcakes."

Irene was feeling good about everything. The crowds were enthusiastic. Flags were waving all around, and she was looking forward to the picnic lunch she planned to share with Theo once this was done.

They stopped two more times.

Theo did his part. "I now pronounce you man and wife. You may kiss the bride."

And the newlyweds kissed to the delight of the folks of Everson, who hooted and hollered their appreciation. They started moving again to do it all over again.

Her aunt said they were running low on cupcakes, but Irene was prepared. She'd just pulled a tray of cupcakes out from under the big wooden wedding cake when the float lurched sideways before slamming into something solid. Irene was thrown down, and cupcakes went flying everywhere. People were yelling and running around.

"What in the world?" Irene could see that Lizzie had fallen down. Matthew was helping her to her feet.

"We're fine," he said. "But I think we're going to go find our families now."

"Thanks for everything, Mrs. Cornwell." Lizzie gave her a hug before they hopped off the float.

Irene looked around. "Is everyone else okay? Where's Theo?" She tried not to panic as she slid off the side of the float and found her aunt safe and sound on the street.

"Are you okay, Irene?"

"I'm fine, Aunt Jo, but I don't see Theo." The alarm she felt was racing through her veins.

"Here I am. I tumbled off the front but caught myself on the front rail, so I'm okay. I went to check on Oliver."

"Oh, thank goodness, Theo. Are you sure you're okay?" She rushed to hug him, not caring who saw.

He hugged her back, rubbing his hand up and down her

back. "I may have a couple of bruises, but nothing serious. Oliver is pretty shook up, though. He ran into the back of the Rise-N-Shine float."

"Oh no." Irene rushed up to the truck. The driver's door was open, and Oliver sat with his head down. "Oliver, are you hurt? What happened?"

"The gol-durned mirrors on that float blinded me when we turned the corner. I couldn't see that they'd stopped and slammed right into them."

"But you're not hurt?"

"Of course not, missy. We weren't going more than three miles an hour when I hit them. We should check on them, though."

"You're right. You sit still. Theo and I will check and be right back."

"Miss Irene?" Oliver said before she could leave. "I'm awfully sorry."

"That's okay, Oliver." She patted his arm and ran up to the Rise-N-Shine float. It was chaos. People wandered around, arguing about what had happened. The first collision had set off a chain reaction, however, and the Rise-N-Shine had run into the back of the Posey Pot float. Flowers were scattered everywhere.

"I saw the whole thing." Arnie Duncan ran up to Irene and Theo, pointing to the Posey Pot float. "After you hit the Rise-N-Shine, they banged into the Posey Pot, and then they banged into Romeo's just as he'd tossed his pizza dough into the air. It landed on one of the horses, spooking it. I think that horse is still running."

"This is a disaster," Irene declared.

People and horses milled around aimlessly. Irene could see the rest of the parade had stopped, too. Word must have gotten to them, and she saw the mayor running across the square toward the mayhem.

The sound of a siren filled the air and Irene's heart sank as she realized someone had been hurt. Speculation flew all around her.

Theo was wandering from float to float, checking on folks. Irene hurried over to where he stood with his hands on his hips.

"Hey, Theo. I just heard someone say Dinah Jones got knocked over and was on her way to the hospital. Do you know if she's okay?"

He nodded. "That's partly right. Her water broke, and she went into labor. That's why Linc took her to the hospital."

The news about Dinah was an exciting, bright spot in the catastrophe that was the Everson parade. "Oh my. That's wonderful. Linc must be beside himself."

"Jake and Marla Jean and her parents went with them."

Irene looked around at the street full of piled-up floats. "Oh, Theo, I broke the parade." She looked distraught, and he threw a comforting arm around her shoulder. She welcomed his act of comfort.

He nudged her under the chin. "I wouldn't be so quick to take the blame. I'd say Nell broke it by blinding Oliver with her big, shiny toy."

"Poor Oliver. He feels terrible. At the very least this probably disqualifies me for the trophy." They started walking back toward the other floats. "I need to talk to the sheriff. I don't want Oliver to get in trouble."

"If Officer Melber sees us, there could be trouble. We aren't on his favorite-person list."

"He's probably going to try to give that poor horse a ticket, knowing him." She laughed in spite of the situation.

Sheriff Watson spotted them and waved them over. "Irene, it's going to take awhile to sort all of this out, but from what I can tell Oliver hit the Rise-N-Shine float. And everything else was a chain reaction."

"That's about right, but I want to take responsibility for any damages. Oliver is my employee, so if he faces any fines, I'll handle that, too." Irene wanted to fix things. Money probably wasn't the only answer this time, but it was always good for soothing ruffled feathers.

"That's all I need for now, but I'll talk to you again in a bit. It might take awhile to sort everything out." With a nod, Sheriff Watson walked over to Romeo to get his version of events.

"Can I have your attention, everyone." They all turned as Mayor Ross Wolfson climbed the steps to the gazebo, speaking into a microphone set up for later festivities. "As of now, the parade is officially canceled."

There were a few scattered boos from the crowd.

"But the picnic, games, and fireworks will go on as scheduled. We apologize for the problems this morning. See you all this afternoon."

Nell came running up with Charlie on her heels. "Irene Cornwell, if it's the last thing I do, you will pay for this."

Charlie tried to settle her down. "Nell, Irene didn't do anything."

"What do you mean? She ran into us." Nell shook Charlie's arm off and tried to get in Irene's face.

Theo stepped between the two women. "Nell, she wasn't driving, so just back off."

Bertie came up to the group, taking her daughter by her arm. "Come on, Nell. This isn't helping anything."

Irene felt terrible. "Is everyone okay, Bertie?"

"Everyone is fine. Whooee. This is a parade we won't forget for a good, long while." Bertie seemed to think the entire thing was funny.

Nell grabbed her neck and let out a moan. "Well, I'm not sure I'm all right. I think I have whiplash. I should sue you for everything you're worth."

Bertie put her hands on her hips. "Girl, you hush your mouth. I didn't raise you to be so nasty."

The girl huffed at her mother. "Oh, sure, take her side. After all the work I did." She looked like she might cry, and Irene felt a flash of sympathy for her.

Bertie dragged her off. "I told you not to use mirrored stuff. You better hope we're the ones that don't get sued, young lady."

Before they got too far, Sheriff Watson was waving them over. "Nell, I need to ask you a few questions."

Irene needed to get back to her float and talk to Oliver. Theo stopped her. "Listen, I need to run over to the hospital and see how things are going with Dinah. I'll see you at the picnic, okay?"

"Sure. Give everyone my regards." Irene gave him a quick hug. "I can't wait to see that baby."

Once Theo left, Charlie fell into step beside her. "Are you okay, Irene?"

"I'm fine, Charlie. Where were you when everything went to hell in a handbasket?"

"I was one of the customers at the diner's counter. I do believe I've finally seen Nell's true nature. Why didn't you warn me?" Charlie looked shocked.

Irene wrinkled her nose. "Well, you seemed to like her, so I didn't want to say anything. Theo found out about Nell after he first got to town."

"What do you mean?"

"She accused me of being a black widow."

"As in killing your husbands?" He laughed.

Irene nodded. "Afraid so."

"That's dumb, but I can't say I'm surprised." He was quiet for a minute. "I have a confession to make."

She stopped to look at him. "What kind of confession, Charlie?"

"Now that I think about it, the black widow thing doesn't surprise me. Nell actually contacted me before I came to town. She said you were misusing my father's money and playing fast and loose with an old boyfriend. I came to town to try to take you down." He looked like he was feeling guilty.

Irene's blood began to boil as she listened to his admission. But then she took a deep breath, giving him some credit for coming clean. "Well, well, I was suspicious when you showed up like a bolt out of the blue."

"The point is, it didn't work like she thought it would. I came to town expecting to find a frivolous woman spending my father's hard-earned money on clothes and cars and fancy shoes."

"I have a few of those things, Charlie. I'm not a nun, you know."

"You know what I mean. But I've studied the foundation, and you do more good work than my father could have hoped to expect."

"Thank you. That means a lot to me."

"So, I wanted to let you know I'll be going back to Dallas soon. I won't be underfoot anymore."

"Why don't we talk about that?" Irene was glad he'd come clean.

He looked surprised. "Really? What did you have in mind?"

"Did you really lose your last job?"

He shrugged. "I quit. I really did want to find something more meaningful."

"If you stay in Everson, your work with the foundation can be as meaningful as you want it to be. I know your father would be happy about that."

Charlie looked a little choked up, and Irene allowed him a moment to collect himself. "Don't give me an answer now. But think about it. I could use another voice to help me keep those Dallas lawyers in line."

He smiled and grabbed her hand. "I'll give it some thought."

"And one more thing. You'll have to move out of the house. Having a grown stepson in the house cramps my style."

He laughed. "Mine, too, Mom."

• • •

"It's a girl." Linc handed Theo a cigar the minute he walked through the waiting room door.

"Congratulations, Linc. Does she have a name yet?"

Linc shook his head. "No, Dinah was sure she was a boy. So we are still discussing things."

"What was the boy's name?" Theo asked.

"Lincoln Junior," Lincoln said like it was obvious.

"I think Junior is a cute name for a girl," Jake volunteered from the couch.

Lincoln grinned like he owned the world. "I'll tell Dinah you said so. Now I'm going to go see if the grandmas will let me hold my daughter."

"Go put your foot down, Dad." Jake got up and goaded his best friend on.

Linc's grin was goofy. "Wait a couple of minutes, then come on back. Dinah will want to say hello."

Jake and Theo sat down in the waiting room. Marla Jean was back with Dinah and the baby.

"That's going to be one spoiled baby." Jake stretched his long legs out in front of him and tipped his cowboy hat up with his thumb.

Theo nodded. "Yep. She's a lucky kid."

"None of the drama we had to face. I wonder what it would be like to have a normal childhood. Two parents that love each other."

Theo couldn't imagine. "If she turns out like Linc and Marla Jean, that'll be okay."

"So, when are you leaving, Theo?"

"I thought I'd wait until after this weekend. Once the holiday is done, we can go over the jobs I finished while you were gone. Bart thinks he has a buyer lined up for my plane. So, once that's done, I'll be on my way."

"Australia is a long way to go." Jake's voice was serious.

"We'll keep in touch." Theo didn't want to get all sentimental.

Marla Jean waltzed into the room, smiling and gesturing for them to come with her. "Get in here and see this precious baby."

As they got up and followed her down the hallway, Theo thought about the baby he might have had with Ree. The baby they'd lost that spurred his decision to join the Navy. He'd wanted to be a good provider, a good dad. And over the years he'd thought about that sweet child and wondered how his life might have been different if Ree hadn't miscarried.

But Jake was right. A baby deserved a life with no drama and two parents who loved each other without question. His life with Irene had turned into nothing but questions, so in the end, things had turned out just the way they were supposed to, he supposed. He walked into Dinah's room and cooed over the pink bundle in her arms.

Chapter Twenty-Seven

~~~

He spotted the basket right away. Yellow napkin and red bow. Just like she'd described it. He didn't see Ree, though. He'd gone home after he left the hospital, showered and changed out of his Elvis outfit, and put on jeans and a T-shirt before heading to the park. The Sven Cornwell Memorial Park was filled with families enjoying the holiday. Kids kicked balls, played with Hula-Hoops, and threw baseballs. Blankets were spread out to enjoy the picnic baskets brought by families.

The baskets up for bid were lined up on a bandstand waiting for the charity auction to begin. The money raised would help fund a new senior center. Theo knew that was close to Irene's heart. It was close to his, too. Folks like Lily Porter could use a place to socialize. He would bid extra for her basket, just to show his support.

He noticed Charlie examining the offerings on the bandstand, too. "Hey, Charlie, have you seen Irene?"

"Not lately. She was filling out more paperwork for the sheriff so he could finish his report about the parade crashes. She should be here soon, though. She asked me to deliver her basket for the auction."

"She did?"

"Yes. We had a nice talk, and she's offering me a permanent place at the foundation. So, to show my gratitude, I'm thinking about bidding on her basket. The house smelled mouthwatering while she was cooking." Theo had expected competition, but not from Charlie.

He gave the man a hard look. "I thought you'd be bidding on Nell's basket."

"Not likely. After today, I've had my eyes opened where that young lady is concerned."

Theo let out an ungracious sound. "Welcome to the club." They paused to share a rare moment of camaraderie.

"So, what basket are you bidding on, Theo?" He had a sly look on his face.

Theo turned to give Charlie a lazy grin. "Ree described her basket in detail, so I think she wanted me to make a bid. I plan to do just that."

Charlie nodded. "I understand you're leaving town soon."

"Next week most likely."

"That's probably for the best."

"Why would you say that?"

Charlie shrugged. "I hate to see Irene get dragged back into a relationship with you if you're not going to be around for the fallout."

"I don't think that's your concern."

"I guess it wasn't my father's, either."

"Now you don't know what you're talking about."

"Maybe not, but I always wondered why Irene married him. She is a young, beautiful woman, so I could see why he'd want her for his wife."

Theo turned away, not wanting to discuss any of this with Charlie of all people.

"I did some digging around since I've been back in town. Did you know that my father paid medical bills for Irene's aunt before they were married?"

"What medical bills? From what she'd told me about her family, her aunt would have never agreed to that."

"She needed an operation. I don't think she knew who paid the bills. The payments were made to the law firm where she worked."

"So, what are you saying?"

"It looks like Irene married my father for completely unselfish reasons. It was for her aunt." Charlie dropped that bomb and then strolled away whistling.

• • •

Irene hurried to the picnic site. After the parade disaster, she had to meet with the company in charge of the fireworks display scheduled for later that night. Everything was ready to go, and the display this year promised to be better than ever.

Now she needed to get there in time for the charity auction. She was looking forward to spending more time with Theo. He'd be leaving soon. She knew it. Accepted it. Hated it. She'd never be able to pass that house on Overbrook Street without thinking of Theo and all the things he'd made her feel.

When she thought of living in Everson without him, she felt like her soul had been scooped out, and the hole left in her chest gaped, and throbbed, and threatened to bring her to her knees. She had ridiculous fantasies of the two of them living together in that small house. And in those fantasies, they were ridiculously happy. She planned weddings, he fixed houses, and sometimes he would take her flying. They'd land in some remote field and make love until they were wrung out, and sunburned, and sated.

She shivered, knowing it wasn't going to happen, but she could hope to share a blanket with him tonight. Snuggle in his arms, drink some wine, and watch the fireworks explode overhead. Good practice being one of the many women he had in the many ports around the world. That meant keeping a smile on her face as she waved good-bye.

When she reached the park, she noticed the parade float judges gathered together discussing the winners and honorable mentions. She ducked her head and hurried past. The Penelope Bottoms Grand Prize trophy wouldn't be hers this year. That was for sure, but she'd had fun building the float, and she'd felt like a real part of the community. So, no regrets. That was her new motto.

Things with Charlie were beginning to sort themselves out. He might never completely accept her as his father's choice for a wife, but he seemed to think more highly of her than when he'd first gotten to town.

And then there was Aunt Jo. They were getting along better than ever. She'd been such a trooper on the float today. And Irene was so happy her aunt wanted to work with her at the wedding shop. And even when she'd told her aunt about the prom dress initiative, she'd been full of ideas, offering to alter some of the donated bridesmaid dresses into younger, more fashionable frocks that would appeal to high school girls.

All in all, her life was heading in a good direction. She waved at Lily Porter and said hi to Hoot and Dooley and their wives. She was trying to find Theo. She'd felt sure he would be here by now. The auction would be starting anytime.

Mayor Wolfson jumped up on the stage, waving to the townsfolk. "Hello, everyone. Welcome to the Fourth of July annual picnic. We'd like to thank the Sven Cornwell Memorial Fund for providing the fireworks this evening. Let's have a round of applause for Irene Cornwell representing the foundation and its fine work."

Irene waved to the crowd as they clapped.

"And now the parade judges will award the prizes for the parade floats. And of course, the Penelope Bottoms Grand Prize trophy for this year. Sarah Lee, will you do the honors?"

Sarah Lee Powers, a member of the city council, took the stage holding a piece of paper that held the names of the winning floats. She waved the paper at the crowd and grinned, trying to build excitement in her moment in the spotlight. She took the microphone and tested it. "Can y'all hear me?"

"We can hear you. Quit stalling," someone yelled good-naturedly.

"Okay, here goes. Honorable mention goes to Romeo's Pizza. Even though you lost control of your dough, the committee didn't think we should hold that against you."

There was a smattering of applause as Romeo jumped onstage and accepted his ribbon.

"Next we have the third place ribbon that goes to I Do, I Do. Come on up here, Irene. Those cupcakes were delicious. Good work."

"Really! Oh my gosh. Thank you!" Irene was thrilled to get anything at all. She skipped up the steps and held her ribbon over her head, waving to the crowd.

"Second place goes to..." There was a long pause. "...To the Rise-N-Shine Diner. Congratulations, Bertie." Bertie climbed the steps slowly, waving to the folks in the crowd.

"Thank you. Thank you. I accept this on behalf of my daughter Nell. She worked really hard on our entry this year as she does every year, and we appreciate it. To show our appreciation to the folks of Everson for your ongoing support, coffee is free all day next Monday." Everyone went crazy applauding as though she'd offered free steak dinners.

Irene couldn't imagine what float would take first with Rise-N-Shine's out of the running. A sudden shiver spread down her spine, and then Theo appeared at her side. Her body seemed to have developed the ability to sense his nearness even before she saw him. "Congratulations, Ree. Third place is pretty good." His deep voice played across her skin like rough magic.

She turned to face him and smiled. Holding out her ribbon, she smiled. "It's better than good. It's great."

Sarah Lee cleared her throat. "Okay, folks. And now for the moment we've all been waiting for. The winner of this year's Penelope Bottoms Grand Prize trophy goes to..."

A hush fell over the crowd.

"The Jones Accounting Firm float and their brand-new baby girl, Harper Mae Jones. She was born this morning at eleven forty-two and weighed seven pounds and six ounces. Congratulations to our grand prize winner. Since they are still in the hospital, Harper's Aunt Marla Jean will accept on their behalf."

Marla Jean darted up the stairs and hoisted the trophy

over her head like she'd just won a wrestling match. "Thanks everyone! Harper thanks you. Her mommy and daddy thank you. And I'll make sure they get this right away."

Theo was laughing at Marla Jean's antics, and Irene felt a moment of jealousy. She would never be part of that family. He would never look at her with such easy acceptance. She tucked the thought away, refusing to feel sorry for herself today.

Touching his arm, she said, "I think that baby's the best winner possible, don't you?"

Theo looked at her and said, "I sure do. A brand-new baby puts things in perspective. Reminds us of what's important in life."

She didn't know where he was going with this. "What do you think is important in life, Theo?"

He put his hands in the back pockets of his jeans and rocked back on his heels. Quietly he said, "Family, connections, belonging someplace. That baby will have all of that and more."

She thought he sounded a little sad. "You're right. That's what we all want."

"And you've found it here in Everson, haven't you, Ree?"

"I'm working on it." But she didn't have everything. Not really. Theo was leaving, and this time at least they were on good terms. She wasn't going to mess that up by being clingy and needy.

The mayor got back up on the stage. "And now we'll get started on our picnic basket auction. So, gather around, folks. The money we raise will help fund a new Everson Senior Center so please be generous with your bids."

"Oh, that's my cue. I have to go get in line by the stage.

Don't forget. Yellow napkin, red ribbon." She smiled and squeezed his arm.

"I won't forget," Theo promised as she hurried away. He pushed his way through the gathered people so he could get a good view of the assembled baskets. Irene's basket was fourth in line.

The auction got under way with a flurry of good-natured bidding. The note on the first basket promised ham, macaroni and cheese, and chocolate cake. Bo Birdwell and Clete Fraser got into a bidding war for the basket. Bo finally won when he upped his bid to fifty dollars. The crowd gasped. And the mayor declared Bo the winner. He smiled a big toothy grin and grabbed the basket, holding it over his head like a trophy. Sylvia Smith giggled while she took his arm, and they wandered off to find the perfect place to enjoy her food.

The next two baskets went quickly, and Theo got ready to start bidding on Ree's. He thought he might start high to discourage competition. Thirty dollars sounded like a respectable amount of money. After all, it was for a good cause.

"Ladies and gentlemen, our next basket offers fried chicken, baked beans, and cherry pie."

Theo raised his hand. "Thirty dollars."

The crowd oohed their approval. "Way to go, buddy," Hoot hollered.

Mayor Wolfson looked pleased. "That's a nice starting bid. Any other takers?"

Theo looked around, thinking this was going to be easy.

"Forty dollars. I bid forty dollars." Charlie stepped out from the edge of the crowd, grinning at Theo.

Theo took a deep breath, grinned back, and prepared for battle. "Forty-five."

"Fifty." Charlie smirked and took a step in Theo's direction.

Theo studied Charlie and figured he needed to get serious. "Seventy-five."

"Oh my." A woman behind Theo cackled. "This is getting good now."

Charlie paced back and forth, looking like he was considering his next move. Theo thought he might have him on the ropes when he declared, "I'll bid one hundred dollars."

"Two hundred," Theo countered without pausing. He glanced up at Ree by the stage. Instead of looking flattered, she looked perplexed and worried. He waved to assure her it was all in good fun.

Charlie rocked back on his heels. "Two twenty-five."

Mrs. Porter toddled up to him. "Theo, come on. Don't let him win."

"Two fifty." Theo winked at Lily. "Don't worry, Miz Porter."

Charlie threw his hands in the air. "All right, that's too rich for my blood."

The mayor announced grandly, "We have a bid of two fifty. Anyone else? Going once. Going twice. Going three times. Sold to Theo Jacobson."

Irene ran down the steps of the stage to greet him while he walked over to pay Carlotta Todd. "Here you go, Carlotta."

Carlotta smiled as big as all outdoors. "Congratulations, Theo. I hope that's some good chicken."

"I'm sure it will be worth every penny."

Theo reached up and got the basket from the stage. The crowd cheered, giving Theo and Irene a wide path as he took her hand and walked toward the picnic tables. He stopped at an empty table and guided her to her seat. Sitting down across from her, he met her gaze head-on.

"You shouldn't have let Charlie goad you, Theo. What were you thinking spending so much?" She was smiling, though, so she must not have minded too much.

"I was thinking I hope your fried chicken is as good as you said it was. Besides, it's for a good cause." He opened the basket and pulled out a sealed container full of chicken. "I'm starving."

She started helping, pulling out the other food. "I can't imagine what got into Charlie."

Theo thought it was obvious. "I think he was trying to make a point. He told me you'd offered him a permanent job."

"So what's his point?"

Theo shrugged. "That I'm leaving, and he'll still be here. He all but warned me not to hurt you."

Irene put her hands on her hips. "He overstepped his place, Theo. We did have a serious talk about his position here. He admitted he'd misjudged me all of these years, and at my invitation, he's agreed to work for the foundation permanently."

"I'm glad to hear it." He took a big bite of a crusty drumstick and rubbed his stomach dramatically. "Can we not talk about Charlie? This is great chicken."

She spooned some baked beans onto his plate. "Eat up. There's plenty."

He handed her a plate. "I'm happy to share."

He wanted to ask her about what Charlie had said

about her aunt's medical bills, but he didn't want to ruin the mood. It made him question what he knew about her marriage to Sven, but maybe in the long run, it was none of his business.

So they ate and talked about nothing in particular.

A few yards away, they could see Lizzie and Matthew Long surrounded by friends and family celebrating the couple's wedding. The two of them seemed deliriously happy. And they'd done that, he thought proudly. Together he and Irene had pulled off a wedding. He could understand the satisfaction Irene got from her new business and it had been fun to be a part of it. Not that he'd want to play Elvis again anytime soon.

In the other direction he saw Lily Porter surrounded by family, too. She was looking very patriotic, wearing a red shirt with a navy-blue skirt. On her head was a red, white, and blue sun hat. She'd introduced him to her daughter Katie and her son-in-law Dan earlier in the day. They'd driven in from Houston to spend the day with her. Her eyes twinkled when she'd introduced her granddaughters, Jenny and Jill, too. They were obviously the light of her life.

He looked across the table at Ree. She was so beautiful. Her face had a glow from the hot sun, while her dark hair was pulled back into a ponytail. She looked about eighteen. His chest hurt with a pressure he couldn't identify. What he knew for certain was she'd been the light of his life these past few days. But the discussion they'd had the night before made it clear that this was a last supper of sorts.

Oliver Barton approached their table. Ree's Aunt Jo was on his arm. Theo had heard him invite her to join him after the parade, and she'd agreed. "Afternoon, Mrs. Cornwell. I hate to bother you, but there is a problem with the fireworks," Oliver said.

"What kind of problem?" Irene stood up from the table.

"Don't worry, ma'am. It didn't sound like anything too complicated. Just something about the location. Ian wanted to talk to you and meet with the fire marshal before they moved anything. He said he'd tried to call, but you didn't answer your phone."

Irene pulled her phone from her pocket and saw she'd missed several calls from Ian Morton, the man in charge of making sure the fireworks display went off without a hitch. The volume on the ringer had been turned down. She'd allowed herself to be distracted by Theo and hadn't been taking care of her responsibilities. "Damn. I better go talk to them. Theo, I'm sorry, but I'll call you later."

Theo stood up. "Don't worry. As long as we still meet up for fireworks."

"I wouldn't miss it." She smiled and hurried off to the parking lot.

"Oliver, Aunt Jo, would you like to join me for some chicken? There's plenty, and I can testify it's delicious. I'd really enjoy the company."

"We'd like that if you don't mind," Oliver said.

Aunt Jo smiled and sat down. "My Irene sure can cook."

"She sure can." Theo's phone rang. Jake was calling to see if he wanted to join them for the fireworks display unless he had other plans. They had a spot staked out, and Sadie was anxious to see him. Jake said Marla Jean told him to add that part as an added enticement.

He told Jake he'd love to. He said he'd be bringing

Irene, and they'd see them shortly. He got off the phone and invited Oliver and Aunt Jo to join them, too. It was turning into a real party.

• • •

After her meeting with the fire marshal, Irene had stopped by her house to get ready for watching the fireworks that night. Theo called, telling her where they were meeting Jake and Marla Jean. She was so pleased that he'd invited her aunt and Oliver, too. There had been many years when Irene had watched them alone from her house up on the hill. She hadn't felt like part of the community and had kept to herself on the holiday. But this year things were different. Today made her realize how many lives she'd touched personally. Not as an extension of Sven. This new relationship with her aunt was an added bonus. Even the change in her relationship with Charlie was a good thing. It sounded like she might have to set him straight when it came to boundaries, but for now she wasn't worried about Charlie.

She took a look around the house Sven had built for her. They'd been married less than a year before his health issues became more serious. A few months when he'd taken her to parties where she'd served as arm decoration. A few months where he'd introduced her to the foundation and taught her the basics. She'd returned to college full-time working on her degree while he spent his days golfing.

He'd paid her aunt's medical expenses through her employer, making certain she didn't know where the money really came from. And except for a short kiss during the wedding ceremony, the marriage had been completely platonic. Sven never made any sexual advances. In fact, he made it clear when he'd asked for her hand that he had no such expectations. But he'd known about his heart condition. And he'd known his time was limited. He didn't want to be alone in a hospital for his final days. Or at home with some hired nurse as his only companion. It had been a trade-off they'd both found beneficial.

Toward the end she's spent hours reading to him. He particularly enjoyed Louis L'Amour westerns and Raymond Chandler mysteries. She discovered that she looked forward to their discussions. When it became clear he didn't have much time left, she'd told him she was calling Charlie. He objected, but she'd told him it should be Charlie's choice to see his father before he died. Sven finally agreed.

Father and son had spent his last days together making some amends, coming to some understandings, while Irene stayed in the background unless Sven asked for her. When he died, Irene had cried like her heart was broken, because it was. He'd been a father figure and a friend who supported her unconditionally. But he'd never been a husband or a lover. So she had cried for all she'd lost. And somewhere in those tears, she had cried for Theo, too.

Chapter Twenty-Eight

Theo met her at her car and helped her carry blankets and an extra cooler to the spot they'd share with Jake and Marla Jean. She was pleased to see Oliver and her aunt already there. As an added bonus her cousins Bonnie and Carrie were there, as well. Everyone sat on folding chairs in the meadow on the east side of the park. It faced the hill Irene lived on and would be the perfect spot for watching fireworks. The night air was warm, but a nice breeze made it comfortable for sitting outside. The city orchestra tuned up, ready to play live music accompanying the display.

"Grab a chair," Marla Jean said in welcome. Jake stood and took the cooler and blankets from Theo. Sadie barked and pranced around, happy to see them.

Her cousins had come down from Dallas to spend the rest of the weekend with their mother. They stood up as she approached and hugged her. "Thanks for inviting us, Irene. Mom said she had a great time riding in the parade this morning."

"Did she tell you we won third place?" Irene couldn't believe they were actually there. She'd invited them on different occasions, but they always had an excuse. "Bonnie, Carrie, you know you are always welcome. Have you met everyone?"

"Everyone except this guy. You must be Theo." Bonnie wasn't shy.

"Nice to meet you," he said, grinning as they arranged chairs.

"Aunt Jo. I see you came prepared."

The quilt spread out in front of her aunt was covered with a cooler of drinks and snacks. In her lap she held mosquito spray, an umbrella, an ice pack, and Chap Stick for her lips. "I like to be ready for anything. I brought lots of food since you missed lunch."

Irene sat. "Thanks, I am hungry."

"And I made cookies. Your favorite, peanut butter bars."

Irene realized she was starving. "Yum, I haven't had those in forever."

"Well, help yourself. Eat something before someone else needs your help with something."

Irene got a ham sandwich out of her aunt's basket. "I don't plan to move from this spot for the rest of the night." She smiled at Theo and settled in.

The band started playing a medley of movie musical songs. Irene smiled as her aunt hummed along. Bonnie and Carrie filled her in on what had been going on in their lives. Irene relaxed and let their voices wash over her. She remembered a few times like this in years past when they'd sat around her aunt's kitchen talking and laughing. In those moments she'd almost felt like a true part of the family. She reached for Theo's hand and he squeezed it. Marla Jean leaned her head against Jake's shoulder and hummed along with the music. It all felt so perfect that Irene was afraid to breathe.

The orchestra moved into "God Bless America," and the crowd stood as one and sang along. It was almost dark. Before long the pyrotechnic display would begin. Sadie woofed at Theo, and he got out of his chair so he could wrestle around with her on the grass.

Charlie wandered up to the quilt and stopped with his hands in his pockets. "Good evening, Irene. Everyone."

Irene felt bad that she hadn't thought to invite him to join them earlier. He didn't know many people in town yet. "Hello, Charlie. You've met my aunt Jo, haven't you? And these are my cousins Bonnie and Carrie."

He said hello.

"And have you met Jake and Marla Jean? Theo's brother and his wife."

Aunt Jo invited him to join them, and he found an empty place on the blanket. Sitting cross-legged he turned to Irene. "Except for that mess of a parade, this has been a nice celebration, Irene. Dad would be proud."

Irene heard her aunt make a sniffing noise at the mention of Charlie's father. She hoped she wouldn't say anything about her feelings for Sven. Her aunt felt strongly about good manners, so Irene hoped that would save the day.

"Who is your dad, Charlie?" Carrie asked.

Oh, dear, Irene realized too late her cousins didn't know Charlie was Sven's son.

Charlie turned toward Carrie with a big smile. "I'm sorry. I should have introduced myself more thoroughly. My father was Sven Cornwell, Irene's late husband."

Silence fell over the group as the two women examined him like he'd crawled out of a test tube. Charlie tried to revive the conversation. "I was saying he would have been proud of the job Irene did with today's celebration."

"You mean her float? Irene just said they won the third-place ribbon," Bonnie said.

"And Mom said Theo made a great Elvis, too." Carrie smiled at Theo.

Charlie shook his head. "Yes, her float was great, but that's not all your cousin does for this celebration."

Irene tried to shush him. "Charlie, really. We don't need to go into all that."

"Don't be modest. Your cousin's foundation helps fund this whole shebang, including the fireworks we are about to watch."

"She does? You do?" They looked impressed.

"Why didn't we know that?" Bonnie asked.

Her aunt spoke up, saying, "It's not really her money."

Charlie looked taken off guard. "Of course it's her money."

"She didn't earn it. Not like the money from her wedding planning business." Her aunt sounded like the entire subject was offensive. "Now that's something she can hold her head up about."

Charlie stood up, brushing off his pants. "I'd think you'd be more appreciative since that money she didn't earn paid for your medical bills."

Bonnie gasped. "What? Irene, is that true?"

"Charlie, hush. Aunt Jo, I'm sorry. I didn't want you to find out." She glanced at Theo. He was looking at her with concern.

Her aunt's face paled, and she announced quietly,

"Bonnie, I'd like to go home, now." They rose, helping their mother to gather her belongings. Oliver stood up and offered to help carry things, too.

"Please don't leave. I'd like to explain." Irene wanted to run after her and make her understand.

"We'll talk tomorrow, Irene. It seems I owe you and Mr. Cornwell my life, but I need some time to process things."

Carrie shot Irene an apologetic look and said, "Come on, Mama." They walked across the meadow toward the parking lot.

Charlie seemed genuinely upset. Once they were gone he said, "She didn't know? I'm sorry, Irene. I just thought she seemed ungrateful, and it bothered me."

Irene buried her face in her hands as the fireworks started exploding in the night sky high above them. She didn't want to talk to Charlie about this. She didn't want to talk to anyone. "Just watch the fireworks, Charlie."

"That's okay. I've made a mess of things, and I'm sorry. I'll get out of here so you folks can enjoy the evening."

They all sat in silence as he left.

Theo leaned over and whispered, "I'm sorry, Ree. Are you okay?"

"I'll be fine. I guess you'd like an explanation, too."

"Don't worry about me right now." His smile was sincere.

"Thanks, Theo."

Another explosion lit up the dark sky. They sat in their chairs and listened to the crowd ooh and ah. It was one of the best displays yet, but Irene thought the day couldn't end soon enough. It built to a crescendo as the music accompanied each explosion. Then finally the display came to an end with an extended succession of loud booms, kapows, and bright crackling lights. The crowd applauded and another Fourth of July celebration was over.

Irene stood up and started gathering her things. "Theo, if you don't mind, I'd like to go home now. I'm sorry, but I won't be very good company until I sort this out with my aunt."

He stood up, too. "That's okay. It's been a really long day already. Don't worry about the cooler. I'll get it to you later."

She kissed him on the cheek. "Thanks for understanding."

Theo stood watching her walk away.

The rest of the group was going to sit and wait for the crowds to thin out before trying to leave. The orchestra kept playing for another hour just to entertain the lingerers. Marla Jean broke out lemonade and poured each of them a glass. "Is she okay?" Marla Jean asked, handing him his lemonade.

Theo sat back down. "I hope so. Her aunt means a lot to her."

Marla Jean patted him on the back. "I hope so, too. I've really come to like her."

Jake was throwing a ball with Sadie. "That sounded like some heavy stuff."

Theo sighed. "Yeah. Stuff she's carried by herself for a long time now."

"Let us know if we can help," Marla Jean said.

"Hey, Theo. Once the traffic clears, Marla Jean is going to take Sadie home, but I'm on park cleaning duty. I could use your help."

"Might as well. I never thought about who cleaned up after the crowd leaves."

"In a small town like Everson, we all have to chip in to help. Most people clean up after themselves, but there is always plenty of trash to pick up."

"Then I'm happy to help, bro."

They got Marla Jean and Sadie into the car and met the other volunteers at the bandstand where Bertie Harcourt was handing out trash bags and trash sticker poles. "All right, folks, let's get this place cleaned up so we can go home. It's been a long day."

Theo couldn't stop worrying about Irene as he worked alongside Jake. They each had a bag for trash and a bag for lost and found. They made good progress when he noticed a rumbling moving through the workers.

"Fire!" a panicked voice shouted. He noticed people were pointing, and he followed their outstretched fingers to see what they were yelling about.

"Where is it?" another voice asked loudly.

"Fire, there's a fire up on the hill."

Theo heart jumped to his throat as his eyes scanned the hill. "Jake, that's Irene's house." He threw down his bags and started running. He could hear his brother's footsteps right on his heels. Jake caught him and said, "Give me the keys. I'll drive."

Theo didn't argue. He threw Jake the keys, and they climbed into the Jeep. Theo had his phone out and called 911 reporting the blaze even as they climbed the hill toward it. Then he was dialing Irene's number, praying she'd answer.

• • •

Irene left the fireworks with Charlie's apologies ringing in her ears. It wasn't his fault. She'd been so full of secrets that she'd known one of them would eventually bite her in the butt. And today was that day. She should have stayed and helped with cleanup, but this was one time she was going to play the privilege card and go home. She drove her Shelby up the hill, planning on going to bed right away.

Tonight she'd bury her head in her pillows because tomorrow she would have to deal with her aunt. She knew her pride would be wounded, and Irene admitted she'd handled it badly. She parked in the rear driveway and let herself in the back door. Without turning on the lights, she dropped her keys in her purse and left it on the kitchen counter before walking down the hallway to her bedroom. She took a quick shower to wash away the day's grime, put on a T-shirt and loose shorts, and fell into bed without drying her hair.

Even though her mind was churning in all sorts of directions, she fell asleep and dreamed she was running, trying to lift Theo's airplane into the air by a rope like a kite but it stubbornly wouldn't budge from the ground.

Chapter Twenty-Nine

Irene's eyes felt glued shut, but the sound of sirens grew louder and closer. She finally sat up in bed, deciding she wasn't dreaming. The air burned her lungs, and she coughed as she climbed off the bed and stumbled to the door. It wasn't hot to the touch, but she could smell smoke and the acrid odor filled her nose and throat.

She ran to the bathroom and wet a towel, placing it over her head before making her way down the hallway and to the kitchen. She stopped long enough to grab her purse from the counter despite all the warnings not to gather valuables in case of a house fire. The nightmare she'd face replacing everything in her purse was too much to consider, and it was sitting right in front of her. Then she opened the door leading out to the back patio and was horrified to see flames leaping from her roof. Oh, God. Her heart was pounding, and she couldn't get a deep breath. She heard the sirens, but she couldn't think straight. Were they coming here? Did she need to call for help?

Panicked, she ran around to the front of the house, her

bare feet sliding on the thick grass. Then she remembered Charlie. Was he inside? She'd gone to straight to bed when she got home and hadn't heard him come in.

"Charlie!" she screamed. She ran around to his bedroom and tried to get close to the window, but a hedge of large bushes blocked the way. She found a rock and hurled it against the window pane. It bounced ineffectively off the double-paned glass and fell to the ground. "Charlie. Are you in there? Answer me, Charlie." She could hear the fire truck getting closer, but she didn't know if she could wait. The whole roof was in flames now.

She could see the flashing lights moving up the hill and ran to meet them at the front driveway. Theo and Jake pulled up behind them, and they raced toward her from the Jeep. She hurled herself at Theo, collapsing in his arms.

"Charlie," she sobbed. "I don't know if he's inside."

Theo fell to the ground holding her, his voice soothing and filled with dangerous emotion. "Thank God, you're okay, Ree. Thank God."

She clutched his shirt at first, but then let her arms snake around his neck, and she let his strength carry her through the moment. She didn't even try to pretend Theo wasn't the person she needed right then.

Jake squatted beside them. "I'll let the firemen know about Charlie. If he's inside, they'll get him out. Hang on, Irene."

The firemen got the water trained on the house, while Theo and Irene sat huddled together in the front yard. A team of men did an inside sweep of the house and didn't find anyone else inside.

It seemed like hours later that the firemen loaded up

their equipment and left. A couple of volunteers from the local Red Cross showed up, offering blankets and coupons for a free stay at a local hotel. Jake declared that they would both come home with him. He'd spoken to Marla Jean, and she insisted as well.

Irene was too numb to argue. She was barefoot wrapped in a blanket, wearing only pajamas underneath, and the thought of Marla Jean's company sounded comforting. All she had was her purse with her car keys inside, but she was in no shape to drive her car. And Jake didn't look like he was in the mood to take no for an answer.

A car screeched to a halt at the end of the driveway, and Charlie came running up. "What happened? Holy cow! The house! Oh my God, did it burn down? Jeez, Irene, are you okay?"

She got to her feet. "I'm fine, Charlie. But your father's house. I'm afraid it's gone."

"Who cares about the house if you're okay? I don't believe this." He ran a hand through his hair.

The Red Cross lady approached him. "Do you live here, too, sir?"

He stared at the smoking ruin. "I did. Temporarily."

"Well, if you follow me, I can offer you a voucher for a free night at a local hotel."

Charlie nodded. "Okay, sure. Are you going to be all right, Irene?"

Jake stepped up. "She'll be fine. I'm going to take her home and let Marla Jean mother her."

Charlie turned and looked at the house once more. "Okay, that sounds like a good idea."

"What about you, Charlie? Do you need a place to bunk?" Jake asked.

"Thanks, but I'll go to the hotel. Do they know what caused the fire?"

Irene shook her head. "Right now, they suspect fireworks, but they have to do an inspection. We'll talk tomorrow, okay?"

He squeezed her arm. "Yeah, try to get some rest if you can."

Jake took charge, hustling her and Theo over to the Jeep. Then he drove them down the hill, through town, and out to his house. Marla Jean met them at the door with hugs and a big robe. She hustled Irene off to the shower where she stood for what seemed like hours letting the hot water wash the smoke and grime from her hair and skin.

She put on some clean pajamas borrowed from Marla Jean and then wrapped herself in the robe. Walking out, she found everyone sitting around the kitchen table. Sadie came over and licked her hand.

"Hey, girl." Irene sank down and buried her face in her soft fur. "Such a good girl."

"Coffee?" Marla Jean asked. Everyone at the table had a cup.

"Sure." She sat down, and Sadie curled up under the table. "I don't think anything will keep me awake once I lay down tonight."

Marla Jean clucked sympathetically. "Just say the word, and you can go to bed whenever you want, sweetie. You must be exhausted."

"I am, but I think tomorrow will be worse. The captain said the house wasn't a total loss, so he seemed to think there would be plenty to salvage. Once I get the okay, I have to get inside and see what's worth saving."

Jake said knowingly, "You can hire companies to do that. They specialize in cleaning things with smoke damage. I used one when we did the remodel after the Miller fire."

She shrugged. "Thanks. I'll look into that."

Theo was quiet, holding on to his coffee mug like it was the only thing anchoring him to earth. His jaw was set and his smile was tight when he looked at her.

"Theo, I want to thank you and Jake for showing up when you did." She sounded formal and overly polite to her own ears. "I was about to come out of my skin not knowing what to do."

Theo finally spoke up, "We'll help you get through the rest of this, too. You aren't alone, Ree. You know that, right?"

She nodded.

Marla Jean brought the coffeepot and an extra mug to the table. "Of course she does. Tomorrow we'll make a list of to-dos, starting with calling your insurance company and getting things under way."

Irene rubbed a hand across her face. "Oh, good gosh, insurance. Yes, I'll need to talk to them and the foundation's board, too. I'll have to let them know what's happened. And then I'll need to find a place to stay while I rebuild, and oh yeah, I'll need to call my aunt." Aunt Jo. They had so much to talk about already, and now this had to happen, complicating everything.

Theo put his hand on top of hers. "Slow down, Ree. Just take it one step at a time."

Marla Jean sat a mug in front of her. "Theo's right. You can stay here until you find a place. There's no hurry. Jake might even have a house you could use."

"Really?" She looked at Jake who nodded. "Oh, gosh, that would be great. Thank you so much. I'd pay rent." Irene closed her eyes, thankful for the generosity, but Marla Jean was wrong. There was a really big hurry. A hurry to get things back to normal. A hurry to fix things.

"You're out on your feet, Ree," Theo said as he helped her up from the table. "Where should I put her, Marla Jean?"

Marla Jean jumped up and led them down the hall to the back bedroom. "Are you going to tuck her in, Theo?"

"Yeah, thanks, Marla Jean. For everything."

"Good night." She enveloped them in a group hug and then disappeared back down the hall.

Theo walked over and pulled back the comforter and the sheet on the bed. He plumped up the pillow and held out his hand. "Come on, Ree. Get under the covers."

She walked to the bed and said, "Thanks, Theo. You were wonderful tonight. You all were, but I can take it from here."

Theo didn't move. "You can, but you aren't. I'm tucking you in like I promised Marla Jean. Then I'm going to sit in that chair in the corner until you fall asleep."

She relented, getting under the sheet, letting him draw it up over her chest. "What are you going to do then?"

He perched on the edge of the bed and smoothed her hair from her face. She leaned in, savoring the feel of his big wide hand on her skin. "I might sit and watch you sleep. Just for a while. You scared the hell out of me tonight." His stormy blue eyes reflected the dark nature of his concern. Concern that cradled her now when she needed it most.

"I'm sorry, Theo." She hadn't meant to scare anyone. She'd been scared, too.

"Ah, Ree. Don't be sorry. When I saw those flames, I

couldn't catch my breath. Just let me stay close for a little while—just until I can breathe again."

She smiled at him sleepily, taking comfort in the heat radiating from his body. "I'd like that, Theo."

He leaned down and kissed her on the cheek. "Good night, then."

She closed her eyes and whispered, "Good night."

She felt him move off the bed, heard him settle in the chair, and knowing he was there, drifted off to sleep.

• • •

Theo woke with a crick in his neck. He straightened up in the upholstered chair in the corner of the guest room and looked over at the bed. Ree was still sleeping, her chest rising and falling in a quiet rhythm. She'd kicked off the covers, revealing her long legs, and her dark hair was a tangled mess against the white pillowcase. She looked beautiful.

So he wouldn't wake her, he rose gently, leaving the room on his tiptoes. He needed a shower and a shave and some clean clothes. If he left now, he could probably make it to his house and get back before Ree was ready to tackle the day ahead. He didn't know if she wanted or needed his help, but he was going to offer either way.

He'd come to a decision while sitting on that chair, watching her sleep. He'd flown away from her a million times in this lifetime, literally and emotionally. But he was done with that now. Her life had been turned on its head. She had the money to fix it, but money wasn't the answer to everything, and it was still going to take time and hard work to get back on her feet, to return to life as she'd known it. And this time he'd be beside her all the way.

He was going all in. He was making Everson his home,

and he was going to become part of the community. Then once she saw his commitment, maybe she'd be willing to take a second chance on him too. A real chance. Not this temporary truce they'd been playing at. He had things to do. He needed to let Mitch know he wouldn't be coming to Australia. He needed to cancel the sale of his airplane. And after that, when the time was right, he needed to tell Ree how he felt. He ran out to the Jeep and headed for the house on Overbrook Street.

· · ·

Irene sat in Marla Jean and Jake's kitchen drinking coffee, listening to the on-hold music playing on the speaker of her phone. She was on hold with her insurance company. But she didn't mind. Thank goodness she'd grabbed her purse on the way out of the house. Otherwise, her phone would be another thing to add to the list of things she'd lost. The whole morning had been a flurry of phone calls. Some she'd made, but many more she'd received. Half the town of Everson called to express their concern and offer their help. The outpouring of sympathy had been nothing short of remarkable. Incredible. Irene had been completely overwhelmed.

She'd slept late and woken up to an empty house. Even Sadie was gone.

A note on the kitchen table from Marla Jean said she had to get to the barbershop. It also said Jake had a meeting with a client, but he was also going to find a house she could use. The note ended saying they'd be home for lunch. It was signed with X's and O's, making Irene smile. She'd also left a pair of jeans, a T-shirt, and a pair of flip-flops for her to wear. Irene got dressed in Marla Jean's clothes feeling coddled and cared for. She also realized she was going to have to buy a whole new wardrobe.

When she'd opened her eyes that morning, she'd been confused. Why wasn't she in her own bed? That moment of disorientation quickly dissolved into a flood of reality. Damn. Her house had burned down last night. And she was at Jake and Marla Jean's house. Theo had put her to bed and slept in the chair in the corner. But the chair by her bed had been empty when she'd woken up. Theo must have finally gone home, and he hadn't left a note.

She jumped when the insurance clerk finally came on the line and told her what she needed to do to file a claim. She promised to e-mail the forms required to get the process under way. Irene hung up and checked another thing off her list.

She needed to get out to the house and take a look at it in the light of day, but she didn't have her car. There was a knock on the front door, and she answered it, finding Theo standing on the front porch.

His smile was gentle. "Hey, Ree. When I left, you were still asleep."

She was so happy to see him. The urge to grab him and hold him was strong, but she didn't. She was afraid she might not ever let go. Instead she asked, "Can you give me a ride to my house?"

He walked inside. "Sure. Whatever you need, Ree. I'm here to help however I can."

"Thanks, you're a lifesaver, Theo. I've done as much as I can on the phone. Now it's time to get back up there and face what's left of the house."

He waited while she grabbed her purse. "Let's go, then."

They drove up the hill, and Irene couldn't sit still. She tried to imagine what was left of the house. Last night it had been too dark to see anything. She held her breath as it came into sight. The charred ruins sat atop the hill like a burnt-out crown. She took a deep breath and got out of the car. "It looks like it's time to get to work."

Chapter Thirty

〜

The following days turned into a flurry of activity. Irene rented a house from Jake on the edge of town. She offered to buy it so he wouldn't lose money, but he wouldn't hear of it. She bought a new bed, but furnished the rest of the house with secondhand stuff. Just enough to function temporarily. It reminded her of the house on Overbrook Street where Theo lived. It was a house, not a home.

She'd finally gotten the all clear to salvage what she could from the house, and at the same time, she'd gotten word that it needed to be done quickly since demolition couldn't begin until that job was completed. It was a daunting task, but it had to be faced. She'd driven up the hill in her Shelby to her house, dreading the work ahead. Every single thing was covered in soot or was soggy from water damage. It was hard to know where to start.

Irene stood on what was left of the front porch, looking down at the town of Everson. The town had truly become her home. The sound of cars approaching the house drew her attention to the road, and she was startled to see a line of cars stretching halfway down the hill.

Theo was in the first car, followed by Jake and Marla Jean.

She rushed to meet him. "Theo? What's going on?"

Theo pushed his cowboy hat up to the top of his head. "I stopped at the diner this morning and mentioned I was on my way here. Before I knew it, we had a whole caravan. Isn't it something?"

Irene clutched her hands to her chest. "It's unbelievable."

More cars parked, and it seemed like half the town piled out of cars and trucks.

Bertie Harcourt walked over hauling empty boxes. "Hey, Irene. We're here to help. Tell us what you need us to do."

She let out a nervous laugh. "I'm not sure."

Bertie was followed by her daughter Nell. Nell carried boxes of bottled water and trays of wrapped sandwiches. "Irene, I'd like to help, too. All these people are going to be hungry. I hope this helps."

"Thanks, Bertie. Nell, I'm touched." Irene looked around at all the townsfolk showing up to help. Showing up for her.

Nell ducked her head. "Nonsense. Everson folks help our own."

Without another word the two women took charge. Assigning people areas to search and providing boxes to place items that looked like they could be saved. Hoot and Dooley showed up with their wives. Etta and Donny Joe came, too. Marla Jean's parents got out of their car with a box of heavy gloves, handing them out to the volunteers.

Irene couldn't believe it. Whole families she'd planned weddings for came in vans. And Charlie arrived, saying he figured he better lend a hand, too. Irene greeted them all, thanking them and promising to find a way to repay their kindness.

Before long everyone was working, pulling things from the ashes, piling trash in one corner of the lot. She kept pausing in the middle of work just to look around and marvel.

She was digging though the remains of her closet when Theo called out to her.

"Ree, look." He stood up and pointed to the front of the house.

Just when Irene thought she couldn't be any more surprised, she looked up and saw a giant beige Buick drive up, park, and then her aunt Jo and cousins got out. They were dressed in matching overalls and sporting kerchiefs on their heads. Irene hadn't had a conversation with her aunt since the Fourth of July. But she'd called Bonnie and left a message on her voice mail.

Irene got up from the pile of clothes she was sorting through and walked over to her relatives. "Aunt Jo. What are you doing here?"

"Where else would we be, girl? You need our help, so here we are." Her aunt opened her arms wide, inviting her for a hug, and Irene melted into her embrace. Her cousins joined in, and soon they were all laughing and crying.

"I'm so happy you're here. You don't know what it means to me."

"You've always taken care of us, Irene. More than your share."

"Aunt Jo, about Sven."

Her aunt waved her hand. "We'll talk about all that later. It doesn't matter a fig anymore. Let's get busy."

Someone turned on their radio to an oldies rock-and-roll station and the gathering of people worked all morning. They took a lunch break, devoured the sandwiches Nell and Bertie supplied, and then got back to work. By early afternoon they'd done a thorough search of the house, compiling boxes and boxes of things that could possibly be saved. Theo instructed everyone to stack them in the back of his Jeep and Jake's pickup truck for transporting them down the hill. Irene personally hugged every single person who'd pitched in that day. Twice. Some of them three times.

Hoot and Dooley folded her up in big bear hugs. "We all care about you, missy." Their wives Linda and Maude extended invitations to dinner as they walked to their car.

"That would be nice, thanks." She laughed. She couldn't possibly make it to all the dinners she'd been invited to. On top of that, the small freezer on her refrigerator was bulging with casseroles from concerned neighbors.

Charlie wandered up carrying some photos of his dad he'd found in the rubble. "Can I have these? I'll get them cleaned up and make copies."

"Of course you can, Charlie. I'd like that. Thanks."

Her aunt and cousins made her promise to let her know what else they could do to help. "Believe it or not, I'm in the middle of planning another wedding. I know I'll need your help with that, Aunt Jo."

"You've got it, girly." Her aunt hugged her tightly.

Bonnie smiled. "Thanks for what you did for Mom."

"It wasn't me. Sven paid her bills because he was a good man, and I wouldn't trade the time I had with him

for anything." Irene was glad things were out in the
open now.

Aunt Jo had tears in her eyes. "I was wrong about you
and Sven. And I'm sorry.

They all hugged again. "I love you all very much."

Carrie smiled and got them all in the car, and they
drove off down the hill waving. A wave of contentment
washed over Irene even while she stood at the edge of the
ruins that had been her home.

After everyone left, Theo lingered. His face was covered with soot, and she imagined hers was, too. He'd
never looked more handsome. He took off the gloves he'd
been wearing to move broken glass and other hazards and
wiped his forehead with the back of his wrist. "We got a
lot accomplished today."

"Thanks to all the help. I never imagined such a thing,
Theo."

"It was pretty remarkable." He squinted up at the hot
summer sun before looking over at her. "Have you picked
a builder yet? What kind of time frame are they giving
you for rebuilding?"

She wondered if that was his way of asking how soon
he could be moving on. Poor Theo wouldn't leave until he
was sure she was okay. "I've talked to some builders, even
started drawing up some plans, but the more I think about
it, the more I'm not sure I want to rebuild."

He put his hands on his hips. "What? Why wouldn't you?"

She looked around and shrugged. "I don't know if I
want to live here anymore."

Theo seemed confused. "Where would you like to live?"

She pointed down the hill. "Down there in the middle
of everything."

Theo squatted down on his haunches, staring down at the town below. "It's a nice place to land."

"I'll think of it as a new adventure," she said, her eyes gleaming with anticipation.

He studied her closely. "Do tell. I have my next adventure planned, too."

"I know. Australia, right?"

He shook his head. "There's been a change in plans."

"Really? Let me guess. South America. Timbuktu?"

"I'm not traveling so far this time." He stood up and faced her, his eyes saying more than his words.

She felt something fragile dislodge from her beating heart. "So, fill me in, Theo."

He widened his stance, placing both feet firmly on the ground. "I'm staying right here in Everson. I'm going to buy that house on Overbrook Street and work for Jake."

She smiled. "So, he talked you into it? He must be thrilled."

Theo shook his head. "He doesn't even know about it yet."

"Why not?" she asked cautiously.

He met her gaze head-on. "I wanted to tell you first."

"Me? If this is about the house fire, you don't have to worry about me, Theo. I'll be just fine."

"I know that. You're one of the strongest people I know." He wiped a smudge from her cheek. "I'm not staying because you need me."

She smiled at the faith he had in her. "Then why?"

"Because, Ree, I need you." His voice was strong and sure, riding over her like a steady breeze. "I want you to understand I'm here for the long haul. That's all."

Irene felt some weight lift and drift away. "That's all?"

"For now." His smile was playful, and his eyes danced with promise.

She studied him thoughtfully. Theo staying in one place? How long would it be before he had to fight the urge to move on? She'd been busy conjuring up the courage to tell him good-bye with a smile on her face, and now this. "That will take some getting used to. I've convinced myself you're only a fleeting part of my life—someone that might pass through on rare occasions."

He grew serious. "I know. And I'm used to thinking of you as someone I used to know. Someone that's always a safe distance away."

She acknowledged his admission with a nod. "I guess we'll both have some adjusting to do, then."

"I guess we do," he agreed readily. "But since we'll be living in the same town, I wanted to warn you that I'll be looking to court you."

A bark of laughter broke from deep in her chest. "Court me?"

He grinned, seeming pleased with himself. "I'm not asking you to go steady or anything. Just give me the time of day when we pass on the street. Maybe let me take you out sometime."

She arched a brow, leaning toward him. "So, you'll be dating other women?"

He shrugged. "No, but you should feel free to see other men if you'd like."

She knitted her brows. "You want me to see other men?"

"Hell, no, but it didn't seem right for me to move to town and start making demands right off the bat."

She let out a deep sigh. "Theo. What am I going to do with you?"

"That's a dangerous question." He moved closer.

"Why?" She ran her hand down his arm.

He let out a low growl. "I'm trying to pace myself."

She smiled. "Pretend you don't have to. What kinds of demands would you make?"

He grinned. "Not demands. Requests. Desires."

She moved until she was standing so close their clothes brushed against each other. "Desires? Oh, I like that."

"Well, in that case I might ask for a kiss. Maybe two." He leaned down and stole two quick kisses, his lips barely brushing hers. "And then I might confess that I haven't slept a full night since you were in my bed."

"I'm sorry—"

"Don't interrupt, woman. I'm explaining how you drive me out of my mind."

Her hand wandered to his chest. "I do?"

His voice was rough. "You know you do. But I plan to wear you down until you can't resist me any longer."

She played with a button on his shirt. "How are you going to do that?"

He shrugged, but his smile was wicked. "The usual. Dinner, dancing, movies, strip Scrabble. Oh, and if you're nice, I'll take you flying, too."

"With or without your plane?"

He laughed. "Maybe I'll skip all the preliminaries and just ask you to marry me."

She grew still. "What? Theo? Are you crazy?"

He moved away and held up both hands. "Too much, too soon? Okay. I jumped the gun. I knew I should have paced myself." His eyes twinkled with mischief.

She knew he wasn't one bit sorry, but she couldn't keep the smile from her face. "I think that's a good idea."

He leaned down until they were nose to nose. "Kissing you again sounds like a good idea, too." He wrapped her up, and she met him halfway, kissing him like he was a sunny day at the beach.

He pulled away reluctantly. "I better go," he said softly. "I smell like the inside of an ashtray, and I could use a shower."

She wrinkled her nose and brushed a lock of hair from his forehead. "Thanks for everything, Theo. You can bring the boxes by whenever it's convenient."

"I'll call. Are you okay up here alone?"

"Yeah. I'll be leaving in a minute."

Theo tapped her on the nose with his finger and started walking to the Jeep.

"Hey, Theo?"

He turned, the sun washing the planes of his face with golden light. "Yeah?"

"If you're staying here, you should get a dog."

His eyes widened. "You think I need a dog?"

She put her hands out in a helpless gesture. "I think a dog needs you. A good dog like Sadie."

He nodded thoughtfully. "I like that idea."

He started to his car again. When he opened the door, he stopped and said, "Hey, Ree?"

"Yeah?"

"I love you. With all my heart." And just like that, he got inside and drove away.

She put her hands over her heart and spoke to his retreating car, "Oh, Theo, I love you too."

Irene watched him leave and then walked around to the back of the house. She sat down by the swimming pool on a wrought iron bench that survived the fire intact.

She looked around, taking a deep breath and closing her eyes.

"Hey, Sven. You already know this, but I'm in love with Theo. Again. Still. And this time he says he loves me too. I don't think he was completely serious today about marrying me, but he will be soon. The next time he asks, I'll say yes. I wanted you to know that. And by the way, you'd be so proud of Charlie. He's going to make a great head of the board because I'm stepping down. I'll stay involved, but I'm a wedding planner now. I think you would be proud of me, too. And Sven, thank you—for everything."

She got up and climbed into her car, driving down the hill, leaving her home behind for the final time.

Chapter Thirty-One

No one had bothered to tell the universe that her life had exploded. Life had gone on even though her house had burned to the ground, and she had weddings to plan, and an amazing man courted her day and night. Irene spent her days working on a million projects and her nights elbow deep in hot, soapy water, making her way slowly but surely through the boxes of salvaged items from her old house. Theo was there most nights helping. And most nights she invited him to stay over. Most nights he accepted.

They talked about their past, but not as much as they talked about the future. Theo made it clear that Everson was his home now. Besides working for Jake remodeling houses, he'd done some work for the Hazelnut Inn piloting guests to and from Dallas. He was most passionate about the handyman service he'd set up with Jake. They'd had a flood of requests, so many that he'd recruited more townsfolk to help fill the needs. Tonight she'd cooked dinner, and after dinner, they'd tackled another box of her smoky knickknacks.

"I'm done," he declared dramatically. He stepped away from the sink. "My hands are all pruney, and I'm not touching any more soapy water anytime tonight."

"But I still have this collection of ducks that have to be cleaned." She laughed and snapped him with a dish towel.

"Watch it, lady. Don't start something you can't finish."

She tried to get him again with the towel, but he chased her around the kitchen until he had her pinned against the refrigerator. She was breathing heavy when she said, "I let you catch me."

"Is that right?" He nipped her ear.

"That's right. So what are you going to do with me now?" She stuck her wet hands inside his shirt.

He squawked and grabbed her hands, putting them over her head against the fridge. "Throw you back. You're a menace."

"I'll behave now. I promise."

He kissed her, murmuring, "Oh, don't do that." That night he stayed over, too.

• • •

Everyone in town gathered for the grand opening. It had taken nine months but the new senior center was now a reality. It was a celebration high up on the hill looking down on the town of Everson. Irene was going to make a speech. Bands would play happy tunes. There were plaques to reveal and lives to make better.

Irene walked around the grounds of the newly rebuilt structure, greeting people and returning smiles and well wishes. Once she'd decided not to rebuild her house, the idea to use the grounds for a dedicated senior center wouldn't leave her alone. She'd talked to the mayor and

town council, and they'd been enthusiastic about the idea.
With the money from the fund-raising the town had held
the past few years, plus her insurance money, the project
had gotten a green light.

There were game rooms, exercise areas, a reading
library, and computer room, plus a small cafeteria. Donny
Joe had serviced the pool, making sure it could be used
for swimming and aqua classes during the summertime.
A van would pick up patrons and carry them up and down
the hill on a regular schedule.

Mayor Ross Wolfson tapped the microphone as he
stood on the front porch, trying to get everyone's attention. "Ladies and gentlemen. I'm happy to see everyone
here today." A horn honked and the group turned to see
the senior center van pull into the driveway. The door
opened and Lily Porter got off waving. She was followed
by a group of enthusiastic seniors who'd made the maiden
voyage up the hill in the van.

The mayor smiled and waved back. "And now that
our special guests are here, we can get this party started.
Irene Cornwell donated the land for our new center, so
I'm going to invite her up to do the honors for our grand
opening."

Irene smiled and took the giant scissors from Mayor
Wolfson. A red ribbon stretched across the front door
waiting to be cut. "Here's to years of fun and frivolity!"
She cut the ribbon with a great whack, and it fell to the
ground. "Before we go inside, I'd like to reveal the dedi-
cation plaque. As you all know, this land belonged to my
late husband, Sven Cornwell. He loved Everson, Texas,
with a lifelong loyalty, and I know he's pleased to see it
being put to such good use." She pulled off the brown

paper guarding the plaque, and everyone cheered when they read the sign. Lily Porter Senior Center.

More applause and calls for a speech filled the air. Irene looked around for Theo wondering where he could be. The sound of a small airplane overhead had them all looking up. It buzzed the house and dipped a wing in acknowledgment of those below. Irene's heart was in her throat. Why was Theo flying at a time like this? For a moment she wondered if he'd decided to leave. She felt as raw and vulnerable as she had the day he'd seen her lying naked on that float in the pool.

Everyone was pointing now, laughing and sending up cheers. The plane pulled a white banner, and when it turned back toward town, the black letters were easy to read.

Marry me, Ree.

Theo appeared at her side. "Well? Say yes, Ree."

She gasped when she saw him. "Who's flying the plane?"

"Bart. He was happy to help. Quit changing the subject."

She couldn't help teasing him. "Bart wants to marry me?"

"Probably, but I'm the one asking." He got down on one knee. "Will you marry me?"

She thought she might faint from the joy cascading through her bones. "Yes. How soon?"

The crowd hooted their approval.

He wrapped his arms around her, pulling her close. "Pushy, aren't you? I thought right now would be good. All of our friends and family are already here, and Mayor Wolfson has agreed to conduct the ceremony. And I bought a big, flashy ring to go on your finger."

She looked around. It was true. Her aunt was there

along with her cousins. Jake and Marla Jean stood by ready to support Theo. "So, now you're the wedding planner instead of me?"

He tilted his head to one side, a dark curl falling onto his forehead. "Do you have a better idea?"

"I do. You could kiss me."

"In front of all these people?"

She jumped into his arms. "Mayor Wolfson, you'd better hurry and pronounce us man and wife. My future husband appears to be a little shy."

• • •

Theo had planned everything. They were married within the hour in the chapel inside the center. He'd asked Etta to provide a wedding cake and enough appetizers to feed a small army. Everyone agreed that a wedding was the perfect way to open the new center.

Theo felt dazed, lucky, and incredibly happy as they waved good-bye to the crowd. He could hardly believe she'd gone along with the plan. He could have ended up looking like a fool, but instead he was married to the love of his life. At last.

He carried his new bride over the threshold of the house on Overbrook Street and kept walking straight to his super-comfy bed. He threw her on the mattress, kissing her until they were both panting and hungry for more. "Are you sorry you didn't get to plan our wedding?"

She smiled. "You saved me a lot of work. Now let's get to the good part." She attacked the buttons on his shirt, peeling it off his shoulders.

He dragged himself away. "Hold on. I'm waiting for a special delivery."

Her lips were bruised and wet. She pouted, reaching out a hand for him to come back. "What kind of delivery?"

A horn honked outside the house, followed by the doorbell ringing, and a loud thump against the front door. "There it is." He hurried to the door, picked up the bundle from the porch, and hurried back to the bedroom.

"What's that? It doesn't look very special." She looked leery.

He unfurled the banner that had been flying behind the plane, spreading it over the bed, letting it pool onto the floor. "I had this fantasy of you wrapped in this banner with nothing on underneath."

She ran her fingers across the letters, and the look she gave him melted any resolve he had to take things slow. She walked toward him, shedding her dress and kicking off her high heels. "I think I'm still wearing too many clothes, then. And just what are you wearing in this fantasy, Mr. Jacobson?"

"Only you, Mrs. Jacobson. Only you."

After her no-good ex-husband
leaves her for another woman—a
Bookmobile-driving librarian
twenty years her senior—Marla
Jean Bandy vows to move on with
her life. And with childhood crush
Jake, this good girl is ready
to be a little bad...

Please turn this page for
an excerpt from

Ain't Misbehaving.

Chapter One

⟋⟍

"Stop it, Donny Joe."

"Come on, Marla Jean. I thought you wanted to."

An hour earlier she would have agreed with him. An hour earlier she wiggled into her tight red dress, tugged on her favorite cowboy boots, and headed out to the local watering hole sure of exactly what she wanted. An hour earlier she'd left her house with every intention of finding a willing man and having her way with him.

Lately she'd felt dried up, dustier than a ghost town in an old Western movie. The swinging saloon doors of her nether portal were rusted shut from lack of use. In other words, Miss Kitty hadn't seen any action in a long, long time.

And now, because she'd decided to rectify the situation, she, Marla Jean Bandy, found herself sitting in the front seat of a Ford pick-up truck with Donny Joe Ledbetter's hand stuck halfway up her skirt.

But it didn't feel right somehow, and that really pissed her off.

Sex had always been something she'd embraced enthusiastically right up until the moment her husband dumped her for another woman. If he'd dumped her for some young bimbo, it would have been embarrassing and humiliating. She would have been mad, outraged even, but no—Bradley left her for Libby Comstock, the fifty-four-year-old, never-been-married librarian who drove the Bookmobile. She'd started to wonder why he ran out the door like a kid who'd just heard the ice cream truck whenever it turned the corner onto their street. But she'd always told him he should read more, and this was the one time in their six-year marriage he decided to listen to her.

Libby seduced him with the Russian classics, challenging him to stretch his mind and feed his soul. He tackled Dostoevsky, Tolstoy, Brodsky, Pushkin, and eventually he tackled Ms. Comstock, too. The fact that he'd left her for someone twenty years older, frumpier, smarter, and fluent in five languages was something she'd never forgive him for.

But back to Donny Joe. He was a stud. A big fish in a small pond. A lover of all things female, and his ability to make the earth move was heralded far and wide by most every woman in and around Everson, Texas.

So when she decided it was time to get back on the horse, he was the natural choice for her to throw a rope around. He would have no problem with a quickie in the front seat of his truck. A quickie, and then they'd never speak of it again. No complications, no angst, no wounded emotional fallout. So why was she getting cold feet? This was the ideal setup, the perfect no-attachment sex she'd been looking for.

She sighed, a petulant, frustrated sigh. "I'm sorry, Donny Joe, but I think I've changed my mind."

"You're just a little skittish, sugar. We'll take it slow. Why don't we go back inside and slide around the dance floor a few times while I coax you back into the right mood?"

He was placing little nibbles on her neck while he whispered his encouragement. His hand took up a neutral position at the edge of her dress, not moving up, but not giving up all the territory he'd gained, either. She tried closing her eyes, tried to let herself be coaxed, but it wasn't working. She was about to agree to a few dances just to ease her way out of an uncomfortable situation when the door on her side of the truck flew open so abruptly that if Donny Joe hadn't had a good grip on her she would've fallen out on her head.

A dark silhouette loomed at her side, and a deep voice commanded, "Take your hands off her, Donny Joe."

If her life followed any kind of normal, predictable pattern, she would have turned to confront her ex-husband, maybe, or her overprotective big brother, but that was not the case. Abel Jacobson—known by everyone around town as Jake—stood just inside the open door, filling up the space with his broad shoulders, glowering like some avenging angel in a cowboy hat. He reached inside and grabbed her arm. "Come on, Marla Jean, get out of the truck."

Donny Joe tightened his grip around her waist. "Get your own woman, Jake."

"That's what I'm doing, Donny Joe."

They were pulling her in two different directions, fighting over her like a prize piece of salt water taffy. She managed to squirm away from Donny Joe, and then shoved at the hard, stubborn wall of muscle that made up

Jake's chest until she could slide past him and get out of the truck. "I'm not anyone's woman. What's wrong with you two?"

Her too-tight skirt had ridden halfway up her ass, and she struggled to pull it back down to a level that wouldn't get her arrested for indecent exposure. She was fuming while they watched. Donny Joe had a cocky grin on his face, and Jake stood with his arms crossed over his chest, glaring like he wanted to put her over his knee and spank her.

That thought sprang into her head from out of nowhere, accompanied by a vivid image of Jake's big, wide hand on her bare bottom. The restless itch that had driven her out of her house dressed like a hoochie mama—only to desert her before she could find the nerve to scratch it—was suddenly back, stronger than ever. She gave her skirt another tug and glared back at him. If anyone could scratch her itch, it was Jake. But she wanted simple and uncomplicated, and there was nothing simple or uncomplicated about Abel Jacobson.

Donny Joe climbed out of his truck and ambled her way. "I'll be inside Lu Lu's if you change your mind, sugar."

"She won't," Jake called after him pleasantly as he watched Donny Joe head back inside the bar. And then before she could blast him for his caveman act, he rounded on her. "Donny Joe? What the hell were you thinking, Marla Jean?"

"I was thinking I might get lucky, not that it's any of your business, Abel Jacobson." She stuck her nose in the air, and stomped off toward the bar.

"You've never had the sense God gave a goose when it comes to men," he muttered as he followed her across the parking lot.

"Excuse me?" She rounded on him this time, not believing the nerve of the man. "When's the last time you dated a woman who had an IQ higher than her bra size?"

"Why, Marla, I didn't think you cared."

"I don't give two figs about your love life, but I'd love to know what brought on this sudden interest in mine."

She was still scowling at him, but she was also more than a little curious about his answer. Growing up, Jake had been her older brother Lincoln's best friend, but as adults she rarely spoke to him. Of course they exchanged greetings whenever they ran across each other in town, but asking "Hey, how are you?" just to be polite was a long way from dragging her out of another man's truck as if he had every right to do it.

He kicked at a piece of gravel with the toe of his boot. "I got a call from Linc before he left town. He said you hadn't sounded like yourself lately, and he was worried. I said I'd keep an eye on you."

"I don't need watching. And Linc can keep his opinions and his concern to himself."

"Aw, give him a break, Marla. He's been worried since Bradley..." His words trailed off like he wanted to spare her from the awful truth.

"You mean since Bradley dumped me? We've been separated for a year, and the divorce has been final for six months. I'm not going to fall apart at the mention of his name."

"Bradley's an idiot."

"Finally, something we can agree on, but I'm a big girl, and I don't need a keeper." She started walking away, feeling put out all over again.

"Where are you going, Marla Jean?"

"I'm going back inside. I'm going to dance with any man who asks me, and I'm going to have a good time. If that's not okay with you and my big brother, then y'all can both kiss my rosy, pink butt."

The smell of stale beer and the sound of country music poured out of the bar as she jerked the door open and stalked inside. She pushed her way through the crowd, but Jake stayed right on her heels. Stopping abruptly, she turned around to face him. "For the love of Pete, what is it now?"

He tipped up the brim of his hat and asked with a lazy smile, "How 'bout a dance, Marla Jean?"

Chapter Two

Jake kept his smile in place as he watched Marla's eyes first widen, and then narrow at his invitation. Without warning, she grabbed his arm and hauled him out onto the dance floor—not exactly the reaction he'd expected.

"Okay Jake, let's dance. I'll talk. You just move your feet and listen."

"Yes, ma'am." She wouldn't get an argument from him. He pulled her into his arms, and they started two-stepping around the floor. She smiled at everyone like she was having the grandest of times, but Jake wasn't fooled. The tight set of her jaw and the scary vein throbbing in her forehead gave her away.

It certainly wasn't any of his business if Marla Jean Bandy wanted to make out with every cowboy in the place. While they were growing up, she'd been a pesky pain in the backside, always trying to tag along with him and her older brother. Since Linc had been his best friend, Jake had become an honorary big brother by default, teasing her, tolerating her when she was underfoot, and now and then, helping her out of the occasional scrape.

But that was a long time ago. They'd both grown up—gone their separate ways. She'd even gotten married. If it hadn't been for Linc's call he certainly wouldn't have been sticking his nose into her affairs now.

But still, Donny Joe Ledbetter? Maybe Lincoln had good reason to worry.

And Marla Jean. If he was any judge of riled-up women, and he'd seen a few in his time, Marla Jean was mad. Mad enough to spit. But that was okay. She could be mad all she wanted. He wasn't going to let Lincoln down.

"First of all, Jake—"

"Wait a minute, Marla Jean—let me talk first. I want to apologize."

She looked a lot surprised and a tad mollified. "I should think so." They made a half circle around the floor before she tilted her head back and said, "Well, I'm waiting."

"For what?" he asked while leading her into an under-arm turn.

"Your apology?" she reminded him as she followed him in a walk-around step.

"Oh, right. I shouldn't have said you were dumber than a goose." He winked and executed a little spin.

"That's what you're sorry for?"

"Yeah, that was out of line."

"And that's it? If you think—"

"Hold your horses, Marla Jean, I'm not done."

"By all means, continue."

He grew serious. "I apologize for mentioning Bradley."

She ducked her head and studied the feet of the nearby dancers. "I told you not to worry about that."

"I know, but since he left you for my Aunt Libby, I feel somehow responsible." Jake never cared for Bradley Bandy. He certainly didn't deserve a woman like Marla Jean, and now this thing with his aunt had everyone in an uproar. His Aunt Libby, on the other hand, was acting like a cat who'd just discovered heavy cream. It was kind of sweet, in a creepy sort of way. But Marla Jean didn't deserve the pain those two had caused her.

"Jake, whatever went wrong for me and Bradley started a long time before he took up story hour with your aunt."

"Humph," he grunted. "My mother's ready to disown her—says she's disgraced the family."

"Can we not talk about Bradley? I came out to have a good time tonight. I've had it up to here with sitting at home feeling sorry for myself, so I'm turning over a new leaf."

"I noticed."

"And if folks around here don't like it they can—"

"I know. They can kiss your rosy, pink butt."

"Exactly."

"But Donny Joe?"

"Don't start, Jake."

"Donny Joe is exactly the kind of thing Linc was worried about." He twirled her around and dipped her as the song came to an end. When he pulled her back upright, she stumbled against his chest. His arms tightened momentarily, and he stared down into her flashing brown eyes.

Pushing him away, she said, "Look, Jake. Leave it alone. I'll talk to Linc and put his mind at ease. You're off the hook. Okay?"

He knew when it was time to beat a tactical retreat.

"All right, I've done my duty for the night." He held up both hands and took a step back.

"Thank you. And when I talk to Linc, I'll tell him you went above and beyond."

"Well, thanks for the dance." He moved back another step, somehow reluctant to walk away, but Harry Beal marched over and inserted himself between the two of them. Back in school, Harry had been in the same grade with Marla Jean and had grown up to be the high school football coach.

"Hey, Jake. How's it going?" Without waiting for an answer, he turned to Marla. "Can I have the next dance, Marla Jean?"

Marla smiled at Harry like he'd invented butter. "Sure thing, Harry. Later, Jake."

Before he could say "alligator," the two of them waltzed away, leaving him alone in the middle of the dance floor. Jake wandered over to the nearest barstool and sat down. He ordered a beer and swiveled around until he faced the crowd of dancing couples. Marla was laughing at something Harry said—her head thrown back—her dark, curly hair cascading down her back.

Christ A'mighty. That dress.

It was short and tight and nothing but trouble.

In the best of circumstances Marla Jean Bandy, being newly divorced and out on the town, was enough to make most red-blooded men sit up and take notice. Especially in a small town like Everson where available women were few and far between. But Marla Jean Bandy poured into that skimpy getup was like waving a red flag in front of every horny bastard in the joint. No wonder Linc was worried. Telling himself he owed it to Linc to keep an eye on her, he took a long draw on his beer and settled his elbows on the bar behind him. It promised to be a real long night.

• • •

Marla tried to pay attention to Harry and ignore the disturbing fact that Abel Jacobson, of all people, was parked on a bar stool across the way watching her. Harry wasn't much of a dancer, mainly shuffling his feet from side to side, but she made an effort to listen as he rambled on about the football team. "I hate to admit it," she said, "but I haven't been to a game this year, Coach."

"You oughta come this Friday, Marla Jean. If we beat Crossville, we'll make it to play-offs."

That was no secret. The whole town was buzzing about the upcoming game. In Everson, like almost every other town in Texas, Friday night during the fall was football night. While they were married, she and Bradley had never missed a game. But that was then. These days she spent Friday nights alone at home watching her mom's old *JAG* DVDs and painting her toenails. But tonight was supposed to be about taking control of her life back, so she smiled and said, "You're absolutely right, Harry. I'll be there with bells on."

"Great! Maybe after the game we could grab some pizza?"

She wasn't really ready to start dating. At least not nice guys like Harry Beal. She'd known him since junior high. They'd been in the same homeroom from seventh grade on, and he had always been sweet and shy until you got him on the football field. Then he turned into a monster. Harry had gone on to play college ball and even had one season in the NFL before a knee injury ended his pro career. After that he moved back to town and no one was surprised when he'd been hired as Everson High's head coach as soon as there was an opening.

But the idea of getting involved with someone she could come to care for scared the blue dickens out of her. Everyone in town would be at the pizza place after the game though, so it wouldn't really count as a date. "Sounds like fun. We can celebrate your victory with pepperoni and extra cheese."

He grinned like he'd landed a three-foot bass. When the music stopped, she thanked him for the dance, but before she could make it back to her table Greg Tucker asked if he could have the honor.

After that she danced with Johnny Dean, Fergus Barnes, and Tommy Lee Stewart. They flirted, and she flirted back. No big deal. A bunch of small town wannabe Romeos checking out the lay of the land. She was smart enough to know her sudden popularity was born of a burning curiosity about her divorce. They all asked basically the same thing, "How ya holding up, darlin'?" and let her know with a wink and a sashay around the dance floor, they'd be more than happy to help her out if she needed anything at all.

She smiled, said "thanks," and kept on dancing.

That is until she saw Donny Joe headed her way, and she made a beeline for the ladies' room. She wasn't ready to go another round with him, or for that matter, to be reminded of her miserable attempt at playing the loose woman.

She splashed cool water on her flushed face and used her fingers to fluff up her hair. Smiling at her reflection, she realized that despite everything, she was having fun—even if she hadn't managed to get laid.

Even before Jake's interference she'd known she couldn't go through with her plan. Damn it all. It had sounded so simple in theory, but in practice she'd run smack dab into reality. For her, sex was tied up with love, and love wasn't something she was likely to find at Lu Lu's on a Saturday night. Not that she was looking. "Love" was a dirty word as far as she was concerned. So while on one hand, she was right back where she'd started—all alone and frustrated—on the other hand, she'd had a blast dancing her fanny off with every man in the joint, and now she had plans that included football and pizza next Friday night. All in all, it hadn't been a complete waste of time.

Wandering back out into the bar, she decided she was ready to call it a night. Jake still lounged on his barstool, but now Wanda Lee Mabry sat by him on one side and Rhoda Foster sat on the other. Both women seemed to be vying for his attention, making it much easier for her to slip out unnoticed.

Walking over to the corner table she'd claimed earlier in the evening, she searched the area for her purse. It wasn't on the table, and it wasn't on the floor, and if somebody was dumb enough to steal it they wouldn't have gotten anything but her driver's license, a twenty-dollar bill, a tube of Ripe Cherry Red lipstick, a just-in-case condom, and her car keys. At the moment, all she cared about were her car keys.

Then it dawned on her. She remembered touching up her lipstick right before she'd gone outside with Donny Joe and having her purse when she got in his truck. Dagnab-it, she'd bet all the beans in Boston she'd left it on the floorboard of his pick-up. Jake's high-handed meddling had ticked her off so much she hadn't given her purse a second thought when she'd scrambled out of that truck. She looked around the room for Donny Joe but didn't see him. The dance floor was still packed with people, so she stood on her tiptoes to see if she could see his head above the crowd.

Lana and Warren Sanders danced by. "Hey, Marla Jean," they said in unison.

"Hey guys. Have y'all seen Donny Joe?"

"Donny Joe Ledbetter?" Lana asked, not hiding her surprise. "Not lately. Sorry."

"That's okay. Thanks, anyway." She moved on around the room asking if anybody had seen him, but she finally gave up and walked over to the far end of the bar, the end farthest away from where Jake still sat surrounded by women. The bartender spotted her and moved down to her end.

"What'll it be, Marla Jean?" An older man with gray hair pulled back in a ponytail and an eye patch over one eye, Mike Benson was as much a part of Lu Lu's as the gravel parking lot and the odor of stale beer.

"Mike, have you seen Donny Joe? I know he was here a minute ago."

He picked up a bar towel and started polishing glasses. "Yeah, he was dancing with Irene Cornwell, and I saw them leave together."

"How long ago was that?"

"Oh, I don't know. A few minutes, maybe."

"Damn it, I've got to catch him." Hitching up her skirt she took off toward the front door. She burst outside, skidding to a stop on the gravel, and scanned the parking lot for his truck. If she was lucky Donny Joe and Irene would just be going at it like squirrels in his front seat. It wouldn't even bother her to catch them *in flagrante delicto*. She'd ask them to forgive the intrusion, grab her purse, and tell them to carry on. They probably wouldn't even notice.

She hurried toward the place where he'd been parked earlier, but she could see before she got there the spot was empty. Son of a bitch. She couldn't believe this. The sound of a racing engine caught her attention, and she spotted his truck at the far exit getting ready to pull out onto the highway.

"Wait, Donny Joe, come back," she yelled, waving her arms about wildly. Hitching her skirt even higher, she took off at a sprint. If she could just get his attention it would save her a world of trouble in the long run. "Donny Joe, hey, Donny Joe, don't leave yet," she hollered at the top of her lungs, but it was no use. She stumbled to a stop and watched his red taillights recede into the dark night. "Crap, horse feathers, and double doo-doo." Cursing her luck and panting, she stood bent over with her hands braced on her knees, trying to catch her breath.

"For God's sake, Marla Jean, don't chase after the guy. Have some pride."

She whirled around at the sound of Jake's voice. He'd followed her out of the bar, obviously, and now he thought she'd lost her mind.

"You!" She pointed a finger and started marching toward him. A smart man would have shown some concern, but he stood his ground until her finger was poking him in the chest. "This is all your fault, mister."

"My fault?" The idea seemed to amuse him.

"Entirely, altogether, and completely your fault." She crossed her arms and stomped her foot like a bratty kid.

He moved closer and leaned down until they were nose to nose. "You should be down on your knees thanking me, missy. I kept you from making a God-awful mistake with Donny Joe earlier this evening. And now this? You go racing across the parking lot screaming like a banshee when he's got another woman in the truck with him? Come on, Marla Jean. You're obviously not yourself."

For the second time that night she marched across the parking lot with Jake hot on her heels. "At the risk of repeating myself, I'll make all the God-awful mistakes I want. And what I am, you big dolt, is stuck."

"Hold up, Marla Jean—"

"I was chasing after Donny Joe, because thanks to you," she turned to glare at him for emphasis, "I left my purse and my car keys in his truck. If I don't seem properly grateful, you can bite me."

"Does that offer involve your rosy, pink butt?"

She marched on, trying for the umpteenth time that evening to yank her skirt back down where it belonged. "Go to hell."

"Before or after I offer you a ride home?" He stopped by his little yellow Porsche Boxster. "Hop in."

"Yeah, right. I'll go ask Harry Beal for a ride."

"That should make his night. He'll think he's hit the jackpot."

She hesitated. She didn't want to give Harry the wrong impression. "I'll call a cab."

"That'd be a waste of good money, if you had any on you. Just get in the car."

She stopped and let out a strangled groan. "Maybe I'll walk. It's not that far."

"Were you always this stubborn? Let me explain something to you, Marla Jean. I don't care if you call a cab, hitchhike, or crawl on your hands and knees—but I'll be driving right behind you, no matter what."

"Now who's being stubborn?"

He shrugged. "I'm not about to tell Linc that because of me, you walked home from Lu Lu's at eleven-thirty at night."

"Linc's got you on a pretty short leash, doesn't he?"

"I owe Linc a lot, and he never asks for much, so for everyone's sake, please get in the car."

She sighed for what seemed like the millionth time that evening, a world-weary, put-upon sigh, and then stalked over to the car. He opened the door for her and didn't even try to pretend that he wasn't looking at her legs when her skirt rode back up to mid-thigh. She was going to go home and burn the stupid dress in the fireplace. After closing her door, Jake loped around the car, and she watched while he managed to fold his big frame into the compact driver's seat. "Wouldn't you be more comfortable in a bigger car?"

"This isn't a car. She's a beloved member of the family, and she handles like a woman in love." He started the engine and turned to face her. "Marla Jean, meet Lucinda."

"You name your cars?"

"Don't you?" He backed out of the space and headed for the nearest exit.

"Of course not. Well, I did have that clunker in high school we called 'Buck'—for bucket of bolts—but these days I try not to get personally involved with my vehicles."

"Hmm." He looked at her as if her answer gave him some important insight into her character before returning his attention to the road.

After the divorce she'd moved into her parents' old house on Sunnyvale Street. They'd retired a few years back and moved to Padre Island. After that, her brother Lincoln lived there until his recent marriage, and then he moved into his bride's place since it was newer and bigger.

The last thing Marla wanted to do was stay in the house she'd shared with Bradley, and her folks' house was empty, so it seemed like the perfect solution until she could find a place of her own. Sometimes, though, moving back to the house she'd grown up in made her feel like she'd failed her first attempt at being an adult.

It was a short drive home, and since Jake grew up on the same street, he knew the way without being told. She closed her eyes and tried not to think about the man sitting by her side. Even when they were kids, he'd always been able to throw her off balance with a look or a word. Apparently, that hadn't changed.

He pulled into her driveway, and she let him walk her to the door. She figured he'd insist anyway, and she was too tired to argue. On the way up the walkway, she remembered her keys, and the fact that they were spending the night in the floorboard of Donny Joe's truck. Jake seemed to realize the problem at the same time. Without missing a beat, he reached into the third hanging basket from the left and pulled out the spare key—the same place the spare key had been hidden the entire time they'd been growing up.

"It's nice to know some things never change." He unlocked the front door and pushed it open. "If you need any help picking up your car tomorrow, let me know."

"Thanks, but I'll manage." It suddenly felt so familiar to be standing in the dark talking with him on the front porch. He was bigger and taller now, but he was still Jake. "Good night, Jake."

"Good night, Marla Jean." He reached for her hand and pressed the spare key into her palm. "Try to stay out of trouble."

She pulled her hand out of his and resisted the urge to stick out her tongue. "Try to mind your own business."

He laughed and brushed his thumb across her cheek. "You haven't changed, either, Marla Jean."

Before she could ask what that was supposed to mean, he bounded off the porch and was gone.

THE DISH

Where Authors Give You the Inside Scoop

From the desk of Lily Dalton

Dear Reader,

Some people are heroic by nature. They act to help others without thinking. Sometimes at the expense of their own safety. Sometimes without ever considering the consequences. That's just who they are. Especially when it's a friend in need.

We associate these traits with soldiers who risk their lives on a dangerous battlefield to save a fallen comrade. Not because it's their job, but because it's their brother. Or a parent who runs into a busy street to save a child who's wandered into the path of an oncoming car. Or an ocean life activist who places himself in a tiny boat between a whale and the harpoons of a whaling ship.

Is it so hard to believe that Daphne Bevington, a London debutante and the earl of Wolverton's granddaughter, could be such a hero? When her dearest friend, Kate, needs her help, she does what's necessary to save her. In her mind, no other choice will do. After all, she knows without a doubt that Kate would do the same for her if she needed help. It doesn't matter one fig to her that their circumstances are disparate, that Kate is her lady's maid.

But Daphne finds herself in over her head. In a moment, everything falls apart, throwing not only her reputation and her future into doubt, but her life into danger. Yet in that moment when all seems hopelessly lost...another hero comes out of nowhere and saves her. A mysterious stranger who acts without thinking, at the expense of his own safety, without considering the consequences. A hero on a quest of his own. A man she will never see again...

Only, of course...she does. And he's not at all the hero she remembers him to be.

Or is he? I hope you will enjoy reading NEVER ENTICE AN EARL and finding out.

Best wishes, and happy reading!

Lily Dalton

LilyDalton.com
Twitter @LilyDalton
Facebook.com/LilyDaltonAuthor

♥ ♥ ♥ ♥ ♥ ♥ ♥ ♥ ♥ ♥ ♥ ♥ ♥ ♥ ♥

From the desk of Shelley Coriell

Dear Reader,

Story ideas come from everywhere. Snippets of conversation. Dreams. The hunky guy at the office supply store with eyes the color of faded denim. THE BROKEN, the first book in my new romantic suspense series, The Apostles, was born and bred as I sat at the bedside of my dying father.

In 2007 my dad, who lived on a mountain in northern Nevada, checked himself into his small town's hospital after having what appeared to be a stroke. "A mild one," he assured the family. "Nothing to get worked up about." That afternoon, this independent, strong-willed man (aka stubborn and borderline cantankerous) checked himself out of the hospital. The next day he hopped on his quad and accidentally drove off the side of his beloved mountain. The ATV landed on him, crushing his chest, breaking ribs, and collapsing a lung.

The hospital staff told us they could do nothing for him, that he would die. Refusing to accept the prognosis, we had him Life-Flighted to Salt Lake City. After a touch-and-go forty-eight hours, he pulled through, and that's when we learned the full extent of his injuries.

He'd had *multiple* strokes. The not-so-mild kind. The kind that meant he, at age sixty-three, would be forever dependent on others. His spirit was broken.

For the next week, the family gathered at the hospital. My sister, the oldest and the family nurturer, massaged his feet and swabbed his mouth. My brother, Mr. Finance Guy, talked with insurance types and made arrangements for post-release therapy. The quiet, bookish middle child, I had little to offer but prayers. I'd never felt so helpless.

As my dad's health improved, his spirits worsened. He was mad at his body, mad at the world. After a particularly difficult morning, he told us he wished he'd died on that mountain. A horrible, heavy silence followed. Which is when I decided to use the one thing I did have.

I dragged the chair in his hospital room—you know the kind, the heavy, wooden contraption that folds out into a bed—to his bedside and took out the notebook I carry everywhere.

"You know, Dad," I said. "I've been tinkering with this story idea. Can I bounce some stuff off you?"

Silence.

"I have this heroine. A news broadcaster who gets stabbed by a serial killer. She's scarred, physically and emotionally."

More silence.

"And I have a Good Guy. Don't know much about him, but he also has a past that left him scarred. He carries a gun. Maybe an FBI badge." That's it. Two hazy characters hanging out in the back of my brain.

Dad turned toward the window.

"The scarred journalist ends up working as an aide to an old man who lives on a mountain," I continued on the fly. "Oh-oh! The old guy is blind and can't see her scars. His name is...Smokey Joe, and like everyone else in this story, he's a little broken."

Dad glared. I saw it. He wanted me to see it.

"And, you know what, Dad? Smokey Joe can be a real pain in the ass."

My father's lips twitched. He tried not to smile, but I saw that, too.

I opened my notebook. "So tell me about Smokey Joe. Tell me about his mountain. Tell me about his *story*."

For the next two hours, Dad and I talked about an old man on a mountain and brainstormed the book that eventually became THE BROKEN, the story of Kate Johnson, an on-the-run broadcast journalist whose broken past holds the secret to catching a serial killer, and Hayden Reed, the tenacious FBI profiler who sees past her scars and vows to find a way into her head, but to his surprise, heads straight for her heart.

"Hey, Sissy," Dad said as I tucked away my notebook after what became the first of many Apostle brainstorming sessions. "Smokey Joe knows how to use C-4. We need to have a scene where he blows something up."

And "we" did.

So with a boom from old Smokey Joe, I'm thrilled to introduce you to Kate Johnson, Hayden Reed, and the Apostles, an elite group of FBI agents who aren't afraid to work outside the box and, at times, outside the law. FBI legend Parker Lord on his team: "Apostles? There's nothing holy about us. We're a little maverick and a lot broken, but in the end we get justice right."

Joy & Peace!

Shelley Coriell

♥ ♥ ♥ ♥ ♥ ♥ ♥ ♥ ♥ ♥ ♥ ♥ ♥ ♥

From the desk of Hope Ramsay

Dear Reader,

Jane Eyre may have been the first romance novel I ever read. I know it made an enormous impression on me when I was in seventh grade and it undoubtedly turned me into an avid reader. I simply got lost in the love story between Jane Eyre and Edward Fairfax Rochester.

In other words, I fell in love with Rochester when I was thirteen, and I've never gotten over it. I re-read *Jane Eyre* every year or so, and I have every screen adaptation ever made of the book. (The BBC version is the best by far, even if they took liberties with the story.)

So it was only a matter of time before I tried to write a hero like Rochester. You know the kind: brooding, passionate, tortured... (sigh). Enter Gabriel Raintree, the hero of INN AT LAST CHANCE. He's got all the classic traits of the gothic hero.

His heroine is Jennifer Carpenter, a plucky and self-reliant former schoolteacher turned innkeeper who is exactly the kind of no-nonsense woman Gabe needs. (Does this sound vaguely familiar?)

In all fairness, I should point out that I substituted the swamps of South Carolina for the moors of England and a bed and breakfast for Thornfield Hall. I also have an inordinate number of busybodies and matchmakers popping in and out for comic relief. But it is fair to say that I borrowed a few things from Charlotte Brontë, and I had such fun doing it.

I hope you enjoy INN AT LAST CHANCE. It's a contemporary, gothic-inspired tale involving a brooding hero, a plucky heroine, a haunted house, and a secret that's been kept for years.

Hope Ramsay

♥ ♥ ♥ ♥ ♥ ♥ ♥ ♥ ♥ ♥ ♥ ♥ ♥ ♥

From the desk of Molly Cannon

Dear Reader,

Weddings! I love them. The ceremony, the traditions, the romance, the flowers, the music, and of course the food. Face it. I embrace anything when cake is involved. When I got married many moons ago, there was a short ceremony and then cake and punch were served in the next room. That was it. Simple and easy and really lovely. But possibilities for weddings have expanded since then.

In FLIRTING WITH FOREVER, Irene Cornwell decides to become a wedding planner, and she has to meet the challenge of giving brides what they want within their budget. And it can be a challenge! I have planned a couple of weddings, and it was a lot of work, but it was also a whole lot of fun. Finding the venue, booking the caterer, deciding on the decorating theme. It is so satisfying to watch a million details come together to launch the happy couple into their new life together.

In one wedding I planned we opted for using mismatched dishes found at thrift stores on the buffet table. We found a bride selling tablecloths from her wedding and used different swaths of cloth as overlays. We made a canopy for the dance floor using pickle buckets and PFC pipe covered in vines and flowers, and then strung it with lights. We spray-painted cheap glass vases and filled them with flowers to match the color palette. And then, as Irene discovered, the hardest part is cleaning up after the celebration is over. But I wouldn't trade the experience for anything.

Another important theme in FLIRTING WITH FOREVER is second-chance love. My heart gets all aflutter when I think about true love emerging victorious after years of separation, heartbreak, and misunderstanding. Irene and Theo fell in love as teenagers, but it didn't last. Now older and wiser they reunite and fall in love all over again. Sigh.

I hope you'll join Irene and Theo on their journey. I promise it's even better the second time around.

Happy Reading!

Molly Cannon

Mollycannon.com
Twitter @CannonMolly
Facebook.com

♥ ♥ ♥ ♥ ♥ ♥ ♥ ♥ ♥ ♥ ♥ ♥ ♥ ♥ ♥

From the desk of Laura London

Dear Reader,

The spark to write THE WINDFLOWER came when Sharon read a three-hundred-year-old list of pirates who were executed by hanging. The majority of the pirates were teens, some as young as fourteen. Sharon felt so sad about these young lives cut short that it made her want to write a book to give the young pirates a happier ending.

For my part, I had much enjoyed the tales of Robert Lewis Stevenson as a boy. I had spent many happy hours playing the pirate with my cousins using wooden swords, cardboard hats, and rubber band guns.

Sharon and I threw ourselves into writing THE WIND-FLOWER with the full force of our creative absorption. We were young and in love, and existed in our imaginations on a pirate ship. We are proud that we created a novel that is in print on its thirty-year anniversary and has been printed in multiple languages around the world.

Fondly yours,

Sharon
+
Tom Curtis

Writing as Laura London

♥ ♥ ♥ ♥ ♥ ♥ ♥ ♥ ♥ ♥ ♥ ♥ ♥ ♥ ♥

From the desk of
Sue-Ellen Welfonder

Dear Reader,

At a recent gathering, someone asked about my upcoming releases. I revealed that I'd just launched a new Scottish medieval series, Scandalous Scots, with an e-novella, *Once Upon a Highland Christmas*, and that TO LOVE A HIGHLANDER would soon follow.

As happens so often, this person asked why I set my books in Scotland. My first reaction to this question is always to come back with, "Where else?" To me, there is nowhere else.

Sorley, the hero of TO LOVE A HIGHLANDER, would agree. Where better to celebrate romance than a land famed for men as fierce and wild as the soaring, mist-drenched hills that bred them? A place where the women are prized for their strength and beauty, the fiery passion known to heat a man's blood on cold, dark nights when chill winds raced through the glens? No land is more awe-inspiring, no people more proud. Scots have a powerful bond with their land. Haven't they fought for it for centuries? Kept their heathery hills always in their hearts, yearning for home when exiled, the distance of oceans and time unable to quench the pull to return?

That's a perfect blend for romance.

Sorley has such a bond with his homeland. Since he

was a lad, he's been drawn to the Highlands. Longing for wild places of rugged, wind-blown heights and high moors where the heather rolls on forever, so glorious it hurt the eyes to behold such grandeur. But Sorley's attachment to the Highlands also annoys him and poses one of his greatest problems. He suspects his father might have also been a Highlander—a ruthless, cold-hearted chieftain, to be exact. He doesn't know for sure because he's a bastard, raised at Stirling's glittering royal court.

In TO LOVE A HIGHLANDER, Sorley discovers the truth of his birth. Making Sorley unaware of his birthright as a Highlander was a twist I've always wanted to explore. I'm fascinated by how many people love Scotland and burn to go there, many drawn back because their ancestors were Scottish. I love that centuries and even thousands of miles can't touch the powerful pull Scotland exerts on its own.

Sorley's heritage explains a lot, for he's also a notorious rogue, a master of seduction. His prowess in bed is legend and he ignites passion in all the women he meets. Only one has ever shunned him. She's Mirabelle MacLaren and when she returns to his life, appearing in his bedchamber with an outrageous request, he's torn.

Mirabelle wants him to scandalize her reputation.

He'd love to oblige, especially as doing so will destroy his enemy.

But touching Mirabelle will rip open scars best left alone. Unfortunately, Sorley can't resist Mirabelle. Together, they learn that when the heart warms, all things are possible. Yet there's always a price. Theirs will be surrendering everything they've ever believed in and accepting that true love does indeed heal all wounds.

I hope you enjoy reading TO LOVE A HIGHLANDER! I know I loved unraveling Sorley and Mirabelle's story.

Highland Blessings!

Sue-Ellen Welfonder

www.welfonder.com

Find out more about Forever Romance!

Visit us at
www.hachettebookgroup.com/publishing_forever.aspx

Find us on Facebook
http://www.facebook.com/ForeverRomance

Follow us on Twitter
http://twitter.com/ForeverRomance

NEW AND UPCOMING TITLES

Each month we feature our new titles
and reader favorites.

CONTESTS AND GIVEAWAYS

We give away galleys, autographed copies,
and all kinds of exclusive items.

AUTHOR INFO

You'll find bios, articles, and links to personal websites
for all your favorite authors—and so much more.

GET SOCIAL

Connect with your favorite authors, editors, and
other Forever fans, and share what's important to you.

THE BUZZ

Sign up for our monthly romance newsletter,
and be the first to read all about it.

VISIT US ONLINE AT

WWW.HACHETTEBOOKGROUP.COM

FEATURES:

OPENBOOK BROWSE AND
SEARCH EXCERPTS

•

AUDIOBOOK EXCERPTS AND PODCASTS

•

AUTHOR ARTICLES AND INTERVIEWS

•

BESTSELLER AND PUBLISHING
GROUP NEWS

•

SIGN UP FOR E-NEWSLETTERS

•

AUTHOR APPEARANCES AND TOUR
INFORMATION

•

SOCIAL MEDIA FEEDS AND WIDGETS

•

DOWNLOAD FREE APPS

Bookmark Hachette Book Group
@ www.HachetteBookGroup.com